PRAISE FOR RANDY SINGER

"Cross James Michener's great historical fiction with a John Grisham legal thriller, and you've got this epic classic by Singer."
PUBLISHERS WEEKLY ON *THE ADVOCATE*

"Singer presents a compelling tale based on two real trials: that of Jesus and that of Paul in Nero's court. This book is a riveting look into ancient Rome and offers parallels to our current political climate."
ROMANTIC TIMES ON *THE ADVOCATE* (TOP PICK)

"Singer, the attorney-author of several solid leg‍ another winner. . . . Singer's many fans will b‍ this one."
BOOKLIST ON *DEAD LAWYERS TELL NO TALES*

"Singer's latest courtroom drama is full of twists and turns, second chances, and spiritual redemption. The author's experience as a trial attorney is evident in the details and realism throughout. He allows the reader an up-close view into the legal system."
ROMANTIC TIMES ON *DEAD LAWYERS TELL NO TALES*

"This riveting and thought-provoking legal thriller is sure to please Singer's fans and earn him new ones."
LIBRARY JOURNAL ON *DEAD LAWYERS TELL NO TALES*

"Singer skillfully loosens the strings and reweaves them into a tale that entertains, surprises, and challenges readers to rethink justice and mercy."

"Another solid, well-crafted novel from an increasingly popular writer. . . . Its nonfiction origins lend the book an air of reality that totally made-up stories sometimes lack."

"*The Last Plea Bargain* is a superbly written book, hard to put down, and easy to pick back up."

"Singer's legal knowledge is well matched by his stellar storytelling. Again, he brings us to the brink and lets us hang before skillfully pulling us back."

"Great suspense; gritty, believable action . . . make [*False Witness*] Singer's best yet."

"A book that will entertain readers and make them think—what more can one ask?"

"Singer artfully crafts a novel that is the perfect mix of faith and suspense. . . . [*The Justice Game* is] fast-paced from the start to the surprising conclusion."

RULE
OF
LAW

RANDY
SINGER

TYNDALE HOUSE PUBLISHERS, INC.
CAROL STREAM, ILLINOIS

Visit Tyndale online at www.tyndale.com.

Visit Randy Singer's website at www.randysinger.net.

TYNDALE and Tyndale's quill logo are registered trademarks of Tyndale House Publishers, Inc.

Rule of Law

Copyright © 2017 by Randy Singer. All rights reserved.

Front cover photograph copyright © Jason Edwards/Getty Images. All rights reserved.

Back cover photograph copyright © Robert Shafer/Getty Images. All rights reserved.

Author photo copyright © 2008 by Don Monteaux. All rights reserved.

Designed by Dean H. Renninger

The author is represented by the literary agency of Alive Literary Agency, 7680 Goddard St., Suite 200, Colorado Springs, CO 80920, www.aliveliterary.com.

Rule of Law is a work of fiction. Where real people, events, establishments, organizations, or locales appear, they are used fictitiously. All other elements of the novel are drawn from the author's imagination.

For information about special discounts for bulk purchases, please contact Tyndale House Publishers at csresponse@tyndale.com, or call 1-800-323-9400.

Library of Congress Cataloging-in-Publication Data

Names: Singer, Randy (Randy D.) author.
Title: Rule of law / Randy Singer.
Description: Carol Stream, Illinois : Tyndale House Publishers, Inc., [2017]
Identifiers: LCCN 2017016378| ISBN 9781496418159 (hc) | ISBN 9781496418166 (sc)
Subjects: LCSH: Special operations (Military science)—Fiction. | Women lawyers—Fiction. |
    Conspiracies—Fiction. | Political fiction. | GSAFD: Christian fiction. | Legal stories.
Classification: LCC PS3619.I5725 R85 2017 | DDC 813/.6—dc23 LC record available at https
    ://lccn.loc.gov/2017016378

Printed in the United States of America

23 22 21 20 19 18 17
7   6   5   4   3   2   1

This book is dedicated to five men and their families:
U.S. Army veteran John Hamen, who was imprisoned
and executed by Houthi rebels after a courageous attempt
at escape. He did not go down without a fight.
U.N. contractor Mark McAlister, who survived six months of captivity
by the Houthis and refused to disavow his Christian faith.
SEAL team member Jeremy Wise, a member of the church I help
pastor. Jeremy gave his life serving his country at the Camp Chapman
CIA base in Afghanistan. He left med school to become a SEAL.
Green Beret Dane Paresi, who served twenty-seven years in the
Army and earned the Bronze Star and various other medals.
Like Jeremy, he died a hero at Camp Chapman.
And SEAL Team 6 member Ryan Owens, another warrior who did not
flinch in the face of death. In Yemen, he laid down his life for his friends.
The story of our freedom is written by men like them.

AUTHOR'S NOTE

I wrote *Rule of Law* in 2016 to address some critical issues lurking on the horizon. Is the president above the law in matters of foreign policy? Should the CIA be fighting shadow wars with drones and Special Forces in countries where we have not declared war? And what happens when the lives of service members are sacrificed for political gain?

To avoid getting bogged down in the political polarization that has gripped our country, I created a president, a cabinet, and a Supreme Court composed of characters who bear little resemblance to the current occupants of those positions. It's fiction, after all, though it's hard to match the entertainment value of the real world. But to at least anchor the story in reality, all historical references—political, military, and legal—are based on actual events. And if that all makes sense, you should probably start writing your own novels.

Most of my stories are inspired by real life. I set part of the story in Yemen because, as a lawyer, I have filed counterterrorism lawsuits on behalf of clients who were kidnapped and tortured by the Houthis. I centered the action around a SEAL team mission because I live in Virginia Beach, the home base for several teams, and have the utmost respect for these elite warriors. Some are my friends and, as a pastor, members of my congregation. I've seen the tragedy of promising lives cut short and the resolve of the SEAL families to carry on. My hope is that this book might reflect the depth of that heroism.

I did not know when I wrote this story that its premise would soon unfold in real life. In January 2017, a SEAL team raid in Yemen resulted in a tragic loss of life. There were reports that the raid may have been compromised.

Though this is a work of fiction, the issues in this book are real. We owe it to our brothers and sisters in the military to think deeply about these topics.

CAST OF CHARACTERS

HAMILTON ADMINISTRATION
Amanda Hamilton—president of the United States
Leroy Frazier—vice president of the United States
Philip Kilpatrick—White House chief of staff
John Marcano—director of the CIA
Seth Wachsmann—attorney general
Roman Simpson—secretary of defense

ATTORNEYS AND JUDGES
Paige Chambers
Wyatt Jackson
Wellington Farnsworth
Kyle Gates—attorney for John Marcano
Dylan Pierce—attorney for Philip Kilpatrick
Landon Reed—attorney for Paige Chambers
Thea Solberg—district judge assigned to the *Anderson* case
Mitchell Taylor—U.S. attorney for the Eastern District of Virginia

MILITARY PERSONNEL AND FAMILY MEMBERS
Patrick Quillen—Navy SEAL
Bill Harris—Patrick's grandfather
Troy "Beef" Anderson—Navy SEAL

Kristen Anderson—Troy's wife
Justin and Caleb Anderson—Troy and Kristen's sons
Brandon Lawrence—drone pilot
Admiral Paul Towers—commanding officer, Joint Special Operations
    Command
Commander Daniel Reese—Admiral Towers's chief of staff

UNITED STATES SUPREME COURT
Cyrus Leonard—chief justice
Augusta Augustini—liberal
Kathryn Byrd—conservative
Barton "the Beard" Cooper—conservative
Taj Deegan—swing vote
William Martin Jacobs III—liberal
Reginald Murphy—liberal
David Sikes—conservative
Evangelina Torres—liberal
Patricia Ross-Braxton—retired

OTHERS
Abdullah Fahd bin Abdulaziz—member of the Saudi royal family
Mokhtar al-Bakri, aka Pinocchio—Yemeni CIA informant
Yazeed Abdul Hamid—Iranian cleric
Cameron Holloman—*Washington Post* journalist
Gazala Holloman—Cameron's wife
Harry Coburn—reporter for the *New York Tribune*
Saleet Zafar—Yemeni cleric

SANA'A, YEMEN

They descended like vultures from the C-17 transport plane, silhouettes against a quarter moon in a tar-black sky. Invisible, silent predators. Arms and legs spread wide, free-falling for the first few seconds, the wind rushing past their arched bodies at 120 miles per hour. Adrenaline surging with every heartbeat.

Twenty men had stepped out of the cargo hold at 31,000 feet, into the frigid air above the sovereign territory of Yemen. Twenty-two seconds later, at 27,000 feet, they snapped their chutes open, checked their NavBoards, and adjusted their flights. They would float through the thin and biting air for nearly twenty minutes, landing within a few hundred yards of the first rally point on a desolate mountain plateau nearly five kilometers outside the city of Sana'a.

The men were part of a Tier 1 Special Forces "asset," the best America had to offer. Among them were a farmer from New York, a swimmer from California, a hunter from Texas, a lacrosse player from Connecticut. They had trained their entire adult lives for a moment like this, a presidential mission, one the suits in D.C. were following in real time. The president herself would monitor progress from the mahogany-lined Situation Room, watching video from the team leader's camera, listening to every spoken word on the command net, the radio frequency used by the team leader and headquarters staff.

These men were part of the famed SEAL Team Six, officially known as the Naval Special Warfare Development Group or DEVGRU, and this team, from the secretive Black Squadron, would be notching their own place in the history books tonight. It wasn't quite bin Laden, but unlike other covert operations, this one would not go unnoticed. In fact, if all went according to plan, the world would later watch select portions of the video. They would see the lethal efficiency of this team. Freedom for condemned prisoners. A statement that America was entitled to respect.

The mission was code-named Operation Exodus, a name Patrick Quillen and his men secretly disliked. They wanted to call it Alcatraz because it would be a spectacular jailbreak, but then the president weighed in, followed by the PR geeks, and a name of requisite nobility was chosen. The Houthi rebels running Yemen had provided no trials or due process for the two noncombatants the SEAL team had been sent to extract. The Houthis had threatened to execute the prisoners by hanging them on Easter Sunday, thumbing their noses at the United States and Saudi Arabia. The president had dispatched this team to put things right, to set the captives free. Operation Exodus was born.

The first prisoner was an American journalist named Cameron Holloman, a flamboyant reporter for the *Washington Post*, one of those pretty boys who inserted themselves into war-torn countries and dreamed of Pulitzers. He had flown into Saudi Arabia and snuck across the border with Yemen so he could report on the plight of the people caught in the cross fire between the Saudi air raids and the Houthis' counterattacks. But after two weeks in Yemen, he had been arrested, accused of being an American spy, and scheduled for execution.

Diplomacy with the Iranian-backed Houthis had long since failed.

In the same prison as Holloman, two cells down, sat Abdullah Fahd bin Abdulaziz, a member of the Saudi royal family, a rebellious nephew who had entered Yemen on his own unauthorized diplomatic mission. Like Holloman, he had been arrested and accused of espionage. And like Holloman, he was scheduled to be hanged on Easter Sunday. The Saudis were desperate to free him, and the mission would be a failure if he died or was left behind.

The intel for the mission came from a Yemeni asset whom the CIA had dubbed "Pinocchio," a twist on the fact that the man had proven himself with his handlers, his information always solid. He had provided the precise layout of the prison down to the cell numbers for the targets. The external layout and the daily patterns of the prison guards had been tracked through drone and satellite imagery.

Floating through the air and inhaling through an oxygen mask while making his flight adjustments, Patrick Quillen thought about the next few hours of his life. Tonight he was leading a platoon of sixteen SEALs, along with two Combat Control Team members from the Air Force and a couple of Air Force PJs, the military's best medics. If all went according to plan, it would be sufficient firepower to overwhelm the unsuspecting Houthi guards and break the targets out of Sana'a Central Prison.

Just a few years earlier, when the U.N.–sanctioned coalition government controlled Yemen, al Qaeda attackers had burst through these same prison walls with a car bomb and freed nineteen of their own prisoners. If al Qaeda could do it, certainly American Special Forces should have no problem. A surprise nighttime raid on a fortified prison in hostile territory. Piece of cake.

A few hundred meters before he hit the ground, Patrick loosened the rucksack strapped between his legs and let it hang below him, attached by a rope, out of the way of his landing. Seconds later he flared his parachute and hit the ground running. He quickly gathered his gear, stripped off his thermal outerwear and mask, and unhooked his chute. Like the other SEALs, he went about his work silently, burying the gear he would not be taking with him.

When the men had all gathered, Patrick spoke into his command net mic and let his CO know that they had hit their first checkpoint. "Roger that," his boss said, and the men were on their way. They were ready. Patrick could see it in their eyes. They were his men, every one of them, and they would have his back.

Operation Exodus was off to a good start. But the fun, Patrick knew, was just beginning.

2

The land was rocky and arid, with windblown sand, sparse desert grasses, and jagged rocks. The wind had a bite, the elevated air thin and brittle. A nocturnal lizard scurried across his path. It reminded Patrick of some training runs he had done in New Mexico—a blend of mountains and desert and ramshackle huts.

The prison was on a dirt road on the outskirts of the city, rising like a fortress from the surrounding slums and rocky hills. Patrick had endured nearly a week of briefings, using a 3-D computer mock-up of the facility. Thick stone walls about ten meters high were topped with coiled barbed wire. An enormous arched steel door served as the front entrance. The outer walls of the compound ran at least four hundred meters on each side, with a number of rounded towers built into each wall like a medieval castle. The towers had small sniper slits on each floor and a guard perch on top.

That was just the first line of defense. Inside the perimeter, the compound was a labyrinth of concrete buildings enclosed by a chain-link fence. In the center, a sniper's platform towered above the entire facility, complete with spotlights and sirens.

Over a thousand prisoners were housed here, separated into sections of forty to fifty each, with only two guards per section. The Houthi guards were mostly new recruits, poorly trained and young, many of them still in their teens. They would be armed with AK-47s but no night goggles and no rocket launchers. Maybe a few hand grenades. Most had never experienced combat.

Patrick and his men arrived at the outskirts of the facility right on schedule, and the snipers settled in. Two rocky ranges provided good cover and clean shots at the guard towers. A third sniper climbed up a fire escape to mount the roof of a nearby abandoned apartment building. A fourth climbed to the top of a warehouse and hunkered down behind a heating vent.

The other men scrambled into position—four per team, each team covering a side of the compound. Despite the brisk air, Patrick could feel the sweat on the back of his neck and the jagged breath of the man behind him. They stopped, checked around, then crouched and sprinted from one rock to the next, down alleys between cramped adobe houses, and across a road, positioning themselves behind some mud-brick utility buildings less than a hundred meters from the prison's outer walls.

The snipers and team leaders checked in on the troop net, the channel used by the SEALs on the ground, monitored by Patrick through his right earbud.

"We're at checkpoint Neptune."

"Roger that, checkpoint Neptune."

"Tex here. Checkpoint Neptune."

"Roger."

And so it went, one after the other. The air acrid and tense, Patrick's breath short. He kept his voice calm on the radio, but his heart was racing. In a few moments they would unleash hell. In less than thirty minutes, it would all be over.

He turned to the man right behind him, his best friend in the SEALs and the undisputed workout champion of the team, a guy named Troy Anderson, known to all his teammates as "Beef." Beef was stockier than Patrick and a few inches shorter, with broad shoulders and a square face. His body fat was a ridiculous 5 percent. Beef was the team prankster, but he was also intensely competitive, and tonight he was in his element. Patrick looked at him and nodded. It was time.

"Clear the towers," Patrick said softly into the radio.

Seconds later, the snipers confirmed their hits on the tower guards. They had code-named them for American patriots.

"Jefferson down."

"Madison down."

"John Adams down."

"Franklin."

"Thomas Paine."

Patrick tensed. The intel said there would be six Houthi guards in the towers. Five had fallen in rapid succession. A sniper cursed into the troop net, and a return shot rang out from one of the guard towers, a brief spark illuminating the night. The responding round from the SEAL sniper was suppressed.

"He's down," the sniper said a second later. "John Hancock."

With a fist to his helmet, Patrick signaled for Beef to move forward. "Set explosives," he said into his mic.

Beef's job, along with the breachers from the other teams, was to scramble to the base of the prison wall and place the explosives. Four simultaneous blasts would open holes in the outer walls, and the assaulters would pour through from every direction. From there they would blast their way through the fence surrounding the compound, blow open the outer doors to the prison, and create chaos inside— grenades, flashbangs, and shots coming at the Houthis from every angle. The SEALs wanted to be in and out in a matter of minutes.

But before Beef could cross the road, the dry night air was split by the sound of sirens. A high-pitched wail filled the skies, accompanied by sweeping spotlights. A hail of gunfire peppered the ground around Beef as he sprinted back behind the utility buildings.

"Thanks for the cover, Q," he gasped, hunkering down with Patrick and the others. "Next time, just tell me if you want to break up."

Patrick kept his head low but could see flashes from the AK-47s inside the slits in the towers. The intel was flawed. There was supposed to be a total of six guards manning the towers, but it looked like there were dozens more, raining fire on the SEALs who had tried to set the explosives.

The other teams radioed in. They were engaged as well, pinned down outside the walls. There was no small amount of cursing.

"Resistance is heavy," Patrick said into his command mic, sounding calm. "Permission to abort Surgery and commence Slingshot."

There was a pause, a disappointed hesitation on the other end of the comm. "Slingshot" meant using a technological advantage, a reference to David's slaying of Goliath. Patrick's orders had been clear. The SEALs were to minimize bloodshed. Take out the snipers, breach the wall, keep the kills to a minimum, clear the cells, and get out. Politically, a targeted Special Ops insertion was preferable to a broader-scale attack. Surgery was preferable to Slingshot.

But not if it meant SEAL casualties.

"Permission granted."

Patrick looked at his watch. It would take the drones at least two minutes. Two *long* minutes with bullets flying. He stuck his head out for the briefest of seconds and fired back at the towers.

This was going to get messy.

3

NAJRAN, SAUDI ARABIA

The room looked like a NASA control center. Dozens of drone pilots sat in rows before high-def digital monitors, eyes glued to the screens in front of them. At the front of the room was a large IMAX screen projecting feeds from multiple drones at once, all flying more than 15,000 feet over the action at Sana'a Central Prison. A CIA operative paced nervously behind the pilots at the joysticks.

Twenty-one-year-old Brandon Lawrence was one of the best pilots in the room. Skinny and pasty-skinned, Brandon had always been a bit of a computer geek. After high school, he'd taken a year off perfecting his favorite video games, then enlisted in the Air Force. He'd completed basic training and had been selected to fly the MQ-9 Reaper, the Air Force's most sophisticated drone, a beefed-up version of the Predator. Working under the command of the CIA in countries outside formal war zones, Brandon had logged thousands of hours and more than thirty-two combat missions in the last two years. He was steady at the controls, clinical in his annihilation of enemy targets, and nonchalant afterward. He never showed how much it tore him up.

In daylight, at 15,000 feet, his drone's light and radar sensors were so advanced that he could zoom in on an object only inches long. He could see what kind of weapon an enemy combatant carried, if not the brand of cigarettes he smoked. With the latest facial recognition software and his drone's 1.8 gigapixel cameras, he could pick enemy leaders out of a crowded city street. But at night, with the infrared technology, the imagery from the ground was more muted, a blur of green hues, fuzzy outlines of buildings, and hazy images of targets.

His job was to take out the guard tower at the center of the prison facility and the half-dozen men who would otherwise open fire on the SEALs once the outer wall was breached. It had to be a precise strike. A few meters off-center, and he would take out part of the prison, killing dozens of inmates.

Brandon zoomed in tight on the tower and pushed a button on his controls that pulled up a computer-generated grid displaying precise coordinates—distance, direction, range. The CIA operative moved in behind Brandon and grunted his approval. Brandon locked on to the target.

The screen provided an overlay showing the anticipated blast radius for the Hellfire missile. Brandon and the other pilots confirmed that they were locked and loaded.

"Commence fire."

On the screen at the front of the command center, the explosions were nearly simultaneous—ten flashes, silent and surreal against the eerie green backdrop of the infrared video. The six towers in the prison's massive outer walls all took direct hits as the missiles incinerated the guards, demolished the towers, and created gaping holes in the walls. Other strikes knocked out the power lines and generators, blanketing the prison in darkness and silencing the siren. Brandon's missile left a smoking crater where the interior guard tower had been, the bodies of six Houthi soldiers cremated in the blast.

"Nice work," the man behind Brandon said.

"Thank you, sir." Brandon stared at the screen in front of him, his hand trembling slightly on the joystick. Here he was, out of harm's way, single-handedly executing men who had no idea what was coming. He was acutely aware that this was no video game. And he felt a little ashamed that he could take another human's life without ever being in danger himself.

He had joined the Air Force because he wanted to serve his country. It seemed the perfect fit, blending his love of technology with his desire to serve.

But he never thought it would play out like this. Working at the direction of the CIA. Sitting at a computer terminal in Saudi Arabia. Killing six soldiers in Yemen, hundreds of miles away. Judge, jury, and executioner. Watching by video as the real warriors stormed the compound.

The wonders of modern warfare.

4

Patrick Quillen felt the shock waves from the explosions. He waited for the "clear" signal, then motioned his men forward. Staying low, they ran across the road and stepped around the smoking piles of charred rubble at the gaping hole created by the missile. He shouldered his HK 5.56 rifle and swept the area, his men fanning out to clear the prison yard.

The place looked more like a refugee camp than a high-security prison. Rows of dusty garments hung drying on clotheslines, and rugs apparently used as canopies for shade stretched from the clotheslines to the chain-link fence ringing the inner compound. There were no trees, just barren ground with a slab of concrete and a basketball hoop at one end.

Basketball. Who knew?

RANDY SINGER

Patrick and his men crossed the prison yard with no resistance. The Houthis had apparently retreated inside the inner walls.

The four teams came together, leaving a handful of members at strategic points in the yard to provide overwatch. A breacher set a small charge at the gate in the fence and blew it open, and the men hustled inside. They divided into two teams of six, with Patrick's team staying at the front entrance to the main prison building.

The thick steel door in front of them required a larger charge. Beef knelt, peeled the backing off the adhesive strip on the two-inch-thick breaching charge, and attached it to the door. He checked the blast area, and the other men backed out of the way.

"Explosives set, south entrance, building 1," Beef said.

Beef rolled out of the way himself, then triggered the charge and the door blew open. Another man threw a flashbang inside, and Patrick was the first to step through, moving quickly away from the death funnel of the doorway, sweeping his rifle in an arc.

There! On a catwalk, trying to regain equilibrium, were two Houthi guards.

He heard the pop of their guns, a few wild shots in the split second before Patrick and another assaulter put several rounds into them. One guard was blown back against the wall. The other slumped over the railing, hung there for a second, then plummeted to the floor below, landing with a thud.

The SEALs fanned out in the entry room. It looked to be an administrative space used for processing inmates.

"Lobby secure," Patrick said.

The other team leader responded. "Alpha Two is in."

The plan was for the two infiltrating teams to converge at the third-floor pod where the targets were being held. But first they had to navigate the steps and breach another steel door on the third floor.

Patrick prepared to open the door to the stairwell but hesitated. He had learned to trust his instincts. The extra guards in the towers had been unexpected and had cost his team the element of surprise. He was

13

sure the Houthis were now waiting at the top of the metal-grate steps and would try to stack his team up on the staircase.

His radio squawked. The team leader was breathless. "Alpha Two engaged in the stairwell. Eagle down."

Patrick heard Beef curse behind him.

"Get that guard over here," Patrick said, motioning to the Houthi they had killed in the admin area.

Two assaulters grabbed the man under his arms and dragged him to the stairwell door. "Toss him in after I kick open the door," Patrick said. "Take cover. Then go."

His men nodded. Patrick kicked open the door, and they tossed the dead guard through. He took a round of fire but no grenades. Two assaulters slid in right behind him, hugging the walls and returning fire at the guards above. Two more SEALs followed quickly behind.

The guards retreated, and Patrick and his men sprinted up the steps, training their rifles on the doors at the second and third levels, leaving two men behind to seal the entrances.

The four remaining SEALs gathered at the landing just outside the third-floor door. Beef attached explosives, and the men retreated down half a flight of stairs. The door blew open, and Patrick launched another flashbang inside. The team followed through the opening and immediately took fire.

"Allahu Akbar!" the guards yelled.

Patrick rolled as bullets cracked over his head. It was pitch black, and he knew the Houthis didn't have night vision goggles. They were at the other end of a pod of cells, retreating and firing, spraying bullets everywhere. The prisoners huddled in the corners of their cells, shouting in Arabic. Patrick and his men stayed low and returned fire. In a matter of seconds, the Houthi guards were lying facedown in their own blood.

Patrick and Beef hustled to the far end of the pod, poked the guards with muzzles to make sure they were dead, and kicked the AK-47s away from their bodies. The prisoners in the cells were wide-eyed, most cowering next to the exterior walls. A few moved gingerly toward the front of their cells, reaching through the bars and calling out to the SEALs.

The team moved quickly along the row of cells. They were less than twenty meters from where Holloman and Abdulaziz were being held when the bad news started pouring in.

"We have seven hot spots moving toward the target," Patrick heard over the command net. "Transport vehicles. Alpha One and Two, do you copy?"

"Roger that," Patrick said.

"Copy," yelled the leader of Alpha Two. He sounded breathless, still under fire. Patrick and his men would have to help in the north staircase as soon as they secured the prisoners.

There was no telling how many Houthis were in the armored vehicles moving toward the compound. They might have RPGs that would make it hard for the extraction helos to land. How had the rebels mobilized so quickly?

The radio traffic picked up.

"Alpha Two still engaged. Resistance is heavy."

"Neptune One engaged," one of the snipers said.

"Neptune Three engaged."

Two snipers under fire. The other breaching team pinned down in the stairway. Extra guards in the towers. Houthi reinforcements on the way. The prison guards had drawn Patrick and his men deep inside the prison. It all added up to a trap.

A few seconds later, when Patrick and Beef reached the cell where Holloman was supposed to be, his worst fears were confirmed.

"Alpha One to Hawk," Patrick said, calling Admiral Paul Towers, the commanding officer of the Joint Special Operations Command. He was the man ultimately in charge of the mission, communicating directly with the director of the CIA and the president. Patrick, like all SEAL team leaders, revered the man.

"Hawk here."

"You need to see this," Patrick said.

He switched on the light attached to the rail system on his helmet, illuminating the cell where Holloman should have been. His camera beamed the visual back to headquarters.

There, in the corner of the cell, smiling, was a full-size cardboard cutout of President Amanda Hamilton.

5

TWO MONTHS EARLIER
CHESAPEAKE, VIRGINIA

Paige Chambers heard the outer door to the restroom open, but it was too late. She let the vomit fly. She was bent over in a stall, the door closed. She would just have to wait this person out. She had read once that the great Roman orator Cicero did the same thing. She hated that she got so nervous before a big hearing like this, putting so much pressure on herself that she literally made herself sick.

This is not me. I'll be fine.

She kept her hair out of her face with one hand and used the other to wipe her mouth with toilet paper. When she was done, she flushed the toilet, and some of her frayed nerves, disguised as this morning's breakfast, circled the bowl and went down the drain.

She waited until she heard the bathroom intruder wash her hands and leave. Paige grabbed her coat from the hook on the back of the stall door and stepped out into the bathroom. She checked herself in the mirror, adjusted her pin-striped suit with the skirt that reached just above the knees, and bent over to get a drink from the faucet.

She stood there for a moment, studying herself, a last-minute pep talk rattling around in her brain. She was blessed with decent looks, though she thought her green eyes were a little buggy. She had straightened her shoulder-length black hair for the occasion instead of tossing it up in a messy bun or pulling it back with a headband like she normally did. She had applied only a thin layer of foundation, a little lip gloss, and some basic eye shadow and mascara—nothing fancy. She wanted to be taken seriously as a professional.

Paige was four years out of law school and had already argued in front of the Virginia Court of Appeals nearly fifty times. She had graduated third in her class and now worked for the attorney general of the Commonwealth of Virginia. She could do this. There was no one better.

She gave herself a quick nod, picked up her briefcase, squared her shoulders, and left the restroom. She took a furtive glance around to make sure nobody was watching and headed straight to the courtroom.

The usual suspects had already arrived. There were a few lawyers, like Paige, who made a living doing appellate work. This court consisted of three-judge panels who decided if the trial court had correctly applied the law. Most of the criminals here were represented not by appellate specialists like Paige but by their trial lawyers, a ragtag bunch who worked for court-appointed rates and seldom offered a real defense. Paige had lost only three times, and she'd seen every one of them coming.

Today, in the back row, sat a reporter for the *Tidewater Times*. She knew he was here for her case, *Markell v. Commonwealth*, the most volatile case she had handled in her short career.

Austin Markell was a twenty-eight-year-old trust-fund child of a wealthy real-estate developer from Portsmouth, Virginia. He had been convicted of raping a nineteen-year-old student from Old Dominion University. She reported it to the police the same night, and the DNA was a match. The woman, Grace Hernandez, had bruises on her arms and neck, where she claimed he held her down with his forearm. Markell said the sex was rough but consensual. The jury convicted him in an hour.

A few weeks after the verdict, a juicy rumor surfaced, fueled by a hearing in a divorce case for one of the assistant commonwealth attorneys. It seemed that Markell's defense lawyer, a young superstar in the defense bar named Lori Benton, had been having an affair with a lawyer in the prosecutor's office. Markell promptly fired Benton and retained sixty-five-year-old Wyatt Jackson, a local legend, a man who hated the government and turned every case into World War III.

Jackson raised an ineffective assistance of counsel defense, arguing that Benton had not told Markell about the affair. Jackson claimed that attorney Benton had pulled her punches. She didn't go after the victim's prior sexual history. She didn't call character witnesses who would have helped Markell. Jackson even submitted an affidavit from Markell saying he would never have hired Ms. Benton if he had known about the relationship.

Paige popped a mint, draped her winter coat over the rail behind her counsel table, and took a seat next to the embattled commonwealth's attorney for the city of Portsmouth. The city was divided along racial lines, and Destiny Brown had been voted in as commonwealth's attorney over her two white opponents. She had fired half the office immediately, and the rest were leaving in droves. The prosecutor caught in the affair had been forced to resign. Defense lawyers like Wyatt Jackson preyed on the chaos.

Austin Markell had already begun serving his sentence and wouldn't be in court today, but Jackson had managed to fill up an entire row with the defendant's family and friends. Before court started, he came over to shake Paige's hand. Jackson was six-five and a full head taller than Paige. She gripped his hand firmly but knew that hers was cold and clammy.

"You nervous?" Jackson asked.

"Not really," Paige said. It sounded unconvincing even to her.

Jackson was rail thin with sharp facial features. He had a formidable mane of silver hair that he shoved behind his ears. He had grown a mustache that could hide yesterday's breakfast, and his piercing blue eyes were sheltered by bushy gray eyebrows. His smile was somewhere between a smirk and a grin. "I'd be nervous too if I were arguing your side," he said.

"Good luck," Paige replied brusquely. "You'll need it."

This caused Wyatt to smile more broadly. "Ah, the bravado of the young." He nodded at Destiny Brown, who had refused to rise and acknowledge him. "Nice to see you again as well, Ms. Brown."

"Get lost," Destiny said.

Wyatt just shook his head. "Didn't realize we were so touchy today. But then again, you are a little short-staffed at the office."

He turned and headed back to his side of the courtroom. Paige sat down, but Destiny couldn't help herself. "What an arrogant jerk," she whispered, loud enough to be heard by those sitting behind her.

Paige knew better than to underestimate the man. Born just this side of the Virginia/West Virginia line, he combined the charm of a Southern gentleman with the hide of a mountaineer. He reportedly lived in an RV at a KOA campground, but the rumor was that he had more money in a Swiss bank account than most Silicon Valley execs. He was the kind of lawyer everyone loved to hate until they needed one.

Then they called *him*.

6

Wyatt Jackson stood ramrod straight as he faced the three judges who would decide this appeal. He gave them little deference, sometimes interrupting as they fired questions at him. Paige admired his tenacity but thought he was alienating the panel. Either way, it didn't help her nerves to have the lawyer for the other side set such a combative tone.

Jackson's main antagonist was Judge Anna Colson, who was also probably the swing vote on the panel. She did not seem to be buying the ineffective assistance of counsel claim.

"I understand we have this relationship going on," she said, peering over the top of wire-rimmed glasses. Judge Colson had a pudgy face and thinning gray hair. "But I'm not seeing where it affected the way Ms. Benton tried the case. What would you have had her do differently?"

"Everything," Wyatt said confidently. "She called no character witnesses. She didn't cross-examine the victim about prior sexual history."

Colson practically snorted at that argument. "Perhaps you've heard of this thing called the rape shield statute," she said.

"It doesn't protect victims if the prosecution puts the victim's prior sexual conduct in play," Wyatt shot back.

"I've looked through the entire transcript and didn't see that happen here," Colson responded.

"Volume 1, page 372," Wyatt Jackson said without consulting his notes. "When Ms. Hernandez was asked whether the sex was consensual, she said, quote, 'I would never consent to sex like that,' end quote. That's a plain statement about her prior sexual conduct, and defense counsel should have jumped all over it."

"You've got to be kidding," Colson scoffed. "If I were the trial judge, that wouldn't be enough for me to let someone like you cross-examine a victim on her sexual history."

"A *zealous* defense lawyer should have at least tried, Your Honor. This case is worse than the *Thornburg* case, and the defendant got a new trial in that one."

Colson leaned back in her chair and crossed her arms, apparently unconvinced. Paige was surprised Wyatt had even mentioned the *Thornburg* case. It was a ruling from a trial court in Richmond that wasn't binding on the court of appeals. In *Thornburg*, a defense lawyer who was married to an attorney in the commonwealth's attorney's office had not only failed to inform his client but had failed to call a single witness. He had fallen asleep during the prosecution's case. Not surprisingly, the trial judge had granted a new trial.

Paige had come across dozens of similar cases during her research, but none of them were from the Virginia Court of Appeals or the Virginia Supreme Court, the only two courts that were binding on this three-judge panel. In her opinion, Wyatt had made a mistake even mentioning *Thornburg*.

Paige watched as the red light at the front of the podium came on, signaling the end of Wyatt's twenty-five minutes. Out of respect for the court, Paige always concluded in a single sentence when that happened.

But Wyatt pulled himself up to his full height and, without asking the permission of the court, continued to plow ahead.

"In Shakespeare's play *As You Like It*, one of the characters says that 'love hath made thee a tame snake.' Here, Ms. Benton was a tame snake. She didn't strike when she had her chance, and my client is entitled to a new trial with somebody not afraid to do so."

"Thank you very much," Judge Colson said curtly.

7

Standing at the podium, before she could get a word out of her cotton-dry mouth, Paige found herself on the defensive.

"Don't you think defense counsel should have at least disclosed this relationship to her client?" The question came from Judge Rahul Patel, a former public defender. He was the judge on the panel Paige knew would be the toughest sell.

"Under the ethical rules, yes. But I don't believe it entitles Mr. Markell to a new trial."

"Why didn't you submit an affidavit from the assistant commonwealth's attorney who had the affair, denying that he ever discussed the case with defense counsel?" Judge Patel leaned forward on the bench. "That would have been an easy way to buttress your argument, no?"

Paige had known that question was coming, but there was no good answer. "He refused to talk to us."

This caused a few raised eyebrows on the panel. "Really?"

Yes, really, Paige wanted to say. Her frustration was beginning to beat back her nerves. "It doesn't actually matter. Mr. Markell was well represented. There is nothing his defense counsel could have or should have done differently."

For the next few minutes Paige found herself on solid ground. "Ms. Benton was smart not to call any character witnesses. The defendant had a long list of reprehensible acts that the prosecutors could have used if Ms. Benton had opened the door by calling character witnesses. As to the matter of the victim's prior sexual history, Ms. Hernandez's claim that she would not have consented to sex that left bruises on her arms and neck is hardly a statement putting her prior sexual history in play. If this court were to hold otherwise, every time bruises are left on a rape victim and she denies that she consented, defense counsel could drag her entire sexual history before the court. That can't possibly be the law."

Paige had now found her zone. It happened this way every time. Nerves. Fear. A rough start. But ultimately her obsessive preparation kicked in, and her adrenaline would fuel focus instead of fear.

Judge Patel asked Paige about the *Thornburg* case. Didn't that case stand for the proposition that any time a defense lawyer had an intimate relationship with someone in the prosecutor's office and the relationship wasn't disclosed, there would have to at least be an evidentiary hearing to see if the defendant was entitled to a new trial?

"*Thornburg* was wrongly decided," Paige said confidently. "If this court adopts the reasoning in *Thornburg*, it will open a huge can of worms."

Judge Colson leaned forward. "Tell me more."

The remark drew a smattering of chuckles, and Paige felt an uneasy chill tingle down her spine. The only one in the room not getting the joke.

"*Thornburg* wrongly holds that any undisclosed relationship between defense counsel and a member of the prosecutor's office is enough for the defendant to have a hearing to determine whether he is entitled to a new trial. What if the prosecutor and defense lawyer had been on a date three months earlier? What if they were friends from law school? What if they went to the same church? What if they played tennis together? What if—?"

"But that's not what we're dealing with here," Judge Colson interrupted. "There's no doubt that Ms. Benton and a member of the commonwealth's attorney's office were having a long-term affair."

"I agree, Your Honor. But I still believe that defense counsel should have to prove some prejudice against his client before he is entitled to a hearing."

"But how does he know if his client has been prejudiced without a hearing where he can examine Ms. Benton, the defense lawyer, under oath?"

Paige felt herself backed into a corner. "We just have to look at the entire record. In a case like this, there's no doubt the defendant was well represented."

"But how do we know Mr. Markell's lawyer wasn't talking to her lover about the case?"

"There's no evidence that she did."

"But there *is* evidence that she was not forthcoming with her client. Why didn't she just tell her client about the relationship?"

The red light flashed. "I see my time is up," Paige said. "May I answer the question?"

"I think you'd *better* answer Judge Colson's question," Judge Patel quipped.

"Courts should not get into the business of second-guessing defense counsel based on the lawyer's alleged motivations. What if Mr. Jackson over there has other clients who pay more than Mr. Markell—though I doubt he does. Should that allow the defendant to second-guess Mr. Jackson's representation here and claim he didn't try hard enough? No. We should look at the record and the conduct of defense counsel during the trial. Because Ms. Benton did an adequate job, the conviction should be affirmed."

★ ★ ★

A few minutes later, Paige learned what the chuckling had been about. During his rebuttal argument, Wyatt Jackson pounced gleefully on her mistake.

"Your Honor's opinion in *Thornburg* should not be brushed aside so quickly," he said to Judge Colson.

Paige felt her face flush, her mind reeling. She had read that case. Surely she would have recognized Colson's name if she had been the trial judge who decided *Thornburg*. Then the panic hit. Paige remembered something about a divorce that occurred before Judge Colson was elevated to the appellate bench. At the time she read *Thornburg*, Paige hadn't been thinking about Judge Colson's prior married name— she didn't even know that Colson would be one of the judges chosen for Paige's panel until this morning. But now it made sense—why the judges had wanted to talk so much about *Thornburg*.

Paige hardly heard another word that Wyatt Jackson uttered. She was too busy replaying her dismissive remarks about *Thornburg*. She would have addressed the matter differently if she had known Colson was the trial judge who had decided that case. Paige would have been far less critical of the reasoning; she just would have distinguished the facts.

"Accordingly, we ask that this court at least direct the trial court to provide the defendant with an evidentiary hearing to see if he is entitled to a new trial," Wyatt Jackson concluded. The red light was on. This time he thanked the judges and sat down.

After the judges left the bench, commonwealth's attorney Destiny Brown shook Paige's hand and told her she had done a good job, but they both knew it was a lie. Wyatt Jackson came over and told Paige she'd had a tough case. She shook his hand and congratulated him, resisting the urge to ask how he could live with himself. She busied herself packing her stuff and grabbed her coat, determined not to make eye contact with anyone else on her way out.

But that proved impossible. First the reporter from the *Tidewater*

Times approached her, though she was able to brush him off with a quick "no comment."

And then, looking over the reporter's shoulder, Paige saw him—the last person she wanted to see on the day of her humiliation. He was standing in the back row, wearing a baggy gray hoodie, hands in his pockets. He must have been there for the entire hearing. He seemed so out of place, like he belonged in an entirely different part of Paige's compartmentalized life.

When she approached him, he broke into a broad smile.

"What are you doing here?" she asked.

Patrick Quillen shrugged. "Scouting out the best lawyers in case I get a traffic ticket."

She couldn't decide whether to laugh or cry. She was already fighting back tears of frustration. And now she felt a whole new set of emotions bubbling up.

8

They'd met through an online dating service. Paige later described their first date to a friend as "awkward and enchanting all at once." Patrick was a little old-school for Paige, like he had stepped off the set of a Western where men held doors for women and protected the fairer sex. He seemed to have a simplistic view of life powered by a sense of unbridled enthusiasm for God and country, a sharp contrast with Paige's cynical lawyer friends.

The enchanting part was his smile. He had deep-set eyes, a model's jaw and cheekbones, and short black hair. Even if she hadn't read his profile, Paige would have known he was military. But when he flashed that smile—and for Patrick Quillen that was a frequent occurrence—he was all Hollywood.

The other thing she liked was that Patrick, unlike the others she had met on that same dating site, didn't try too hard to impress. He actually seemed to care more about Paige than he did about himself. It wasn't until their third date that she learned he was a SEAL.

"Why didn't you tell me that before?" she asked.

He shrugged the question off. "That's just the way we roll."

That same night Patrick told her about his parents, killed in a car accident when Patrick was only three. He was raised by his grandparents on a dairy farm in upstate New York. His grandmother had died from cancer just three months before Patrick headed to BUD/S.

"She was the bravest person I've ever known," Patrick said. "She fought through chemo and weight loss and hair loss. I never heard her complain or get angry at God. If someone asked how she was doing, she would just say she was blessed."

"She sounds incredible," Paige said. "I wish I could have met her."

"So do I," Patrick said.

By now they had been seeing each other for a month—long enough for Paige to close her online dating account and develop real feelings for Patrick. But not long enough for him to see her at a moment of weakness like this.

They rode together down the escalator to the first floor, and he told her how impressed he was with her argument.

"Thanks. But let's not talk about it."

He asked her out to lunch, but she politely refused. She had too much to do, other cases that needed attention. Honestly, she just wanted to be alone and pout.

But he wouldn't take no for an answer, and the smile eventually worked its magic. They settled on a compromise. He would buy her lunch at the hot dog stand in front of the Chesapeake courthouse. She could take it back to the office and lick her wounds.

He held her briefcase while she put on her coat, helping her slip one arm in the sleeve. "Thanks," she said. He held the door on her way out, and she braced for the January wind.

It was a bright day with a few thin clouds and a strong breeze that cut through layers of clothing. The poor guy running the hot dog stand was layered with a hooded sweatshirt inside a down jacket. Patrick ordered three dogs and grabbed two bags of chips and two drinks. He slathered mustard on his.

"Cookie?"

"No thanks."

They walked side by side to the parking lot. "For a lawyer, you're a cheap date," Patrick said.

"How did you even find out about this hearing?"

"You mentioned it a few days ago. It sounded interesting. I wanted to see you in action."

The comment made Paige smile. The guy walking next to her was a Navy SEAL. He probably wasn't all that impressed with what her profession considered "action."

"Not my best day," Paige said.

"I thought you were awesome."

Either he was trying to make her feel good, or he had been clueless during the hearing. "Except for when I missed the fact that Colson was the same judge that had written the *Thornburg* opinion they kept asking about."

"I thought you handled it well," Patrick said. "You had an answer for everything. There's no way this case should get a new trial."

This was part of what attracted her to Patrick. Like her, he was a crusader. There were good guys and bad guys, simple as that. In their own ways, Paige and Patrick were both doing their part. It wasn't about the money or fame. She couldn't imagine arguing for a criminal defendant any more than he could see fighting for ISIS.

She was already starting to feel a little better just being around him. Lunch with Patrick would beat brooding alone.

"Maybe we could eat lunch together in your truck," Paige said. "You could give me more details about how brilliant I was and cheer me up a little."

"Sounds like a date."

★ ★ ★

It took him three more weeks and eight more times together—two movies, three dinners, one walk on the beach, and two seven-mile runs—before he kissed her. He did it on the same night that he told her he would be deploying in a little over a month. "Basically a cruise in the Med. Nothing dangerous."

He was dropping her off after a date, and he walked her to the front door of her condo.

They had grown comfortable with hugs, but he had never tried to kiss her. Others from the same dating service, especially after a few drinks, had tried much more than that on the first date.

Yet on this night, just before he said good night, he gave her a hug but didn't pull away. He gently brushed a lock of hair behind her ear and traced her cheek with his finger. She looked at him intently, her breath catching in her chest.

She closed her eyes as he leaned in to kiss her. And when he pulled away, his little romantic mission completed, he flashed that irresistible smile. "Was that okay?" he asked.

She could hardly breathe. Things were spinning. "It's about time," she said. Then she leaned in and kissed him again.

When he left that night, she stepped inside, closed the door, slumped against it, and felt her knees go weak. She smiled and slid slowly to the floor.

Get a grip, she told herself. *It's only a feeling.*

But it was a feeling, and a night, that she knew she would remember for the rest of her life.

9

The opinion in *Markell v. Virginia* was released on Tuesday, March 13, and it was as bad as Paige had feared it would be. All three judges agreed that Lori Benton had a conflict of interest that she should have disclosed to her client. The judges were not willing to assume that the conflict was harmless error, as Paige had argued. "Instead, given the overriding importance of a defendant's Sixth Amendment right to competent legal counsel free from bias, and given the flaws in defense counsel's handling of this case, we hold that the conviction is tainted and the defendant is entitled to a new trial."

Paige stewed about the opinion for an hour before she called commonwealth's attorney Destiny Brown. "You did everything you could," Destiny said unconvincingly. "But there won't be another trial. The victim is not willing to go through this again, particularly with Wyatt Jackson as the defense lawyer."

The call, along with the opinion, made Paige sick. The attorney general's office was in Richmond, two hours from where Paige lived, so they allowed her to work from home. She normally loved the arrangement because if she wasn't in court, she could dress casual, work on briefs, go for a run in the middle of the day, and never have to worry about office politics. But on a day like today, she needed the companionship. Instead, she fumed in isolation.

That night, she was supposed to go with Patrick to dinner at his friend's house. Patrick talked a lot about Beef Anderson and his family, and now he was taking Paige to meet them. Under normal circumstances, Paige would have been excited to go. But after reading the opinion, she didn't really feel like putting on a happy face for Beef, Kristen, and their two little boys. On the other hand, it was just a few days before Patrick's deployment, and she knew she would regret not spending the evening with him.

In midafternoon, she texted him to let him know that she wasn't feeling great.

He replied quickly. **You want to just hang out? Call off dinner?**

She stared at the text for a long time. The thought of spending time alone with Patrick was tempting. But it would mean a lot to him for her to meet his friends. She had heard that the SEAL community was a tough group to crack.

No, I'll be fine.

★ ★ ★

By seven thirty that evening, Paige was glad she had decided to go. The Andersons lived in a crowded neighborhood on a nondescript cul-de-sac in Virginia Beach. Their two boys, four-year-old Justin and three-year-old Caleb, had pretty much taken over the small house. There were toys and shoes and plastic guns scattered around, the walls and shelves crammed with pictures. The Andersons had a big German shepherd named Tiny, and he was a licker.

"That's why Patrick brought you here," Kristen Anderson told Paige. "To make sure you passed muster with Tiny."

Paige liked Kristen from the moment she met her. Kristen was a little shorter and frumpier than Paige had imagined she would be. The word on the street was that SEALs' wives were all "government issue," beautiful and athletic. But Kristen didn't fit the mold. She was plain, easygoing, down-to-earth, and very welcoming of Paige. She wore a fitted T-shirt, Bermuda shorts, and sandals despite the chilly weather. Paige liked the fact that Kristen couldn't cook, or so she claimed. Beef and Patrick spent the first twenty minutes manning the grill.

"How many deployments have you been through?" Paige asked as the two women stood at the kitchen counter making a salad.

"Probably ten or fifteen," Kristen said. She tossed a slice of cucumber to Tiny, who was sitting obediently at her side. "But some of them were pretty short."

"What's the hardest part?"

"Three days after he comes home. The first two days—and nights—are awesome." Kristen smiled at the thought of it. "But then Troy starts messing up the routine I've established while he's gone. He wants to fly back in and take over the house, and I'm thinking, we've done pretty well while you were gone, thank you. Plus, the first few days he's back, he lets the boys get away with murder. So yeah, by day three we always have our knock-down, drag-out. Once I win that, we're good again."

A few seconds later, Kristen was mediating an argument between the boys, and Paige was working on the salad solo. She tried to picture herself like this. Was it even possible to be married to a SEAL and still have a normal family and career? Somehow the warmth of this home and the sheer normalcy of it—right down to the boys competing with each other for her attention—were oddly comforting.

Dinner could only be described as high energy, the boys relentless with their questions. Justin had jagged blond hair that looked like Kristen had cut it while the kid squirmed. He was wide-eyed and polite with a Dennis-the-Menace smile and mischievous blue eyes. Little brother Caleb was nearly the same size, though where Justin was all sinew and bone, Caleb was roly-poly. Caleb was also more sensitive than Justin, looked like his mom, and had already hugged Paige three times by the time they started dinner.

Much of the conversation centered around Beef's exploits, which Kristen described in coded PG terms so that little ears wouldn't pick up any ideas. There were more than a few barroom brawls and a couple of pranks that had gotten out of hand. Patrick grinned sheepishly as Kristen exposed some of his shenanigans as well.

The real entertainment started after the meal. It came at the insistence of four-year-old Justin, though at first Patrick and Beef politely declined. "Please, Daddy! Please, Uncle Q!"

When little Caleb started chiming in, Paige knew it was over. The men would be deployed soon, and she could tell that they didn't have the heart to say no.

"Sorry about this," Beef said, and Paige knew she was in for a treat.

Kristen just shook her head. "Miss Paige is going to think we're all nuts." But her two little boys were already scurrying off down the hallway.

Beef followed them, and Patrick just leaned against the counter, arms crossed, a smirk on his face.

"Where are they going?" Paige asked.

"You'll find out."

While the boys got ready, Patrick moved into the family room and started pushing the furniture up against the walls, pulling a coffee table out of the way. A few minutes later, Beef's deep voice came booming down the hallway that led back to the bedrooms in the single-story ranch.

"And now, weighing in at a svelte 185 pounds!"

Kristen almost spit out the water she was drinking. "Add another forty!" she shouted.

"A nuclear physicist hailing from Transylvania, Pennsylvania, the Incredible Hulk!"

Following the introduction, Beef Anderson sauntered into the living room, posing and flexing his muscles. He was quite a sight—shirtless and wearing a tight pair of green sweatpants he had cut off at the knees. He had a huge tattoo of an American eagle on his chest, wings spread across his impressive pecs. His face was painted green, and the man could strike a pose.

"Booo!" Kristen shouted. "Throw the bum out!"

But Beef just went on posing, undeterred. He was used to being the villain. "Hulk's partner, from a dairy farm in upstate New York," he announced, gesturing toward Patrick. "The American doughboy, soft and pudgy and cuddly, also known as Patrick 'Q' Quillen!"

Patrick glanced at Paige, giving her a quick roll of the eyes. Then he moved to the center of the room and bounced around, shaking out his limbs like a true wrestler. He might have been a little embarrassed, but she could tell he loved it.

"And now, weighing in at forty-three pounds wringing wet, Captain America!"

Justin Anderson came running down the hall in his Captain America outfit, missing only the trademark shield. He pointed at his dad and started trash-talking. He yelled back to his brother. "Hurry up, Caleb!"

A few seconds later a chubby little Spider-Man came running down the hallway, his mask skewed to one side, and the fight was on. Patrick and Beef dropped to their knees and rolled around with the boys while Kristen and Paige watched, smiling. The boys liked to jump from the arms of the couch onto the backs of the big men, and the big men liked to twirl the boys around until they got them dizzy and then lie on top of them. Tiny barked and circled the melee and darted in and out of the action. There was a lot of roughhousing and laughing and tickling. At one point, Caleb got kicked in the face and came running to Kristen, crying. Kristen healed him with the magic of a mother's kiss and sent him back into the fray.

After a spectacular fifteen-minute cage match, the little boys finally pinned the Navy SEALs, and Beef called the festivities to an end.

That night did something to Paige that she couldn't quite describe. She had been at war with her own father since he left when she was in middle school, and she had always felt a little jealous of friends who could turn to their dads for advice. But something about the way Beef was not just a father but also a friend to his little guys made her think that maybe someday she could rise above her own past and experience something like this in her family too. Especially with a guy like Patrick, someone who would not cut and run when things got tough.

10

Two days later, on the night before his deployment, Patrick took Paige out for dinner at a fancy restaurant on the boardwalk named Catch 31. It was the first time Paige had seen Patrick in a button-down shirt, along with a dress sweater and his normal jeans. He had wanted to sit at the outside tables with the fire pits, but there was a steady drizzle and a stiff March breeze that forced them to go with plan B.

They found a cozy booth, and Paige allowed herself to enjoy the time together, chasing away thoughts about the deployment and how long it would be until they saw each other again. When the main course came, they talked about the Anderson family, and Patrick asked Paige if she ever saw herself as a mother. He took a bite of his steak—in a seafood restaurant—and waited for her response.

"Sure. Someday. But right now I'm more focused on my career." She turned the question on him—"Have you ever thought about having kids?"—and took a sip of wine.

"Oh yeah," Patrick said. "I'd like to have an entire basketball team."

Paige stopped mid-bite. "You're dating the wrong woman for that."

Patrick shrugged. "I figured I would start high and leave room to negotiate."

Aren't we skipping a few things? Paige wanted to ask. They had never even talked about marriage, and now they were negotiating kids?

"Let's take it one step at a time," she said.

"It's a hypothetical," Patrick said, grinning. "And if we needed to, I could be a player/coach and settle for four."

It wasn't the only time that night that things got personal. Patrick had a way of asking soft, probing questions, his dark eyes oozing empathy, and Paige would surprise even herself in the way she let him in. They talked about how her father left the family and how her mother had abruptly moved to Nashville in order to marry a pastor as soon as Paige graduated from high school. "That's the year I stopped going to church," Paige said.

There were two boyfriends in college, and one in law school who had proposed to Paige before he graduated and moved to New York City. Six months later he moved in with a coworker, and the wedding was off. "He told me in a phone call," Paige said. But she knew it was for the best; the guy was on his third female roommate now. "I've probably got serious abandonment issues," she said.

"Just a poor judge of men," Patrick said.

"Undoubtedly."

Patrick reached over and took her hand. "You can trust *me*, Paige. I'm not perfect—you've probably figured that out—but I would never hurt you."

Paige leaned a little closer. "I know that," she said.

★ ★ ★

Later that night, Patrick pulled into the parking lot of Paige's condo. They had this thing going where Patrick would jump out of his truck, run around to the passenger's side, and try to open the door for Paige.

But she never waited for him. Instead, she would hesitate for just a moment, then open her own door seconds before he careened around the front bumper to get his hand on the handle.

But tonight, neither of them got out.

"You want to come in?" Paige asked.

He turned to her. "I don't think I should. I don't trust myself."

They were in the front seat of his truck with a console between them. He reached over it and put his arm around her shoulder, and she scooted toward him. She remembered how awkward it had been on their first date.

"Can I ask you a question?" Patrick said.

"Sure."

He thought for a moment, as if rehearsing the words in his mind, making sure they came out right—editing, revising, restating. "What would you think about getting married?" he asked.

The question stunned Paige and, frankly, confused her. Was he proposing? Was it one of those I'll-ask-you-to-the-prom-if-you-say-yes questions? After just three months?

"I'm not . . . really sure," Paige stammered, the surprise evident in her voice. "It seems like everything is happening so fast."

There was an awkward silence as her mind reeled. *Married?*

"In my world," Patrick said, "we make quick decisions and trust our instincts. Plus, I've prayed about this, and I knew we were right for each other from that first kiss—actually, from the first time we met."

Paige had no idea what to say. She leaned toward him, over the console, her head against his shoulder. In her world, she acted on logic, not instincts. And certainly not emotions.

"I just . . . I don't know," Paige said, looking out the front windshield. "I love the thought of it, but I would want to make sure it's right, not just something we do because you're going away and we want to lock something in."

"Think about it," Patrick said. "I don't need an answer tonight. I wasn't really expecting one." He hesitated. "Well, to be honest, I did have this plan of proposing on the boardwalk right after dinner. But then the weather . . . and our dinner conversation about that guy who dumped you in law school."

The hint of disappointment in his voice stung Paige. The last thing she wanted to do was hurt him.

"I guess I just wanted you to know before I head out that I'm ready to spend the rest of my life with you," he said.

Paige faced him, inches away. "I love you," she said. She gave Patrick a long kiss, one that connected them in a way she had never felt before. And when he got out and walked around to her side of the car, she let him open the door.

"See, that didn't hurt," Patrick said.

He walked her to her front door. She asked him again to come in but he said he couldn't . . . shouldn't. This time she sensed the slightest distance between them—or maybe she was just imagining it.

He leaned down and she stood on her toes and they kissed again. They said their good-byes, and he wiped her tears away and waited as she entered the condo.

She watched through the peephole as he turned and walked away. She got ready for bed, her mind still whirling. And finally, when she had sufficiently dissected the man's character and made lab slides out of every piece of information she knew about him, every date they had shared, and especially the last few minutes together tonight, she typed a text message.

If the offer is still open, I would love to.

But she didn't want it to be just an emotional reaction to the disappointment she had detected. Or a desire to nail things down when they were staring at a few months apart. This was too important, and she had been burned before. That law school relationship had felt right too. At the time, she was sure they had been created for each other. She crawled into bed, placed the phone on the sheets next to her, and stared at the message for a long time.

Was this how it was supposed to be? Were her feelings real and lasting, or were they just because she knew that she wouldn't see him for three months? And if they were real, couldn't they pick up where they left off when he returned?

Was she worried because he was a SEAL and she didn't want to spend her life married to someone who would be in and out every six months? Was she ready to live with the thought that somebody could knock on her door in the middle of the night and tell her that her husband was gone? But then she thought about Troy and Kristen and how they made it all work.

These and a hundred other questions plagued her as she lay on her back and stared at the ceiling, trying to imagine the next three months without Patrick. At nearly two in the morning, she started to doze off. She woke after a few seconds, set the alarm on her phone, and placed it on the dresser. She left the text message unsent. She didn't trust her emotions; right now they were just too raw.

For a few more minutes, her thoughts bounced around in that no-man's-land between wakefulness and sleep, jumbling together in a swirling mix of bad court opinions, giggling little boys, and the earnest eyes of a man she was sure she loved. Finally, at 2:30 a.m., she rolled onto her right side, fluffed up her pillow, and fell into a fitful but welcome sleep.

11

For the next ten days, Paige and Patrick exchanged texts and e-mails, though they didn't have a chance to Skype. According to Patrick, they didn't allow it at the base where he was stationed.

All of this was new to Paige and a far cry from seeing Patrick face-to-face. His messages came in bunches, at erratic hours because he was in a different time zone, and it wasn't unusual for a full day to pass before he could respond to a single e-mail or text.

She wasn't too worried about his safety, due in large part to the influence of Kristen Anderson. Paige and Kristen met twice for coffee, and it was clear Kristen thought the men were in no danger. Paige loved Kristen's easygoing personality, and she was buoyed by the way Kristen talked about Patrick.

"I've known Q for a long time, Paige. He's never dragged anybody over to our house before. When a guy on the team brings a woman over and introduces her as his 'girlfriend,' it means something."

Kristen took a sip of coffee. "These guys live fast, Paige, even the good ones like Patrick. And when they decide to start a relationship, they don't mess around. I saw the way he looked at you."

Paige took it all in without saying a word about Patrick's quasi-proposal. She wondered if he'd had a ring in the car the night before he deployed. Either way, she had already decided to throw caution to the wind. She might never meet another man like Patrick Quillen. She was better just being around him. She couldn't count how many times each day she would pull up his picture on her computer and think about the time they had spent together.

They occasionally talked on the phone, but the calls were disjointed because of the brief time lag caused by the distance between them. And Patrick seemed somewhat distracted, sometimes cutting the calls short with a promise that they would talk longer next time. That worried Paige, but Kristen was a help there, too. She said Troy was the same way. "When the guys are on deployment, they've got a one-track mind. It's all part of the package."

Paige was guarded by nature, especially when it came to trusting someone with her deepest feelings. But when she decided she was all-in on something, nothing could stop her. By the tenth day of Patrick's deployment, she was mailing care packages and counting down the days just like the rest of the Navy wives and girlfriends. The next three months would go agonizingly slow, but when he came back in the summer, they would make up for lost time. She would be waiting at the airport when he returned, and they would pick up where they'd left off. She would tell him about the text message she had typed the night he left. This time there would be no hesitation.

★　★　★

WASHINGTON, D.C.

Philip Kilpatrick, White House chief of staff, was fifty-four years old and a veteran of fourteen political campaigns. He had seen it all—heck, most of it he had choreographed. His black-rimmed glasses sat on a short, squat boxer's nose. By campaign eight, he had lost every strand of hair on his head, magnifying his ears, which probably belonged on a bigger skull anyway. He kept his gray beard neatly trimmed, so short that it never looked like it had fully grown in.

He had become accustomed to being the smartest man in the room, even when that room had a legendary history, like the wood-paneled Situation Room where he now sat, and even when the room was populated with the president's top advisers. He could remember by how many votes the president had come up short in the second precinct in Warren County in the Iowa caucus and by how many votes she had unexpectedly won in Beaver County, Pennsylvania. And that's why the governor of Pennsylvania was now the secretary of the interior and the governor of Iowa was shaking hands at the Dubuque County Fair.

It was 7:00 p.m. on Palm Sunday, and Kilpatrick watched intently as President Amanda Hamilton conducted a meeting of the Security Council with her usual efficiency and decisiveness. Hamilton was a young-looking forty-six, a female version of JFK minus the affairs, an image that Kilpatrick had gone to great lengths to plant and cultivate. She was five-ten and muscular, a former member of the Harvard women's crew team, and determined not to let the world's hardest job completely wreck her health. But her first fifteen months in the Oval Office had already aged her about four years, spawning crow's-feet at the corners of her piercing dark eyes and two small grooves on her forehead that became more pronounced when she frowned.

Amanda's path to the presidency had taken her through the Manhattan district attorney's office, where she prosecuted Wall Street executives, followed by a term as attorney general of New York and later as attorney general of the United States. She was a natural prosecutor, but the country hadn't hired her to prosecute; they had hired her to govern.

And on that score, the jury was still out. Her administration had tried to do too much too soon on the domestic front, including reforming prison sentences for nonviolent offenders, and the Republicans in control of the House had fought Amanda at every turn. Internationally, Iran had been thumbing its nose at the United States and exposing the weaknesses in the nuclear deal that her campaign opponent had called the worst ever made in the history of the planet. She once told Kilpatrick that she was beginning to think her opponent was right.

Most of her chief advisers in the room, including Kilpatrick, were at least ten years older than her and still getting used to taking orders from a woman. Sixty-five-year-old Roman Simpson, her secretary of defense, was a granite block of a man carved from the horrors of war who made little effort to conceal his contempt for the president's lack of foreign-policy experience. Kilpatrick had advised against putting Simpson in a cabinet post, but the man had the respect of the Pentagon brass, and President Hamilton had a fondness for the Abraham Lincoln approach—appointing a "team of rivals" in key cabinet positions.

Simpson had bushy black eyebrows, jowls that had long since lost the fight with gravity, and a humorless demeanor. The president and Kilpatrick had already decided that Simpson would not be around during a second term.

Sitting across the table from Simpson, and his chief adversary on the Security Council, was CIA director John Marcano. The director was a lifetime member of the agency, an analyst who had never put his own life on the line. He was emotionless and unflappable. He had wisp-thin gray hair, and his skin was red and blotchy. His long forehead sloped down to thin eyebrows and a long beak of a nose. Simpson called him "the CPA" and chafed at the fact that the pencil pusher had so many military assets at his disposal, including an army of drones, in countries like Yemen where the U.S. was not officially at war.

Director Marcano was briefing the council on the latest intel from Yemen, and he spoke with an air of certainty that came from reading everything his field operatives and analysts had produced. He confirmed reports that the Houthis planned to execute both Cameron Holloman and Abdullah Fahd bin Abdulaziz in one week, on Easter Sunday, in a symbolic political and religious statement to the world.

The asset providing information about the prison, a man nicknamed "Pinocchio," had never been wrong before. Drone and satellite imagery had shown an uptick in security at Sana'a Central Prison during the last week. A few intercepted Internet and cell phone communications had confirmed what Pinocchio was telling them.

"What's your confidence level in the intel?" the president asked.

"Ninety-five percent."

"What about the negotiations?"

"Not great," Marcano reported. "The Houthis are convinced Holloman is a spy. They originally thought he was going to write a piece highly critical of the way we've been using drones in Yemen. Lots of civilian casualties, that type of thing. They even set up a meeting with a few Houthi leaders, including one who allegedly lost his family in a drone attack. Eight days later, one of our drones took out the compound where the meeting occurred, killing those leaders and their families."

"Was Holloman in fact working for us?" Vice President Leroy Frazier asked. Frazier had been Hamilton's surprise pick for veep. Good-looking, energetic, and not quite forty years old, the African American senator from Florida was by far the best orator in the room. His father had been a famous preacher in the AME Church, and young Leroy had the cadence.

"Of course not," Marcano said quickly.

And if he was, Kilpatrick thought, *Marcano would never admit it to you.*

Kilpatrick knew all too well that Marcano trusted no one outside the agency. The president might have pulled together a bunch of rivals just as Lincoln had done for his cabinet, but nobody would accuse them of being a team.

They discussed the matter for thirty minutes until the president came to the one conclusion everyone knew was inevitable. "Let's keep working every diplomatic channel we can," she said. "Keep me informed of any developments. If Holloman's not out by Friday, we'll send in an extraction team. I'll want a full mission briefing in three days."

The president stood, signaling an end to the meeting, and the other members of the Security Council followed suit. As they were packing, Kilpatrick stole a quick glance at Marcano, who returned an almost-imperceptible nod. The negotiations were going to fail. It was time to send in the SEALs.

12

On Wednesday, waiting at a U.S. base in Saudi Arabia near the border with Yemen, Patrick and his team still had doubts about whether the mission would go forward. They were less than forty-eight hours from launch, and there were rumors that the State Department was still trying to negotiate a diplomatic resolution. The prior Sunday, the president had authorized a surgical extraction for the early hours of Friday morning. But Patrick and his men had been to the brink of important missions before and had the rug pulled out from under them at the last minute. He was starting to think it might happen again.

Tonight they were scheduled for a video briefing that would involve JSOC commander Admiral Towers and the president herself. Patrick had never been on a presidential mission before and had found it impossible to sleep the night before the briefing. Admiral Towers, a highly respected former SEAL, already knew the mission by heart. He had told Patrick to keep his briefing short and to the point. Fewer details meant fewer questions and fewer opportunities for the president to get cold feet.

Like his teammates, Patrick spent most of the day packing and repacking his gear. He had ten pockets in his Crye desert digital combat uniform, and each had a specific purpose. He made a handwritten list in his pocket journal and went through the items one by one. His camera. His fixed-blade knife. A tourniquet and rubber gloves. A video camera. Plastic infrared lights that could be seen only through night vision and would be activated in rooms the SEALs had cleared.

He checked and rechecked the rest of his equipment. The body armor. The night vision goggles. His rifle, laser, and helmet. He leafed through his laminated mission booklet with a diagram of the prison's layout and pictures of both Holloman and Abdulaziz. And lastly, he ran his fingers over the small photograph of Paige he had taped inside the back cover.

He was ready. He was a thousand times ready. The next thirty-six hours, waiting for authorization to proceed, would be the most agonizingly slow and gut-wrenching hours of his young life.

The briefing took place at 2100 Yemen time, 1400 in Washington, D.C. Patrick and his men sat in a tent in front of a secure camera feed with two large monitors, one on each side. At precisely 2100, the faces of Admiral Towers and President Hamilton, flanked by their respective chiefs of staff, flashed on the two screens. Vice President Frazier was also in the room with the president; Patrick couldn't tell if there were other VIPs off camera.

The president thanked them for taking time for the briefing, as if they had a choice. The whole thing seemed surreal. Admiral Towers was dressed in his battle fatigues, his face thin and angled, his gray eyes unforgiving. Patrick had seen the president a thousand times on television. He had voted against her and griped about her to his buddies. But now here she was, the commander in chief, looking intently into the video feed and waiting for Patrick to describe the mission.

Admiral Towers introduced Patrick and asked him to begin the briefing.

In the last three days, Patrick had gone over it multiple times with Towers's chief of staff, and he had it down almost word for word. Because it was the military, he'd integrated lots of PowerPoint slides, but the goal was to have the whole thing described in five minutes or less.

He could feel his voice cracking as he described the high-altitude, high-opening parachute entry, the various rendezvous points, the plans for breaching the compound, the extraction of the prisoners, and the contingency plans if things went bad. By the time he was halfway through, he had settled down, and his words came out crisp and confident. He finished in four minutes and asked if the president had any questions.

She did. "Whom did you vote for in the last election?"

Patrick's heart froze. He had prepared for every question . . . except *this*. What difference did it make?

"I voted for your opponent," Patrick said. "But that was before I knew you would authorize a mission to kick the Houthis' collective butts."

He saw a brief smirk on Towers's face and knew he would get props for the answer later.

Hamilton smiled broadly. "I thought that might be the case. Maybe I can earn your vote for the next election."

"Anything's possible," Patrick said because he couldn't think of anything else.

Hamilton stared into the camera, and the smile left her face. "Actually, I have no questions. I didn't ask you men to give me a briefing so that I could second-guess your tactics. I don't call you for advice on the State of the Union, and you don't need my advice on how to extract prisoners."

That statement somehow changed the dynamics on the call. She had instantly earned some of Patrick's respect. He had heard that the president had an aura about her, that once you spent time with her, you wanted to trust her, to follow her lead. It was gravitas, and he was sensing it now.

"I asked you men to brief me because this is one of the hardest decisions I have to make as your commander in chief. I'm not sure how the other presidents approached it, and we all have our own styles, but if I'm going to ask good men to put their lives on the line, I want to look them in the eye and tell them how grateful I am for their service.

"I want you to know that your country is behind you. I want you to know that our prayers are with you. I know that you have families and that many of you are somebody's dad and most of you are somebody's husband. You are not just another piece on the global chessboard to me. This mission is about some very important principles like freedom and due process and respect for American citizens. I wouldn't put your lives on the line for anything less."

She hesitated for a moment and it seemed to Patrick like she might be choking up a little. He and his teammates liked to joke around about these missions or downplay their significance. *It's all part of the job. This is what we get paid to do. No big deal.*

But in moments like this, they knew it was a *very* big deal.

"I will be monitoring every minute of this mission from the Situation Room at the White House. While Americans go safely about their business, your team will be showing the rest of the world why this is still the land of the brave."

She leaned back a bit, and Patrick wanted to salute. But he didn't know the protocol and thought he should wait for her to stand. When she did, he gave her a crisp salute. He sensed his team rising behind him and doing the same.

The president saluted back. "God bless you," she said, and the feed was terminated.

For a few seconds, nobody said a word, the gravity of the moment engulfing them.

As usual, it was Beef Anderson who broke the reverence. "You suck-up!" he said, pounding Patrick on the back. "'I'll be sure to vote for you next time!'" he squealed. "'You are such an awesome leader!'"

The other men chimed in, mocking Patrick and his interaction with the commander in chief.

But Patrick didn't care. The mission was on! And a farm boy from a small town in upstate New York had just spoken to the president of the United States of America.

13

On Maundy Thursday, Philip Kilpatrick began his day, as he always did, at 6:30 a.m. with President Hamilton in the Oval Office. Kilpatrick was an inch or two shorter than the president and about twenty pounds overweight, ten of which had been added during the first year of her presidency.

He remembered the first day of Hamilton's term, when they had met in this room so rich with history, so ripe with the smell of luxury—freshly polished wood and shampooed carpet. He had watched as Amanda Hamilton ran her hand over the finish of the president's *Resolute* desk, made from the timbers of the British frigate HMS *Resolute* and presented as a gift from Queen Victoria in 1880. There were the busts of Abraham Lincoln and Martin Luther King Jr. flanking the fireplace, the portrait of Washington centered just above it. Kilpatrick had walked to the bookcase and picked up the program from the August 28, 1963, March on Washington when Martin Luther King Jr. gave his "I Have a Dream" speech.

Watching the president that day, Kilpatrick had felt himself getting caught up in the same sense of history that Amanda must have felt. But those days seemed far away now, a distant memory of a time when governing seemed full of possibilities. The first year of her administration had humbled them both. Her domestic agenda had been thwarted by Republicans in the House. On the international front, ISIS was gaining ground, and Iran was suspected of violating its nuclear deal without remorse. Midterm elections were still seven months away, but the president's popularity had dipped below 50 percent. History, which showed that presidents accomplished the most during the first eighteen months of their administration, was not on their side.

Coffees in hand, Kilpatrick and his boss took their respective seats in front of the fireplace. They were studying the printout of the president's schedule, shuffling events so she could monitor the mission that evening. They would postpone some arm-twisting meetings with senators about judicial appointments. The vice president could take a ceremonial appearance at a local elementary school. They could use that time slot to meet with Democratic party leaders who had been previously scheduled for dinner. And so it went, juggling this event and sliding that event over so that the busiest woman on earth would have nothing on her calendar from 6 p.m., when the men would be parachuting into Yemen, until whatever time the mission was concluded.

When they finished, Kilpatrick handed the president copies of three speeches. "They're all short and to the point."

"Good," she said, leafing through them.

"The top one is for a mission with no American casualties and the successful rescue of both Holloman and Abdulaziz. The second is a successful rescue but with American casualties."

Hamilton looked at the speeches as Kilpatrick talked, flipping pages and then setting each one aside. They were no longer than five minutes each with just the facts. For a successful mission, the president's speechwriter knew there was no point in boasting. Let others do it for you.

"The third one is our disaster scenario. Americans killed or captured. Holloman and/or Abdulaziz still in prison. As you requested, it goes into Iran's role in backing the Houthis. Lots of talk about the bravery of our troops, of course. A call to action to get tougher with Iran." Kilpatrick stopped talking and gave the president a few moments to look it over.

The signature frown told him everything he needed to know. She looked at her schedule again. "We need to free up another hour. I need to work on this."

Kilpatrick rubbed his stubbly gray beard, took off his distance glasses, and looked again at the schedule. He thought about all the political fallout if he canceled or shortened even one more event. He knew the speech wasn't a masterpiece, but then again, nobody would remember exactly what was said after a disastrous mission. The important thing would be for Amanda to be seen as presidential, which meant proposing strong and decisive action. This speech was perfect for that.

"What don't you like about it?" Kilpatrick asked. "Maybe I can work on it this morning and you can look it over first thing this afternoon."

In response, Amanda handed the first two speeches back to her chief of staff but kept the third. "I need an hour," she said in a tone that made it clear there would be no debate. "We've got to get this right."

The routine was always the same with John Marcano, director of the CIA. Kilpatrick would go to CIA headquarters, pass through the CIA's metal detectors, and be wanded by the guards. There would be a staffer waiting on the other side of security who would stay at Kilpatrick's side as they turned around and left the building, climbing into a waiting sedan. Kilpatrick would be ferried to a different spot in the capital each time, dropped off, and pointed toward a park bench and a waiting

Marcano. Whether it was snowing, raining, or a hundred degrees, they always met outside, at a place of Marcano's choosing.

Today, the director wore a dark suit and a raincoat, his umbrella at the ready. The sky was dark and ominous, the sidewalk wet from the brief showers that had passed through earlier. Kilpatrick had brought his own umbrella; Marcano did not like to share.

Kilpatrick sat down, keeping some space between himself and Marcano, and crossed his legs. They gave each other their usual stiff greetings, and Marcano didn't waste any time getting to business.

Their meeting lasted all of ten minutes. Marcano, as usual, never looked at Kilpatrick when he talked. He kept his voice low and even. Kilpatrick suspected they were being videoed and that Marcano would watch the video later to study Kilpatrick's facial expressions. At times Marcano covered his mouth with his hand or rubbed his face so that lip-readers would never be able to make out what he said. The man was paranoid in the extreme and one of the few people who made Kilpatrick nervous.

When the meeting was finished, both men stood and walked to the curb, where a black sedan pulled up. The director shook Kilpatrick's hand, said, "I'll see you tonight," and climbed into the car.

Instead of hailing a cab, Kilpatrick decided to walk the seven blocks back to the White House. It had started to sprinkle, and he had a thousand things to do, but none of that mattered right now. He needed time to think, and the walk might clear his head.

As he passed other pedestrians on D.C.'s busy sidewalks, tourists and government workers, students and businessmen and -women, for a brief moment he envied all of them. The normal cares of an average life. *What did the boss think of my project? When will I have time to study? What museum will we go to today?* He longed for a time when he could finally retire, read the news about the misfortunes of others, and have no more pressing issues to address than choosing a restaurant for dinner. But even as he thought about such things, Philip Kilpatrick knew he would never retire. This was what he hated and what he craved at the same time. The weight of the world on his shoulders. Along the journey, he had sacrificed even his own family for this.

He was seeing a side of the world that few people knew existed. He felt alive with power and influence. There were politicians and leaders, up-front people who came and went. But there were also strategists behind the scenes, puppet masters who pulled the strings. John Marcano was one of them and, with his quiet and paranoid ways, one of the best. But Philip Kilpatrick was another. And he wasn't about to let the bookish director of the CIA get the better of him.

As he walked faster, his thoughts came with more clarity. They all had secrets, things they would do differently—you didn't get to the top by playing it safe. All he could do now was navigate the way forward. Amanda Hamilton was depending on him. And he was not about to disappoint the president of the United States.

★   ★   ★

VIRGINIA BEACH, VIRGINIA

Paige Chambers had sent two text messages and one e-mail to Patrick Quillen since the last time she had heard from him. In that text message, Patrick had been upbeat and witty, telling her how much he appreciated his taxpayer-funded vacation to the Med. He said he might not be able to contact her for a couple of days and asked her to say a prayer for him. And that was all.

She called Kristen and received some reassurance. It was not unusual for the boys to go a few days without responding to messages. It was all just part of the drill. "I know Patrick will call on Easter," Kristen said. "It's his favorite day of the year."

Paige went for a run, took a shower, and began fixing dinner. Since Patrick's deployment, she had started watching the news again. A year and a half ago, Paige had voted for Amanda Hamilton, optimistic that a former prosecutor would have the guts and wisdom to turn things around in Washington. But Paige had been disappointed when one of the president's first domestic initiatives was to soften federal sentencing guidelines for first- and second-time drug offenders. There were a couple of missteps abroad as well, in Paige's opinion, and Paige had pretty much decided to tune the whole thing out. But now, with Patrick overseas, her interest in foreign affairs had been rekindled.

Mideast tensions were at an all-time high as Holy Week reached its conclusion. There were reports of ISIS attacks on Christians and fighting in the West Bank. Yet that was nothing out of the ordinary, as far as Paige could tell. She finished her dinner and retreated to her study to put in a few more hours on a brief that was due the next day.

14

Philip Kilpatrick had been in dozens of meetings in the Situation Room, but there was a different tension in the air tonight. The president arrived just before six, wearing a sweater and jeans, her hair pulled back and her sleeves pushed up. Others stood as she entered, but she briskly signaled for them to sit down.

Amanda Hamilton prided herself on running informal meetings, and the younger members of the National Security Council took full advantage. Vice President Frazier was in khakis and an untucked button-down shirt. The secretary of state, a forty-two-year-old whiz kid who had worked his way up through the ambassador ranks, sported a golf shirt. But the older men, like Director Marcano, all wore ties or open-neck shirts with sport coats. Roman Simpson, the bulky secretary of defense, was in full uniform, his colorful array of ribbons splattered across his chest.

Kilpatrick wore a white shirt, red tie, and gray pants. There would be a presidential speech later tonight in one form or another. As White House chief of staff, he would help herd the press, and there would be no time to change before that took place.

For the first ninety minutes, the president was restless. She spent some time working on her speech in a side room with a fully equipped desk and frosted privacy windows. She popped in and out of the main conference room as the SEALs landed, buried their equipment, and made their way to the prison. She finally settled in, leaning forward with eyes unblinking, as the snipers took their places.

A large digital display on the wall opposite the president was divided into four separate screens. The first showed Admiral Paul Towers at the command headquarters in Saudi Arabia. The second showed a satellite feed of the prison facility. The third contained an aerial photo of the prison and surrounding area that had been taken in daytime. Flashing markers on this screen represented the SEALs as they moved across the landscape. The fourth screen showed a ground-level view, alternately taken from the helmets of the various team leaders.

Kilpatrick and the others had a similar array of video feeds on their laptops and could switch feeds whenever they wanted, including some that were not displayed on the wall. The audio from the command net came into the room over the loudspeaker.

Kilpatrick watched the third screen as the snipers surrounded the prison at a distance of about a hundred meters. He waited for the snipers to open fire and heard the calls as the guards in the towers fell. He found himself holding his breath when it was obvious the last sniper had missed and return fire came from one of the towers. But then the sniper found his mark.

"All six towers have been secured," Admiral Towers said over the video screen. "The breachers are up next."

All eyes in the Situation Room were glued to the ground-level view on screen four when it became obvious that the mission would not go according to plan. They saw chaos on the ground, the breachers racing toward the prison walls and then scrambling back for cover. They heard

Patrick Quillen call for permission to commence Operation Slingshot. They heard the momentary pause before Towers granted permission and then looked at the camera, his eyes boring into the men and women in the Situation Room.

"I've authorized drone strikes," he said. "This will complicate the mission, but we planned for this contingency."

"How long until the drones arrive?" the president asked.

"Two minutes."

"Very well," said the president, although nobody thought for a moment that Towers had been asking her permission.

This mission was technically a CIA operation, and for tonight, Towers was reporting to Director John Marcano. America was not at war in Yemen and could not send in its troops without violating international law and the Constitution. But it could send in "civilian" CIA operatives, even if they happened to be expertly trained Special Forces who had been deputized only for the evening. It was the same logic, and the same method, that Obama had employed when sending the SEALs after bin Laden in Pakistan.

But in reality, given Towers's ego and battlefield experience, he was the one calling all the shots. Marcano was just window dressing.

In precisely two minutes, just as Towers had said, the video feeds showed explosions in six guard towers nearly simultaneously, and for a brief moment Kilpatrick allowed himself to bask in the pride of American ingenuity.

But the feeling was short-lived. The action unfolded so quickly it was hard to keep up. Two of the four screens at the front switched to grainy infrared ground feeds from the helmets of the team leaders, and Kilpatrick's eyes darted from one to the next. The calls came in on the command net, and Towers provided brusque commentary.

"Alpha One has breached the compound and secured the front entryway. Alpha Two is securing the stairs. Both teams are engaged."

Kilpatrick could see pieces of the chaotic firefight, the dead Houthi guard being thrown into the stairwell, drawing fire, followed by the

SEALs. He heard the sounds of gunshots and explosions over the command net. A chilling cry of *"Allahu Akbar!"* could be heard in the background. The team leaders on the command net were out of breath; a SEAL on Alpha Two had been gunned down in the stairwell.

General Simpson, normally impassive, had his lips pursed and was slowly shaking his head. Towers was too busy talking with his men to provide commentary for the Situation Room. Kilpatrick stole a quick glance at the president, who had her fist to her mouth.

A photographer had been allowed in the opposite corner of the Situation Room to capture the historic moment, but the president told him to put the camera down. This was no longer a photo op; it was a life-and-death mission with a serious risk of failure. A sense of helplessness permeated the room, settling over the hunched shoulders and strained faces of the most powerful people on the planet, who could do nothing but watch.

The calls came in from the snipers that they were all under fire, followed a few minutes later by the chilling moment when Patrick Quillen called to his command.

"Alpha One to Hawk."

"Hawk here," Towers said.

"You need to see this."

At first the feed from Quillen's camera showed the jail cell in the green hues of a night vision camera. Then he switched on his helmet light, illuminating the scene before him.

They froze around the table. The life-size cardboard cutout of the president filled the video screen. Several in the room gasped. The vice president cursed under his breath. General Simpson sat straight up in his chair and commanded Towers to get the men out. The Houthis obviously had known they were coming. Then, remembering that this was not his mission, Simpson looked at CIA director John Marcano.

"I agree with General Simpson," Marcano said to the president, his face expressionless. "We have no choice."

"All right," said the president. "Abort the mission."

"The birds are on their way for extraction," Towers said crisply. "I'm sending in the QRF."

Simpson turned to the others in the Situation Room. "The Black Hawks are on their way. We had planned to use them for extraction. They're about seven minutes out. The QRF is our Quick Response Force. A total of sixty SEALs and Delta Force members."

"Can we get these men out without using the QRF?" the president asked, her voice calm but commanding. She was talking to Simpson, but the response came from Admiral Towers on the video screen.

"We don't want to take any chances," Towers said.

To Kilpatrick, it sounded dismissive. He watched the president bristle.

"What are the chances that the Black Hawks will be shot down by surface-to-air missiles?" she asked.

"We don't believe they have that capacity at the prison facility," Towers said. The man exuded confidence, but he had lost a fair amount of credibility. This mission was crumbling as he spoke, the tension in the room escalating.

Kilpatrick knew that the president had dealt with some tough FBI agents and cops in her days as a prosecutor. He had never known her to back down.

"I hope you're right," the president said. "We've had enough surprises for one night."

★   ★   ★

VIRGINIA BEACH, VIRGINIA

Kristen Anderson was trying to persuade her boys that it was time for bed. They were employing the usual excuses. *One more story. Can we call Daddy? I'm not tired. Can Tiny sleep with me tonight?* It was always this way the first two weeks after Troy deployed. He was the one who had bedtime responsibilities when he was at home. She had been with them all day; it was the least their father could do. When he deployed, it was hard for the little guys to adjust their routines.

But she took it one night at a time, one excuse at a time. And tonight, after fifteen minutes of arguing, she tucked them in bed and said a prayer for their dad. And then, before she went to bed herself, she crossed off another day on the calendar hanging on the refrigerator.

★ ★ ★

Paige Chambers shut down her computer for the night and turned on the television. It was eight o'clock, and she was already tired. It seemed like she was twenty-nine going on sixty. In college, she would go to bed at two in the morning, but now she was lucky to stay up until eleven. She curled up on the couch and pulled the blanket over her legs.

She switched mindlessly from one channel to another, her thoughts drifting to Patrick. Maybe she should send another e-mail before she went to bed. But she didn't want to seem like a stalker. By her count, she had three unanswered text messages and two unanswered e-mails in the queue. She smiled sleepily. She would give him a piece of her mind when he finally answered.

15

SANA'A, YEMEN

The reports came in so quickly Patrick was having a hard time assimilating everything. The snipers were all surrounded and engaged. The other assault team, Alpha Two, was trapped in a stairwell and under heavy fire. Houthi soldiers were approaching the prison in trucks and transport vehicles. Drones would be unleashing more Hellfire missiles soon. And inside the prison itself, Patrick had no idea how many Houthis were lying in wait as part of this trap.

Patrick had four team members cornered with him in this third-floor pod, with two others providing cover in the stairwell at the other end of the hallway. Even now, those men were taking fire.

Patrick knew he and his men would have to fight their way out of the prison facility. The Black Hawks were on the way and would be there in a matter of minutes. Reinforcements from the QRF would take longer, but if he could just get his men out to the prison yard, there was a chance they could get extracted.

He decided not to go back to the same stairwell they had used to access the third floor. That's what the Houthis would expect because that stairwell was still partially secured. Instead, he motioned two of his men forward to the nearest stairwell, at the west end of the prison. They would shoot their way down these stairs and then circle back to the north end of the building to exit.

He signaled for two of his men to approach while he and Beef provided cover, their sights trained on the two intersecting hallways that led to the stairwell. Once this near stairwell was secure, Patrick would radio the men at the other end of the hallway to retreat and join them.

He glanced over his shoulder as one of his men kicked open the door, but the Houthis were one step ahead. The opening door triggered a blast that filled the pod with heat and shrapnel and light. The force of it knocked Patrick to the ground and staggered Beef. Patrick felt piercing pain in his left shoulder and a burning sensation where the shrapnel had gouged his right cheek. He knew his two buddies at the doorway had not survived.

"Eagles down, west stairwell," he gasped into his mic, struggling to get to his feet. "You okay?" he asked Beef.

Beef had his gun trained on the gaping hole where the stairwell door had previously been. He was expecting Houthis to pour through, but so far none had entered.

"Let's make those bastards pay," Beef said.

The reports of casualties were coming in too quickly for Patrick to process. Alpha Two was losing members fast. One of the men Patrick had left behind to secure the stairwell was down. Patrick and Beef decided to join the lone surviving member of the team. They would go out the same way they came in.

They moved quickly to the east-end stairwell, where their teammate was just inside the frame of the door they had blown off its hinges on the way up. He was stepping through, spraying rounds at the Houthis, and then stepping back.

"Up top and below," he said breathlessly as Patrick and Beef came up behind him. The left arm of his shirt was drenched in blood.

"Beef, drop a grenade on the men below. I'll step through and give you cover with the ones upstairs. You two take the steps and blast your way out." It wasn't much of a plan, but they were out of options.

Without hesitation, Beef tossed a grenade down the steps. The explosion rocked the stairwell, and the three men stepped onto the third-floor landing. Patrick began emptying rounds into the Houthis one flight up. They were returning fire wildly, a shower of bullets clanging off the grated metal staircase. Patrick was stacking them up, picking them off one at a time as his rounds slammed into their bodies, his night goggles providing a decisive edge.

But then a light flashed from the landing above him, some sort of battery-operated spotlight that lit up the stairwell for a split second before Patrick could shoot it out, enabling the Houthis above and below to find their marks on the three SEALs caught in the middle.

The world slowed down, frame by frame, as Patrick squeezed off a last round and felt the pain sear through the right side of his neck, just above his body plate. He stumbled down a step, dropping his rifle, and braced himself with his left hand, slumping onto the step below. He could hear the triumphant shouts of the Houthis mixed with the roar of blood rushing to his ears as they clambered down the metal staircase to execute Patrick and his fallen teammates.

The images were blurred, but his last sight was of his best friend sprawled across the steps below him, his mouth open and his gun still in his hand. Somehow Patrick pulled himself down a step, draped his body over that of his friend, and grabbed the grenade from his own belt. He pulled the pin free with his teeth. And just before the world went dark, he placed the grenade under his body, sandwiched between him and Troy.

His last thought was about the smallest of victories. There would be no desecration of these bodies. No weapons or information would fall into enemy hands. He had lived to be a warrior. Now he would die like one.

16

WASHINGTON, D.C.

Like the others in the Situation Room, Philip Kilpatrick had changed his computer to what he euphemistically called the "death screen." It was a real-time aerial view of the prison compound with superimposed data that not only showed the location of each member of the extraction team but also their respiratory rate and heart rate. Each SEAL wore a monitor strap around his chest, relaying via satellite vital signs that were displayed on the screen in front of Kilpatrick. He had found it fascinating as the men went through segments of their mission to see the ones who remained the most calm. But now, he and the others watched in mounting horror as digital readouts all over the map began changing to zeroes.

In the last few minutes, the radio traffic had gone from calm reports of the enemy being engaged to more urgent calls for backup to total silence from the men on the ground. The members of the National

Security Council had fallen silent as well, listening and watching as Admiral Towers took charge, calling in the drones for strikes against the personnel carriers that were delivering more Houthis to the scene, preparing the Black Hawk helicopters for their insertion, talking to the QRF.

The overhead infrared views on the big screen showed the prison yard full of Houthis scampering around, and there was no telling how many troops were inside the building. With an estimated fifteen hundred prisoners in their cells, the drone strikes would have to be carefully calculated.

When the Black Hawks came under fire from surface-to-air missiles, Towers backed them off. The men on the ground were all dead. It was useless to land the extraction birds without the backup QRF troops who could secure the prison facility long enough to drag the bodies out.

"Pull back and stand down until QRF arrives," Towers said, and Kilpatrick could see the fury on his face. Within minutes, a second strike force would descend on the prison yard. Special Forces teams would fast-rope to the ground, engage in a vicious firefight, and retrieve the bodies of their dead friends. There was no doubt in Kilpatrick's mind that Towers would take out as many Houthi rebels as possible in the process.

Kilpatrick watched the second round of drone strikes do its damage, annihilating transport vehicles and pulverizing Houthi guards running across the prison yard. But after the smoke had cleared, dozens more were running to the roofs of the houses surrounding the prison facility and scrambling for cover inside the prison walls. There were hundreds of enemy troops, with more converging on the prison every minute.

"Insert at contingency coordinates," Towers said to the commander of the QRF team.

The president looked at General Simpson. "What does that mean?"

Simpson was ashen. His voice was low and gruff, devoid of the bravado that usually characterized the big man's tone. "The quick-response forces will fast-rope in at various locations about a mile from the prison compound. That way they can avoid the shoulder rockets the Houthis have at the compound."

"What's the likelihood they'll meet resistance trying to get to the compound?" the president asked icily.

"Strong. But they should be able to blow through the resistance and secure the compound. The helicopters can land for extraction once the yard is cleared."

The president turned her ire on Director Marcano. After all, it was technically his mission, and the faulty CIA intelligence had already cost twenty men their lives. "I thought there weren't supposed to be any shoulder rockets," the president said.

Marcano's blotchy skin turned red, and his eyes narrowed. He wasn't used to being addressed in such curt tones, even by the president. But he was smart enough to keep his own voice measured. "Our assets on the ground failed us," Marcano admitted. "We checked them every way we could."

It was a weak concession, but there were more important matters at hand. Kilpatrick knew the president would deal with the blame fallout later.

For now, she studied the video screen in front of her. "Admiral Towers, can you confirm that there are no survivors from the initial team?"

"That is correct, Madam President."

"So now we risk another sixty lives to retrieve the bodies?"

Towers gave the president a wary look. "We have never in the history of Special Forces left a team member in hostile territory," he said. Every muscle on his face was taut. "We're not about to do so now."

"I authorized a surgical extraction," the president said. She looked at Towers on the screen and then directly at Director Marcano. "I didn't authorize a military invasion, and I have no authority to do so."

Towers didn't wait for Marcano to respond. "Events have obviously escalated. We don't leave our men behind."

"You don't make that decision," the president shot back. "I do."

For a moment, nobody spoke. The command net radio crackled as the Black Hawk operators changed course. "Five minutes from insertion," one of the pilots said.

On the screen, Towers stared at the president and spoke into his mic. "Roger that," he said.

The president slid back her chair and stood. She swiveled from Towers to Marcano. "Call them off."

"With respect," Towers started, "we're not just retrieving the bodies. There is classified technology in the equipment—"

"Paul," General Simpson said, cutting off Towers. "The president knows that."

"Darn right I know that," Amanda Hamilton said, her voice laced with indignation. "And I'll take the blame for it. But if we lose sixty more men because we don't have the guts to admit when we failed, I'll get crucified for that, too."

"Two minutes to insertion," a pilot said over the command net.

"There will be no insertion," the president said to Admiral Towers. "Tell your men to stand down."

"Do as she says," Marcano piped in. "And do it *now*."

In response, Towers spoke to General Simpson. "General?"

"It's not my mission. You have your orders."

Towers waited just long enough to make his point. "Command to Hawk One, Two, Three, and Four," he said. "Abort insertion. Return to base."

There was a stunned silence over the command net as the pilots absorbed the order. "Roger that," one finally said. The others did the same.

Towers took off his headset and leaned forward on his elbows, his presence looming larger than life on the screen at the end of the Situation Room. "With respect, Madam President, I think you're making a serious mistake," he said.

"On the contrary, Admiral Towers, I'm just trying to clean up yours."

17

The phone call came at 9:05 that evening.

As soon as Paige answered the phone and heard Kristen's voice, she knew something was wrong. Kristen was speaking in harsh, staccato bursts, her words racked by sobs.

"I just—just got done meeting with a chaplain—" She couldn't speak for a moment, overwhelmed with grief.

Paige's heart sank, her knees buckling. Something had happened to Beef!

"I wanted you to know," Kristen continued between short and jagged inhalations. "But I hated to be the one to call you. Troy and Patrick's team were on a mission tonight—"

Hearing Patrick's name stunned Paige. She reached out a hand to steady herself, bracing her emotions.

"They were all—they were all killed, Paige." Kristen inhaled sharply. "Twenty of them. I'm so sorry. So, so sorry."

The words knifed into Paige, disorienting her, jumbling her thoughts. *Killed?* They were all *killed?* Patrick said it was going to be a routine mission.

Paige slumped into a chair. Her world shattered, she could find no words to respond.

Killed.

"Some of Troy's friends and the families of the other men are coming over to the house," Kristen said. She seemed to have regained a shred of composure. "We want you to come, Paige. You shouldn't be alone."

Paige tried to gather herself, to keep the emotions at bay. The shock settled over her. "What happened?" she asked, her voice thin and fragile.

"I'm not sure about the details. The chaplain didn't know. I just know . . . I just know they're not coming back."

Something about the way Kristen said it, her husky voice hollow with resignation, made the horrific finality of it sink in. Paige moaned and felt the weight on her chest—the pangs of regret and loneliness and nightmarish sorrow making it hard to even breathe.

"I'm so sorry," Kristen said. "I still can't believe this is happening." She managed to murmur a few more words of comfort and regret and disbelief. She asked if Paige needed someone to come by and drive her, but Paige said she would be okay.

"You are coming over, aren't you?" Kristen asked.

"Yes," Paige said, though she just wanted to be alone.

She hung up the phone and the grief consumed her, ripping her heart from her chest.

She thought about calling her mother, but they were so distant that she had never even talked to her mother about Patrick. Her friends knew Patrick and loved him, but she had been guarded around them, and they could bring no words of comfort now. And so she curled into a fetal position on the couch, clutching a pillow, tears streaming down her face, her sobs coming in jagged, gasping fits.

The one person who could comfort her was gone. And just as Kristen had said, he was never coming back.

18

When Paige arrived at Kristen Anderson's house forty-five minutes later, the driveway, the cul-de-sac, and the street leading up to the cul-de-sac were all lined with cars. Paige had expected a few extended family members and friends. But this looked like half of Virginia Beach had crammed themselves into the Anderson house. Paige immediately felt overwhelmed and had an urge to go back to her condo, where she could mourn in peace. But she forced herself to park and walk past all the other vehicles up to the Andersons' front door.

She was let in by a man she did not know, who introduced himself. The place was jammed with other young women and kids and men whom Paige could tell were SEALs. She was struck by how young the women looked. They were all pretty much Kristen's age—late twenties and early thirties—way too young to be widows. She didn't know if all of the other team members' spouses were here or whether the same type of thing was happening in other homes all over Virginia Beach.

She made her way to Kristen, and the two women hugged for a long time. Even without words, it was the first time Paige found any solace. She allowed herself to weep quietly on Kristen's shoulder and she felt the sobs shaking Kristen's body as well.

"Troy loved Q," Kristen whispered. "They both would have died for each other."

The two women separated and tried to wipe away their tears. Kristen introduced Paige to the others as "Patrick's girlfriend," and Paige learned that the widows of two other men who had died that night were also in the house. Most of the men were drinking in the kitchen, and the women were hanging out in the living room. The air was heavy with a mixture of unspoken sorrow, resolve, and a game attempt to put on a brave face. These were SEALs and the families of SEALs. They could not flinch even in the face of death.

Paige overheard the men telling stories about their buddies, the combat missions and the pranks, the fallen men already being lionized into legendary status. Some of the SEALs were playing with the kids, especially the boys, doing everything they could to keep them distracted. The women were assuring Kristen and the other widows that they would never be left alone, that the team members would be there for Kristen's sons, that if she ever needed anything done around the house, all she had to do was ask.

For her part, Paige mostly listened, sipping quietly on a Coke. She had never experienced a community like this—so close, so free with one another, bonds that came from facing danger together. It was something beyond loyalty, the threads of individual lives woven together into a tapestry even tighter than family blood.

Yet Paige felt like she was on the outside looking in. Everyone was kind to her and quick with a story about Patrick, but she knew instinctively that she wasn't really part of this community. She was a girlfriend—not even a fiancée and certainly not a wife. Without anyone saying a word, or even hinting at it, there was a sense in the room that she would be able to move on and find another man. But the three widows in the house would forever be part of *this* community, gold-star families who would be linked to the SEALs for life.

The house quieted dramatically at eleven o'clock, when the president began her speech. Men leaned against the walls and doorjambs, sipping their beers, the living room crowded. A few of the moms took the kids into the back bedrooms. Paige found a place next to Kristen, sitting on the floor.

President Hamilton was grim-faced and to the point. She sat behind her desk in the Oval Office, the American flag and president's flag flanking her. She told the nation that her heart was heavy with the news she had to bear.

She explained that American journalist Cameron Holloman and an innocent member of the Saudi royal family had been falsely accused of espionage in Yemen. They had been arrested by Houthi rebels and sentenced for execution without even a hearing, much less a full-blown trial.

"It was," the president said, "an intentional and blatant violation of international law and a direct insult to American and Saudi sovereignty." The president explained that diplomatic channels had failed and that, as a last resort, she had authorized a Special Forces team to free the innocent prisoners.

"Unfortunately," she said, her eyes unblinking as she stared at the camera, "the mission did not succeed. Resistance was heavy. Even though our brave men fought with the courage and skill of the best forces in the world, they were eventually overcome by resistance that outnumbered them at least ten to one. We lost twenty of our bravest warriors in the conflict, men who loved their country and believed in our mission of freedom. It is estimated that more than a hundred and fifty Houthi rebels were killed in the firefight."

The president paused, and it seemed she was struggling to keep her composure. Her lip trembled ever so slightly before she began again. Nobody in the Anderson living room moved. The only sound was the muted noise of the children in the bedrooms.

"Our thoughts and prayers are with the families of the brave men who gave their lives in an attempt to save others. I take full responsibility for this action. The decision to send in this team and protect the life of a fellow American was mine and mine alone. Tonight I am demanding that the Houthis call off the scheduled executions and return both Cameron Holloman and Abdullah Fahd bin Abdulaziz to their home countries. I am also demanding that the Houthis return the remains of our service members so that we might properly mourn them and provide a measure of closure for the families."

"Screw that," one of the SEALs said. "They should never have been left."

Paige watched as the man walked back into the kitchen with his beer, trailed by a few of his buddies, mumbling curses at the president. There had been rumors circulating earlier that the president had called off a large force of SEALs and Delta Force members sent to extract the bodies and finish off the remaining rebels. None of the men and women gathered that night had made any effort to hide their disdain for the commander in chief.

The air was tense as the president continued. She said the nation would mourn but that America would also exact justice. "We *cannot* shrink back. The lives of these men demand more. America, by the grace of God, does not possess a spirit of fear. Ours is a spirit of justice, of freedom, and of a resolute mind. We will not rest until justice is served."

Though she felt the resentment in the room, Paige could not be mad at the woman. The president had taken full responsibility and then articulated values that Paige embraced. Sure, the president was older and more liberal than Paige. But like Paige, the president had started her career in law enforcement. She understood the pain of victims and the righteous pursuit of justice. Paige trusted her. At the right time, in the right way, she would hold the Houthis accountable.

After the president finished, an awkward silence settled over the room. Eventually, in fits and starts, conversations broke out. There was a lot of speculation about whether the Houthis would go forward with the planned executions and, if so, what America's response would be. Not surprisingly, there was a consensus among the men that the response should be swift, forceful, and heavily dependent on the Special Forces.

Less than thirty minutes later, Paige decided it was time to leave. She hugged the Anderson boys, her heart wrenched by the thought that they would never again wrestle with their daddy. She embraced Kristen one last time in the front hallway. After the hug, she tried to think of words to express the emotions bubbling up inside her. But there was nothing she could say.

Instead, she thanked Kristen for including her.

"Patrick loved you," Kristen said. "That makes you family."

19

The next morning, Paige lay in bed for a long time, her eyes open, sorrow and loneliness pressing her into the mattress. Even after the Ambien, she had slept fitfully and woke with a twisted stomach, the sadness sweeping over her as soon as she opened her eyes. He was gone. He was never coming back.

Patrick had not been shy about his faith, and Paige tried to tell herself that he was in a better place. On one of their last dates, when Paige had expressed concerns about Patrick's safety during his deployment, he had brushed it off. "Believe it or not, God is in control of the Mideast, too. He won't let anything happen to me before my time. And if I die . . ." He had shrugged as if that, too, was fine by him.

"Don't talk that way," Paige had said.

"Paul said that to live is Christ and to die is gain. I'm just saying—that's the way I look at it too."

"Can we not talk about it?"

From that point on, Patrick had gone out of his way to assure Paige that he would be fine—a cruise in the Med at taxpayer expense.

As she thought about him, tears rolled out of her eyes and down her face, soaking her hair and pillow. There were so many regrets. That last night together, shutting down the talk about marriage. Why hadn't she just said yes? She had hurt him, though he had tried not to show it.

One more day. She would give anything for just one more day.

Eventually she forced herself out of bed and made a cup of coffee. She felt heavy and sluggish, her body weighed down with grief, her chest literally hurting from so much sobbing the night before. She still couldn't believe this had happened. And the honest truth was that she didn't care if her own life went on or not.

She tried praying, but it seemed pointless now. She had prayed for Patrick's safety, and then he had died. The God she had given her life to as a child—the one who had walked the earth and healed the lame and come back from the dead—felt so distant now. Yet this thin and frayed strand of faith was the only thing that gave her any hope—the thought that she would see Patrick again someday.

She checked her phone and saw a text from Kristen. **Are you up? Don't turn on the TV. They're showing bodies. Troy's and Q's were destroyed by bombs.**

But like the rest of America, Paige could not look away. Sitting in her pajamas on the couch, she tuned in to CNN. The anchors were discussing the botched raid, interviewing a Republican congressman who put all the blame at the feet of the president. Within minutes, they were showing grainy footage of the bodies of sixteen SEALs hanging in the bombed-out ruins of the Sana'a Central Prison yard. The Houthis had removed the men's helmets and night goggles and left them hanging by the neck in full uniform, their bodies rotting in the desert sun.

It nearly made Paige vomit even though the news feed was careful to show the images at a distance so the viewers could not see the faces of the men.

"The president has promised an appropriate response," the congressman was saying. "But she missed her opportunity. She called off a second response force that would have retrieved the bodies of our servicemen. Nobody who does that is fit to be commander in chief."

★　★　★

WASHINGTON, D.C.

Philip Kilpatrick was an adrenaline junkie who loved chaos, but even he had never seen anything quite like this. The White House was a flurry of activity the day after the failed raid. Like the president, Kilpatrick had slept only a few hours. Details of the raid were trickling out, though the press had still not caught wind of the cardboard cutout of President Hamilton inside the Sana'a prison cell, placed there by the Houthis to mock the Americans.

For its part, the White House had released statements and sent the president's spokesperson out to talk with the media. It was a stalling maneuver while the president worked the phones with American allies and held high-level meetings in the Situation Room. The administration had a plan in place, but they would have to weather this day first.

The president's critics took to the airwaves and second-guessed both her decision to send in the assault team and her decision to call off the QRF. But the criticism was mixed with a heavy dose of rhetoric about the country standing together. With the bodies of American SEALs hanging in the prison yard, the public was in no mood for politics as usual.

At 4:00 p.m., the president and Kilpatrick stepped into the Oval Office, where their two guests were waiting. Admiral Paul Towers and his young and gung ho chief of staff, Daniel Reese, had just flown in from Saudi Arabia. They both stood, snapped to attention, and saluted.

The president returned the salute, and everyone took seats in front of the fireplace.

Towers looked exhausted. He had dark circles under his eyes and a weariness on his face that seemed to go bone-deep. Kilpatrick found it ironic that the legendary Towers, known for being an iron man who survived on little or no sleep, looked more haggard than the president.

"I think you know why I called this meeting," President Hamilton said, her legs crossed, forearms resting on the arms of her chair, her voice calm and authoritative. "After a lot of soul-searching, I have asked General Simpson and Director Marcano to remove you from command for tonight's activities. Your behavior last night bordered on insubordination."

"I followed your orders, Madam President," Towers said.

"But not without questioning them first. And not without making it clear that you had lost confidence in my leadership."

"The orders were a mistake," Towers said bluntly. "Those bodies should be home right now. Instead, they're being desecrated by our enemies."

Kilpatrick saw the steel in the president's eyes. He knew the president expected some sort of apology, but Towers was as belligerent as ever.

"I've heard that after I called you back for this meeting, you told some of your officers what I could do with that request. Is that true?" the president asked.

"That would appear to be accurate, Madam President."

"Do you care to explain?"

"I think it's self-explanatory."

The man wasn't going to make this easy. As Kilpatrick sat there, watching this extraordinary exchange, he knew that the strength of the country depended on men like Towers, men who would never back down, who brooked no compromise. But he also knew that the president would not tolerate it.

She let the silence hang for a moment, a stare-down of sorts between the president and one of her top commanders. "I'm asking for your resignation, Admiral Towers. You are a gunslinger, sir, and we don't need gunslingers calling the shots for our Special Forces. I believe that your arrogance was at least partially responsible for last night's fiasco."

Towers started to protest but she cut him off. "Let me finish," she insisted. "We should have sent in a much larger force. We should have at least called in the Quick Response Force as soon as we knew they had more men in those towers than we first anticipated. You think your men are invincible, Admiral, and last night it cost us."

"Permission to speak freely," Towers said.

"You've never needed my permission before, but go ahead."

"The mission was appropriately planned," Towers snapped. "The intelligence was *seriously* flawed. You should be having this conversation with Director Marcano, not me. He cost those men their lives. His agency should be held accountable. My men performed honorably and followed the mission with integrity."

Towers's face, tanned and wrinkled from the desert sun, was a deep shade of scarlet now. It was clear to Kilpatrick that there would be no reasoning with him—the same traits that made him such a confident commander would sink him now.

The president must have sensed it too, because she responded in a softer, more conciliatory tone. "Paul, I want to give you an honorable way out. Your service has been extraordinary. But I can't leave you in command when you denigrate this office and publicly criticize your commander in chief. I'm asking you to submit your resignation from your current post. I'll see to it that you're reassigned to something befitting your record. But if you don't resign, I'll have no choice but to have General Simpson relieve you of your command and put you at a desk job pushing paper."

Towers rose, and Daniel Reese hopped up with him. The admiral stood ramrod straight and looked over the president's head as he spoke. "I will not resign, Madam President. I cannot do that to my men."

She stood as well and let out a sigh. "Very well," she said. "You'll be hearing from General Simpson."

Towers and Reese saluted, waited for the salute to be returned, then pivoted and left the room.

20

Paige spent all day Friday trying to get a grip on her emotions. She called her mother, but the conversation was awkward and stilted. The two women had grown far apart over the years, and a boyfriend's death wasn't going to fix it.

Her friends brought food and drink and sat with Paige in her dark condo. She had the shades pulled and the overhead lights off, lamps throwing shadows across her living room. It was a cloudy day, but Paige wasn't about to let one of the few rays of sunlight break through the windows.

Mostly she just wanted to be alone. Finally, late in the afternoon, she said it to them bluntly. She couched it in apologies, of course, because she didn't want to hurt her friends' feelings. After they left and quietness descended, she immediately regretted sending them away.

Between crying spells and rereading Patrick's old text messages and after prayers that brought more questions than comfort, Paige sat on the couch and surfed through the news channels. The talking heads rehashed the same story from the night before, over and over, wondering when the president might speak again and address the mess she had created in the Middle East. There were unconfirmed rumors that she had fired the commanding officer of JSOC, an outspoken former SEAL named Paul Towers. The networks ran old footage of the admiral, a thin and determined-looking man wearing khakis, strolling among the troops. The blame for the botched mission was apparently being laid at his feet.

Some of the commentators didn't think that was fair. John Marcano, the bookish head of the CIA, did not have a lot of media fans. Sources close to the situation were reporting that he was in the hot seat as well. Faulty CIA intelligence had cost the lives of twenty good men.

All of it was just noise to Paige, making her angrier and more frustrated by the minute. The president and her cabinet had already shifted into blame mode, and none of it was going to bring Patrick back.

It was almost midnight when the breaking news scrolled across the bottom of her screen. U.S. Special Forces had conducted another nighttime raid and had successfully retrieved the bodies of the dead SEALs. This time, the U.S. had used overwhelming force. There were no reported casualties for the Americans and more than two hundred Houthi rebels confirmed dead. The president would be holding a press conference at nine on Easter morning.

★　★　★

WASHINGTON, D.C.

Philip Kilpatrick stood to the side of the stage, his arms crossed in satisfaction, watching the press conference unfold. This was President Amanda Hamilton at her best. She confirmed reports from Friday night that the bodies of the SEALs had been recovered. The mission had involved air attacks followed by a Special Forces team of more than 120 SEALs and Delta Force members inserted at various positions around Sana'a Central Prison. The American forces, supported by targeted drone strikes, had converged on the prison yard and retrieved the bodies of their fallen brothers.

Hamilton stood to her full five feet ten inches, her jaw jutting forward, eyes blazing. Many criminal defense lawyers had tested this woman's mettle and regretted doing so. And now, representing the greatest country in the world, President Hamilton was warning the Houthi rebels not to do the same.

"The United States is a peaceful nation," she said brusquely. "But when one of our citizens is arrested and condemned without a trial, we will act. When the bodies of our soldiers are desecrated, we will act. And when our allies are threatened, we will act."

She paused, her lips pursed. It was great theater, and the press was lapping it up. "It is no secret that the Houthi government in Yemen receives material support from Tehran. I am warning both the Houthi leaders and the Supreme Leader of Iran that if Cameron Holloman is not released unharmed, we will consider his execution a hostile act of war by enemy nations."

She gripped the sides of the podium and looked around the room. This was vintage Amanda Hamilton, and Kilpatrick could feel the momentum beginning to swing.

"In Yemen, we will increase our support for the legitimate coalition government, backed by the Saudis, including an increase in air strikes against the Houthis. And with regard to Iran, we will treat this hostile act as a violation of the treaty negotiated by the Obama administration, and I will personally request that our allies join us in a renewal of sanctions against a rogue country."

This caused a murmur and a flurry of scribbling among the reporters. They scooted forward in their chairs, waiting for a chance to ask questions.

The president looked down and softened her voice. "Next Friday we are planning a joint memorial service at Arlington National Cemetery for the service members who died in Yemen. On this day, when so many Americans are celebrating the promise of eternal life, I would ask you to take a moment and remember the families of our fallen heroes in your prayers."

As soon as the president stopped speaking, before she could draw a breath, the questions started flying. She handled them all beautifully. She confirmed that Admiral Paul Towers had been relieved of his command before the Friday-night raid. She refused to provide details about why the first mission had failed—"There will be time for that after a full investigation." She stoked the fires of resentment against Iran for supporting not just the Houthis but Hezbollah and Hamas and Islamic Jihad.

All in all, Philip Kilpatrick could hardly keep himself from smiling. It was a somber affair, and he was not unmindful of the lives that had been lost. But deep in his bones, he loved politics most of all. And as he stood there watching this amazing spectacle, he realized that this was one of the reasons why. Fame and popularity were fickle and fleeting. The reversal of fortune that he was watching with his own eyes—no, that he had in fact orchestrated with his own hands—was devastatingly sudden.

By day's end, if the Houthis followed through on their threats, President Hamilton would have the political capital to renew sanctions on Iran, effectively isolating the country and further stalling its development of nuclear weapons. In the process, she would strengthen ties with Saudi Arabia and other more moderate Islamic countries. And eventually, if the pieces all fell into place the way Kilpatrick envisioned they would, President Amanda Hamilton would be in a position to actually achieve what every other president since Jimmy Carter had attempted and failed. She could broker peace talks between America's Muslim allies and the nation of Israel. And in the process, she could unite moderate Muslims and cripple the radical networks intent on jihad.

The press conference ended at 10:05 a.m. The Houthis waited two hours, until just before sunset in Sana'a, to respond. Their video went viral as soon as it hit the Internet. Cameron Holloman and Abdullah Fahd bin Abdulaziz were executed by hanging. The crowd cheered and began chanting in unison. It was Arabic, but in America, the words were displayed in block letters for the entire country to see:

"Death to America! Death to Saudi Arabia!"

21

For a few days, Paige thought she might not get tickets to the memorial service. Each family was allotted twenty VIP tickets, and there would be thousands of people trying to attend. Paige and her friends had planned to arrive at five in the morning to get a seat. Kristen Anderson had been trying to finagle a ticket for Paige in her own family section but found it hard to tell members of Troy's large family that they couldn't attend.

All that changed when Paige received an unexpected call on her cell phone Tuesday morning. She didn't recognize the number with the 607 area code, and she let it go to voice mail. When she checked the message, she heard the raspy, halting voice of a man who introduced himself as Bill Harris, Patrick's grandfather, and asked Paige to call him back. She wasted no time doing so.

"Hello."

"Mr. Harris, this is Paige Chambers. I am so very sorry for your loss."

Paige hesitated because she didn't know what else to say. But the voice on the other end was surprisingly upbeat. "Thank you, Paige. And thank you for calling me back. You meant so much to Patrick."

She'd had no idea that Patrick had discussed their relationship with his grandfather.

"You raised a remarkable grandson," Paige said. She found herself choking up. "You should be very proud."

"Patrick talked about you a lot. And you probably know that he didn't have much family left. The folks in D.C. were kind enough to give me twenty tickets to the memorial service, and I was thinking that I would like to meet you and hoping that maybe you could use one."

For the first time since Patrick's death, Paige felt something other than unmitigated sorrow, and it momentarily left her speechless.

"Of course, if you've already got a ticket or wanted to sit with some-body else, I can certainly understand that," Bill Harris continued, his voice warm. "Either way, I would love a chance to get to meet you. Patrick thinks—" He stopped for a second. "Patrick thought that you basically hung the moon."

"I would love to attend the service with you," Paige said. "There is nothing I would like more."

For the next few minutes, they worked on arrangements. But before he hung up, Mr. Harris had another bombshell. "The families are sup-posed to meet with the president at the White House at nine that morn-ing. If you're not too busy, maybe you could join me there as well."

Surprising even herself, Paige smiled. *If I'm not too busy!* "I might be able to fit it in," she said.

This brought laughter from Mr. Harris. "That's the same thing I told them. I said I'd been meaning to get with the president and give her some advice anyway, so this will work out perfect."

"Did you really?" Paige wasn't sure how to take this guy.

"Sure did. But the staffer I was talking to didn't have much of a sense of humor. He said the president would look forward to it."

By the time she hung up the phone, Paige found herself almost excited about Friday morning. It seemed like Patrick's grandfather was going to at least make things interesting.

★ ★ ★

WASHINGTON, D.C.

As if it knew the entire world was watching, Washington, D.C., was at its best the Friday after Easter. The cherry blossoms had not yet turned white, but the rest of the city was in the fullness of its glory. Puffy clouds floated across the sky on a brisk spring breeze. The sun pushed the temperature into the sixties early in the morning. The grass on the National Mall was thick, lush, and freshly mowed. Even the monuments seemed to dance in the sunlight, reminders that this was a country built to last.

Paige joined Bill Harris for breakfast at the Hyatt hotel and found him to be fascinating company. He was full of stories about Patrick's childhood, and Paige couldn't get enough. He insisted that Paige call him Bill and drop the "Mr. Harris routine." His face was weathered and tanned, his gray hair wispy and combed over, but the man was in great health for someone in his seventies.

Paige could see Patrick's eyes in his grandfather's face and the same big smile and firm jaw. Bill wore bifocals with big lenses that he must have purchased fifteen years ago, along with a baggy suit and an unfashionably broad tie, but he didn't seem the kind to care about how he looked. He was thin, with long arms and hands that were calloused and bony and crisscrossed with veins like spiderwebs.

Bill asked Paige if she minded if he blessed the food, and of course she did not. He said a brief prayer that included a request for God to grant Paige comfort and peace and courage to live the kind of life that Patrick would have wanted. When he finished, Paige could feel her eyes watering.

They took a taxi to the White House, and Bill made a friend of the cabdriver, a man with a thick Indian accent that Paige found difficult to understand. Bill had apparently been to India on some kind of trip with his church, and the two men hit it off talking about the driver's homeland. Bill slapped the man on the shoulder when they got out of the cab and gave him a generous tip. And then Paige and Bill stood on the sidewalk for a moment, just staring at the White House, lost in their individual thoughts. "Feels like *Mr. Smith Goes to Washington*," Bill eventually said.

They headed to the VIP entrance, where a staff member met them and took them to security clearance. Eventually they were ushered into a large waiting room in the West Wing with the rest of the families.

For the next hour, Paige and Bill talked quietly with the family members of the other fallen men while waiting for their turn with the president. They ended up going last. They were the only representatives from Patrick's family.

They met with the president in the Oval Office, and Paige still had a hard time believing this was real. The president had a firm handshake; Paige knew that her own hand was cold and clammy.

A staff member introduced them. "This is Patrick Quillen's grandfather, who raised Patrick," he said. "And this is Patrick's girlfriend."

"Please, have a seat," the president said. She looked larger and older in real life. And everything felt so staged, with cameras lurking all around them, capturing every move.

"Patrick was a brave man," the president said. "He and his teammates were some of the finest men in our nation's military, and I want you to know how sorry I am for your loss."

Bill thanked the president and told her that he prayed for her every day. Then he told her that Paige was a prosecutor, just like the president had been—and from what Patrick had said, a darned good one.

Paige felt herself blush, but the president seemed genuinely interested. She asked Paige about the kind of work she did and then launched into a few stories about her own days as a prosecutor. She told Mr. Harris that his grandson obviously had good taste in women.

"You can call me Bill," Patrick's grandfather said as if he were on a first-name basis with all the great world leaders. "And I agree 100 percent."

Before they left, they had a few pictures taken even though Bill had earlier refused to sign a release so that the White House could publish the pictures. He said that he didn't want his grandson's death to be used for political purposes, and the staffers in charge of procuring the forms didn't quite know what to say.

But now he stood on one side of the president with Paige on the other, and he smiled for the camera. "Thank you for your family's sacrifice," the president said after the photographers were done. "And thank you for being part of the ceremony today."

"It's an honor," Bill said. They all shook hands, and another staff member escorted Paige and Bill out of the office and down the hall.

Paige waited until they were on their way out of the building before asking her question. "You're part of the ceremony today?"

"They asked me to do the closing prayer," Bill said. "I think my pastor wrote to somebody and suggested it. If you ask me, they probably just have a hard time finding somebody in this town that knows how to pray."

Paige stole a glance and saw the smirk on his face, a look she had seen often on the man's grandson.

"I wonder how much we're paying to heat this place," Bill Harris mused.

22

Arlington House, a Greek revival mansion, was the former home of Robert E. Lee and towered over Arlington National Cemetery and its inspiring garden of white stones. In front of the house was the elliptical Memorial Amphitheater, constructed of stark white marble with low marble benches that would seat four thousand and leave room for another thousand people to stand. The amphitheater was bordered by enormous colonnades inscribed with the names of forty-four major battles from the American Revolutionary War through the Spanish-American War. The main stage of the amphitheater, constructed in the shadow of Arlington House, was an enormous three-level structure, recessed into a richly carved marble dome. A quote from Lincoln's Gettysburg Address could be seen just below the peak of the roof: "We here highly resolve that these dead shall not have died in vain."

The stage had been prepared for the president to address a nation still in mourning, though the seven days since the failed mission had allowed time for some of the tears to morph into clenched jaws of defiance and revenge. The Houthi rebels were now under relentless air attacks from the combined forces of the United States and Saudi Arabia, and the president's team was strong-arming allies to join in reimposing sanctions against Iran.

The flag-draped coffins of the twenty Americans killed in Yemen lined the front of the stage, and three enormous American flags provided the backdrop to the podium where the president would speak. Paige sat with a number of people she did not know, all friends of the Quillen family from Delhi, New York. Bill Harris sat in one of the few dozen seats on the elevated stage.

The whole scene created a lump in Paige's throat, a mixture of emotions that were hard to unravel. There was the suffocating sadness brought about by the finality of this ceremony and the growing acceptance that she would never see Patrick again. But there was also a measure of pride in what he stood for and the courage he had shown. This was America at its patriotic best. Patrick and his friends had died to set other men free. Wasn't that why he had joined the SEALs in the first place?

The president's speech was equal to the occasion. She captured the right tone, and after meeting her that morning, Paige felt a certain affinity with her. For the most part, Paige managed to hold it together, except when the president spent a few minutes describing the essence of each of the fallen men.

"Patrick Quillen was raised by a grandfather who also served this country in the Korean War. Mr. William Harris, who will give our closing benediction, taught Patrick that there was no greater honor than serving our country, and his grandson distinguished himself as the very best of the very best.

"Patrick was a man of tremendous character and faith. His commanders tell me that on the battlefield Patrick always carried a small Bible with his life's philosophy written just inside the front cover. It was a quote from a missionary named William Borden, a young man who left America and the wealth of his father's large company to serve on the mission field. He died at the age of twenty-five, and when Borden's Bible was given to his mother, she found he had penned three phrases inside the front cover—'No retreat. No reserves. No regrets.' These were the same phrases Patrick had written in his Bible, and like his hero, Patrick lived it out."

The president moved quickly to the next man, but Paige reflected on the words. She dabbed at her eyes and sniffed back some tears. Family members of the other SEALs were moved as the president shared kind words about their loved ones, including Beef Anderson, whom she called the best prankster in the unit, a "happy warrior," and a loving father and husband. Paige stole a glance at Kristen, seated about fifteen chairs over, clutching the hands of her little boys. Her bottom lip was trembling as tears streamed down her face, but her head was held high.

When the speech was over, Bill Harris walked slowly to the podium, pulled a copy of his prayer out of his suit coat pocket, and asked the crowd to bow their heads. He thanked God for his country. He prayed for the president and the country's leaders. He thanked God for the privilege of raising Patrick. For a moment his voice quivered, and Paige wasn't sure if he would be able to finish. But then he cleared his throat and asked for God to help his country use its power for justice and not revenge, that its people would not meet evil with evil but overcome evil with good.

He ended by saying, "And without any disrespect to the other religions gathered here today, including the followers of Islam, I ask these things in the name of Jesus. Amen." There were a few muttered *amens* from the crowd as Bill took his seat.

With her emotions already running high, the pageantry and symbolism of the rest of the ceremony nearly tore Paige apart. The crowd stood in reverent silence as the twenty flag-draped caskets were loaded onto separate caissons, each pulled by six beautiful white horses. A lone soldier walked in front, and the family members of each SEAL fell in behind. Paige rejoined Patrick's grandfather as they walked side by side behind Patrick's coffin.

They walked nearly a mile down the tree-lined road with thousands of people standing on each side. It was a national show of respect that made Paige realize, perhaps for the first time, just how important these events were for her country. The spectators included people of every race, age, and social standing. They all stood quietly, tears visible on some of the faces. There were servicemen and -women standing at attention, their uniforms gleaming in the sun. There were kids on the shoulders of their dads and men with hats over their hearts and older men and women who had probably served their time in the military saluting as Paige walked by. She felt honored and unworthy all at the same time.

They reached the grave sites, and the caskets were carefully lifted into place at a row of twenty open graves. There were a few chairs facing each grave, and Paige took a seat next to Bill Harris in the front row at Patrick's grave. Everything was done with military precision. A flyover started the interment service. A chaplain stood in front of each casket and said a brief prayer. A cannon salute was fired in the distance.

A loud voice called out, "Present arms!" and at each grave, a team of soldiers with crisp, sharp movements initiated a rifle volley that echoed through the cemetery. When the salute was complete, a single bugler played taps. It was a haunting sound, stirring emotions that Paige didn't even know she had.

Two soldiers at each grave then lifted the flag from the casket and began the precise and exacting folding ceremony, every movement perfectly timed across the twenty graves, so that the flags were all reduced into neat, compact triangles in the same way at the same precise moment. The two soldiers in front of Patrick's grave handed the flag to a captain and saluted sharply. The captain turned and knelt in front of Bill Harris, presenting him with the flag, telling him how much the country was indebted to him and to Patrick for their sacrifice. Bill thanked the man, remaining stoic, but Paige felt tears running from behind her sunglasses, and she didn't even care.

The chaplain then said a few words of comfort and offered a prayer of commitment. Friends stepped forward, one at a time, to place a single rose on the casket. Paige watched as Patrick's grandfather approached the casket and placed his right hand on it, bowing his head in prayer. It was perhaps the saddest sight she had ever seen. The man had already lost his daughter and son-in-law in an accident. His wife had died from cancer. And now the pride of his life had been snuffed out before he reached his thirtieth birthday.

Paige felt overwhelming sympathy for this man whom she already loved. She rose from her seat and joined him, gently placing a hand on his shoulder. He looked over at her and straightened, an old man gathering strength to leave a graveside one more time.

"He belongs to the nation now," Bill Harris said. "God gave him to me for a season. But he belongs to the nation now."

And with that, he gave Paige a squeeze on the shoulder and walked away from the empty casket.

23

Paige spent that night at the Hilton Garden Inn in Alexandria, Virginia. She had agreed to meet Bill Harris for breakfast the next morning before she returned to Virginia Beach and made an effort to reclaim some type of normal life.

She woke the next morning and squinted when she turned on the hotel room lights, heading toward the bathroom. That's when she noticed it—a manila envelope that someone had slid under the door. It was thicker than the hotel room bill lying next to it and had Paige's name typed on the label.

She picked it up and opened it, sliding the contents out one document at a time. She furrowed her brow and studied the papers. She walked to the desk, moved some of her stuff to the side, and spread out the sheets.

She opened the curtains, flooding the room with light. Then she returned to the desk, pushing her hair out of her face, and sat down in her thin cotton pajamas to inspect the documents more carefully.

There was no letter here to explain things, and nothing to identify whom the documents were from. There was, however, a grainy photo of a poorly lit prison cell with a life-size cardboard cutout of President Amanda Hamilton. At the bottom of the picture, somebody had pasted a caption that read: *Sana'a Central Prison, March 30.*

Whoever left the package had also paper-clipped together three documents that appeared to be three separate drafts of a speech by President Hamilton. The first announced a successful mission to free Cameron Holloman and Abdullah Fahd bin Abdulaziz. The second announced that those same prisoners had been freed but that the U.S. Special Forces had suffered casualties. This speech contained a section offering condolences to the families. It was obviously prepared before the raid because there were blanks for the names and number of men killed.

The third draft, the only one that had handwritten edits, informed the American public that Operation Exodus had been unsuccessful. Paige recognized the language from when she had watched the speech at Kristen's house. She assumed she was looking at a copy of that speech with the president's handwritten revisions.

Paige opened her computer and searched for a video of the president's speech. She watched for a few moments, checking the president's language against the words written on the page in front of her. It was pretty much a final draft. Still, Paige didn't really see the point.

The other documents were photocopied articles about the president's Mideast policies. There was an interesting piece from *Foreign Affairs*, discussing the "disastrous" Iranian agreement President Hamilton had inherited from her predecessor. It outlined the same types of criticisms of the Iranian deal that Paige had heard in the presidential election eighteen months earlier. Inspectors had to give twenty-four days' notice before they viewed Iran's uranium enrichment facilities. The only punishment for Iranian violations was a "snapback" of international sanctions, but first the U.N. Security Council had to agree. In addition, the U.S. and Iran were prohibited from reintroducing alternative sanctions unilaterally, meaning that the U.S. had its hands tied to the

United Nations from then on. From following the news, Paige knew President Hamilton was now ignoring this part of the deal based on Iran's failure to act in good faith when it had funded the Houthis but failed to help the U.S. negotiate Holloman's release.

But the article also discussed some aspects of the Iranian deal that Paige had never heard about or at least had never understood. The deal not only tied the hands of the United States with regard to sanctions, but it committed the United States to assist Iran in the development of "energy, finance, technology, and trade." The author said the agreement was "truly historic," a turning point in America's Mideast policies from one that supported Israel and the Sunni Arab states, such as Saudi Arabia, to one that would now equally support a longtime enemy like Iran. In essence, the agreement committed the United States to help build Iran into a regional military and economic superpower.

Prior to her involvement with Patrick, Paige had never cared much about U.S. policies in the Mideast. The whole thing was a mess, and she could never keep the Shiite and Sunni Muslims straight. She knew the U.S. needed to support Israel and get troops out of the Muslim countries, but that was about as deep as she got. Even when Patrick was deployed and Paige started researching the sectarian violence in the Mideast countries, it still seemed like a maze.

So she couldn't understand why anyone would take the time to copy these articles and slide them under her door. Who even knew she was in this room?

The answers would undoubtedly be found in the last item that she had shaken out of the manila envelope. It was an unmarked thumb drive, and against her better judgment, Paige plugged it into her computer.

There were only two items on the drive. The first was a PDF that expressed condolences for Patrick's death but then claimed there were some disturbing things that Paige and Bill Harris should know. It said a similar package of materials had been delivered to Bill's room. The writer, without identifying himself or herself, asked for a meeting at the

Falls Church Marriott hotel at three o'clock that afternoon, executive suite 301.

> Patrick and his team were good men and deserve the truth to be known. I'm sorry if what I must tell you adds to your grief. However, if I were in your place, I would want to know. Please do not talk to anyone else except Mr. Harris about this information. If you decide not to come to the Marriott, I will understand and will never contact you again.
>
> The video on this thumb drive shows a meeting between Philip Kilpatrick, the president's chief of staff, and John Marcano, the director of the CIA. That meeting occurred less than twenty-four hours before the SEAL team was sent into Sana'a. If you come to the Marriott later today, I will tell you why that meeting is important.

Paige opened the video and watched as the two men sat on a park bench and talked, both holding umbrellas. One kept a hand over his mouth most of the time. There was no audio, and it was impossible for Paige to understand anything either of the men was saying.

When the meeting was over, the men stood and walked to a black sedan at the curb. They shook hands, and one of them climbed into the car. The other watched as the sedan pulled away, then turned and walked in the opposite direction.

Paige knew immediately that she would be showing up at the Marriott that afternoon. She thought about contacting the authorities but worried about scaring this person off. Paige wasn't into conspiracy theories, yet when she searched the Internet, she wasn't able to find the picture of the cardboard cutout of the president. Somebody had access to inside information.

The implication was that the mission in Yemen was not for the purpose she and the rest of the American public had been led to believe. Paige thought about her meeting yesterday with the president. She instinctively trusted the woman, another crusader who had come up through the ranks as a prosecuting attorney. Yet how could Paige not show up at the Marriott? She would spend the rest of her life wondering what this had all been about.

She pulled up a picture of Patrick on her laptop. If for no other reason, she owed it to him to at least check this out.

24

Bill Harris met Paige for breakfast wearing jeans, work boots, and a tucked-in short-sleeved button-down shirt. His gray hair was combed over, and he smelled of an old man's cologne. Paige caught glimpses of Patrick in his grandfather's mannerisms and a few of his figures of speech. It made her feel closer to Patrick just being around this guy.

They took Uber to the Falls Church Marriott. It was the first time Bill had used Uber, so he hopped up front with the driver and asked an endless series of questions. By the time they reached Falls Church, Bill had told the Uber driver all about Patrick and the services from the prior day. The driver told them the ride was on the house.

The hotel was an elegant building that bore a slight resemblance to the White House. It featured a large fountain in the middle of a circular drive, perfectly trimmed hedges, and a Southern porch with white oval columns. Whoever this source might be apparently liked to go first-class.

Paige and Bill walked through the revolving glass doors, nodded at the bellboys, and headed straight for the elevators. Bill had received a room key in his package, and Paige was anxious to meet the person feeding them this information.

They entered executive suite 301, turned on the light, and realized they were the first to arrive. Bill looked around, even checking out the bathroom, as if he were some kind of trained detective. There was a note in the middle of a conference table with a computer next to it. Following the instructions on the note, they turned on the computer and entered the password. A video screen that resembled Skype popped up. The instructions said that a video call would start at precisely 3:00.

They pulled two chairs to the same side of the table, looked at their watches, and waited.

"This place is prob'ly bugged," Bill said softly as he surveyed the ceiling, apparently looking for video cameras.

"Probably," Paige said.

A few minutes later, just before three, they heard someone else insert a key to the room. They both hopped up and turned around, and Paige felt her jaw drop as Wyatt Jackson entered the room, followed by Kristen Anderson.

Wyatt Jackson?

"Paige!" Kristen said. "What are you doing here?"

"I'm not sure," Paige said. "I suppose the same thing you're doing." The two ladies hugged, and Wyatt shook hands with Bill.

"This is Mr. Jackson," Kristen said to Paige. "He represented Troy on some . . ." Kristen hesitated for a moment as if she didn't want to spill the details of Troy's former troubles. "Some legal matters."

"We've met before," Paige said icily. She shook Wyatt's hand but wanted to knock the arrogant smirk off his face. It was the same haughty look from that day in the Virginia Court of Appeals, when Wyatt knew he would spring another rapist on a technicality. Paige would need to tell Kristen to stay away from the guy.

"Did you get an envelope too?" Kristen asked.

The four compared notes. Kristen had received the same information. She'd called Wyatt because he had represented Troy in the past. Wyatt, intrigued by what Kristen told him, came to D.C. for the meeting.

Paige wondered whether some of the other SEAL families had received envelopes and would be joining them momentarily, but when three o'clock rolled around, they were the only ones in the room. They all took a seat at the conference table, and when the call started, Paige clicked the icon to answer.

The figure on the other end was a silhouette, a black shadow against a white screen. The outline seemed to suggest a man wearing a hat and sunglasses. His voice was distorted and mechanical.

"Thank you for coming," he said. "Sorry for all the cloak-and-dagger stuff. I know my voice sounds like Darth Vader."

For a second, nobody spoke. What do you say to a silhouette?

"Don't worry about it," Bill said. "If what you tell us makes sense, we don't necessarily need to know who you are."

As a lawyer, Paige didn't agree with that for a second. But this was no time to argue.

"Who's the older gentleman sitting next to Mrs. Anderson?" the man on the screen asked.

"Wyatt Jackson. I represent the Anderson family."

"Welcome, Mr. Jackson."

Wyatt stood up and moved behind the others. Paige couldn't tell if the camera on the laptop was picking him up or not.

"I know you didn't come here for small talk," the man on the screen began, "so I'll get right down to it. But first I want you to know how sorry I am for your loss."

Kristen and Bill thanked him, and the source began a stilted monologue. He apologized for being anonymous but said he might have to provide classified information that could cost him his job if his identity became known. He explained that he had chosen each of them, with the exception of Wyatt Jackson, for a reason. Kristen, Bill, and Paige were the only ones who had received the manila envelopes.

He called himself the Patriot and said he was concerned that the president and her cabinet were misleading the American people. He hoped that he was wrong, and he didn't want to add any more grief to the families, but he had dedicated his life to serving his country, and he couldn't stand idly by if U.S. Special Forces had been sent on a mission by a government that knew ahead of time that they would fail.

As he talked, Paige felt a growing uneasiness in the pit of her stomach. The Patriot's distorted voice made the whole thing seem eerie, and a shadowy figure on a computer screen was hard to trust. Out of the corner of her eye, she glanced at Kristen, who had a sideways tilt of her head that telegraphed her skepticism. Bill had grabbed some hotel stationery and a pen so he could take notes. Wyatt Jackson paced behind them, making Paige even more nervous. She didn't like having a man like that at her back.

"I want to make one thing clear," the Patriot continued. "I do not know for a fact that the president knew this mission was compromised. The worst case is that she intentionally sent the SEALs into battle knowing they would be killed so that the country would support what she wanted to do in the Mideast. But at the very least, she probably knew the mission was at great risk and decided to proceed anyway."

"What's your evidence?" Wyatt asked abruptly.

"Of course," the Patriot said calmly. And for the next ten minutes he laid out his case.

25

He began by reviewing the evidence he had already provided. He started with the video of Philip Kilpatrick and John Marcano.

The director of the CIA had learned the most important lesson of D.C. politics, the Patriot said: cover your butt. Like others at the CIA, he had learned it the hard way. During the Obama administration, when the CIA's waterboarding program became the focus of congressional hearings and investigations, the White House stood idly by even though the Bush Justice Department had earlier authorized the interrogation technique. In the military, when you followed a legal order, you were protected. But the CIA was a civilian agency, and it had a history of operating under justification from one president's Justice Department only to be questioned by the next.

So John Marcano had learned a valuable lesson.

"You'll notice," said the Patriot, "that in the video, Director Marcano is covering his lips with his hand, but Philip Kilpatrick isn't."

"What's the significance of that?" Paige asked.

"Marcano is protecting himself. My guess is he was recording the entire conversation on a hidden audio recorder. But even if not, with this video a good lip-reader can still tell exactly what Philip Kilpatrick is saying."

"Which is?" Wyatt Jackson asked.

The Patriot nodded, as if his guests had finally asked the right question. "Kilpatrick asks if the source is compromised. He asks Marcano to put a figure on it—what level of confidence does Marcano still have. He asks Marcano if the director has independent corroboration. Remember, all of this occurred roughly twelve hours before the mission took place."

The Patriot paused, giving that a second to sink in, and Paige immediately understood the implications. Marcano was making sure he had video evidence that the president's chief of staff had been informed that the mission might be in jeopardy. But he was obviously not sharing this same information in the cabinet-level meetings with other officials, or this park-bench meeting would not have been necessary.

"I have sources who know what happened in the Situation Room later that day," the Patriot claimed. "Marcano said he had a 95 percent confidence level in the intel. He didn't raise any cautions. I can also tell you that the president was handed three speeches that day before the mission started. I included copies of the drafts in your envelopes. She only made changes to the one that would be given if the mission was a total disaster."

The Patriot then turned to a lesson in Mideast politics. He explained that the president had grown increasingly frustrated with Iran's activities in violation of its treaty and was looking for a reason to get tough with President Rouhani. "Think about it. First Hamilton wants to crack down on Iran. Then this failed mission takes place—hours after the director of the CIA informs the White House chief of staff that the mission intel is likely compromised. After the mission, the president gives a speech—the only speech she edited—calling for renewed sanctions against Iran. Is it all just coincidence? Maybe, but I don't think so. At the very least, it makes you wonder."

After a pause, the Patriot asked, "Did you know who Patrick and Troy were working for when they conducted Operation Exodus?"

Nobody answered. It seemed like an obvious question to Paige, but she didn't want to sound stupid.

"SEAL Team Six," Bill Harris eventually said. "The United States Navy."

"Not that night," the Patriot answered. "Our country has no authority to wage war in Yemen. The Authorization for the Use of Military Force Act that was passed right after 9/11 only allows us to conduct traditional military activities in declared war zones, or against al Qaeda and its affiliates anywhere in the world. Yemen and the Houthis don't qualify. So in order to send Special Ops troops inside Yemen, they had to be deputized by the CIA under Title 50 of the U.S. Code. That way they would be performing covert action, not military operations. They call it being sheep-dipped as spies. It's the same thing they did with the bin Laden raid in Pakistan."

The shadowy figure on the screen leaned forward. He lowered his voice to a metallic whisper. "That's one reason the president didn't want to send in another sixty men to retrieve the bodies until she had the support of the American people. She couldn't make it look like an act of war."

All of this information began scrambling Paige's thinking. It seemed that the Patriot knew precisely what he was talking about, but what could *she* do about it? And why did it matter? Patrick was dead and he wasn't coming back.

"I want to show you one more thing," the Patriot said.

His image was replaced by a picture of several men in battle fatigues in the middle of the rubble of a destroyed building. The oldest man, a slim and intense-looking figure, was kneeling over a lamb, preparing to slit its throat.

"This is a United States military officer sacrificing a lamb at a house in Yemen," the Patriot said. "Do you know who that officer is?"

The Patriot's silhouette appeared back on the screen. "That's

Admiral Paul Towers, the former commanding officer of the Joint Special Operations Forces. He's sacrificing that lamb as an apology to the family whose loved ones were mistakenly wiped out by a CIA drone strike. A copy of that picture is in the top desk drawer in the room that you're in now."

Paige was stunned by the image. A high-ranking U.S. official engaged in an Islamic ritual to apologize for an act of war? What if this got out?

To Paige's surprise, Wyatt Jackson didn't seem that intrigued by it. "Why does it matter?" he asked, his voice skeptical.

"It shows the connection between the CIA, who supervises the drone strikes, and the Special Forces in Yemen," the Patriot said. "It shows that our Special Forces were involved in that country long before the Easter weekend mission."

"What are you asking *us* to do?" Bill Harris asked. "I trusted the military to do what's right by my grandson. I would have preferred to leave it that way."

"The reason I chose the three of you is because I know you have integrity and will have credibility with the public. All I am asking is that you think about the evidence I've provided and, if it seems like the right thing to do, take it to your congressmen or senators. Ask them to launch an investigation and get to the bottom of it. I can't do this directly, but America will listen to the voices of gold-star family members. If I were sitting in your seats, I would want to know the truth."

"I've tried a lot of cases," Wyatt said, his arms crossed. "And they usually hinge on the credibility of the witnesses. I'm not going to recommend that Kristen take this anyplace unless we can meet with you in person and weigh your motives and access to information."

"I can't do that," the Patriot said. "I wish I could. But I've given you everything I have. Now, you might want to back away from that computer because it's going to self-destruct."

Surprised, Paige and the others slid their chairs back from the table.

"Just kidding," the Patriot said. "In truth, if you want to go to the police and take that computer with you—go right ahead. There will be nothing helpful on it. All I want is for someone with authority to look into this."

With that, the screen went dark, and the four people in the room stared at it for a very long time.

26

Smooth. That's the way people described Dylan Pierce. Smooth. Brilliant. Sophisticated. Philip Kilpatrick would add one more descriptor: expensive.

At forty-five, Pierce was one of the top litigators in the country's largest law firm. He billed at $1,500 an hour. He once told Kilpatrick that he wanted to raise his rate to $2,000—"five hundred for each of my ex-wives and five hundred to live on."

Pierce was everything Kilpatrick was not. He had a full head of jet-black hair, movie-star good looks, and Ivy League credentials: Harvard undergrad, Yale law, Supreme Court clerkship, and now a corner office in Washington, D.C. He also had a photographic memory. Pierce had argued five times at the Supreme Court and had never taken a single note to the podium. He had only lost once, and he still wouldn't concede that the justices got that one right.

He showed up in the West Wing in a formfitting Brooks Brothers suit and made himself at home sitting at the polished conference table in the Roosevelt Room. One of the clerks brought him a bottle of water without even asking. Pierce and Kilpatrick traded barbs for a few minutes before they were joined by Vice President Frazier, CIA Director Marcano, and Attorney General Seth Wachsmann.

In any other administration, this would have been the AG's show. But Seth Wachsmann disliked these meetings and had delegated most of the heavy lifting to Pierce. Seth was introverted, melancholy, and a stickler for details. His grandfather had been a Holocaust survivor, and that heritage had colored nearly every aspect of Seth's worldview. He was sixty-one with a receding hairline, a long sloping forehead, an oversize nose, and a closely cropped gray beard.

The whole concept of a "kill list" had always bothered Seth, and in the first months of the administration he had worked hard to narrow the parameters. Amanda Hamilton had inherited a kill list of thousands from the Obama administration and some fairly loose criteria for inclusion.

What really grated on Seth were the so-called "signature strikes" based solely on the intelligence signatures of the targets. In much the same way that cops could recognize drug-running houses by the traffic patterns of people visiting, the CIA could establish that the occupants of a certain building were assisting terrorist organizations by looking at patterns of behavior established through aerial surveillance, cell phone signal intercepts, and other nonspecific sources. Drone strikes could be authorized based on such profiles even if the occupants' identities weren't known—wiping out not just the persons assisting the terrorists but everyone in the house.

Seth had argued that the new administration should go back to a rule that allowed drone strikes only against known terrorist leaders. He had eventually convinced the president but used a lot of political capital in the process.

That's when the senior leadership team had brought in Dylan Pierce. He'd put together a ninety-page document called the "Authorization Memo" that justified the continued use of drones under both domestic and international law. He now attended these meetings as a counterbalance to Wachsmann—one lawyer justifying the nonjudicial killings intellectually, the other serving as the country's conscience so that things didn't get out of hand.

The president arrived last, briskly shook hands, and took her place at the head of the table. Pierce and Wachsmann sat down opposite each other, and Philip Kilpatrick settled in for the show. The issue today was whether they should add a Muslim cleric from Iran named Yazeed Abdul Hamid to the list.

According to sources that John Marcano called "eminently reliable," Abdul Hamid was scheduled to deliver a sermon at a mosque in Aden. It would be a rare trip inside Yemen, and the CIA had the capability to take him out using drones or Special Forces on loan from JSOC. It could be done at night and be made to look like a highway bomb or an attack by coalition forces from northern Yemen. All they needed was the green light.

The problem was that Abdul Hamid could not be connected to al Qaeda or ISIS in any operational sense. His hate-filled sermons had inspired many suicide bombers and terrorist attacks. But was that enough?

Dylan Pierce had already circulated a lengthy memo to everyone in the meeting arguing that Abdul Hamid fit the established criteria. He went through the high points now, using the factors that had been established under the Obama administration. The capture of Abdul Hamid for detainment and trial was not feasible or politically wise. The operation to take him out would be conducted in a manner consistent with applicable law-of-war principles. He posed an imminent threat of violent attacks against the United States. This last point, Kilpatrick knew, was quite a stretch.

"We killed Anwar al-Awlaki in Yemen with a drone strike for motivating and recruiting terrorists, and he was a U.S. citizen," Pierce argued. "Is a man like Abdul Hamid, who inspires thousands of terrorists, less dangerous than a soldier who sets off a single bomb? We have verifiable intelligence that he met with ISIS leaders shortly before three terrorist attacks. Just because he's a cleric doesn't disqualify him from the list. Otherwise bin Laden would still be alive."

"You can't compare Hamid to bin Laden," Seth Wachsmann contended. "Bin Laden planned the attacks, recruited soldiers, and ran a terrorist organization. He was the leader of a terrorist group and just happened to be a cleric. Hamid is an imam whose sermons we don't like. But every time a drone takes out a leader like Hamid, ten thousand others take his place. This is dangerously close to assassinating someone for free speech."

That comment got an immediate rise from several others, and the argument escalated. Free speech didn't include inciting terrorist activity. Besides, Abdul Hamid was doing more than preaching sermons and spewing hate. He was meeting with terrorist leaders shortly before known terrorist actions. How much more evidence did they need?

Philip Kilpatrick watched the president's face as the debate intensified. This was exactly what Hamilton wanted—the best thinking of smart people with the freedom to speak their minds. And as a former prosecutor, she was perfectly equipped to make the final call.

But she also had a schedule to keep, and it was Kilpatrick's job to make sure she did.

"Madam President," he interrupted. "The senators have been waiting for ten minutes."

She frowned, resentful that she had to bring the meeting to an end. "It's a close call," she said. "Whenever I'm tempted to say no, I think about the innocent lives that will be lost because a man like Abdul Hamid recruits and inspires terrorists. But when I think about saying yes, I go back to this nation's core principles. Anwar al-Awlaki was an American citizen whom we killed in Yemen. But he had been tried in absentia by the Yemeni courts and found guilty of being a member of al Qaeda. A Yemeni judge ordered that he be captured dead or alive. We don't have that same kind of judicial basis for taking out Hamid."

She surveyed the men at the table, cognizant that Dylan Pierce and

John Marcano would be the most disappointed. "As you know," she said, "on close calls we err on the side of restraint."

"I understand," Director Marcano said quickly. "But I would assume there is no objection to our sharing intelligence with the coalition army in Yemen."

Kilpatrick watched as the president thought about this for a moment. Could they do indirectly what she had chosen not to do directly?

"They are our allies," the president finally said. "Let's treat them like it."

★　★　★

Later that day, there was a meeting between Philip Kilpatrick and John Marcano on a park bench overlooking the Potomac River. It was a beautiful spring day, but Marcano was not in a chatty mood. From start to finish, the entire meeting lasted fifteen minutes.

Less than forty-eight hours later, on the other side of the planet, Yazeed Abdul Hamid delivered a stem-winder of a sermon at a mosque in Aden, calling on Shia Muslims to join the jihad against the United States, Saudi Arabia, and Israel. The sermon was immediately posted on the Internet and distributed throughout the Arab world. The tall cleric cut an imposing figure with his long black beard and blazing eyes, speaking with a cadence and conviction that his followers found mesmerizing.

That night, as Hamid's caravan traveled along the bumpy roads of a mountain range near the Yemeni coast, it was ambushed by a group of eighty soldiers who gunned down everyone in the entourage. One of the men, who had been shot and feigned death, survived. He would later describe the attackers—men wielding AK-47s, their faces hidden by black scarves. They had on the telltale garb of the coalition Yemeni forces—khaki pants, broad belts, and aviator jackets.

But it was dark, and the survivor didn't notice the feet of his attackers. If he had, he would have seen the black low-top Salomons worn by nearly every one of the men who had killed Abdul Hamid.

27

After their meeting with the Patriot, Paige Chambers and Bill Harris agreed to spend a few days researching the matter. If the information the Patriot had given them checked out, they would return to Washington and approach Congressman Mason from Virginia's second congressional district. Paige also agreed to meet with Wyatt Jackson, though she wasn't happy about it.

A few days after returning to Virginia Beach, Paige went to see Kristen and the boys. It was sad watching the boys play without their father. Kristen seemed less patient with them and finally herded them back to the bedroom so that she and Paige could talk alone.

They talked about the ceremony at Arlington, and both teared up. Kristen told a few more stories about Patrick's and Troy's exploits. She said that it if wasn't for Patrick, Troy would never have made it through BUD/S.

It didn't take long for their conversation to turn to the Patriot. Kristen didn't know what to think. Paige shared her misgivings about Wyatt Jackson. She told Kristen about the rape case and how little respect she had for the way Jackson went about his business. She tried to keep her remarks measured, but she knew she wasn't hiding her animosity very well.

"I hear you," Kristen said, fiddling with her coffee cup. "But Troy loved Wyatt, and that man bailed Troy out on about three different occasions. I mean, you're probably twice as smart as him, but the guy's been around the block a few times, and I would just feel better with him involved."

Paige wrestled with whether she should push the point. She had talked with Kristen almost every day since Patrick's death, and the friendship meant so much to her. She didn't want to jeopardize it over the involvement of Wyatt Jackson.

"Just think about it," Paige said. "It's fine with me either way, but I wanted to make sure you knew about my concerns."

Kristen seemed content to let it drop, and Caleb came running out of the bedroom crying. Between sobs, he claimed that Justin had hit him and knocked him down. Tiny was standing next to Caleb, his tail wagging as if he were vouching for the little guy's story. Kristen hugged her youngest son, told him he would be all right, and called for Justin to come out and face his accuser. Under cross-examination, Justin claimed total innocence. It was just an accident, and besides, Caleb had hit him first.

After she had restored some semblance of order and the two women were alone again, Kristen's eyes filled with tears. Everything was still so raw. "I keep asking God why they have to grow up without a daddy," she said.

★　★　★

Nobody would confuse the three lawyers who gathered at the KOA campground on General Booth Boulevard in Virginia Beach with the high-powered crowd that had gathered two days earlier in Washington,

D.C. A few years ago, Wyatt Jackson had sold his house in an upscale golf course community, socked some of the money away in an offshore account, and used the rest to purchase a luxury motor home. He took it on the road when he tried out-of-town cases and lived at the KOA campground the rest of the year. Tonight, he had suggested that Paige meet him and his associate at "his office," and she had reluctantly agreed.

It was a chilly April evening the first time Paige met Wyatt's associate—a pudgy young lawyer named Wellington Farnsworth. He looked all of nineteen years old, with soft, pale skin, light-blond hair, and a round face that looked like he hadn't started shaving yet. He wore a hoodie as the three lawyers pulled up chairs around a campfire Wyatt had built.

Despite Wellington's boyish looks, Paige knew he should not be underestimated. He had graduated from Southeastern Law School at twenty-one at the top of his class. His job was to do Wyatt Jackson's research, prepare outlines for Wyatt's examination of witnesses, and compose legal briefs. In other words, Wellington did all the grunt work.

The three of them were joined by Wyatt's golden retriever, a friendly mess of a dog that Wyatt called Clients.

"Clients?" Paige asked.

"Yeah," Wellington said. "My cell phone is the firm's general number, and when people say they need to talk to Mr. Jackson, I tell them he's meeting with Clients."

"And my RV is named Court," Wyatt said.

What a crew, Paige thought.

Like Paige, Wellington and Wyatt had done some research on what the Patriot told them. Wyatt was convinced the information was legit. He lit up a cigar and puffed on it as they talked.

"What makes you so sure?" Paige asked. It was seven thirty, and the sun had just disappeared behind a row of trees.

"That stuff about the SEALs working for the CIA checked out," Wyatt said proudly. He took a sip of beer and leaned back in his webbed chair, cigar smoke swirling around him. He was staring at the fire as he talked. "I had Wellington apply for some death benefits for Troy that are available only to CIA members. Sure enough, they confirmed that he would be eligible."

Paige made a note to get that information later from Wellington. She should have thought of that herself.

"I did some research on the president's Mideast policies," Paige said, not to be outdone. "What I found lined up with the Patriot's information."

"Wellington did a short memo on that," Wyatt offered. "At least it was supposed to be short. Turned out to be about fifty pages. Wellington, why don't you send a copy to Paige?"

Wellington had his computer on his lap and typed in some notes. He had positioned himself under the lights of the RV so that he could see the keyboard better. "Done," he said.

They talked for nearly an hour about the best course of action. Wyatt was on his third beer. Paige explained that she and Bill Harris were prepared to take the information to Congressman Mason. She would be happy for Kristen and Wyatt to join them.

"You too, Wellington," Paige quickly added when she realized she had left him out.

Wyatt shrugged. "Actually, I was thinking about just filing suit."

Paige gave him a courtesy chuckle, but he didn't appear to be kidding. Wellington kept his head down, typing like mad.

"Wellington here tells me we don't have much chance of success," Wyatt said. He snuffed out the stub of his cigar and flicked it in the fire. "Says the president has absolute immunity. Says that soldiers involved in combat activities can't file suit against government officials. Something called the Feres Doctrine. He's got all kinds of reasons a lawsuit won't work."

Paige hadn't even considered a lawsuit. What was the point in that?

"It doesn't sound like a lawsuit would stand a chance," she said.

"I told Wellington to find some exceptions," Wyatt said. "I'm not about to turn this over to some congressional committee that we don't control. If I file a lawsuit, I'm in control of the investigation."

"Not if it gets thrown out on a motion to dismiss," Paige countered. "It will just make the Anderson family look bad."

"You don't have to join us. In fact, it'd probably be better if you didn't."

"You don't have to worry about that," Paige said.

This was exactly the kind of thing she was concerned about. Wyatt Jackson was in it for the publicity. He was going to use this tragedy to get his name out there and claim his fifteen minutes of fame. And Paige couldn't talk him out of it. Even though Wellington lent some tepid support, all of her arguments fell on deaf ears.

Wyatt finished his beer and tossed it toward a trash can, missing badly. "You sure I can't get you one?" he asked Paige.

She just shook her head. His act was getting old.

"Sometimes you've got to start a fight to figure out how to win the fight," Wyatt said.

"What's that supposed to mean?"

Wyatt had his hands burrowed in the pockets of his windbreaker now. He was rubbing Clients's belly with his foot.

"I'm not going to some congressman so they can nibble away at this in endless committee meetings. I'm going to sue these clowns for a few hundred million and get their attention. We'll just punch them in the nose and see what happens. Like I said, sometimes you can't figure out your strategy for winning a fight until the fight gets started. And this . . . well, this should be a heckuva good fight."

The whole thing was nonsense to Paige. She told him as much, thanked him and Wellington for their time, and excused herself.

★ ★ ★

On the way home Paige called Kristen and told her about the conversation.

"I know he wants to file suit," Kristen said. "I haven't decided yet whether I will let him."

"It's got no merit. It'll get dismissed, and Wyatt will get sanctioned," Paige said.

"I'm not worried about any of that. I just don't want the whole SEAL community turning against me."

Paige hadn't even thought about that angle. "You need that community," she said. "They'll be your lifeline long after Wyatt Jackson has moved on to the next case."

"I get all that. But sometimes I just want to fight back against somebody."

28

On Friday, Bill Harris drove all the way to Virginia Beach so that he and Paige could meet with Congressman Mason, who was spending time in the district. Paige had asked Kristen to join them, but Kristen begged off.

The meeting was scheduled for 9:00 a.m. Saturday morning. Paige was surprised at the nondescript nature of the storefront space the congressman rented for his district office. Mason was a moderate Republican who had been in Congress for nearly thirty years and knew how to work the system. He was gracious and low-key with a reputation for good constituent service.

When Paige met him that morning, she was struck by how tired and haggard he looked. She'd only seen him on TV and in campaign flyers. He looked so much older in real life. His hair was thin and dark, the product of a poor coloring job, his eyes were red, and he had tiny goose pimples on his cheeks. Republicans were having a tough time in Washington these days, and the despondency of that fact seemed to be written all over Mason's face.

He expressed his condolences to Paige and Bill and offered them coffee. A couple of staffers sat at the table while the congressman filled the air with small talk about how moving the ceremony at Arlington had been and how much Patrick's sacrifice meant to the nation.

Bill Harris seemed truly grateful and humbled by the words. "Thank you, Congressman," he said. "That means a lot to me, sir."

Paige wanted to skip the sentimentality. "Congressman, would it be okay if Mr. Harris and I met with you privately?" She fired a quick glance at the staff members, who looked like they had been caught in some horrendous crime. She didn't mean to embarrass them, but she wasn't sure about the protocol for something like this.

"Of course," Mason said. "But I can assure you that my staff would keep everything very confidential."

Once the room was clear and it was just the three of them, Paige pulled out the folder of documents from the Patriot and the research she had compiled and began filling the congressman in. She showed him the picture of the president's cardboard figure in the Sana'a prison cell and the copies of the president's speeches. She went through her understanding of how the failed mission had advanced the president's Mideast policies. She slid the thumb drive across the table with the video of Philip Kilpatrick meeting with John Marcano. She explained how the SEALs had been working for the CIA on the night of the mission and how the president had called off the Quick Response Force. The only thing she didn't give the congressman was the picture of Admiral Towers sacrificing a sheep.

Through it all, Congressman Mason took plenty of notes and asked polite clarifying questions. When Paige finished, he studied the documents she had placed in front of him and watched the video while an uncomfortable silence blanketed the room.

"Where did you get all of this?" Mason asked.

"I can't really say," Paige responded. "An inside source. He seemed credible."

"There are some disturbing things here," Mason said carefully, weighing each word, "but at this point it would be quite a stretch to think that the president authorized a mission knowing it would fail. Or even that she kept relevant intelligence from the men in charge of the mission. I mean, that meeting on the park bench might just be the president's chief of staff and the CIA director getting their heads together on how best to communicate the CIA's intelligence to the president. Or maybe the president had some questions and sent her chief of staff to get the answers. Who knows?"

Paige shrugged as it became obvious that Mason wasn't impressed by her inside information. He must have read her expression, because he changed his tone into one of political resolve.

"But I can assure you of this," he said. "I will look into it. And if there's anything here, I'll make sure it gets brought to light. I go to bed every night and wake up every morning thinking about the men and women serving this country and families like yours who have lost a loved one. This information here—" and for good measure, the congressman tapped the documents on the table in front of him—"will be my top priority."

"I really like that guy," Bill Harris said as soon as they got outside. "I think he'll get to the bottom of it."

Paige kept her misgivings to herself.

★   ★   ★

"You cannot sue the president of the United States." This was the advice Wyatt Jackson received from Wellington Farnsworth after the young associate completed all of his research. "The president has absolute immunity while in office from a suit like this."

Then it got worse. Members of the military couldn't bring any lawsuits against government officials for things incidental to military duty. Otherwise, civilian courts would be interfering with military discipline and affairs.

Wellington wrote a memo reducing all the bad news to a mere eight pages, barely a tweet for a guy like him. Part of the memo was dedicated to *United States v. Stanley*, a 1987 U.S. Supreme Court case that was, in the view of Wyatt Jackson, one of the most ridiculous decisions he had ever read.

In *Stanley*, some soldiers sued the Army for using them as human guinea pigs in an experimental chemical warfare program where they had secretly been administered LSD. But the Supreme Court threw the suit out. Servicemen could not sue, the Court said, because it might undermine "the unique disciplinary structure of the military establishment." The dissenting justices criticized the majority opinion, claiming that the government had "treated thousands of its citizens as though they were laboratory animals, dosing them with this dangerous drug without their consent."

Wyatt wasn't all that concerned about the *Stanley* case. The Supreme Court had changed a lot since 1987. If he could get his case reviewed, he was pretty sure he could carve out an exception for cases when service members were sent on a doomed mission solely for political purposes. And even if he couldn't, he would make a good name for himself trying.

But Wellington's memo didn't end there. The state secrets doctrine would prevent any lawsuit that might reveal confidential information vital to the security and defense of the country. Anything having to do with the CIA was generally covered. Plus, they didn't really have enough information to file suit yet. At most, they had a few pieces of intriguing evidence and a lot of speculation from an anonymous source.

Wyatt reviewed the memo carefully while sitting on the pullout couch in his RV, chewing on an unlit cigar. He pulled up the cases cited by Wellington and read every one of them. He popped a beer and paced back and forth in the RV, walking in tiny circles as he played out the scenario in his mind.

He took Clients outside and played a game of fetch using an old, grungy tennis ball while he enjoyed a smoke. Then he picked up his cell phone and called his young associate.

"I want you to draft a lawsuit on behalf of the estate of Troy Anderson against Philip Kilpatrick and that CIA guy, Marcano. Refer to the president as an unnamed coconspirator."

Wellington began to sputter out reasons why such a suit could never succeed. But Wyatt had made up his mind.

"I want you to allege, on information and belief, that the president knew the mission would fail but authorized it anyway so she could blame Iran. Attach those draft speeches as exhibits and a still photograph of the Marcano and Kilpatrick meeting. Put in that stuff about the president not authorizing a Quick Response Force and anything else to make her look bad. I want to file it Monday afternoon.

"And I'll need you to come out and take care of Clients on Monday night. If all goes according to plan, I'll be in New York City."

29

Wellington Farnsworth put in a superhuman effort over the weekend, staying up nearly all night on Sunday to finish the complaint. Wyatt made a note to give the young man a raise. The lawsuit spanned 102 pages and asked for $30 million in damages. Wyatt wanted to ask for more, but Kristen had put her foot down.

The complaint contained lots of speculation and paragraphs that began with the magical words "Upon information and belief," a lawyer's way of saying that he didn't know whether the information was necessarily true but he had to allege it for a good lawsuit.

Wyatt carried the thick document to the federal court building in downtown Norfolk himself. Because the case accused the president of wrongdoing and involved the greatest disaster for American Special Forces in modern history, he knew there would be plenty of media interest. He had alerted the local press that he was filing the case and would have a few comments on the courthouse steps. When you don't have a traditional office, you have to improvise.

He wore his best gray pin-striped suit and red power tie. He had stuffed his briefcase full of extra copies so he could hand them out to the local reporters. He filed the suit early in the afternoon so they would have plenty of time to get their stories together for the evening news.

He emerged from the courthouse to a bank of microphones and at least a dozen reporters. He began by talking about Kristen and Troy Anderson and the brave men from SEAL Team Six. It pained him to file this lawsuit, he explained, but he had learned disturbing information from reliable sources that the SEAL team's mission had been compromised before it began. Worse yet, he had learned—upon information and belief—that the president's chief of staff knew the mission had been compromised and had conveyed that information to the president herself. Troy Anderson's family deserved answers, and Wyatt Jackson was going to get them some.

He took questions for a few minutes, but he wanted to save the good stuff for the national news. He had included a picture of the meeting between Marcano and Kilpatrick in the lawsuit but had held back the video. Wellington was on the phone with the big networks in New York at that very moment. The young associate promised to send them electronic copies of the complaint and, if they agreed to interview Wyatt Jackson the next morning, a video of the park-bench meeting. They could get their own experts to read the lips of Philip Kilpatrick.

The plan worked to perfection, and the next morning Wyatt Jackson was making the rounds on the cable networks and morning shows in New York City. Predictably, the news had exploded the prior night, and legal experts were already predicting the lawsuit would be quickly tossed. But when the morning hosts confronted Wyatt with those predictions, he had a surprise for them. The Feres Doctrine didn't apply, according to Wyatt, because the SEAL team actually hadn't been working for the Navy at the time of the mission. That's right, they had been "sheep-dipped" by the CIA. They were civilians, not members of the military.

And once the networks started showing the video, the merits of the suit were no longer the center of public debate. Everybody had an opinion on what Philip Kilpatrick said or didn't say. Everybody also had an opinion on why the wily Marcano kept his hand over his mouth. Soon the press corps was descending on the White House, demanding a comment.

Wyatt Jackson took an early-evening flight back to Norfolk with a smug half smile on his face. He was sixty-five years old. He would probably never have another case like this. He might not win, but he was sure going to have fun trying.

★ ★ ★

Philip Kilpatrick learned about the case on Air Force One. He printed two copies of the entire complaint and huddled with the president at thirty thousand feet to review it. It contained mostly conjecture and speculation and paragraphs that began, "Upon information and belief." Kilpatrick had been around the block a time or two, and the president had seen her fair share of lawsuits, but neither of them had heard of Wyatt Jackson. The whole thing had the stench of an ambulance chaser trying to get lucky.

"What do we know about this lawyer?" the president asked. Pointedly, she had not used his name. He had not yet earned that much respect.

"Basically a solo practitioner. Criminal defense. Virginia Beach. Unorthodox trial lawyer who will say and do anything."

"Sounds dangerous," Amanda said. Kilpatrick knew what she meant. The big D.C. firms were predictable. But guys like Wyatt Jackson could be the legal equivalent of suicide bombers.

"Do you think one of those conservative crusader groups is behind him?" the president asked.

"Don't know. I'll do some research."

The president set her copy of the lawsuit on the table in front of her with a sigh. She took off her reading glasses and placed them next to it. She never wore them in public, preferring contacts so that the good people of the United States would always remember she was the youngest president since JFK.

Kilpatrick could see the weariness in her eyes. This was day one of a four-day international excursion—first to Europe, then the Mideast. Allies had to be cajoled. Giant egos had to be massaged. Promises had to be made and explanations given for those that had not been kept. The president hated trips like this.

"You'll have to take care of this, Philip," she said. "We won't be able to talk about it. If the case ever makes it to trial, which is highly unlikely, they'd be able to ask about any of our conversations. We don't have attorney-client privilege, you know."

"I can handle it," Philip assured her.

The president looked out the window for a second and then blew out a breath. This lawsuit was not in the plans. "Do you think this story has legs?"

"I'll call Dylan Pierce. He'll file a motion to dismiss. It'll be gone at the first hearing. You've got immunity, and we've got the Feres Doctrine to fall back on. Plus, we'll plead national security and say the courts shouldn't pry into these matters."

"I know all that. But we need this thing to die quickly. We can't wait two months for a court ruling. The timing couldn't be worse."

The whole conversation had a familiar ring to it. *Take care of it, Philip. Do the impossible, Philip. Make it go away.*

"We'll need to issue a firm denial," Philip said. "We'll be careful in the wording so it doesn't look like we're taking a shot at the widow of the SEAL who filed this thing. We'll reaffirm how much you love the military and how you would never send men into harm's way knowing that they weren't going to make it out. You'll have to be ready to take questions at the press conference in London tomorrow night."

"I know," the president said. She sounded more determined now. Nothing about this job was easy. "I heard this guy left behind a wife and two little boys. Is that right?"

"Yeah. It was the Anderson family."

"I remember them," the president said, looking out the window. There was a wistfulness in her voice. "Cutest little boys."

"We'll take care of it," Philip said.

The president turned back to him. "Sometimes I hate this job."

★ ★ ★

If Philip Kilpatrick was good at one thing, it was opposition research. His team was the best in the business at digging up dirt on campaign opponents. So after he called Dylan Pierce and hired Washington's most expensive law firm, he called his opposition research team. They had two assignments—first Wyatt Jackson, then Troy Anderson.

Philip googled Jackson and knew his boys would have fun with this guy. By the time Air Force One landed, his team would have enough dirt to bury the man twice over. A divorced defense lawyer with a checkered legal career who liked to push the envelope on ethics. It would be, in the parlance of the military, a target-rich environment.

30

Two days after he filed suit, Wyatt Jackson rolled out of bed in his RV, fed Clients, and made coffee. He was getting ready to boot up his computer and check the day's headlines when Clients started pawing at the door. Wyatt threw on his spring coat and opened the door to let the dog out. Clients hesitated, noticing the drizzle, and decided suddenly that he did not have to go.

"C'mon," Wyatt said. He nudged the dog with his foot, and Clients tiptoed out onto the wet grass. Wyatt noticed a newspaper in a plastic bag at the bottom of the RV steps and picked it up. He didn't subscribe to the paper—why bother when you could get your news online? Besides, they probably didn't deliver to campgrounds.

He pulled the paper out of the bag and read the note attached to the front. It was typed in large font.

You've been playing in the minor leagues. Welcome to the big-time.
    The Patriot

Clients finished his business, and the two of them went back inside. The paper was the morning edition of the *Washington Herald*, and Wyatt immediately wondered how the Patriot had managed to deliver it to the KOA campground so early in the morning. He must have been right outside Wyatt's door just a few hours ago. He knew where Wyatt lived.

The article about Wyatt began on page three, where the paper ran national political stories that didn't make the front page. The headline: "SEAL Member's Lawyer Leaves Trail of Unhappy Clients."

It was a classic hit job that made Wyatt fume. Any lawyer who had practiced for nearly forty years had a few skeletons buried. But this reporter had dug up every bone and made it seem like Wyatt was a walking malpractice suit.

There had been about a dozen clients who alleged ineffective assistance of counsel on appeal. Wyatt was actually proud of that record. When criminal defendants got convicted, their appellate lawyers almost always argued that the trial lawyers had been ineffective. But Wyatt had put up such fights that it had only happened a few times in his career.

The reporter had talked to clients who complained from their jailhouse cells that Wyatt had not interviewed the right witnesses or made the right legal arguments or, in one case, had fallen asleep during trial. Wyatt remembered that case—a white-collar defendant with lots of testimony from accountants. Wyatt hadn't missed a thing during his short nap, but the appellate lawyer made him sound like Rip Van Winkle. The article contained a quote from the client, who said that Wyatt nodded off so much he "looked like a bobblehead doll" during the testimony of an expert witness.

Several other clients complained that Wyatt had dropped their cases on the eve of trial. They said Wyatt had promised them he would handle their entire case for a flat fee but then made demands for more money. When they didn't pay, he made a motion to withdraw and left them high and dry.

Like the best hit stories, it had a grain of truth. Wyatt *had* left a few clients on the eve of trial, but that was because he was supposed to be paid by the hour and he had already burned through their retainer. Their families couldn't come up with additional funds, and Wyatt was not going to spend weeks of his life working for free. At least not for the guilty clients—he had done it a time or two for the innocent ones who couldn't come up with more money.

Toward the end of the article, the reporter quoted a few clients who were actually satisfied with Wyatt's work and a couple of lawyers who said what a tough old codger he was in the courtroom. The reporter noted that he had attempted to contact Wyatt by phone and e-mail but had received no response.

The whole thing felt like a vicious sucker punch, and there was nobody Wyatt could punch back. He couldn't file a defamation suit against the *Herald*, both because he had thrust himself into the public spotlight and because everything in the article was technically true. The only thing he could do was use the article to feed his venom against the people who had undoubtedly set this up—Philip Kilpatrick and John Marcano.

He lit up a cigar and glanced through the article a second time, highlighting the most incendiary sentences. He went online and read comments from those who were predictably trashing his good name and all other lawyers along with him. For about thirty minutes, the hit job had thrown him off-balance. But soon the old Wyatt was back, plotting ways to exact his revenge.

The problem was that he had a weak lawsuit. He had filed it primarily to draw attention to the allegations the Patriot was making. Apparently the Patriot didn't like that approach. But Wyatt had learned in nearly forty years of trying cases that the other side fought most viciously when you were really onto something. And this article had required a lot of investigation.

"Looks like we've struck a nerve," he said to Clients.

31

Paige quit work early on Thursday so she could watch Justin Anderson's soccer game and talk to Kristen. The two women pulled up lawn chairs near the end of the field and out of earshot of the other spectators. Three-year-old Caleb was running around on the sidelines, playing with other kids, which gave Paige and Kristen a chance to talk, punctuated by occasional cheers when Justin kicked the ball.

Like all soccer games at this level, the kids bunched around the ball in a great moving amoeba. Only occasionally would the ball squirt loose and make progress toward a goal. Justin was more coordinated than the others and scored a goal in the first half, knocking three other boys down in the process.

"He gets that from his dad," Kristen said. "And honestly, he's been a lot more aggressive in the last two weeks."

It was a good chance for Kristen to unburden herself about how hard things had been since Troy's death. "I always thought I could handle anything. A Navy wife and all of that. But, Paige . . ." Kristen's voice trailed off, and Paige just let the silence linger.

The hardest times, Kristen said, were after the boys had gone to bed and she was alone in the house. She would dwell on the life she had with Troy and think about how she would never find another man like him. She worried about the future.

"I know what you mean," Paige said. "I've never met anybody like Patrick."

It was the kind of heart-to-heart that both women needed. Paige had resisted counseling because she couldn't stand the thought of somebody prying into her life and feelings. Plus, she had this nagging fear that the counselor would unearth all of those other life issues that Paige had worked so hard to tamp down.

But out here, with the shouts of kids playing and parents yelling, it seemed like a safe place to talk about the hurt. Though she had only dated Patrick for a few months, he had filled such a big void in her life. Just having someone who cared about what she did every day, someone she could trust, made her feel needed and secure and connected in a way she hadn't felt in a long time. From the moment her mother had moved to Nashville, it had seemed that nobody had her back. Even with her law school fiancé, she felt like she had to constantly prove herself, to show that she was his equal in terms of intellect and wit and ability to cope with life's challenges. It was like they were some kind of power couple in training, and she could never relax around him the way she did around Patrick.

Kristen waited until the second half was nearly over before bringing up something that had apparently been on her mind. "Did you see the story about Wyatt Jackson?" she asked.

"Yes," Paige said. Then she quickly added, "But he's a good lawyer." Even though Paige didn't like the man, Kristen had decided to stick with him, and it wouldn't serve any purpose to undercut him now.

"Oh, I know he's a good lawyer. I saw him in action when he represented Troy."

There was a flurry of excitement on the field as a kid from Justin's team had a wide-open shot on goal. It flew wide of the net, and the parents let out a collective groan.

"I talked to him yesterday," Kristen continued, then shouted, "Let's go, Justin!" Then, without missing a beat, and proving again that Navy moms could multitask with the best of them: "He called and said we have a problem. A reporter for the *Washington Herald* contacted him and has been snooping around about Troy's prior criminal cases. Wyatt thinks they're going to run a story."

It took Kristen only a few minutes to explain the background, but Paige could tell it made her exceedingly uncomfortable. She never glanced at Paige as she talked, following the action on the field and keeping her voice low. Several years ago, Troy had been involved in a bar fight. A woman had accused him of sexual assault. Fondling and groping, that type of thing. Troy said it was all a lie, that one of his buddies had been hitting on somebody's girlfriend and a fight had broken out. The woman had mistaken Troy for his friend.

At court, it would have been the woman's word against Troy's. But Troy couldn't testify without ratting out his buddy. So Wyatt Jackson had come in and negotiated a deal. Troy pleaded guilty to misdemeanor assault, and the judge entered a suspended finding. The entire case was eventually dismissed after Troy kept out of trouble for six months. The deal allowed Troy and his buddy to stay in the SEALs.

Out on the field, Justin dribbled the ball down the middle, juked past one person, and headed toward the goal. But Kristen didn't seem to notice.

"So now we get hit with this article about Wyatt, and it will be followed by something bad about Troy." She stopped talking and swallowed hard. "It just all looks like—I don't know. That's not who Troy was at all."

Goal! Justin had done it again. His second of the day. Paige jumped out of her seat, and Kristen belatedly joined her, just in time for Justin to look over and smile at his mom's approval.

When they settled back down, Kristen asked the question that must have been on her mind the entire game. "Would you ever consider coming into my case as cocounsel? I know I can trust you, and I think it would be good to have a female lawyer on the team to fight some of these accusations. I've already asked Wyatt about it, and he said he would welcome the help."

The request caught Paige off guard. There were a thousand reasons she couldn't get involved. The case was on shaky ground legally, and Wyatt had filed it against Paige's advice. It would be impossible to work with Wyatt Jackson. Besides, Paige had a job with the attorney general's office in Virginia. It wasn't like she could sue all the president's men on the side.

"It's okay if you can't," Kristen added, to fill the silence. "I just thought I would ask."

"I'd like to help," Paige said, trying not to hurt Kristen's feelings. "But I'm not a private lawyer. I can't work for the state and represent private clients too."

"I understand. I didn't really expect you could. I just thought . . . well, it couldn't hurt to ask."

★   ★   ★

Paige hardly slept that night. Was she being selfish in telling Kristen no? How crazy would it be to leave a well-paying job just to help with one lawsuit that would probably be dismissed in two months? She believed in the cause, but she didn't think the law supported their arguments. And she certainly couldn't stomach the thought of working with Wyatt Jackson.

But then she thought about the relationship between Troy and Patrick. Those men were there for each other. They would have each other's back. Each man would lay down his life for the other.

Was it too much for her to give up a job, even temporarily, to help out a person who was quickly becoming her best friend?

For a week she wrestled with the decision. And when the article came out exposing Troy's prior run-ins with the law, quoting the woman whom he supposedly assaulted and excoriating the judge for ultimately dismissing his case, Paige knew she couldn't stay on the sidelines. She called Wyatt Jackson and he welcomed her to the team. She knew he would view her as another Wellington—an associate to help with grunt work—but at least she was in the game. She called Bill Harris, who told her he had been praying for her that morning and that God had put her on his heart. Now he knew why. That whole conversation gave her chills. Then she called Kristen, who choked up when she tried to express her gratitude.

Finally Paige wrote an e-mail to her boss. She requested a leave of absence so that she could help represent Kristen Anderson in her lawsuit against the director of the CIA and the president's chief of staff.

Her boss was understanding, but the office had its policies, and his hands were tied. She could resign, and he would do everything within his power to make sure she was hired back when the Anderson case was over. But he couldn't give her a leave of absence; the AG's office didn't work like that. Paige thanked him and told him that she needed to do this. He said he understood, and they worked out a transition plan.

Paige thought she would feel a certain sense of euphoria and relief the night after she had settled things at work. She thought she would sleep well for the first time in weeks. One of the hardest decisions in her life was behind her, and she had chosen the right path.

But none of those things happened. Instead, she lay awake, staring at the ceiling, her mind racing. There were lots of questions and very few answers. The future had never seemed quite so uncertain.

Patrick, what have you gotten me into?

32

Paige woke up the next morning feeling very much alone and very much unemployed for the first time in her life. It would do no good to feel sorry for herself, she decided. She had made her decision, and there was no turning back.

Instead, she charted a new course for the next few weeks. She would get up and run every morning. When she got back to the condo, she would spend the rest of the morning job hunting or perhaps working on setting up her own firm. The afternoons would be reserved for research on Kristen's case and reading about the geopolitical situation in the Mideast. She would only let herself think about Patrick in the evening.

At least that was the plan.

But there were reminders of him everywhere. Her screen saver. Pictures in her study. Old text messages. Plus, he was completely intertwined with the very case that she was now researching. His ghost was ubiquitous, and it would rise up at the most unpredictable times, strangle her heart, and leave her emotionally exhausted.

She began the week by polishing up her résumé and sending cover letters to law school friends who had landed jobs at private firms. By her third day of unemployment, she started spending more time investigating what it would take to start her own firm. Letterhead, malpractice insurance, setting up an LLC, registering with the state bar—the list was endless. Plus, she had no idea where she would find the clients.

Yet it still seemed like the best path. If Kristen's case got thrown out early, Paige would be right back at the attorney general's office, asking for her old job back. If she got it, she could shut down her fledgling firm. But if she had started a new job, it wouldn't be fair to her employer to leave a few months after she started.

By Friday, she had drafted the operating agreement for her new LLC and ordered business cards. Paige Chambers, Managing Member. It had a certain ring to it.

★　★　★

On Wednesday, May 9, the managing member of the Chambers Law Firm took a break from her legal work and met Bill Harris at Patrick's old apartment. They planned to spend the day together, packing Patrick's stuff in a U-Haul that Bill would tow up to New York. Paige had been dreading the day all week.

It was the first time Paige had been to Patrick's apartment since before the deployment. The place had a musty smell, and Paige sucked in a deep breath. She stood there for a moment, almost paralyzed as the emotions came rushing back to her. That was the couch where she'd slid next to him and he had put his arm around her shoulder. There was the table where they'd eaten undercooked steaks and debated whether steaks were better with A.1. sauce. She had been sitting in that recliner when he gave her a back rub and put her to sleep.

She stared for a moment at the pictures lining the living room shelf. Patrick and his SEAL buddies. Patrick's grandmother and grandfather in happier times. And a picture of Paige that hadn't been there the last time she was in this room.

"He always kept his place neat like this," Bill Harris said, snapping Paige back to the present. He flipped on a light switch and wandered around for a few minutes. "Not as much stuff as I thought there would be."

For most of the day, Paige withdrew into her own world and said little as they packed Patrick's clothes, kitchen utensils, sports equipment, and personal items. Being around Bill meant she didn't have to say much. He provided a running commentary filled with Patrick stories triggered by various items that Patrick had left behind.

It wasn't much of an apartment. Patrick had never really cared about the finer things in life, and Paige had teased him about it. He'd duct-taped one of the cushions on the old, worn-out leather couch. He had picked up his kitchen table at a yard sale. His television and Xbox were the only things in the living room he had spent any money on.

But to Bill Harris, it might as well have been the palace of Solomon. He carefully boxed up everything, and Paige labeled the boxes with neat block letters.

It was almost noon when Bill knelt down and started cleaning out the nightstand. He came across a small box tucked away in the corner of the drawer, and Paige pretended not to notice as Bill pulled it out and opened it. She continued packing clothes from the dresser, catching the scent of Patrick, but watched with one eye as Patrick's grandfather paused for a moment, removed his glasses, and wiped his eyes with the back of his hand.

He put his glasses back on, closed the box, and stood. He walked over to Paige and handed it to her. "I think Patrick would want you to have this."

Paige took it gingerly, knowing what was inside. She opened it with the greatest care, as if it were a sacred artifact.

It was a simple ring with a round-cut diamond, a four-pronged setting, and a yellow-gold band. Traditional. Elegant. The most beautiful thing Paige had ever seen. But she couldn't keep it—that wouldn't be right.

"He asked me about marriage on the night before he left," Paige said, her voice brittle. "I told him I needed time."

"I know," Bill said, looking at the ring. "He called me about it."

"He did?"

"Yep. He was mad at himself. Thought he might have pushed too fast. Too hard. I told him it took me three tries with his grandmother. Good women are worth the wait."

Paige gave him a wan smile. "Three tries?"

"That woman had a stubborn streak."

Paige touched the ring. "What did Patrick say?"

"He thought he could do it in two."

"He was right," Paige said. "But I still can't keep this."

She tried to hand it back, but Bill wouldn't take it. "It's not my size," he said. "Besides, it's yours. Patrick bought it for *you*."

Paige closed the box and gave Bill a hug. "I miss him so much," she said.

"I know. But this is something to remember him by."

Paige put the ring in a large cardboard box that had her name on it. It joined a few of Patrick's T-shirts, his ball cap from Auburn University, and a few dozen photographs that Paige had asked Patrick's grandfather if she could keep.

They went on packing, and a few minutes later Paige broke the silence. "I should have said yes."

Bill stopped packing and looked over at her. "He knew it was only a matter of time. He wouldn't want you to beat yourself up about it."

Bill was right, but it didn't change the way she felt. She would forever regret their last night together.

Thirty minutes later, four men from SEAL Team Two showed up. Two of them had gone through BUD/S with Patrick. They had somehow heard, probably though Kristen, that Paige and Bill Harris were packing the apartment today. In no time they had finished loading the U-Haul, tied everything down, and cleared out the apartment.

The men also brought a whole different atmosphere to the endeavor, lifting Paige's spirits. She could tell they were subconsciously competing with each other about how many boxes they could take at a time or how light various items of furniture were. Paige insisted on grabbing one end of the couch when one of the men took the other. She wouldn't allow anyone to help her, and they all joked about her being an honorary female SEAL.

The stories were different now too. Bill had gone on and on about all-American Patrick, but Patrick's SEAL buddies talked about more colorful exploits. All good-natured and harmless, but Patrick obviously enjoyed a good prank.

When the last box was packed, the men and Paige hung out at the counter area in the kitchen, finishing off some energy drinks that somebody had brought. "We all appreciate what you're doing for Kristen," one of the men said. "Every one of us on the teams knows this isn't easy for you guys. But we all want the same answers that you're trying to get."

The others murmured their agreement and told Paige that if she ever needed anything, she should just ask.

"Anything," one of the men emphasized. "Just call us."

When she got home that night, Paige felt better than she had for a long time. She was still unemployed and alone. But today it felt like she had somehow crossed a threshold into the SEAL community. *If you need anything,* they had said, *we'll be there.* And Paige didn't doubt for one second that they meant every word. That was the thing about these guys. They were rough-hewn and full of themselves. They had obnoxious amounts of testosterone and egos the size of Texas. But they were there for each other, and that was something that had been missing in Paige's life.

She placed the box of Patrick's stuff next to her bed. She pulled out the small box holding the diamond ring and put it on her night-stand. Before she crawled into bed, she put on one of his T-shirts. She was emotionally exhausted, but that night, at least until the phone call came, she slept better than she'd slept in weeks.

33

The call startled Paige out of a sound sleep, her mind full of cobwebs. She looked at the time as she answered: 2:16 a.m. She felt the sickness lodge in the pit of her stomach. Nobody called with good news at that time of night.

"Hello," Paige said, her voice husky.

"This is the Patriot," came the metallic voice from the other end. "Are you awake?"

"I am now."

"Why did Jackson file suit?"

"I don't know. He didn't check with me."

"You've got to get him to back off. The judge will dismiss the case, and the whole thing will be over. They'll block any congressional investigation by saying the court has already ruled."

Paige didn't know what to say. The Patriot sounded frustrated. She was still trying to get her bearings. Should she tell him that she was getting ready to sign on as cocounsel?

"I can't talk Wyatt Jackson into much of anything," she protested.

"You've got to try."

Paige sat up, her mind clearing. "I'll do what I can."

"There's another thing," the Patriot said. "You should know that a Muslim cleric named Yazeed Abdul Hamid was killed by our Special Forces inside Yemen. The coalition army took credit for it, but it was definitely our guys."

Paige was scrambling for a pen and paper. "Spell that name for me," she said.

The Patriot carefully listed each letter.

"What does that have to do with anything?"

"He's nothing more than a Muslim imam preaching hate in a country where we are not even at war," said the Patriot. "It was an illegal assassination."

Paige still didn't get the connection, but then again, everything seemed unclear when you were jolted out of a sound sleep at this hour.

"Tell Congressman Mason about it," the Patriot said.

"How can I prove it?" Paige asked.

"Get Mason to launch an investigation. Have him put the commander of the Joint Special Operations Forces under oath in a closed hearing and question him about it. But you've got to get Jackson to drop that suit."

"I already said I would try."

The line went dead, and Paige wondered whether the whole thing was just a nightmare. Why didn't the Patriot call Wyatt directly? Why was it so important to drop the case? And what did this Muslim cleric have to do with anything?

She got up and googled the imam's name but learned nothing more than what the Patriot had already told her. Abdul Hamid was supposedly killed by Yemeni coalition forces a little more than two weeks ago. She made some notes, then lay down and eventually drifted back to sleep. Her last murky thoughts were of American Special Forces killing an unarmed Muslim imam on his way home from preaching his last sermon.

34

After a brutal weeklong trip to Europe, Saudi Arabia, and Israel, followed by another week of strong-arming congressional leaders, President Amanda Hamilton woke on a rainy Friday morning to a new domestic crisis. Following a two-day deluge, the Susquehanna River in northeastern Pennsylvania had flooded its banks at a level not seen in a hundred years, forcing the evacuation of nearly a hundred thousand people and causing more than forty casualties. At Scranton, the river had crested at forty-seven feet, five feet higher than the 1972 flooding from Hurricane Agnes.

Other presidents would have just declared a state of emergency, clearing the way for federal aid, and then toured the damage with local officials. But Amanda Hamilton and members of her staff believed in getting their hands dirty. The day after the waters began subsiding, she was on the ground in Scranton, working at a Red Cross disaster-relief outpost, serving meals for people who found themselves homeless. Amanda and her husband, Jason, a professor at Yale University, served the lines for more than two hours, slapping food on plates and talking to the beleaguered residents.

That afternoon, they put on waders and worked with "mud-out" crews, helping to remove limbs and other waterlogged debris from nearby homes. It was a reminder that Amanda Hamilton was young and healthy and a woman of the people. By the end of the day, she was covered in mud and seemed happier than she had been in a long time.

She toured a shelter in a high school gym that evening. Some local kids had started a pickup basketball game, and soon the president and her husband joined them. Secret Service members stood nervously to the side as the president showed she could still hang with the guys. She ended up taking a blow to her left eye that resulted in profuse apologies by the embarrassed young man with the sharp elbow and a nice shiner for the president.

Once the medics were done looking her over, she insisted on finishing the game, and Kilpatrick figured her poll numbers went up a half-dozen points based on that decision alone. With a little luck, he thought, they would soon be able to put the lawsuit behind them, build a real coalition of allies in the Middle East, and cripple the Houthis and Iran.

The press had other ideas. Amanda Hamilton's swollen face graced the front page of the *Washington Herald* the next morning. They must have stayed up late working on the headline: "A Bruising Week for the President."

★ ★ ★

While the president was getting elbowed in a pickup basketball game, Paige Chambers met with Wyatt and Wellington in the RV that Wyatt had dubbed Court. Clients kept coming over and rubbing against Paige's leg until she scratched him under his chin. He lay down for a few minutes and then circled back for some more attention. This was not the way Paige had envisioned things in law school.

She told Wyatt about her conversation with the Patriot, but Wyatt wasn't about to drop the lawsuit. Handing it off to the political hacks in D.C. was a guaranteed way to make sure nothing happened, in Wyatt's opinion. He didn't know what to make of the information about Yazeed Abdul Hamid, so he did what he always did when he was in doubt—asked Wellington to research it.

"It wouldn't surprise me if the CIA deputized a couple of SEALs and took that guy out," Wyatt said. "This shadow war is out of control."

They batted around legal arguments for a while, and then Wyatt broke out a fat cigar and started chewing on the end of it. Paige shot him a glance—this place was cramped enough without somebody smoking.

"Don't worry," Wellington said. "He never lights them up inside."

They analyzed the meager evidence they had mustered, with Wyatt doing most of the talking. Paige interjected a few times, but Wellington was conspicuously quiet.

"What's your theory?" Wyatt asked his young associate. He spit some of the cigar's outer wrapping into an ashtray.

Wellington spoke softly, hesitantly, as if he didn't want to rain on everybody's parade. "I've been thinking about this a lot," he began, "and I keep asking myself the same question: What if Cameron Holloman really was a CIA agent just like the Houthis said?"

He looked from Wyatt to Paige, waiting just long enough for the thought to sink in. "What if he used his journalistic credentials as cover and pretended to be sympathetic to the Houthi cause? That way he could interview a few of their top leaders, and the drone pilots would know which houses to hit.

"Maybe the president and Marcano didn't want anyone else in the cabinet to know, so she sent her chief of staff to talk to Marcano privately about what they should do. Maybe the CIA had some concerns that the SEALs' mission was compromised, which explains why she worked so hard on the speech that she would only give if the SEALs died. But maybe she felt like she had to send in the SEALs because the CIA doesn't leave its operatives behind any more than the SEALs leave their men behind."

Paige thought it through, and despite the fact that there were a lot of maybes in that theory, it made some sense. It was the truth hiding in plain sight. And it would explain a lot of things.

"No chance," Wyatt said. "Have you read any of Holloman's articles?"

"Over a hundred of them," Wellington said.

"Then you know he's a real liberal wacko. No way he's working with the CIA."

"Did you know that the CIA has set up fake news organizations in the Mideast to spread propaganda?" Wellington asked. "They've also paid millions of dollars to Mideast news outlets so they would weave in favorable stories about America from time to time. The CIA believes in the long game. I wouldn't put it past them to have somebody like Holloman write articles critical of the United States and Saudi Arabia for a year or two just to gain credibility."

"Was he married?" Wyatt asked.

"Yes. His wife is Muslim. Immigrated to the United States from Lebanon."

Wyatt chewed on his cigar and thought about it. He stood up and began pacing.

"He always does this when he's thinking," Wellington whispered to Paige.

"I think we should go pay the missus a visit," Wyatt said. "She'll know if he was a spy."

Wellington was sitting across the table from Paige and gave his head a little shake as if to tell Paige that spouses seldom knew whether their significant others worked for the CIA. But he didn't say anything to Wyatt.

"All right then, we've got a plan," Wyatt said. "This calls for a smoke."

He stepped outside and lit up his cigar. But a few minutes later, he was back, the lit cigar still in his mouth.

"Where are you working now?" he asked Paige.

"I'm setting up my own firm."

"That's a bad idea. It's hard to get clients in this environment, especially ones that pay. Plus, you've never worked in a private firm before, so the learning curve will be steep. You ought to come and work for me."

"Thanks. But I'm good."

"Wellington, how much are you making?"

"Um, about sixty grand."

"That's what I thought. Paige, I'll pay you sixty thousand, take care of your malpractice and health insurance, and you can start first thing next week."

"Again, like I said, I'd rather start my own firm."

"Five-thousand-dollar signing bonus, plus I'll teach you how to be a real trial lawyer."

"What part of *no* don't you understand?"

"I don't understand any part of *no*," Wyatt said. He smiled with the cigar wedged between his teeth. "And that's why we're going to win this case."

35

The next Monday, Paige woke early, made a cup of coffee, and put together her list. Today would be the official launch of the Chambers Law Firm. She had already ordered the letterhead, settled on a snazzy logo, and put together a website that, despite Paige's best efforts at buffing up her meager experience, still seemed embarrassingly hollow. Today she needed to open a trust account and an operating account, set up QuickBooks, and take the website live. Then she would be in business.

She felt a small rush of pride. This was the American way. Sure, she had only one client—and one with whom she had never discussed fees—but you had to start someplace. Big dreams, high risk, and the freedom to be your own boss. She still couldn't believe she was doing this.

After she finished her coffee, she put on her running gear and headed out for her morning run. The ground was wet from thunderstorms the night before, and there was a chill in the air. She shivered for the first half mile or so but then warmed up as she neared the boardwalk, about a mile and a half from her house.

She turned right and ran into a stiff breeze, the ocean air clearing her head of worries and fears and responsibilities. She nodded to folks walking or running in the other direction and glanced out at the surfers in wet suits riding erratic waves. She passed hotels and restaurants and condos on her right. In a few months, the vast concrete boardwalk would be teeming with people, but right now, it was just Paige and the other locals. Her own private oceanfront practically in her backyard.

It was a good run, one of the first she'd had in the last thirty days. The emotional roller coaster and lack of sleep following Patrick's death had drained her, causing her to skip the exercise she needed, thus draining her even more. But this morning she practically sprinted the last half mile. She finished strong and bent over, hands on knees, gasping for air. She walked around the parking lot of her condo to catch her breath.

Back inside the condo, still sweating from her run, Paige picked up her cell phone and saw two missed calls from Kristen along with a text asking Paige to call. She knew it couldn't be good, and she felt the sudden crush of pressure again.

"Have you seen the news?" Kristen asked.

"No. I've been out running."

"Can you come over?" Kristen's voice sounded fragile, like she had been crying.

"Sure."

"That woman who accused Troy of molesting her is all over the news this morning—" Kristen's voice broke off.

Paige waited, not knowing what to say.

"I'm just really struggling."

"Let me change. I'll be right there."

Paige toweled off and changed into some jeans and a T-shirt. She pulled her hair back and gathered it into a ponytail with an elastic band. She could put on her makeup later. Her friend needed help.

Before heading out the door, she paused to check one of the national morning shows. The host was interviewing a woman named Jordan Johnson, who apparently went by the nickname JJ. She looked like she had walked off the set of an extreme makeover show—bright-red lipstick, lots of eye shadow, stylish brown hair. Her dress was modest, just above the knees, though she wore three-inch heels. She wore a cross necklace and folded her hands in her lap.

She claimed Troy Anderson had molested her in a bar. Groped her and said things to her she couldn't repeat on the air. She had told him to stop a couple of times, but his hands were all over her.

She talked as if she might break down at any moment, and Paige wondered how many times she had repeated the same story already that morning on different shows, hitting the perfect emotional tone, one of pain mixed with anger. She hesitated, and the host gently prodded her to continue.

"Finally some of the other guys in the bar came over and told him to leave me alone. But this SEAL guy told them to get lost and started pressing himself against me. That's when the big fight broke out."

"Why are you coming forward to tell your story now?" the host asked. "Some will say this is just a move by the president's political supporters to smear the reputation of a man who died for his country."

JJ looked offended and then, as if she were a seasoned actress, turned to the camera. "Nobody asked me to come forward. But I believe our president is a good woman. And I also know that the lawyer who filed this lawsuit against the president's chief of staff is the same man who defended Troy Anderson and did everything he could to smear my reputation just for telling the truth about what happened. Before our entire country judges President Hamilton, I think they ought to know the kind of man making these accusations."

Paige had heard enough. She texted Kristen, telling her to hang in there and that she was on the way. She remembered what Wyatt Jackson had said. They must be onto something, because the president's team was pulling out all the stops to shut them down.

36

When Paige arrived at Kristen's house, several reporters were already camped out in the street and driveway. Paige parked in front of a satellite truck and walked through a small gauntlet of cameramen, thinking about how horrible she was going to look on TV. The half-dozen reporters apparently recognized Paige and started asking questions. She kept her eyes straight ahead, not even tossing them a "no comment." Surely they wouldn't put her silent walk on the news, would they?

The front door was locked, and Paige rang the bell. Kristen cracked the door, peered out, and let Paige in.

The women hugged, and Paige was struck by Kristen's puffy eyes and the dark circles underneath.

"When will they go away?" Kristen asked.

"I have no idea."

The boys came running out, and Paige gave them a hug. She noticed that the television wasn't on.

"I can't believe she's saying these things about Troy," Kristen said. "It's all lies. The prosecutor would have never agreed to a suspended sentence if he believed that woman for one minute."

"I know," Paige said. They retreated to the kitchen table, out of earshot of the boys, and talked while Kristen checked text messages and ignored incoming calls. They decided to put together a written statement that would deny the allegations. Paige was jotting something down when Wyatt called Kristen's cell.

Paige listened to one side of the conversation. Kristen was mostly nodding and fighting back tears and saying that she understood. She asked Wyatt if she could put him on speaker because Paige was there with her.

"Are the reporters out front?" Wyatt asked. His voice was raspy, and Paige imagined that he was recovering from a hard night of drinking.

"The local stations," Paige said.

"Good. That'll be a perfect opportunity to tell them our side of the story," Wyatt said.

Paige tensed up. She could see where this was heading; as usual, Wyatt was about to make a bad situation worse.

"We've got the goods on this woman," Wyatt said. "Two friends of Troy's were prepared to testify that she was hitting on them that night. She's been married and divorced twice. Plus, she brought another charge once against some Navy guys at a bar up near Little Creek, and those charges were also dismissed. She cleaned up her Facebook page, but we have copies from my file that we can provide to the press. Paige, I can e-mail all this stuff to Kristen, and you can have an impromptu press conference right there on her front porch. Just go out and tell the press that you'll be releasing a statement in an hour or so in order to make sure they don't leave."

Kristen looked at Paige, who shook her head. She leaned toward the phone to speak. "I don't think that's a good idea. Attacking this woman will just add fuel to the fire. And I don't know the case well enough to start making statements I can't back up."

"I'll give you everything you need. We've got to get this stuff out there *now*. If we don't, the press will move on to something else and it'll be too late."

"That's my whole point. Let the press move on. People will see this as a desperate woman trying to attack a dead war hero."

But Wyatt was insistent. "Kristen, do you see what I'm saying?" he asked, ignoring Paige. "They're trying to play the woman's card. They're saying that I'm a misogynist who hates women and wants to bring down our first female president. Troy deserves better than this."

Paige could tell the words were having an impact on Kristen, and she despised Wyatt for it. Of course Kristen wanted to strike back. Who wouldn't? But Paige was only two weeks into private practice, and she wasn't about to start trashing the reputation of women who claimed they were victims of sexual assault. Not even women like JJ, though Paige was tempted to make an exception for her. "I'm not comfortable with it, Wyatt. We'll play right into their hands if we do that."

"I'm asking Kristen," Wyatt said. "I want to know what *Kristen* thinks."

Kristen stared at the phone. "I don't know," she said at last. "I mean, it sounds like something we should do, but if Paige isn't comfortable with it, then maybe we shouldn't."

Paige felt sick. She had come to the house to comfort Kristen, and now it looked like she wasn't willing to help her friend. But this was why people needed lawyers. Clients got too emotional to make good, objective decisions.

"Maybe we could just issue a statement or something," Kristen suggested. "I don't know. I just feel like we ought to do something."

"Look, this needs to be answered," Wyatt said. Paige could hear the exasperation in his voice. "Paige, if you're not willing to say something, I will. I just think it would be better coming from a woman."

"It's not that I'm not willing. I think it's a bad idea."

"We can talk about this all day but we've got to *do something*. Kristen, are you okay if I go out there and defend Troy?"

Kristen looked up and caught Paige's eye. Paige shrugged. She had said enough. Maybe too much.

"Go ahead, Mr. Jackson. Do whatever you think you ought to do."

When they got off the phone, Paige tried to get Kristen to talk it through. Kristen kept saying that she wasn't mad at Paige and that she understood where Paige was coming from, but she seemed disappointed, like the phone call with Wyatt had taken the fight out of her.

After a while, Paige shifted course and decided she was going to say something after all. She tried to call Wyatt, but he didn't answer. She and Kristen jotted down a few statements that sounded good, and Paige rehearsed them a few times. At eleven thirty, Paige gave Kristen a hug and stepped out onto the front porch.

There were only three camera crews left. Paige announced she had a brief statement to make, and they gathered around. Paige swallowed hard and tried to look as confident as possible.

"As you know, a woman named Jordan Johnson is making the rounds today, accusing Troy Anderson of sexually assaulting her in a bar several years ago. These allegations are entirely false, and that's why the commonwealth's attorney ultimately dropped the charges. Mr. Wyatt Jackson, who was serving as Troy's attorney at the time, had lined up several eyewitnesses, and the commonwealth could find no one to support Ms. Johnson's version of events."

Paige watched the reporters jot down notes. She licked her lips and continued. "Troy Anderson is a decorated war hero who gave his life defending our country. He died so that people like Ms. Johnson could have freedom of speech, even if they use it to unfairly tarnish someone else's reputation. I am proud to represent Mr. Anderson and his family, and I would ask the members of the press to please give them their privacy as they try to move forward without a husband and a father."

When she finished, a couple reporters asked questions. Paige politely refused to answer and requested again that they give the Anderson family some privacy.

She walked back in the house and let out a deep breath.

"Thanks," Kristen said. "That was perfect."

★　★　★

None of the news shows that day aired Paige's statement on behalf of the Anderson family. They didn't need to. They had a much more colorful denial from Wyatt Jackson, standing on the steps of the federal courthouse after filing what he described as "an important legal document."

"This isn't the first time this woman has lied about being sexually assaulted, and it probably won't be the last," Wyatt said nonchalantly. "I'm not saying that the president's political team put her up to this, but the timing sure is suspicious. The only regret I have about that case is that we didn't go to trial. I had plenty of witnesses, and she had nobody to back her up. But even if we had won that trial, the allegations alone would have been harmful to Troy's career as a SEAL, and all he ever wanted to do was serve his country."

Wyatt Jackson shook his head as if he couldn't understand the depths to which people would stoop in these troubling times.

"What evidence do you have that the president's supporters put her up to this?" a reporter asked. "She said she came forward of her own volition."

Wyatt smiled as if that were the dumbest question he'd ever heard. "Let me just say this. Sometimes you see a little creature running in the shadows of your basement, and you can't really tell what it is. But one thing you saw was a furry little tail. That's probably a squirrel. But sometimes you see a nasty little creature scurrying around your basement and all you notice is a long thin slimy tail on its backside. You don't need DNA to tell you that creature is a rat. Bringing up discredited charges against a man a month after he gives his life for his country—that's just slimy, folks. That's a rat if I ever saw one."

37

On Tuesday morning, lawyers for Philip Kilpatrick and John Marcano filed motions to dismiss the wrongful-death suit with long briefs arguing that the case had no merit. Both asked for sanctions against Wyatt Jackson and Paige Chambers personally for filing the frivolous case. Paige was notified of the filings via e-mail through the court's electronic filing system. She sat at her kitchen table and read through the legal documents, growing more pessimistic by the minute.

As expected, the defendants relied heavily on the Feres Doctrine and the Supreme Court case that threw out the lawsuit by military members who had been used as guinea pigs for LSD testing. The defense lawyers scoffed at the notion that the *Anderson* case was different just because Troy Anderson had been working for the CIA.

Whether or not Mr. Anderson, a longtime member of SEAL Team Six, was technically deputized by the CIA for this mission is of

no consequence. His team leader was Patrick Quillen, also a Navy
SEAL. Mr. Quillen reported to the commanding officer of SEAL Team
Six, who in turn reported to the commanding officer of the Joint
Special Operations Command. All of these men were members of
the military. Moreover, as the Supreme Court noted in the *Stanley*
case, the question is not whether the plaintiff is technically working
for the military but whether the case is "incident to military service."

The briefs also claimed that the case would jeopardize state secrets,
though that issue was downplayed. They were well-written briefs,
authored by lawyers from two of the largest firms in the country, and
it gave Paige a new realization of how monumental the challenge was
before her. It also made her consider, for the first time, what this suit
might personally cost her. If a federal judge got mad and levied sanctions, both she and Wyatt could be fined tens of thousands of dollars.
Typically, lawyers asked that the sanctions include the legal costs they
have billed responding to the case. Just these briefs alone would probably cost $20,000 each, given the billing rates of the D.C. firms. Where
could Paige get that kind of money?

She fretted over the briefs for a while and then called Wellington. He
asked if they could meet later that day to parcel out the work for their
response. He also told her that the court had set a hearing for Friday,
May 25, the day before Memorial Day weekend.

"What did Wyatt think about the briefs?" Paige asked.

"He said they're both crap," Wellington replied. "He was in one of
his I-told-you-so moods. He'd predicted the defense lawyers wouldn't
push the state secrets defense because it would be like hiding behind the
Fifth Amendment and would make the president look bad. And sure
enough, he was right—they only spent a few pages even referencing the
national-security concerns."

"Has Wyatt ever seen a case he thought he would lose?" Paige asked.

Wellington thought about that for a long time. "Not since I've been
with him."

★ ★ ★

NAJRAN, SAUDI ARABIA

Brandon Lawrence couldn't live with himself if he didn't say *something*. In the past six months, two of his Hellfire missiles had destroyed houses where the CIA later learned that only civilians had been present. One had killed a pregnant twenty-three-year-old mother, and another had wiped out three children under the age of ten. "Collateral damage," they called it. But for Brandon, it was the failure of the CIA to do its job. They were so busy using drone pilots to kill people that they could no longer be trusted to know where the enemy's leaders were actually hiding.

When he enlisted in the Air Force, it had seemed like the perfect job. Though he never learned how to fly a real plane, he had become one of the best drone pilots anywhere, his expertise in computer games finally coming in handy. Plus, he was patient and didn't mind sitting through hours of drudgery as the drones flew over Yemen and looked for patterns representative of Houthi command and control.

But he had not signed up to work for the CIA. It had started during the Obama administration and accelerated with President Hamilton. CIA operatives were now in charge of most drones, using Air Force drone pilots like Brandon to gather information and take out enemy commanders. He found the operatives to be haughty, demanding, and always secretive. They treated him like a creature of lesser intelligence, one who could not be trusted with sensitive information.

All of that was bad enough, but it was the duplicity that finally spurred him to action. Less than twenty-four hours after the SEALs died at Sana'a, two CIA operatives had sat down with Brandon and made a request. About three weeks before the SEAL mission, another drone operator had launched a successful strike against some Houthi commanders holed up in a compound on the outskirts of Aden. Brandon and two other pilots had been watching the house for two days in order to verify the identity of the Houthi leaders.

The CIA operatives explained that there might be some

investigations about that strike. For purposes of national security, Brandon should tell anyone who asked that they had been monitoring that site for nearly a month. It's complicated, he was told, but failure to do so would compromise several CIA assets in Yemen. The CIA director, who had discussed it directly with the president, was making the request.

At the time, Brandon had agreed. It wasn't his job to ask questions. And though there had ultimately been no investigation, over time he felt less comfortable with the directive. He had discussed it with the other pilots who had been part of the two-day surveillance, confirming that they had received the same directive.

"It's not unusual," one of them said. "That's the way the CIA works. Their first priority is to never compromise an agent."

Brandon couldn't figure out how it all fit together, but he somehow felt exposed. If there was an investigation, he might have to answer questions in some kind of official capacity. Who would be in charge of such an investigation? And what would happen if he lied to them?

The more he thought about it, the more uncomfortable he became. His drinking, already a problem, became heavier. He couldn't sleep. He went to the doctor and obtained a prescription for anxiety.

But when he saw the lawsuit against the CIA director, he believed he had found a way out. He could call the plaintiff's lawyers anonymously and provide a tip. That way, if he ever got in trouble for being part of some cover-up, he could have the lawyers confirm that he had exposed the CIA. It wasn't perfect, but it seemed like the right thing to do. It was one thing to be part of a killing machine that all too frequently took out civilians. Perhaps that couldn't be avoided. But it was another thing to lie about it to the authorities. He knew his history well enough to realize that the cover-up was usually worse than the crime.

The phone numbers for the lawyers were in the pleadings. On one of his off days, he picked up a burner phone in the city of Najran.

Wandering the streets, he called the number for Wyatt Jackson. Just his luck, the man didn't answer and his voice mail was full.

Before he lost his nerve, he dialed Paige Chambers.

★　★　★

She was groggy and confused—another phone call in the middle of the night. The display said *Unknown Caller*.

"Hello."

"Is this Paige Chambers, the lawyer who represents Kristen Anderson?"

"Yes. Who is this?"

"I can't say. But I need you to know something that might be helpful to your lawsuit."

The man sounded young and scared. He was definitely American, but Paige couldn't place the accent. "I'm listening."

"The CIA is telling its drone pilots to lie about how long some of their targets have been under surveillance," the man said. "This whole thing is all screwed up. Civilians are dying and the CIA is covering something up."

"How do you know this?"

"I can't say."

"Are you in the CIA?"

"I can't say."

"I've got to have some specifics. I can't just go into court and tell them I got a phone call in the middle of the night."

There was a long silence as the man on the other end of the line thought it through.

"There was a drone strike on March 11," the man said, his voice shaky. "Three Houthi leaders were killed. That's the one you need to focus on."

Paige was wide awake now. She needed to keep this man on the phone. "Why are you telling me this?"

"Because the CIA will lie to cover it up."

"Cover what up?"

"That's all I can . . ." The man's voice trailed off.

"How do I get in touch with you?" Paige asked.

"I'll call you back when I find out more information."

"Wait. I need—"

The man hung up. Paige's mind raced with questions. She quickly went to her computer and searched for information about the drone strike he had referenced. She found some articles about an alleged bombing on March 11 that had been credited to the Yemeni coalition government. It was probably a drone strike, and maybe that was the one this man was talking about. It fit a pattern—the Patriot had said that the assassination of Yazeed Abdul Hamid, which had also been credited to the Yemeni coalition government, was actually the work of U.S. Special Forces.

The drone strike had occurred two weeks prior to Cameron Holloman's arrest. Maybe Wellington Farnsworth was onto something. Maybe Holloman *was* working for the CIA. Maybe he had provided the intel that led to the killing of these Houthi leaders. That would mean the Houthis were right all along in accusing Holloman of being a spy. It would also explain why the CIA was lying about how long certain targets had been under surveillance—they didn't want them linked to Holloman.

Paige stayed up the rest of the night searching for more information. But when the morning sun replaced the dark shadows of her condo with the first rays of sunlight, Paige still had more questions than she did answers. She wondered if the phone call had been made by the Patriot but without the voice disguises. Or maybe it was just some nut with a grudge against the CIA.

She felt like she was wandering around in the dark, playing a high-stakes game where everyone was wearing night vision goggles except her.

38

In the ten days prior to the hearing, Paige and Wellington put together notebooks full of cases for Wyatt to study. Paige thought it would be good for them to practice the argument like a moot court panel in law school, but Wyatt apparently didn't do those types of things.

"Is he even reading the cases?" she asked Wellington.

"Probably not yet. But he'll have them all read by the morning of the twenty-fifth."

Meanwhile, Paige's fledgling law practice was not exactly off to an explosive start. She had put her name on the court-appointed list and had picked up one client during her second week in business. He was appealing a fifth DUI conviction and had received a ten-year sentence. Paige was supposed to somehow find him a loophole to slide through on appeal. The case would pay $500.

A few friends had hired Paige to draft wills, and another friend had tried to send Paige a medical malpractice case, but Paige didn't have the foggiest idea where to start. All of this gave her plenty of time to focus on her one big case—*The Estate of Troy Anderson v. Philip Kilpatrick and John Marcano.*

Three days before the hearing, Paige spent the morning at Kristen's house, waiting for an important visitor from JSOC. His name was Daniel Reese, and he served as the chief of staff to Admiral Paul Towers, the former commanding officer of JSOC. Reese had been a Navy SEAL himself and had been a training officer in BUD/S when both Patrick and Troy paid their dues. Kristen didn't know why he was coming, but she assumed it was good news. "They never send the brass when it's bad."

Paige arrived fifteen minutes early because she had learned that these Navy guys always started on time. She played with the Anderson boys for a little while and answered Kristen's questions about the case. Kristen was nervous about meeting Daniel Reese, a man whom both Troy and Patrick had deeply admired.

Commander Reese arrived right on time wearing his dress blues, and Paige was immediately struck by how young he looked. He was tall and handsome with a colorful array of ribbons on his chest. He gave Kristen a polite hug, told her how great it was to see her, and gave Paige a firm handshake. Kristen introduced Paige as Patrick's girlfriend. Reese expressed his condolences to both women and noticed the boys standing a few paces behind Kristen. He walked over to them and knelt down in front of them. The two little guys seemed like they were in awe.

"This is Commander Reese, a good friend of Daddy's," Kristen said.

Reese nodded. "Your daddy was a great man," he said, looking from one boy to the other. "One of the bravest men I have ever known. I'm sure glad he was my friend."

Kristen said, "Say thank you to Commander Reese, and then I need you guys to go back to the bedroom. I've got to talk to Commander Reese for a few minutes."

The boys said thanks, and Caleb reached out to touch the shiny brass buttons and medals on Reese's chest. Tiny got in on the action, and Reese gave him some love while the dog licked at his face. The man had hardly said more than two words to her, yet Paige already felt comfortable around him.

Once they had settled at the dining room table, Commander Reese got down to business. "Because Troy and the others were working for both the CIA and JSOC at the time of their death, we made an appeal to the pension board that the families receive additional death benefits typically paid to CIA families. Earlier this week we received notification that the payments were approved, and I wanted to deliver them personally."

He slid an envelope across the table to Kristen. "Kristen, I know money can't begin to replace Troy or even bring you much comfort, but I wanted to come so I could express how much we miss these men and how much of a hero your husband was."

Kristen dabbed at an eye with the back of her hand and blinked several times. "He would have never made it in the SEALs without you," she said.

"That's not true. Troy wouldn't have quit no matter who his instructor was. I don't think he ever quit anything his entire life."

"Thank you," Kristen said. She picked up the envelope. "To be honest, it feels wrong to take money like this. I feel like it's some kind of payoff for Troy's death."

Commander Reese assured her that it wasn't. Instead, it was just a small token of appreciation from a grateful nation.

Reese told Paige that Patrick's grandfather would be receiving similar benefits for Patrick. Paige said nobody deserved it more. She had known from Wellington's research early in the case that it was likely the benefits were coming. Still, it was kind of Commander Reese to deliver the funds himself.

"I appreciate what you're doing for Kristen in the lawsuit as well," Reese said to Paige. "You've got an excellent reputation as a lawyer, and I know that if Q was dating you, you've got to be in the top point-one percent of women in the world. Q was known to be the pickiest SEAL on the entire team."

Paige flushed a little and was surprised that Commander Reese knew about her role on the legal team. "Thanks. I guess."

"I meant it entirely as a compliment. Q was one of the best."

After a few minutes of conversation, Kristen offered Reese a drink, and to Paige's surprise, he accepted. The three of them nursed iced teas while they talked, and the topic turned to law school.

"I always wanted to go to law school," Reese said. "But I wasn't smart enough to get into the good schools, and it turned out that all I needed to be a SEAL was to be stubborn as a mule. So I end up in Special Forces, and now I'm the chief of staff for Admiral Towers, formerly commanding officer of JSOC but presently one heckuva pencil pusher at the Pentagon."

Paige knew about the demotion of Admiral Towers. It had only made him more of a hero with the rank-and-file men.

"Your boss is a good man," Kristen said. "Every SEAL family I know thinks he got a raw deal."

Eventually they finished their iced teas, and Daniel thanked Kristen again. "Can I tell you something in confidence?" he asked.

"Sure," Kristen said.

"I hope the court lets your case go forward. There are a lot of us who want to know what really happened that night. If I can do anything to help, short of sharing classified information, just let me know."

They all exchanged phone numbers, and Kristen told him again how grateful she was for everything he had done for Troy.

"You both have my greatest condolences," he said. Before he left, he went back into the bedroom and said good-bye to the boys.

★ ★ ★

WASHINGTON, D.C.

This time there was no park-bench meeting. Marcano had requested a private conference room in the West Wing of the White House. For Kilpatrick, it meant the CIA director would not be secretly recording this meeting—that he was more interested in total deniability for what he was going to say. They had already signed a joint defense agreement, meaning that their conversations could be kept confidential even if the litigation blew up.

Kilpatrick started off with some news of his own. "The president has signed off on a state secrets defense," he said. "But only if your lawyer carries the water. She wants you to file an affidavit at the hearing on Friday. She wants Pierce to argue only the Feres Doctrine. Your guy can argue the state secrets issue."

"Very courageous of her," Marcano deadpanned. "'I'll fight to the last drop of your blood.'"

"She's got to run for reelection in two and a half years. And you'd better hope she wins so the public can have four more years to forget about this mess. You don't need votes, John. She does. She can't look like she's hiding behind state secrets."

"Okay," Marcano said. "But assuming we get this case dismissed, I'll need your help to tie up a few loose ends."

"I'm not a big fan of loose ends. What is it?"

"Saleet Zafar needs to go on the list."

Kilpatrick knew that Marcano was talking about the president's kill list. And this one would be a tough sell. The president didn't like adding Muslim clerics to the list if they weren't tied into the operations side of ISIS.

"I'll see what I can do."

39

This time the phone call came late in the morning. It was the metallic voice that Paige immediately recognized as the Patriot.

"Are you ready for the hearing tomorrow?" the Patriot asked.

"Yes. We've been prepping Wyatt Jackson for the last two weeks."

"They're going to try to sandbag you," the voice said. "Make sure you're ready on the state secrets defense. That's why I didn't want Jackson filing this case to begin with. You are almost certain to lose on that point."

Paige was tired of playing games. They were one day away from the most important hearing of her life, and she needed more than dire predictions of gloom. "Who is this? And why should we trust you?"

"Have I been wrong yet?"

Before Paige could answer, he was off the phone.

She immediately called Wellington and briefed him about the phone call. Wellington decided they should patch in Wyatt, and before long Paige was describing her conversation with the Patriot again. She could picture Wyatt, pacing around the RV, chewing on a cigar, taking it all in.

"So let me get this straight," he said. "We get an anonymous phone call from a guy who may or may not have inside information about the legal strategy for the defense lawyers, and we're supposed to drop everything and focus on an area of the law that those defense lawyers have spent about two pages on?"

"We don't have to drop everything," Paige said. "I just want to make sure you've read those cases we've been sending you on state secrets privilege and that you're ready to argue the point."

"I've been in court on another matter the last three days, and the Feres Doctrine has kept me plenty busy. Why don't you prepare for the state secrets defense?"

Wyatt said it as if he were ordering a cup of coffee, but Paige felt her heart jump into her throat. "Me?"

"It's either you or Wellington. And no offense, Wellington, but that's an easy choice."

"I don't know," Paige said. "The hearing's tomorrow."

"Right. You've got almost twenty-four hours. We're going to make you a star."

I don't want to be a star, Paige wanted to say. She hated the way Wyatt had waited until the last minute and then dumped this on her. But at the same time, she was a litigator, and this was why she'd gone to law school. Besides, it wouldn't do any good to argue with the man. Knowing him, he would tell the judge that Paige was going to address the state secrets doctrine tomorrow even if she refused to accept the assignment today.

"Wellington, can you come over and help me get ready?" Paige asked.

"Sure."

"I still don't think they're going to actually make the argument," Wyatt said. "It looks bad for the president to hide behind state secrets under these circumstances. But if they do, you can address the case law and I'll handle the Feres Doctrine and any rebuttal."

"You sure you don't have time to read these cases?" Paige asked.

"Positive."

★ ★ ★

Paige spent the next sixteen hours in a state of mild panic that eventually gave way to full-blown exhaustion. She spent the first thirty minutes after Wellington arrived railing on Wyatt Jackson. "Why didn't *he* read these cases?" "What good is it if we provide all this research and he never reads it?" "Why wouldn't he already be prepared for the biggest hearing of his career?"

Wellington tried to calm her down by explaining that this was just Wyatt's unorthodox way of mentoring young associates. "He knew that if he gave you something to do a month ahead of the hearing, you would work yourself into a frenzy. He's confident that you've mastered the cases already."

Paige didn't want to hear it. "Some of us don't fly by the seat of our pants. Some of us like to actually be prepared."

"He tried the same thing on me when I first joined his firm," Wellington confided. His pale cheeks blushed as he told the story. "He threw something at me for a hearing at the last minute. But I'm like you—I need lots of time to prepare."

"How did it go?"

Wellington hesitated for a moment, choosing his words carefully. "Let's just say that afterward he decided I should stick to writing briefs and he should do the oral arguments."

"At least you didn't have the whole world watching."

Though Paige had already read the cases once, reviewing them now made her realize how few cases actually supported her argument. It seemed that every time the executive branch claimed that a case involved state secrets, the judge threw it out.

"Maybe he just wanted to take the best argument and give me the loser," Paige complained.

She was hoping Wellington would take exception. She was hoping he would argue that the state secrets issue was not necessarily a loser. She wanted him to show off that famed legal mind. Instead, he just said, "That wouldn't surprise me."

By two o'clock in the morning, when Wellington finally left, Paige had an outline of an argument. It took her another hour to settle down enough to try to get some sleep. She set the alarm for 6:00 a.m. and noticed the small box with her engagement ring where she had left it on the nightstand. She thought about Patrick and did something he would have been proud of—she said a heartfelt prayer.

The state secrets doctrine was complicated, but one thing was crystal clear: If they were going to win tomorrow, it would take a minor miracle.

40

On Friday morning, Paige picked up Kristen at her house, and they rode to court together. Kristen was talkative and relaxed. She apparently had no idea how difficult it would be to win this motion.

Kristen had decided that she, Paige, Wyatt, and Wellington should call themselves SEAL Team Nine. Even though there was actually a SEAL Team Eight and a SEAL Team Ten, the Navy had for some reason skipped nine. There were lots of legends about the missing SEAL team, and now Kristen decided they would create their own lore.

"ST-9, that's us."

Paige smiled nervously and thought this must have been what it felt like for Patrick to go into battle with Troy. Patrick's wingman was always joking, taking life as it came, not fretting about the consequences. Kristen was doing the same thing now, keeping Paige somewhat loose.

While the women were on the way, Wellington called to inform Paige that they had drawn Judge Thea Solberg, a first-generation immigrant from Norway who had been a constitutional law professor before she was appointed to the bench by Obama.

"She was at the top of my list," Paige told Wellington. "But I didn't get my hopes up because we had a slim chance of drawing her."

"Actually, our chances were one in three," Wellington said. "Two of the judges recused themselves because they've hit Wyatt with sanctions in the past and he routinely files recusal motions against them."

"I should have known," Paige said.

The women arrived thirty minutes early and parked in the underground garage near the Norfolk Scope Arena. When they turned the corner onto Granby Street, which ran in front of the outdated block fortress that served as the federal courthouse, Paige almost stopped in her tracks. The street was jammed with satellite trucks, reporters of every stripe, and spectators who were lined up out the door and down the steps of the courthouse.

"Must be a slow news day," Kristen said.

"Maybe they're here for another case," Paige said.

In truth, she had expected a lot of media, though nothing this big. But it was the perfect storm of political controversy—a sitting president and her cabinet members accused of using U.S. troops for political purposes. Twenty members of the Special Forces gunned down. A high-ranking admiral reassigned. The CIA and the president's chief of staff accused of a cover-up. Midterm elections later in the year.

Yet it was more than just political. In many ways, the case seemed to be pitting the families and commanders of SEAL Team Six against a civilian administration that had not always been on the best terms with its military leaders. There were a lot of dynamics swirling around, and Paige felt like she was in the vortex of a hurricane.

The two women didn't break stride as they walked down the sidewalk toward the front steps of the courthouse. A few of the cameramen recognized them and whirled around to capture footage. Like a swarm of locusts, other crews and reporters rushed toward Paige and Kristen, shouting questions and sticking microphones in their path. Neither of the women said a word as they plowed ahead, hoping the media Red Sea would part before them.

There was a scuffle caused by a group of men coming from the opposite direction, and soon the mass of humanity in front of Paige and Kristen was pried apart by a number of SEALs in civilian clothes, men Paige recognized from the night she had met them at Kristen's house. They shielded Paige and Kristen down the sidewalk and to the front of the security line. They had apparently already talked to the federal marshals, who allowed Paige and Kristen to cut in line and go through the metal detector. The SEALs passed through right behind them, thanked the marshals, then encircled Paige and Kristen again as they made their way to the elevator and the large courtroom on the third floor where Judge Solberg presided.

Paige thanked the men, who told her that there were plenty more SEALs in the courtroom—"the first three rows on your side." They had all taken a personal day to show their support.

"Right now would probably be a good time for somebody to attack the country," one of the men quipped.

★ ★ ★

The defense lawyers were already in place when Paige entered the courtroom. Wellington was there as well, though Wyatt was nowhere to be found.

"He usually gets here just before the judge hits the bench," Wellington whispered to Paige.

"Great."

Paige crossed the aisle to shake hands with opposing counsel. The first man introduced himself as Dylan Pierce, the lead lawyer for Philip Kilpatrick. Paige had done her research on the man and knew he could not be trusted. He looked like a lawyer from central casting—slick dark hair and handsome face, designer suit. He had a bit of a five o'clock shadow that would make him appear hip and casual during the post-hearing news interviews.

The other lawyer, Kyle Gates, was six inches shorter with broad shoulders, a blocky face, deep-set eyes, and a noticeable scar over his left eyebrow. Gates had an Army haircut, and Paige knew from her research that he had been a Green Beret before going to law school, ultimately becoming one of the best litigators at one of D.C.'s largest firms. He was only forty years old.

He shook her hand and handed her an affidavit.

"This is from my client, Director Marcano," Gates said. "It supports our state secrets defense."

"A little late, isn't it?" Paige asked.

"We raised the defense in our brief several weeks ago. This is just a supporting affidavit. I've also filed a classified affidavit under seal to explain the basis for our defense in more detail."

Paige flashed back to her conversation with the Patriot. There was no doubt now the man had insider access.

Paige noticed that neither Kilpatrick nor Marcano had bothered to show up. "Are your clients planning to attend?" she asked.

"They're a little busy," Pierce said.

As Wellington had predicted, Wyatt Jackson did not saunter into the courtroom until about 9:28. He shook hands with the defense lawyers and sat down next to Paige.

"Did you see this?" Paige asked, sliding the affidavit toward him.

He glanced it over. "They just file that?"

"This morning."

He frowned. "I usually like to be the one with the surprises."

He placed his briefcase behind him and pulled out a single legal pad with a few handwritten notes. Paige had two large black notebooks in front of her, filled with cases and analysis. She had also typed an outline of her state secrets argument. The defense lawyers had a wall of notebooks lining their table as well. And her cocounsel, Wyatt Jackson, had a single legal pad.

He leaned over to Paige. "Think I have time to hit the bathroom?" he asked.

"No," Paige said, though she was feeling a little sick herself.

He checked his watch. "Yeah, you're probably right."

41

Judge Thea Solberg had been appointed to the bench at age sixty-two and was now approaching the mandatory retirement age of seventy. She was diminutive (it was rumored she sat on a pillow to see over the bench), quirky, and energetic. Her lean, angular form was covered by white Norwegian skin, her thin face framed by straight blonde hair. She wore bifocals over pale-blue eyes—eyes that could drill a hole through renegade lawyers. She ran, by all accounts, a tight ship.

Her life and love was the law. She had taught constitutional law at William & Mary for nearly thirty years before taking the bench. She specialized in writing law review articles about arcane aspects of the Constitution that famous professors at places like Harvard and Yale ignored. If you wanted an expert on free speech, you went to the Ivy League schools. But if you wanted to know about the Article 6 clause prohibiting a religious test as a qualification to any office or public trust under the United States, then Professor Solberg was your scholar.

A few minutes before she took the bench, a clerk came out and plopped down a large pile of papers with yellow stickies jutting from the side. The clerk disappeared out the back and reappeared a minute or so later with a large cup of coffee that she placed next to the papers. The bailiff then announced that court would come to order and everyone stood.

Judge Solberg breezed in the back door, pleasantly asked everyone to take their seats, and climbed into her chair behind the bench.

She peered out at the courtroom, taking in the spectacle. "Looks like we have a full house today," she announced. "Probably some kind of fire code violation. We have a few rules here for the purpose of decorum, and you should know that I'm a stickler for rules.

"If there's any talking from the gallery, I'll have the marshals escort you out. I don't allow people to run in and out during the proceedings. If you choose to stay after I complete these remarks, then I'll assume you're staying for the entire hearing. Those of you standing along the back walls, this is going to be quite a long hearing and you're welcome to have a seat on the floor when you get tired."

She looked at the clerk and asked him to call the case. When he was finished, Judge Solberg explained she would be hearing arguments on the defendants' motions to dismiss. She told the lawyers that she had read every word of every brief—so there was no use repeating those arguments—and invited defense counsel to begin.

Dylan Pierce argued first, addressing the Feres Doctrine. His voice sounded like a polished radio show host's, and he spoke with great confidence, as if it were just a matter of formality for the court to enter judgment on his behalf. It would create absolute chaos if military members could file suits arising out of combat activities, he argued. Commanders would be hesitant on the battlefield, worried about losing their savings accounts and homes. Courts would be second-guessing military decisions. Other military officers would be called as experts by plaintiffs to testify, pitting one commander against another. To avoid all of this, Congress had granted generous military pensions and death benefits for men and women like the SEALs who bravely gave their lives in Operation Exodus. He actually spelled out the amount of money that the Anderson family had already received, totaling more than three hundred thousand dollars.

He argued the case law in great detail, emphasizing the *Stanley* case, which held that a serviceman could not file suit even when the government had secretly administered doses of LSD to that serviceman as part of an experimental program.

Lastly, he pointed out that the test under the Feres Doctrine was not whether the serviceman was technically employed by the military at the time of his death, as opposed to the CIA, but whether the injury was "incident to service." Troy Anderson was part of SEAL Team Six, he reported to the command structure for SEAL Team Six, and he had received the benefits of being a serviceman. His tragic death was certainly incident to his service as a member of the military, and the case should therefore be dismissed.

It was, Paige thought, a performance worthy of Pierce's exorbitant hourly rates. Judge Solberg paid rapt attention, jotting down notes and sipping her coffee. She occasionally twisted her face into a look of quizzical skepticism but for the most part seemed unsurprised by what Pierce said.

When Kyle Gates rose to speak about the state secrets doctrine, Paige felt her palms go sweaty and heard her heart beating in her ears. She still couldn't believe Wyatt had passed this argument to her on less than a day's notice!

By comparison to Pierce, Gates seemed choppy and strident. Pierce had been conversational, but Gates had a military cadence and an intense tone that made it feel like he was lecturing the court. According to Gates, the classified and unclassified affidavits he had submitted spelled out in great detail why this case would result in disclosure of state secrets detrimental to national security.

The state secrets doctrine had been part of the country's juris-
prudence for over two hundred years, he said, dating back to the treason trial of Vice President Aaron Burr. Just up the road in Richmond,
Chief Justice John Marshall had acquitted Burr. During that trial, Burr's
lawyers had tried to subpoena papers from President Thomas Jefferson,
but Jefferson argued that it was his executive privilege to decide what
papers should be produced and what papers should not be produced so
as to protect state secrets.

"And two hundred years later, in the case of *El-Masri v. United States*,
the Fourth Circuit Court of Appeals, sitting in the same city, threw
out the case of an innocent man who had been wrongly captured by
the CIA during the Bush administration and allegedly blindfolded,
drugged, and tortured. In that case, the director of the CIA submitted
two sworn affidavits just like the ones I have provided, explaining why
a trial might expose state secrets about the CIA's interrogation program.
That case was dismissed, and this one should be as well."

Gates took his seat, and there was a stir of anticipation in the courtroom. The defense lawyers had done fine, but people hadn't crowded
into the courtroom to hear the high-paid lawyers from D.C. recite
predictable quotes from prior cases. They had come to hear the irascible
Wyatt Jackson, and the air became thick with tension as the old man
rose, buttoned his suit coat, and stepped grandly to the lectern.

"I remember the Aaron Burr case," he said. "I believe I was a young
lawyer at the time, and Your Honor was probably still in law school."

Though she probably tried to suppress it, Solberg's mouth twisted
into the faintest hint of a smile.

"And if I remember correctly, Chief Justice Marshall, may he rest
in peace, decided that the subpoena for documents could be issued to
the president *despite Jefferson's protests*. Marshall vowed to give some
deference to Jefferson's office and avoid what he called 'vexatious and
unnecessary subpoenas,' but he didn't just defer to the president and
dismiss the case. His ruling was significant because it made clear that
the president, like every other citizen, was subject to the law, not above

the law. That's why we're here today, Your Honor—to uphold the rule of law. And you should reject the invitation from my distinguished opponents over there to rule that the courts have no authority in matters of foreign affairs and that we should just trust the executive branch to do the right thing."

Wyatt pulled himself up to his full height, grasping both sides of the podium without a single note in front of him. Paige had already been impressed that he knew something about the Aaron Burr treason trial. Maybe she could relax a little.

"But we are here precisely because this president *cannot* be trusted. We are here because we believe *this president*, in conspiracy with the director of the CIA and her own chief of staff, sent Troy Anderson on a dangerous mission *knowing* he would die. She did it for political reasons, and it is insulting to both this court and every member of our armed services to suggest that we are not even allowed to question the president or her henchmen about this. That we are *required* to simply take their word that things have been done lawfully when it comes to matters of foreign affairs. That is a good argument for dictators and despots but not one that should sit well in a constitutional republic, one with checks and balances that require the president to be accountable under the law just like everyone else."

Wyatt paused and took a deep breath. And Paige could sense that the SEAL team members and their families, sitting right behind her and hoping to see politicians held accountable, were ready to stand up and applaud. It made Paige sit up just a little straighter to be on Wyatt's team. He had certainly thrown down the gauntlet. He was right about one thing—even if they lost, they would go down swinging.

42

Wyatt's logic was simple. The United States was not at war in Yemen. "Unless, of course, I missed a declaration of war from Congress in the last few months." Accordingly, it would be a violation of the U.S. Constitution and international law for U.S. military members to go on a mission in Yemen unless they were taking action against al Qaeda under the 2001 Authorization for Use of Military Force Act. But this mission was against the Houthis, and that's why the Special Forces had been deputized by the CIA.

"The CIA does not employ servicemen; it employs civilians. They're called operatives, not soldiers. And the CIA can insert its operatives anywhere in the world. On this mission, it happened to pick twenty operatives with Special Forces training and military background. But when they set foot in Yemen, they were civilians employed by the CIA, and that was an intentional choice by the president of the United States and the director of the CIA. It is the height of hypocrisy for them to say to the world that they were civilian CIA operatives but to say to this court that they were servicemen."

"Let me interrupt you for a moment," Judge Solberg said. It was the first time she had asked a question in the hour-long proceeding. "How do we know these men were acting as operatives for the CIA?"

Wellington was sitting behind the counsel table and passed a note to Paige. *CIA benefits paid to families.*

A scene flashed through Paige's mind: Daniel Reese coming to Kristen's house to personally deliver the news that Congress had approved CIA death benefits for Troy. In that moment, she realized that Reese had not merely been doing a kind act for a widow; he had also been slyly providing evidence that he knew could be used in these court proceedings.

Paige tried to get the note to Wyatt, but he ignored her. "We will prove it through the testimony of Director Marcano," Wyatt said.

"Doesn't that expose state secrets?" Solberg asked.

"The test is not just whether state secrets are exposed," Wyatt responded. "The test is whether state secrets are exposed in a way that would jeopardize national security. The world already knows that the CIA deputizes SEAL team members for missions in countries where we are not at war. Dozens of books have been written about the bin Laden mission where the same thing was done."

"Go on," Judge Solberg said.

Paige pulled the note back and placed it on top of her own legal pad.

Wyatt closed his argument with a flurry. He turned to the SEALs and their family members in the first three rows and made a sweeping gesture. "The Feres Doctrine tells these good folks that the doors to the courthouse are closed for them. The Feres Doctrine says that equal justice under law does not apply if you risk your life to protect our country."

He turned back to Judge Solberg, his voice low and dramatic. "I'm not saying that Your Honor should ignore the doctrine; I'm just saying it doesn't apply to CIA operatives, because they're civilians. Troy

Anderson died as a civilian, defending our rights. His family should not be denied their day in court."

Wyatt took his seat, unbuttoned his suit coat, and leaned over to Paige. "We're on a roll," he said. "Don't screw it up."

"Thanks."

Paige stood, and she could sense that her argument would be anticlimactic. The reporters already had their quotes. Wyatt had been Wyatt, and he had brought raw emotion to the surface. But Paige had a role too. Wyatt was flash; she would provide substance.

"If I may, I'd like to briefly address the Feres Doctrine before I turn to the state secrets issue."

Solberg nodded and Paige thought she detected a hint of empathy from the judge.

"A few days ago, a representative from the Joint Special Operations Command paid a visit to the family of Troy Anderson. The purpose of the visit was to give Kristen Anderson an additional check representing death benefits payable to families of CIA operatives. My client was grateful for the help, and I mention this only because our government has made a conscious decision to treat Mr. Anderson and his colleagues as members of the CIA for all purposes except for their arguments in this case. Interestingly, when Mr. Pierce told you the amount of death benefits the Anderson family has received, he conveniently left out the CIA death benefits because those benefits are proof positive, even without the testimony of Director Marcano, that the government is treating Troy's death as the death of a civilian employed by the CIA."

Paige watched as Judge Solberg made some notes. Then Paige transitioned into her state secrets argument. Relying heavily on case law and reading most of her argument, Paige made two main attacks.

First, she noted that the state secrets doctrine was an evidentiary privilege that only rarely required throwing out an entire case. Even if there were state secrets involved, the court should decide whether the case could proceed without disclosing sensitive military secrets or whether those secrets were so central to the case that any attempt to proceed would threaten disclosure.

"Our evidence does not rely on state secrets," Paige said. "We are prepared to prove our case without disclosing any sensitive military information."

There were ways the court could test whether state secrets would be critical in the litigation of this case, Paige argued. For example, Paige and Wyatt could be granted leave to take the depositions of the defendants in the presence of only the judge, and those proceedings could be kept under seal. The defense lawyers could object to anything that might involve a state secret. In other words, the court should dig deeper into the matter and not just throw the case out at the beginning.

And second, a state secrets defense did not apply anyway, because this mission was a thing of the past and the trial wouldn't expose any secrets about future missions. The bin Laden mission, which also involved SEAL teams deputized by the CIA, had been talked about—no, make that bragged about—by the Obama administration ad nauseam.

"They provided a minute-by-minute account of what they knew in the Situation Room and how they knew it. And nobody suggested that the Obama administration was somehow divulging state secrets. That's all we want—historical information about who knew what and when they knew it. Congressional committees investigate these types of things all the time.

"The court can protect the names of CIA operatives in Yemen. We just want to know whether the president and these two defendants had information before the raid started about the mission being compromised. If they did, that's not a state secret whose exposure would jeopardize national security. That's treason."

There—she had said it. Paige had wrestled until two in the morning about whether she should be so bold as to label this *treason*. But in the heat of the moment, she had decided to show them that Wyatt Jackson wasn't the only one who could provide a quote.

43

After an hour-long recess, Judge Solberg returned to the bench. She had told everyone that she would rule from the bench and follow it up with a written opinion a few days later. Paige had spent the recess preparing Kristen for the worst. She reminded Kristen that even if they lost, they could appeal this case to the Fourth Circuit and ultimately to the Supreme Court.

Solberg studied her handwritten notes, then surveyed the courtroom. "This is an important case, and it raises substantial constitutional issues," she began. She adjusted her glasses and peered down at her paper. "The inquiry today pits the role of the courts in our search for truth against the role of the executive branch in keeping this nation secure. As plaintiff's counsel has pointed out, the president cannot just say 'Trust us' and expect the court to drop the matter. On the other hand, this court must be careful that by adjudicating the case, it does not expose military matters that might jeopardize national security.

"I will begin my analysis with the question of whether the Feres Doctrine prevents this case from going forward. As defense counsel has pointed out, the Feres Doctrine is an absolutely critical part of our national security because it keeps the courts from second-guessing military decisions made on the field of combat and also because our troops are provided benefits in other ways. And as defense counsel has also noted, the ultimate test is whether the death of Mr. Anderson was incident to military service."

As Judge Solberg delivered her opinion, Paige jotted notes. She was so tense that she could hardly write. She couldn't bring herself to look up as the judge continued.

"The court finds that the Feres Doctrine does not apply under the unique facts of this case."

There was a murmur in the rows behind Paige. She heard someone whisper a forceful "Yessss." For the first time since the judge had started reading her opinion, Paige looked up.

"The integrity of the courts requires that litigants not be allowed to make a claim in legal proceedings that is inconsistent with what they claim elsewhere. If the SEAL team had gone into Yemen as an act incident to war against the Houthis, they would have been violating our nation's laws. Instead, the president and CIA director sent them in as CIA agents—civilian operatives in a country where Congress has not declared war.

"The government cannot have it both ways. They cannot say the action was lawful because the SEALs were acting as civilians but then come into this court and claim they were actually working for the military. Accordingly, I am denying the motion to dismiss based on the Feres Doctrine."

Judge Solberg flipped a page, and Paige stole a glance at Dylan Pierce. He had leaned back in his chair and was no longer taking notes. He eyed the judge with thinly disguised contempt, his look promising that she would be reversed on appeal. But the judge didn't seem to notice. She had already moved on to her second point, the most important roadblock in the way of justice for the Anderson family.

"But there is a second matter." Solberg's voice was conversational but firm. Her ruling might get reversed, but there was no doubt that she believed she was doing the right thing.

"The court finds that the defense has raised a valid claim of state secrets," she said.

Paige felt the roller coaster drop and her stomach lodge in her throat. They had lost on the issue *she* had argued. Though she had expected it, she still felt like she had just been run over.

"I have considered both the unclassified and classified declarations from Director Marcano. There is no doubt that litigation of this case will touch on matters that are considered state secrets."

Solberg paused, surveyed the lawyers, and then continued. "But that doesn't end the inquiry. The test is whether the case can be fairly litigated without resorting to state secrets or whether the state secrets are so central to the case that moving forward will threaten national security. This court is not required to take Director Marcano's word for that. At the very least, in a case that calls into question the integrity of the very man who signed the affidavit, this court should try to find a way that the lawsuit can proceed while keeping privileged information from being disclosed."

Paige's emotions took another dramatic swing. What was Solberg saying? Were they going to be allowed to proceed?

"For example, the plaintiff may be able to prove the allegations set forth in her complaint without reference to any state secrets at all. She could do this by using nongovernmental witnesses to show that the president or her chief of staff or the CIA director knew that this mission was doomed. Perhaps there are documents that don't contain state secrets but will help prove the case.

"And as Ms. Chambers argued, we debrief missions like this all the time without disclosing classified material. Nobody thinks that Secretary of State Clinton violated national security when she talked about the discussions leading up to the bin Laden raid and how she argued to move forward with the raid while others were against it. Isn't that the same kind of thing we're talking about here?"

Another flip of the page as the judge's remarks picked up steam. "On the other hand, the defendants may be right that they can only show us what the president knew by exposing state secrets about CIA operatives. But how will we know any of this if I just dismiss the case?"

She let the question hang in the air for a moment and Paige let out a breath. Out of the corner of her eye she saw Dylan Pierce stand at his counsel table as if he wanted permission to answer the questions the judge was posing.

"Sit down, Mr. Pierce. I'll give you a chance to respond in a moment." Pierce sat, but he wasn't happy about it.

"This court has a duty to proceed as far as possible in its search for the truth. The court will therefore grant the plaintiff the limited right to conduct discovery and depose witnesses. However, for any witness who is now or has in the past been a government employee, those depositions will be done under seal in my closed courtroom, and I will preside as judge. Defense counsel may object to any question they feel violates state secrets and I will rule on it immediately.

"Mr. Jackson and Ms. Chambers, let me make this clear. If I find that matters of state secrets pervade the depositions, I will have no choice but to dismiss this case. Is that understood?"

Wyatt stood immediately. "We understand, Your Honor."

"Your Honor." Dylan Pierce was standing again.

"Yes, Mr. Pierce."

"In the *El-Masri* case, the court noted that allowing litigation when the executive has asserted a state secrets privilege may force disclosure of the very thing the privilege is designed to protect. In light of that, we would ask you to reconsider or, at the very least, mandate that anyone who attends these closed depositions have top-level security clearance."

Solberg thought about this for a moment. "I won't reconsider my ruling. But I do think it's reasonable that anyone attending these depositions, including the lawyers for the plaintiffs, have clearance to view classified information. I don't think top-secret clearance is necessary, and I will order the government to expedite its review of any clearance applications that need to be filed."

"I object," Wyatt said. "The court has already said that we won't be getting into state secrets in these closed proceedings, so—"

Solberg held out a hand. "No, no. I think he's right, Mr. Jackson. At the very least, plaintiff's counsel and the court reporter should have security clearance. I'm instructing the government to process security clearance applications for all of you expeditiously."

Wyatt started to speak again, but Solberg tilted her head and warned him off. "If I were you, Mr. Jackson, I would be grateful for today's ruling. I've gone as far as I can go."

"Thank you, Your Honor," Wyatt said, sitting down.

Under the table, Kristen reached over and squeezed Paige's hand. SEAL Team Nine was still in the game.

★ ★ ★

That afternoon, Wyatt took a nonstop flight from Norfolk to New York and did the cable news tour. He was his usual bombastic self, crowing about the court's ruling and promising the good people of America that he would get to the bottom of what had happened that fateful night when the SEALs died.

Paige went to Kristen's house and helped put the boys to bed. Afterward they sipped glasses of wine in the living room sitting face-to-face on the couch, their legs curled under them. They swapped stories about the magnificent events of the day and made fun of Dylan Pierce and Kyle Gates and Wyatt Jackson. They thanked God for Daniel Reese, and Paige made a note to call him in the morning. And most important of all, they raised their glasses in a toast to the boys from SEAL Team Six.

44

This time the anonymous call came in the middle of the day, just before noon. Paige expected the voice of the Patriot, but she was surprised by the thin and reedy voice of the nervous young man who had told her about the drone strike.

"Congratulations on your win yesterday."

"Thank you."

Paige pressed 4 on her keypad. After the last call, Wellington had enabled the call recording function on Paige's smartphone. Now she just had to keep this guy talking.

"I was hoping you would win. The government is definitely hiding something."

"How do you know this?"

"Like I told you last time, they asked me to lie about some things."

"Are you being honest with me now?"

"Of course. I don't have any reason to lie."

He sounded a little defensive, Paige thought. "Can you tell me your name?"

"No."

"How can I get in touch with you?"

"You can't. It doesn't work that way."

"Last time you said that you and some other drone pilots were asked to lie about a drone strike that occurred on March 11. I researched it like you asked me to do."

Paige waited for a response. The last time they spoke, this man had not revealed that he was a pilot—only that he and others had been asked to lie about drone surveillance.

"What did you find out?" he asked

Paige smiled to herself. He *was* a drone pilot. "That three Houthi leaders were killed. That the Yemeni coalition government took credit for it, but that you or one of the other pilots fired the missile."

"That wasn't my mission."

"Why did the CIA want you to lie about the surveillance associated with that strike?"

He hesitated. "I don't know. They didn't say."

"Have you killed civilians? Is that why you're calling me? Too many civilians have died?"

"No. It's got nothing to do with that."

"Then what does it have to do with? And how do I know this is connected to my case?"

"Get the actual surveillance footage. It'll show how long we had been focusing on that compound."

"I can't do that—the surveillance footage is protected. So you have to tell me. How is it connected to our case?"

The man hesitated before answering. "I don't—if I figure it out, I'll call back. But you can't tell anyone that I've called. Not even your client."

"I understand," Paige said. She tried to keep her voice reassuring. She was going down the checklist that Wellington had prepared, question by question.

"Who asked you to lie? Can you give me his name?"

"No, but I can tell you that the conversation took place the day after the SEALs died."

Paige's heart started beating faster. "Let me get this straight—you're saying that the conversation in which you were asked to lie happened one day after the SEALs died?"

"I can't talk anymore. I'll call back if I get more information."

"Wait—" But it was too late. The drone pilot was already gone.

Paige immediately dialed Wellington. "Get over here," she said. "I just got a call from our friend at the CIA."

★ ★ ★

Though the number itself was untraceable, the recording was clear enough to hear every word and every inflection. Paige watched Wellington hunch over his computer, his face a few inches from the screen. He had installed voice stress analysis software that served as a sort of crude lie detector for audio recordings. Wellington swore that the accuracy rate was above 90 percent.

He worked for about ten minutes, then called Paige over. "Watch this graph," he said.

As the audio played on Wellington's computer, they watched the stress level in the drone pilot's voice. He was incredibly nervous, and the meter registered consistently high, but for most of the conversation the software concluded that he was telling the truth. It spiked into the fabrication range on only two questions. The first was when Paige quizzed him on why he had been asked to lie about the surveillance.

"I don't know," the pilot had said. *"They didn't say."*

And on the very next question, even though the pilot hadn't hesitated before answering, it registered a fabrication again. *"Have you killed civilians? Is that why you're calling me? Too many civilians have died?"*

"No. It's got nothing to do with that." The meter spiked again.

"He lied," Wellington said matter-of-factly. "But you asked him a compound question. It's hard to know which one he was answering."

They finished listening to the tape, and Wellington typed some notes, thinking out loud as he did so.

"Here's what we know. Drone pilots running missions in Yemen were asked to lie about how long the CIA had been doing surveillance on the compound that was bombed on March 11. Our guy was told to lie the day after the SEALs were killed. They told him *why* they wanted him to lie, though the pilot for some reason wasn't willing to tell us. And he's probably killed a bunch of civilians."

Wellington and Paige stared at the notes for a moment. "I keep coming back to my theory that Holloman was a CIA agent," Wellington said. "Holloman gets arrested shortly after this drone strike on March 11. The Houthis claim he's a spy. Maybe he discovered this compound while he was in the country doing interviews. The CIA wants people to believe that they had been watching that compound for nearly a month, well before Holloman came into the country."

"That all makes sense," Paige said tentatively. "But it still doesn't explain why the president would send SEAL Team Six in if she knew it was a trap."

"Maybe she didn't know for sure it was a trap. Maybe she was worried about Holloman giving up state secrets and wanted to rescue a CIA agent."

"Whose side are you on?"

"I'm just trying to figure out what happened," Wellington protested.

For Paige, there were still too many pieces that didn't fit. Who was the Patriot, and why was he giving them information? Why hadn't Marcano discussed this directly with the president instead of meeting with Philip Kilpatrick on a park bench? Why hadn't the president sent in the Quick Response Force? Why did she work exclusively on the speech that she would give in case of a disaster?

"We're missing something, Wellington," Paige said. "We may be missing a whole lot of things."

★ ★ ★

Things got even more confusing on Saturday when Paige got in touch with Daniel Reese. She thanked him again for personally meeting with Kristen Anderson to give her the CIA pension benefits. "As you probably know, that came in handy at our hearing."

"Yes, ma'am, I heard that it did."

Paige couldn't decide if she loved or hated the "yes, ma'am" routine, so she let it go. "You said I could call if I needed help. Do you have a moment for me to bounce something off you?"

"Actually, I'm extremely busy right now, Ms. Chambers. And given the fact that the case appears to be proceeding forward into litigation, it might be best if we didn't talk after all."

Paige was stunned by the sudden turnaround. Somebody had gotten to him. "I'm sorry. I was just following up on something you said at Kristen's house."

"I appreciate what you're doing for Mrs. Anderson," Reese said stiffly. "But I really think it would be best if we didn't talk."

45

He was only thirty-nine years old, but the mantle had fallen to him. First, Anwar al-Awlaki, a dual American and Yemeni citizen, was martyred by a drone in 2011. Two weeks later, his sixteen-year-old son and nine relatives were killed by a drone in an open-air café in Shabwah, Yemen. U.S. officials claimed it was a mistake—the intended target was supposedly an Egyptian who was nowhere near that location.

Seven years later, the Great Satan struck again. This time the victim was an Iranian imam named Yazeed Abdul Hamid, killed in Yemen when more than eighty soldiers ambushed his caravan. The Yemeni coalition government claimed credit for the assault, but everyone knew it was American Special Forces.

The Great Satan would never learn that the death of one martyr only gave birth to a hundred more. And now Saleet Zafar, an imam from Saudi Arabia, had taken up the cause, his sermons blazing across the Internet, inspiring tens of thousands to great deeds for Allah.

Zafar seemed an unlikely choice—an intellectual and an introvert, a reader of books and a student of current events. He had committed the entire Quran to memory before his twelfth birthday. One hundred fourteen suras. Six thousand two hundred thirty-six verses. Eighty thousand words. There was nothing more important than the word of Allah.

He was a thin man with a black, wiry beard who always wore the long white robe of a cleric. He had bad eyesight and thick, round, wire-rimmed glasses. But when he preached, those imperfect eyes blazed with the glory of Allah.

He was also a man on the run, shuttled from one host family to another, seldom sleeping in the same house on two consecutive nights. He often went for a week without seeing his family. But his two sons, aged twelve and ten, would be at the mosque tonight. Even Saleet did not think America would strike a mosque full of innocent women and children.

But when he left, he would tell his boys good-bye. He did not want them sleeping under the same roof as him when the Hellfire missile came.

There were times he would stay with members of ISIS; they had little fear of death. He knew his sermons on YouTube had inspired many to become part of the great jihad, but he was only doing the will of Allah. He had not asked for this mantle, but if it was Allah's will, he would carry it with great zeal.

He followed events in America closely. The infidels had turned on each other in the American courts, an entirely predictable occurrence. But the subject of his sermon tonight was something far more important—the upcoming trip of the Israeli prime minister to America. It was part of President Amanda Hamilton's plan to construct an axis of power between the Americans, the Israelis, and the Saudis that would end up destroying all true followers of Islam. But these were the last days. What else should one expect?

As he rose to speak, his two sons listened from the front row, their eyes expectant, their faces proud. There were hundreds of others jammed into the mosque, some recording the message with their phones so it could be posted on various Internet venues.

Saleet began by reciting the Quran's description of those who died at the Battle of Uhud: "'Never think of those who have been killed in the cause of Allah as dead. Rather, they are alive with their Lord, receiving provision, rejoicing in what Allah has bestowed upon them of his bounty.'"

Saleet, preaching without notes, expounded on the great bounty given by Allah to his martyrs. The remission of one's sins. Avoiding the torment of hell, where the skin was literally burned from your body. Marriage to beautiful heavenly virgins. A crown set with priceless rubies. The right to intercede with God on judgment day on behalf of seventy relatives. Entry into the highest gardens of heaven. It was an impressive list, and therefore, according to Saleet, the tragedy was not in dying; the tragedy was in failing to live life fully surrendered to Allah.

Partway through his message, he pivoted from theology to the recent events unmasking the agenda of the Great Satan. He condemned the alliance between the U.S. and Israel but saved some of his harshest language for the moderate infidels in Saudi Arabia who helped advance the Great Satan's agenda.

He ended by pleading with his listeners to study the Quran: "The life of a true Muslim flows from the ink of our Quran and the blood of our martyrs. Our history has been colored with these two streams: one of them black and the other red. The infidels cannot harm true believers. Even in our death, they can only guarantee that the great bounty of Allah will flow unhindered to those who truly believe."

When Saleet had finished, he looked down at his boys. They had soaked it all in, even concepts they could not yet understand. He knew in their hearts they were ready to die for Allah. And though it pained him to consider such a possibility, he trusted the words of the Quran over his own emotions. Allah demanded great sacrifices. And if this was the sacrifice Saleet was called upon to make, he would do it willingly, though his heart would break in the process.

★ ★ ★

WASHINGTON, D.C.

Najir Mohammed knew the video was his call to action. The twenty-one-year-old Georgetown University student would color history with his own red blood. He had been planning his attack for nearly a year, but now events had aligned. In a few days, the Americans would be celebrating Memorial Day, and the leader of Israel would be visiting American soil. It could not be coincidental. He prayed Allah would give him an opportunity to act, and he prayed for the courage to do what needed to be done.

46

Early in the morning on Memorial Day, Paige parked her car in the gravel lot that overlooked Broad Bay at First Landing State Park. The rising sun was spraying watercolor purples and oranges on the river. The trail through the woods would be deserted and half-lit, but Paige knew her way by heart—every stump, every rut, every turn. By the time she finished, the sun would be fully up, and this day, which promised to be one of her hardest in a long time, would officially begin.

First Landing State Park was one of Virginia Beach's hidden treasures—sprawling, undeveloped land between Atlantic Avenue on the oceanfront and Shore Drive on Chesapeake Bay. The Cape Henry Trail was broad and fairly even, surrounded by swamp and lined on both sides by cypress trees that provided shade for mornings like this one when it was already eighty degrees and humid.

She had put together a playlist that reminded her of Patrick. She would use it during her run to flush out all of her emotions so they wouldn't sneak up on her and paralyze her in the middle of the day's events. She placed her keys on top of her left front tire and popped in the earbuds. She stretched, too quickly to make a difference, and began her run. For the next thirty minutes she would be alone on the park trail with her memories, her tears mixing with sweat as she focused on the world of what might have been.

Half an hour later, she completed her run emotionally spent. She took out her earbuds and walked around for a few minutes to cool down. She felt better—psychologically prepared for the day ahead.

She wiped her face with her shirt, grabbed her keys, and unlocked the door. On her seat was a plain manila envelope. She quickly surveyed the parking lot, but there were only a few cars and nobody looking in her direction. She pulled out the envelope. In the upper left-hand corner, where the return address would normally have been, were two words: *The Patriot.*

Inside the envelope were a few sheets of paper and a thumb drive. The first page was the cover of the Senate Intelligence Committee's report on the CIA's detention and interrogation program that took place during the Bush administration. Through her research, Paige was aware of the six-thousand-page report, much of which had been declassified and released to the public. The second and third pages were excerpts from the report. She quickly scanned the documents to see if she could figure out why the Patriot had provided them. There, toward the bottom of the first excerpt, was a list of names that included current CIA director John Marcano.

The next document was an excerpt from a speech given by Marcano when he first took over as director. He was talking about why the CIA mattered. Everyone had their own reasons for doing the thankless work of the agency, he said. For him, it was a good friend, a man who had been in his wedding, a man who was working on Wall Street when the towers fell. He was believed to be one of the men shown free-falling from the building, jumping to his death when he could no longer take the hellish fire inside. It was impossible to know for sure, Marcano said, but he had watched the video a hundred times, and he was almost certain the grainy image was his friend.

"I do this for Eric," Marcano had said. "I do it for his family."

Paige had a hunch that when she plugged in the thumb drive, she would see the image herself—the horrific sight of a man plunging to his death.

But how was this connected to her case? And more disturbingly, how did the Patriot get inside her vehicle?

He must have followed her to the park and watched as she put the keys on the tire. It gave her chills to think he had been watching her this morning, alone in the parking lot. How many other days had she been followed? How many other times had she practically rubbed elbows with the man, not knowing who he was?

And why wouldn't he make himself known? Why was he helping in the lawsuit now instead of complaining that they had filed one?

None of these questions had answers, but she and Wellington had begun a methodical profile on the Patriot. They had started writing down everything they knew about him and hoped, through the process of elimination, to figure out his identity. Now, in addition to the fact that he was a high-ranking official with inside knowledge about the president's National Security Council meetings and the tactics of the defense lawyers, he was also someone who could make at least two trips to Virginia Beach unnoticed. He was likely some kind of professional spy, and he obviously wanted to see the president brought to justice.

Paige decided she would call both Wellington and Wyatt later and tell them about the Patriot's latest delivery. If nothing else, these materials would help them understand more about Marcano and better prepare for his deposition.

But other than that, the package raised a lot more questions than it answered.

47

For President Amanda Hamilton, Memorial Day was not going to
be easy. For the first time since the ceremony for the fallen SEALs,
she would be back at Arlington. It was tradition for the president
to speak there in honor of America's fallen soldiers, and for obvious
reasons, she couldn't miss it.

But the optics, as Philip Kilpatrick liked to say, would be awful.
The White House had invited each of the families of the fallen SEALs,
including Kristen Anderson, but each had respectfully declined to
attend. Adding insult to injury, they had decided instead to go to a
local service at the Virginia Beach oceanfront, and organizers of that
event had secured Admiral Paul Towers, former commanding officer of
JSOC, as their keynote. There was no telling what the man would say.

The news shows would juxtapose her speech against his, and she
would be hit with questions all day about the pending lawsuit. It was,
Amanda knew, going to be a long day.

If she could just get through it, things were looking up for the rest of the week. Israel's prime minister would be in the nation's capital for two days, speaking to a joint session of Congress and meeting with the president. The symbolism would not be lost on the American public. The last time Israel's prime minister had visited the United States, he had done so at the request of the Republicans in the House of Representatives and had avoided meeting the president altogether.

Amanda Hamilton's recent hard line against Iran had helped raise U.S.–Israeli relations to a new level. And later this week, she would be able to bask in the warm glow of a grateful ally thanking her in front of a joint session of Congress.

But first she had to get through today. Her speech was prepared, her words chosen carefully. Now she needed time to think and burn off some of the nervous energy.

The Secret Service hated it when she did this, but once a month or so, weather permitting, she liked to head down to the Potomac Boat Club, dust off her one-person shell, and go for a row. Agents went ahead of her and behind her in small motorboats, giving the president space while they watched the banks. Early in her administration, they had tried to talk her out of it altogether. But she could be stubborn, and the water did something for her that she couldn't describe, something not just physiological but nearly spiritual. There was something about gliding across the surface of the Potomac, heart pumping and muscles aching from the strain of her relentless pace, that somehow opened her thinking and allowed her mind to focus. It was on the water that she gained perspective and courage, returning to the dock both exhausted and renewed for the challenges before her.

She carried her own shell to the water and slid into it, chilled by the brisk air not yet warmed by the rising sun. She started slow—stretching, gliding, getting a feel for the water. But soon, like a kid set free at recess, she was rowing at full strength, her muscles instinctively recalling every precise movement that had made her stroke so smooth and powerful twenty years earlier. She reached forward with her long arms, sliding her seat, catching the water at just the right angle, and then exploded with her legs and torso as the seat rolled back on its track before she feathered the oars and repeated the process. Her pace climbed to forty strokes a minute. Reach, grab, slide, feather, and repeat. Stroke after stroke, the boat surging forward, the oars slicing into the water and skimming back across the surface for the next stroke. Her breathing and heart rate accelerated. She was a competitor, and competitors could never row just for fun. She leaned into it and picked up the pace, feeling the fatigue set in earlier than she thought it should. *You're forty-six,* she told herself, *not sixty.*

Her shoulders started burning first, then her thighs and hamstrings, and soon her arms felt like rubber. Her form began to break, and she told herself to sit up straighter.

★　★　★

On the west bank, hidden in the bushes out of sight of the agents in the boats and the helicopter flying overhead, sat Najir Mohammed. The president was out of range right now, but she was rowing toward him. He had been waiting a year for this moment, and he took deep breaths to calm himself, eyeing her through the long-range scope, his finger trembling slightly on the trigger. He wore a suicide vest so that he could kill as many of the infidels as possible when they tried to apprehend him afterward. It was Memorial Day, and what could be more heroic than to become a martyr for the cause of the Prophet in a holy war on Memorial Day?

"Allahu Akbar," he whispered. *"Allahu Akbar."*

48

Amanda Hamilton had been going for nearly twenty-five minutes and still wanted to do some sprints on the way back. She began slowly turning the boat around, catching her breath, giving her tired muscles a break.

"Haven't lost a stroke, Madam President," one of the agents in the trail boat called out.

"You get paid to protect me, Caleb," she called back. "No bonuses for lying to make me feel better."

For the most part, she had a great relationship with these men. Like the Pope, she preferred being among the people, and that made their job harder. But she wasn't a diva, or at least that's what they told her, and she knew most of them by their first names.

These early-morning rows were the things they hated most. They had to keep the event off the official schedule, of course. And they had agents crawling the banks on both sides of the river and others in boats, looking for anything suspicious. It took a lot of manpower, so she didn't do this often.

Yet occasionally she still insisted on this one indulgence. Clinton went jogging on public streets three times a week and always had a dozen or so agents in tow. Bush was a runner too. Obama played on public golf courses. And Hamilton had her rowing.

★ ★ ★

Najir Mohammed prayed the president would change her mind and come a little closer. Instead, she started turning. Her strong back, which had been squarely within his sights when she was rowing, was now replaced by a sideways moving target. She might be slightly out of range, but it wasn't going to get any better. When she completed her turn and the trail boat motored slowly past the line of fire, he sighted the crosshairs on her heart. Always go for the body mass—even if he was slightly off, the bullet would still find flesh. And if Allah wanted her to be dead, she would be dead.

Either way, today *he* would die a martyr. There was no turning back.

★ ★ ★

The president started her countdown timer and caught a long stroke. The first few would be powerful and deep, churning the water and lifting her boat to glide on the surface. Then she would settle into a hard pace, clipping off two-minute sprints as fast as she could go, feeling the burn.

It was on her third stroke that she heard something hit the water behind her, a few feet from the end of the boat. The agents must have seen it as well because they pivoted in their seats, guns drawn. Another stroke and something hit the stern of her Kevlar hull, the cracking noise startling her, the bullet slicing through the boat.

"Over there!" somebody yelled.

"Get down, Madam President!"

She dropped the oars and rolled out of her boat, the cold water sucking her breath away. She dove under, her mind reeling, her breath short. She tried to go deeper, thinking that if she stayed beneath the surface long enough, it would give the agents time to react. Someone was trying to kill her! How many assassins were out there? She was running out of breath. She would surface, quickly take stock, and figure out the next move.

As she broke through, one of the agents dove into the water next to her. He grabbed her by the arm—"Keep your head down!"

The two boats protected her—one on each side, positioning themselves between the president and the riverbanks. The agents in one of the boats grabbed her and pulled her in, pushing her down on the deck of the boat.

"I'm sorry, Madam President," one of them said. "There's an active shooter."

The pilot gunned the engine as the boat whirled in the water and headed back toward the boathouse. Lying flat on her stomach, Amanda could hear the radio traffic. They were calling in backup. Block the roads. Search the riverbanks. Alert the aircraft.

She said a prayer of thanks. There would be no more morning rows on the Potomac—she knew that much. And this would be a Memorial Day that she would never forget.

★　★　★

VIRGINIA BEACH, VIRGINIA

Paige was getting ready for the Virginia Beach service when she received the text from Kristen.

Have you heard about the pres?

Paige turned on the TV. The anchors were breathless. The president had been rowing on the Potomac when a lone gunman had tried to kill her. That man was now dead, killed by a Secret Service sharpshooter from a nearby bridge. The would-be assassin had been wearing a suicide vest. The president was not hurt.

Paige thought about the upcoming service at Neptune's Park on the boardwalk. Things were getting crazy in this country. The families of twenty slain SEALs would be in attendance, and the former commander of JSOC was speaking. She hoped the organizers had a handle on the security risks.

She was genuinely relieved that the president was not hurt. It was moments like this that brought the country together. Despite the lawsuit, Paige wanted to believe the president would not have intentionally sent Patrick and his team into Yemen knowing they would be killed.

She remembered how moved she had been by the president's kindness just a few short months ago when she met with every family at the White House. Her speech at Arlington Cemetery had brought Paige to tears. She still couldn't bring herself to believe that it was all a fraud.

Philip Kilpatrick and John Marcano were a different story. As far as Paige was concerned, they were obviously lying and needed to be held accountable. But the president? Paige had her differences with the woman, but she thanked God that Amanda Hamilton was still alive.

49

The news out of Washington dominated the chatter in Virginia Beach prior to the Memorial Day ceremony. Admiral Paul Towers and his chief of staff, Daniel Reese, spent a half hour before the service in the ballroom of a Hilton hotel next to Neptune's Park mingling with the families of the slain SEALs. Daniel was cordial to Kristen and Paige, as if the awkward phone call two days earlier had never happened, but he was also stiff and formal. It seemed to Paige that he was uncomfortable around her, perhaps because she had mentioned his prior visit at the court hearing.

The security for the event that day was airtight. The FBI and local police had cleared out every guest room in the Hilton overlooking the park. Police snipers were stationed on the roofs of nearby buildings. Uniformed officers by the dozens mingled with the crowd and established perimeter entry points, where they searched guests for weapons or explosives.

The place was packed, the sun was blazing, and Admiral Towers delivered a stirring speech. It had been rumored that he was going to blast the president by talking about the bravery of the SEALs who had died and the fact that no SEAL should ever be left behind. He was also supposedly going to ask the president to stop using the state secrets doctrine as a shield in the Anderson lawsuit and voluntarily testify about what she knew and when she knew it.

But none of that happened. Perhaps Towers was too much the soldier to criticize his commander in chief, or perhaps he had changed the speech after the assassination attempt. Either way, his remarks were devoid of any political overtones or references to the president.

For Paige, it was good to be back with the family members of the other SEALs. It wasn't until she was leaving the ceremony and bumped into Wyatt Jackson that her mood soured.

"They're saying it's a lone gunman," Wyatt said, his voice so low that only Paige could hear. "Another Islamic terrorist."

"I know. I saw the reports."

"Bad break for us. In one day, the president goes from Richard Nixon to JFK. She's lucky—what else can you say?"

Paige didn't even bother responding to the tasteless comment. She had actually been impressed that despite the assassination attempt, the president had still delivered her speech at Arlington. But why should Paige waste her breath trying to convince Wyatt Jackson of anything?

"I'll talk to you later," she said, peeling off and walking in another direction. It had already been a stressful day, and she didn't need Wyatt making it worse.

★ ★ ★

WASHINGTON, D.C.

Philip Kilpatrick got a call from the president at nine o'clock that night.

"I need you to free up one of my evenings in the next two weeks," Hamilton said.

Kilpatrick sighed. He spent half his life negotiating the president's schedule. Every minute was accounted for. He would squeeze crucial meetings into tiny slots and find ways of turning down thousands of important people. It was easier to pass a piece of major legislation than to free up a night of the president's schedule.

"What's the occasion?" he asked.

"I'm throwing a pizza party for our Secret Service detail. I want to invite all of their spouses and kids. I should have never put them in the position that I did."

"That's a good idea. I'll see what I can do," Kilpatrick promised. "And by the way, Madam President, I've ordered an indoor rowing machine."

50

The Tuesday after Memorial Day, Philip Kilpatrick's lawyers filed an emergency motion for a stay with the Fourth Circuit Court of Appeals. If granted, the motion would prevent Paige and Wyatt from taking any depositions until the Fourth Circuit could rule on a full appeal. Accompanying the motion was a long brief that the lawyers had apparently been working on the entire three-day weekend. As an attachment to the brief, they had filed an affidavit from Daniel Reese.

In the affidavit, Reese told the court that even though the SEALs had received CIA benefits, they were still directly accountable to the Joint Special Operations Command as part of their military service. They were subject to military court-martial and were still drawing a salary from the Navy during the mission. Moreover, Reese said that he had been on a video call and had personally heard Director

Marcano tell the president that the CIA had a 95 percent confidence level in its sources. To his knowledge, the president had never been told anything different.

For Paige, the affidavit raised a lot of questions. She assumed they'd had Reese sign it only because Paige had mentioned him during her argument in front of Solberg, and the defendants wanted to make it clear that Reese supported them.

As for its substance, the affidavit ignored the fact that the president might have been told one thing in official meetings and another through backdoor channels like the park-bench meeting between Marcano and Kilpatrick.

A few hours after she had reviewed the affidavit, Paige got a call from Wyatt Jackson.

"Let's depose Daniel Reese right along with Kilpatrick and Marcano," Wyatt said.

It was typical Wyatt Jackson—lash out and strike back.

He was also upset about the application for security clearance he was filling out that day. "You might as well prepare to take these depositions yourself," Wyatt griped. "They'll never give me security clearance. I'll just work on the appeal to the Fourth Circuit."

"If you got security clearance, I'd lose all faith in the system," Paige said.

"That's the problem," Wyatt shot back. "You still have faith in the system."

★ ★ ★

WASHINGTON, D.C.

Two days later, in his West Wing office, Philip Kilpatrick fired up his computer and opened a chart that he consulted religiously. It had the inconspicuous label *Popularity*, and on this day Kilpatrick proudly plotted a new point—the first time the president's approval rating had broken through the 50 percent barrier in nearly a year. It had been that kind of week.

The president's Memorial Day speech following the failed assassination attempt had been a big hit with a nation starved for heroism. Investigators had discovered that Najir Mohammed had been stalking the president for almost a year. He had been inspired by ISIS and a half-dozen radical Muslim clerics whose sermons he had watched on the Internet.

The Israeli prime minister's visit and his glowing words about the president's get-tough stance on Iran had also provided an aura of international respect that had been previously lacking. Though the president was having difficulty rallying allies to support the new Iranian sanctions, Israel's PM had reminded the joint session of Congress that leadership sometimes required standing alone. Who knew that better than Israel? He was grateful that the United States had not bowed to those countries made of lesser stuff. It was a rousing speech with a number of ovations, and the president's popularity had surged in its aftermath. If they could stay above 50 percent, the midterm elections in November might not be so bad.

Later that day, after watching the president's joint press conference with the Israeli prime minister, and before the Secret Service pizza party, which had become the talk of the West Wing, Kilpatrick slipped into a conference room to meet with a half-dozen others who would determine the fate of Saleet Zafar, the most recent radical Muslim imam to be considered for the kill list. Zafar now had the additional qualification of being one of the clerics who had inspired Najir Mohammed's assassination attempt.

"This is the new face of ISIS," Dylan Pierce argued. "Religious leaders spew their hate on the Internet, and lone wolves carry out terror attacks in our country. San Bernardino. Orlando. Fort Hood. And now an attempt on the president of the United States. And it's not just preaching jihad. We know for a fact that Zafar has met with leaders of the Houthi rebels *and* ISIS. Preaching is one thing, but acting in concert with terrorist groups who kill Americans is another."

Seth Wachsmann slowly shook his head. Kilpatrick could sense that the taciturn attorney general, with his trim gray beard and receding hairline, knew the tide was turning against him. But he would not be dissuaded—not by the visit from the Israeli prime minister, not even by an attempt on the president's life.

In a measured tone, the scholarly Wachsmann pleaded his case as if he were a defense attorney trying to spare the life of a client facing the world's new electric chair. "First it was Anwar al-Awlaki. Then Yazeed Abdul Hamid. Now Saleet Zafar. Don't you see? When one dies, another rises up to take his place. We cannot win a war against terrorists by becoming like them."

Wachsmann stopped and looked around the table, one person at a time. "This cannot become a religious war," he argued. "I detest the ideology of Saleet Zafar. That man will not rest until he annihilates my people. But if you think we will silence him by killing him, you are badly mistaken. We will only give him a megaphone. Najir Mohammed was not listening only to Muslim imams who are alive. He was also listening to those who have died for the cause."

Wachsmann turned to address President Hamilton directly, knowing she was the only person in the room who really mattered. "Madam President, I have never been more proud of this administration than I was last night, when the prime minister of Israel addressed the joint session of Congress and expressed his thanks for the way we have stood for the peace and security of Israel. And we must continue to do so, fighting enemy combatants and isolating radical regimes like Iran. But we do not stand tall as a nation when we stoop to drone attacks on a religious leader, carried out under cover of darkness, especially when we have no hard evidence that he is part of the operations or command of any terrorist group. I respectfully urge that we not subvert our ideals for the sake of expediency."

"Thank you, Seth," the president said. "Your restraint and principled analysis of these issues is why I believe you are one of the best attorneys general this country has ever had."

Listening to that statement of thanks, Philip Kilpatrick knew what was coming. From the look on his face, so did Seth Wachsmann. First you compliment; then you hit them with the bad news. The president was about to authorize adding someone to the list whose main transgression was that he preached jihad. Other imams had been added to the list, but they had all been conclusively linked to the operations side of terrorist groups, not just their ideology. This was a turning point, and everyone around the table knew it.

"I am trying not to be swayed by the fact that Zafar's sermons were found on the computer of the man who tried to kill me," the president said. Kilpatrick could see the weight of this decision on her face. "But we can't ignore the evidence. He preaches a strident form of Islam and calls on its followers to become martyrs. We know he has at least met with ISIS leaders and Houthi rebels. We also know that somewhere in this country, even now, someone is probably listening to one of his sermons and planning the next attack on American soil."

Hamilton paused and looked into the distance as if seeking guidance from some of the great leaders who had occupied her chair. These were the kinds of moral issues that defined a president's legacy.

"My first responsibility is to protect the American people and our way of life. Seth, we can either let these leaders bring the fight to us, or we can take it to them. This is a different kind of war—one we didn't want but one we cannot run away from. And if there is a more persuasive spokesman for our enemies, I'm not sure who it would be. How can we kill the foot soldiers and not strike the head of the serpent?"

Seth looked down and subtly shook his head.

The president turned from him to Director Marcano. "You have my authority to use a targeted strike against Saleet Zafar," she said softly. "But I don't want his family to be collateral damage. Do you understand?"

"Yes, Madam President."

A few minutes later, the meeting was adjourned. Philip Kilpatrick followed the president out of the room and glanced over his shoulder at the head of the CIA. Marcano was watching them leave, his eyes cold and calculating.

The thought of the power vested in that one man chilled Kilpatrick. And there was something else eating at him as he headed down the hall, one step behind the president of the United States.

There had been three people in the conference room who knew things about Saleet Zafar that the others did not. Himself, Director Marcano, and the woman he was now following. Kilpatrick had no way of knowing how much her decision had been influenced by the role Zafar had played not in the assassination attempt but in the events of the past three months.

And as he tried to mentally shift gears for the next meeting, he couldn't erase that look on Marcano's face or something that Marcano had said to him on multiple occasions, only partly in jest: "Two people can always keep a secret—as long as one of them is dead."

51

For over thirty days, armies of lawyers hired by the defendants did their best to stop the scheduled depositions of their clients. They had already requested that Judge Solberg stay her ruling so that they could appeal to the Fourth Circuit before the depositions commenced. She had refused. Now they had petitioned the Fourth Circuit for an emergency stay postponing the depositions until the case could be fully briefed and considered by the appellate court.

Wellington and Paige responded to each filing with briefs of their own, arguing that the case should be allowed to proceed on the limited basis that Judge Solberg had outlined. Every time the defense firms filed a brief, there was a string of about six lawyers for each firm in the signature line. But when briefs were filed on behalf of Kristen Anderson, they had the same three lawyers every time. And one of them—Wyatt Jackson—hadn't actually written a word.

By the beginning of July, Paige and Wellington were sleep-deprived and jumpy.

As it stood, the first deposition was scheduled for Friday, July 13, when Director Marcano would be deposed by Paige. As predicted, Wyatt had not obtained security clearance and could not even be in the courtroom when Paige questioned the director. Wyatt wanted to file a motion claiming that the government improperly denied him security clearance, but when Paige saw his long list of contempt citations and ethics complaints, she talked him out of it. No sense picking a fight they couldn't win.

Two days prior to the deposition, the Fourth Circuit issued a one-paragraph order denying the emergency stay. The order said that the procedure proposed by Judge Solberg was fair and would adequately protect state secrets while she made the determination of whether the case should proceed.

The very next day, the defendants filed a thirty-five-page petition with the U.S. Supreme Court, requesting that the justices halt all discovery until such time as they could hear a full appeal and consider whether the case should proceed on its merits. The petition claimed that if the Court didn't stop discovery in the interim, state secrets might be exposed, causing irreparable harm.

Under the Supreme Court's procedural guidelines, the emergency petition would first be considered by the one justice who had jurisdiction in the Virginia area—Chief Justice Cyrus Leonard. In theory, he could issue a temporary stay without even consulting the others, though such actions were exceedingly rare, especially when the Court was in summer recess.

"He might grant some type of expedited review," Wellington told Paige. "But he's not going to act in the twenty-four hours before we start our depositions."

Wellington sounded sure of himself, but Paige had a question. "How many cases have you and Wyatt had at the Supreme Court?" she asked, though she already knew the answer.

"This would be our first."

★ ★ ★

The call came at 11:05 p.m. on the night before Marcano's deposition. Paige had finished reviewing her outline of questions and had just crawled into bed. As soon as she recognized the voice, she started the recording software Wellington had loaded onto her phone.

"Deposing Daniel Reese is a bad idea," the Patriot said, his voice the same metallic blend as before.

"Why?"

"There are things I can't say over the phone. We will need to meet in person."

"When can we do that?" Paige asked, her heart racing. This was the first time he had mentioned an in-person meeting.

"I've got to figure a few things out first. I'll give you the details soon."

"Do you have anything else on Director Marcano?" Paige asked.

"You received my package of materials?"

"Yes."

"Then you've got it covered."

"That's debatable," Paige said.

"I'll be in touch. But stay away from Reese."

As always, the Patriot hung up without saying good-bye. But this time Paige had it recorded.

She dressed and called Wellington. "I'm on my way over," he said.

When he arrived, Wellington set up his computer at the kitchen table and transferred the recording to his hard drive. For the first hour, Paige watched and listened as he tried to reverse the voice scrambler that disguised the Patriot's natural tone. But it was now past midnight, and tomorrow would be a very long day.

"I'm going to bed," she told Wellington. "Good luck."

"Okay," he said without looking up.

When she arose the next morning, there was a handwritten note on the kitchen table.

No success yet. Still working on it.

52

Hearing no word from Chief Justice Leonard, Paige and Wellington showed up in Judge Solberg's courtroom on Friday morning to take the deposition of CIA director John Marcano. The vast courtroom that had been so jammed with people in May was now nearly empty. Dylan Pierce was there, of course, accompanied by three other associates from his large firm—a total of four white males with freshly pressed suits and power ties, all sporting Ivy League degrees no doubt, ready to pounce with an objection at the first opportunity.

Their client, Philip Kilpatrick, sat at the defense counsel table. He slouched in his chair, and the big ears, black glasses, and closely trimmed gray beard made the man seem less dangerous than he was— less conniving. But Paige knew he didn't miss a thing. He would be scrupulously studying her style because his deposition would be next.

Kyle Gates was there too, but he didn't bring a pack of associates like Pierce. He greeted Paige with an aggressive handshake and a crisp

"Good morning." The muscles were tense on the former Green Beret's broad neck; he was ready for combat of a different type.

Paige was battling her own nerves and ready to get the testimony started. She had spent her young career arguing cases in the court of appeals, not examining witnesses. This was one of the few times she wished Wyatt Jackson could be by her side.

Judge Solberg took the bench, placed a large cup of coffee in front of her, and called the proceedings to order. She asked the court reporter to swear in John Marcano, who walked to the well of the courtroom, his black suit hanging on his thin and rounded shoulders. He raised his hand and took the oath, then settled into the witness box, his bird-like eyes peering out from under his long, sloped forehead, following every move Paige made. His skin was blotchy this morning, his brow furrowed in a perpetual scowl, his thin gray hair combed back. Paige had watched films of a few congressional hearings where Marcano had testified. His arrogance and defensiveness would make him an unlikable witness.

"I will begin by reminding everyone that this proceeding is under seal," Judge Solberg said. "No portion of the transcript may be shared with anyone who is not listed in the protective order."

Paige knew the remarks were an oblique reference to Wyatt Jackson, who was not listed in the protective order because he had not obtained the requisite security clearance.

"You may begin, Ms. Chambers."

Paige took her place behind the large wooden podium and began with some easy questions on background matters. But before long, she got right to the crux of the matter.

"Did you provide any information to the president or her chief of staff prior to the commencement of Operation Exodus on March 30 indicating that the mission had been compromised or that your intelligence sources were not reliable?"

Kyle Gates sprang from his seat. "Objection. That question would require that Director Marcano reveal state secrets about ongoing CIA operations in Yemen and would jeopardize the national security of this country."

"I'm not asking him to talk about CIA operations in Yemen," Paige shot back. She had anticipated the objection. "I'm asking what he told the president about a past mission. And I'm not asking for names of operatives—just what he told the president or Mr. Kilpatrick."

"It's still state secrets," Gates insisted.

It was playing out exactly as Paige and Wellington thought it would, exactly as Wyatt had scripted it. And before Solberg could rule, Paige preempted the judge. "Your Honor, I'll temporarily withdraw the question. But I intend to show that providing information about past operations has never been considered a state secret when it serves the administration's political agenda."

Solberg told her to continue, and Paige began the next phase of the plan.

"You were in the CIA during the Obama administration, weren't you?" Paige asked.

"Of course."

"And you never objected to the disclosure of information about the Osama bin Laden raid, did you?"

"No. We were careful not to divulge state secrets."

It was the answer Paige wanted.

One by one, she took him through Obama's speeches about the raid, speeches that revealed details about the deliberations and tactics used. "Did you believe the president was revealing state secrets?"

"Nobody asked me."

"I'm asking you now."

"I would rather not have the president talking about the deliberations leading up to the raid. But he was careful not to reveal state secrets."

Next Paige took Marcano through a detailed account of the raid itself that was published in a *New Yorker* article titled "Getting bin Laden: What Happened That Night in Abbottabad." Published shortly after the raid, the article included authorized interviews with Ben Rhodes, a deputy national security adviser, as well as Obama's counterterrorism adviser and the chairman of the Joint Chiefs of Staff. The article revealed details about the deliberations leading up to the raid, the Black Hawk helicopters' routes, how the SEALs entered bin Laden's compound, how they moved from room to room, the weapons they used, how security was maintained around the perimeter, the killing of bin Laden, the communications between the SEALs and the bigwigs in D.C., the hunt for intelligence documents, and the decisions made in the Situation Room.

"Did you or anyone else in the administration object because state secrets were being revealed?" Paige asked.

"That wasn't my role."

Next Paige handed the witness a book titled *The Finish*.

Gates objected. "What's this got to do with anything?"

"I'm about to show you," Paige said, and Solberg overruled the objection.

The book was the story of the bin Laden raid told from Obama's perspective. Paige had highlighted various passages, and she took nearly forty-five minutes dragging Marcano through them page by page, having him read into the record various aspects of Obama's decision-making on the night of the raid, what he was told, and what happened in the Situation Room.

"It has been reported that President Obama and the commanding officer of JSOC cooperated at length with the author of this book, the same man who wrote *Black Hawk Down*. Do you know if that's true?"

Marcano sneered at her. The blotches on his skin had grown, his lips pursed and his eyes narrowed. "I have no idea."

"How else might this author have obtained this information about President Obama's thoughts and deliberations?"

"As I said—I have no idea."

"Does this book reveal state secrets?"

"If the president wanted to reveal certain information, that was his prerogative. As director of the CIA, it is not mine."

Paige ignored the answer and moved to her next line of questioning. She was starting to have fun. "What about the movie *Zero Dark Thirty*, also about the killing of bin Laden? The CIA cooperated with the producers on that movie, didn't they?"

Paige knew he couldn't deny it. CIA staff members had provided unprecedented access in return for favorable treatment in the movie. That cooperation had triggered two internal investigations and a critical report authored by the CIA itself.

"Certain CIA employees worked with the producers to make sure the information was accurate," Marcano grudgingly admitted. "As I'm sure you know, the CIA produced a guidance report later that was critical of those actions and detailed how such situations should be handled in the future."

Paige spent the next half hour showing scenes from the movie and asking if the scenes revealed state secrets. Marcano denied that they did.

Having beaten the bin Laden horse to death, Paige moved on to the Benghazi disaster. She questioned Marcano about statements by then–Secretary of State Clinton to congressional committees investigating the incident. She walked him through Clinton's book *Hard Choices* and the information Clinton had revealed in it. There were detailed statements about what the secretary of state knew, when she knew it, and who told it to her. True to form, Marcano denied that the accounts revealed state secrets.

It had taken her nearly three hours, but Paige was now ready to circle back to the most important question in her case. "In light of the fact that all of this information has been revealed in after-action reports and books and movies for other missions, let me ask my question again: Did you tell the president or Philip Kilpatrick prior to Operation Exodus that the mission had been compromised or that you had lost confidence in your intelligence sources?"

Gates was on his feet again, noting his objection, but his voice was less strident this time. Paige kept her eyes on Solberg, holding her breath for the court's ruling.

Solberg let the silence linger for a moment as she studied her notes. "The state secrets doctrine typically protects classified information in documents as well as sources of information, such as the names of CIA operatives," Judge Solberg began.

She turned to the court reporter, watching as her words were typed into the record, carefully choosing each one. "But the state secrets doctrine only protects those secrets that would compromise our national security if they are revealed. That is why the type of information we have spent the last three hours covering—such as the release of details about past missions that have failed or succeeded, when that information does not include names of CIA operatives or specifics about how the classified information was obtained—is not the revealing of state secrets.

"If it were, as Ms. Chambers has demonstrated, there would be a number of high-ranking former officials in a lot of trouble. That hasn't happened. Accordingly, I am instructing the witness to answer the question, but he is not to reveal any secret details about CIA operations in doing so."

Paige glanced back at Wellington, who was practically smiling. This was the best ruling she could have imagined.

"I strongly object," Kyle Gates said, his voice brazen. "Once state secrets are revealed, they are impossible to put back in the bottle. I respectfully request that this court suspend the deposition and give the Fourth Circuit an opportunity to rule on this question."

"Request denied," Judge Solberg said. There was a sharpness to her voice for the first time in the proceedings. She turned to the witness. "Answer the question, please."

Marcano leaned back in his chair, still eyeing Paige. "I did not tell the president or her chief of staff that the mission had been compromised or that our intelligence was in doubt."

"You're sure?" Paige asked.

"Positive."

Paige walked to her table and picked up the affidavit of Daniel Reese. "Your attorneys have filed an affidavit that says the president was told one week prior to the mission that you had a 95 percent confidence level in the intelligence you had provided. Was that assessment ever changed?"

"That number was not changed," Marcano said.

"Did you consider it a violation of state secrets when your attorney filed that affidavit with the Fourth Circuit Court of Appeals?" Paige asked.

"Objection," Kyle Gates said. "Argumentative."

Solberg sustained the objection though Paige thought that the judge seemed amused by the question.

"Your Honor, this might be a good time for a lunch break," Paige suggested.

The judge agreed, and for the first time that morning, Paige relaxed and took a deep breath. She had laid the foundation in the morning—locking Marcano down on what he had communicated to the president. She would blow it up in the afternoon.

As she and Wellington gathered some papers to review during lunch, Marcano brushed past her table on the way out, murmuring something under his breath.

Wellington watched the CIA director and his counsel leave the courtroom. "I think you got under his skin," he whispered.

53

John Marcano had an unnerving stare that was in full force during the afternoon session. He repeatedly hesitated and locked his eyes on Paige for just a moment before answering her questions. Judge Solberg seemed oblivious to it as she diligently took down notes.

Marcano's eyes narrowed when Paige asked if his friend had jumped to his death from the World Trade Center. "What's that got to do with anything in this lawsuit?" he snapped.

Kyle Gates stood and objected. Better late than never.

"It goes to Director Marcano's motivation," Paige argued. "It shows that he has a personal vendetta against terrorists."

"That's a stretch," Solberg ruled. "Let's move on."

Wellington handed out copies of a bulky exhibit that Paige identified as the Senate Intelligence Committee's 528-page summary of its report on the CIA's detention and interrogation program carried out during the Bush administration. At the time of the events detailed in the report, Marcano had been head of CIA operations in Lebanon.

Paige directed Marcano to a page where the names of CIA agents who had participated in the program were redacted. She knew from the documents provided by the Patriot that Marcano was one of those names.

"Did you participate in this enhanced interrogation program during your time in Lebanon?" she asked.

"That's classified information. That's why the names are redacted."

"Did you do the things in this report?" Paige asked. "Did you strip prisoners down, chain their wrists to the wall, deprive them of sleep for days, and feed them rectally?"

Gates stood but Solberg didn't wait for an objection.

"You do not have to answer that question," she said to Marcano. And then, turning to Paige: "This case is not about enhanced interrogation techniques. Let's move on."

"I understand, Your Honor," Paige said, though she really didn't. Marcano's role in the torture program revealed a lot about the man's character. But she and Wyatt could make a bigger deal about that during the jury trial—*if* there was a jury trial.

Paige looked down at her outline, flipped a few pages, and began the next set of questions.

"What is the date of the report you're holding, sir?"

Marcano checked the publication page. "December 3, 2012."

"During the Obama administration?"

"Obviously."

"The report was filed six years after the events detailed in it?"

"That's not unusual. In some cases, the delay is even longer."

"So then, whether or not you are named in the report, isn't it true that the CIA felt like it had been hung out to dry during the Obama administration? Like you had done what President Bush authorized but then risked being prosecuted for war crimes under Obama?"

Marcano placed the report on the broad rail in front of the witness box and pushed it a little to the side—creating some psychological distance from it. "Those techniques were authorized by the Bush Justice Department, by the DOD, and by the White House. And yes, CIA operatives felt like they had been hung out to dry when the next administration came in and tried to paint those same techniques as criminal."

"Sounds political to me," Paige said.

"Everything is political," Marcano replied.

Now Paige was getting somewhere. She and Wyatt both believed that the real reason Marcano had met with Philip Kilpatrick on that park bench was to create a video recording of the meeting that would keep the White House from disavowing knowledge later.

"Didn't you, when you became director of the CIA, take steps to permanently document White House approval of any controversial CIA programs?"

"I don't understand the question."

"Isn't it true that you met with Philip Kilpatrick on a park bench in Washington, D.C., on the Thursday right before Operation Exodus?"

"Yes."

"Was that location secure?"

"It was a public place, but nobody overheard our conversation. We took pains to be careful."

"Did you have CIA agents secretly video that session?"

Marcano stared at Paige for a moment. Then he looked over at Kyle Gates, prompting the lawyer to rise.

"If the CIA did video that or any other meeting, those tapes would contain state secrets," Gates said.

"I'm not asking for any tapes right now," Paige responded. "I just want to know if they exist."

Solberg took off her glasses and looked out into space for a moment. "The witness will answer the question," she said.

"It would not surprise me if there were videos of some of my meetings. I would have to check."

"In fact, a video was indeed made of your meeting with Kilpatrick before Operation Exodus, isn't that correct?"

Marcano hesitated. He couldn't deny the existence of a video that had already been released to the media. "Somebody released a video. It wasn't me."

"Do you have an audio recording of that meeting?"

"I would have to check."

"That meeting is a central part of this lawsuit, and you don't know if you have an audio recording of it?"

"I said I would have to check."

"Then let me do the next best thing," Paige said. "I'm going to play the video of that meeting and ask about some of the statements that were made."

This prompted another round of objections and a lengthy argument. Eventually Judge Solberg ruled that because the meeting took place in broad daylight and at an unsecured location, the state secrets objections would be overruled.

Wellington controlled the video from his computer.

"Is that you and Mr. Kilpatrick?" Paige asked, pointing to a monitor next to the witness stand. They were simultaneously streaming the same video to a monitor on Judge Solberg's bench as well as one for the defense lawyers.

Marcano admitted that it was.

For the next several minutes, Paige played the video and grilled Marcano about the meeting. When did it occur? Why did he keep his hand over his mouth? Why were they meeting in such a public place?

Her lip-reading experts had confirmed what the Patriot had told her: that Kilpatrick asked if the source had been compromised. She played the segment of the tape showing that question and glanced at Philip Kilpatrick, sitting at counsel table. "Is that what he said?" she asked. "He wanted to know if your source was compromised?"

Marcano shook his head. "I don't remember exactly what he said."

Paige ran another part of the tape. "Did he ask you right there about the level of confidence you still had in your source?"

"Maybe. That would be a natural question to ask the day before an important mission."

"What did you tell him?"

"Objection, state secrets," Kyle Gates said.

"As I ruled before, he can testify as to what he remembers about the conversation but should not reveal names of CIA assets in the field," Solberg said.

"I don't remember exactly what I told him," Marcano said defiantly.

"Do you remember *generally* what you told him?"

"I'm sure that I would have given him an honest assessment of what we knew. I would have told him that I had confidence in our sources."

"Why would you need a one-on-one meeting to tell him that? Why not just tell him that in the Situation Room with everybody else from the Security Council listening?"

"Objection!" Gates called out. "Calls for speculation."

Solberg sustained the objection, but Paige knew she had made her point.

She rolled another part of the tape. "Did he ask you right there if you had independent corroboration of what you were telling him?"

"I don't remember that question."

And so it went, Paige quizzing Marcano about the conversation and Marcano acting like he didn't remember a thing. His denials rang hollow, and Paige could see that Solberg wasn't buying it.

"This is a secret meeting with the president's chief of staff just one day before the U.S. was about to launch one of the most daring missions in SEAL history. That mission was totally dependent on CIA intelligence, and now you're telling me you don't remember anything about this meeting?"

Marcano stared at Paige for a moment. "I'm a busy man," he eventually said.

Paige smirked at the answer and asked Wellington to shut down the video. She returned to her notes, ready to close it down.

"What does the term *eyewash* mean in the CIA?"

Marcano shot his lawyer a look, but Gates didn't object. He would probably hear about it later.

"That's not a term I use."

"I didn't say it was. But do you understand what it means?"

"Yes, I know what it refers to."

"Then please tell the court."

Marcano sighed and took a sip of water. "The term is used primarily by journalists when they accuse the CIA of not being truthful with its own operatives."

"Didn't the Senate Intelligence Committee and the CIA's inspector general both conclude that leaders at CIA headquarters had routinely sent eyewash cables to agency operatives in places like Pakistan?"

"A cable sent to a remote office will be read by every operative at that location. Sometimes the agency needs to conceal information even from some of its own field agents. To do so, it sends a general cable that is untrue and finds other ways to communicate the truth to particular agents."

"Didn't the Senate Intelligence Committee report find that the CIA had lied to the White House and State Department—had eyewashed them, so to speak?"

"That report is not accurate," Marcano said stubbornly.

"Is it the CIA's position that it can lie to its own agents as well as the State Department and White House, all in the interest of national security?"

"Objection!" Kyle Gates said.

"Overruled. I would like to know the answer to that," Judge Solberg said.

Marcano shifted in his seat. "The safety and security of this country depend on the quality of our intelligence information," he said, emphasizing each word. "It should not surprise you that obtaining reliable information sometimes requires misdirection. We are accountable to the president of the United States and ultimately to the American people. And those people are smart enough to know that intelligence gathering is not an undertaking for Boy Scouts and choirboys. Yes, we use misdirection and mischaracterizations and sometimes even outright lies to protect our agents in the war on terror. That is our job, Ms. Chambers, no matter how repulsive it might seem to you. And I will not apologize for it."

"Is that what you're doing today?" Paige asked. "Eyewashing?"

"Objection!" Gates said.

But Marcano did not wait for the judge to rule. "I have testified truthfully under oath. I can't help it if they are not the answers you were hoping to hear."

★　★　★

After the deposition, Philip Kilpatrick and John Marcano rode together in a black sedan to Washington, D.C. Kilpatrick spent most of his time on his cell phone or responding to e-mails. Marcano was in a foul mood and spent his time pretending to read important CIA briefs. Though soundproof glass separated them from the driver, they spent little time talking about the case.

Marcano was dropped off first at his home on the outskirts of Arlington. It was a large brick house with a circular driveway, illuminated at night with soft porch lights, lamps for the driveway, and walkway lights on the sidewalks.

"You did a good job today," Kilpatrick said.

Marcano turned to him before getting out of the vehicle. "I won't take the fall for you," he said. "And I won't take the fall for the president. Make sure she knows that."

"Nobody's taking a fall on this," Kilpatrick said.

Without another word, Marcano gathered his briefcase and stepped out of the vehicle.

Kilpatrick was on his cell phone before they got out of the driveway.

"How'd it go?" the president asked.

"It was a disaster."

54

It was one thing to know that the parties of most presidents suffered significant defeats in midterm elections, but it was quite another to be in the middle of it. Yet now, with Congress out for the summer and the campaign season in full swing, the Democrats were looking at some serious losses.

With Republicans controlling the House, the president's domestic agenda had stalled. Gun control, income equality, regulation of banks, and tuition relief were all progressive causes that were dead on arrival. That left the president nibbling at immigration reform, tinkering with reducing entitlement programs, and trying to modify the criminal justice system so that minorities were not warehoused in prisons for minor drug offenses. It was a compromise legislative agenda that made the liberals mad and the conservatives furious. Not even two years into her term, and the far-right talk-show hosts were referring to Amanda Hamilton as "the Mouth," a reference to her compelling oratory but lack of substantive accomplishments.

And Philip Kilpatrick, for all his political finesse, felt powerless to change any of it.

The one thing that had salvaged the first half of this term was Amanda's surprisingly adept hand at foreign policy. She had repositioned the United States in the Mideast as a stronger ally of Israel and the main tormentor of Iran's president. She had managed to stifle ISIS and stand up to Russia. And she was aggressively renegotiating America's unfavorable trade deals.

All in all, it was a mixed bag. After the president's temporary approval bump from the assassination attempt, her approval rating had quickly dipped back under 50 percent and seemed destined to stay there.

It was in this context that Philip Kilpatrick began obsessing over the *Anderson* case, playing out various scenarios and fretting about its lethal potential. Prior to the Memorial Day incident, Kilpatrick was fond of telling the president that "it's always the bullet you don't see that gets you." He meant it in a symbolic sense and was smart enough not to use the saying anymore. But that didn't make it any less true. All presidents had skeletons in their closets. Richard Nixon and the tapes. Bill Clinton and the blue dress. It was Kilpatrick's job to make sure every skeleton in Amanda's closet stayed safely in its place. And there was no greater risk than *Anderson*.

On the campaign trail, for example, she had been speaking to a group of elementary school students, a classic photo op, when the case reared its ugly head. An adorable first grader with blonde curls and big puppy-dog eyes sweetly asked the president, "Why did you make the soldiers die?"

The president got down on one knee and used her softest voice. "Oh, sweetie, I didn't make the soldiers die. Our soldiers are brave men and women who love this country. I would do anything to keep them from dying."

It was a beautiful and touching response, but that didn't matter.

Republican PACs turned the little girl's question into the campaign's hottest attack commercial. Even in July, months before Election Day, the ads were everywhere. "Why did you make the soldiers die?" became a rallying cry for conservatives. There was talk that in November, the Democrats would lose additional seats in the House and maybe lose control of the Senate. That would make life more difficult in general but particularly when it came to judicial appointments.

That's why it didn't surprise Philip when the call came early in the afternoon on Monday, July 16. He was in the Oval Office with the president and several other staffers when someone discreetly entered and handed him a slip of paper. Eighty-six-year-old Supreme Court Justice Patricia Ross-Braxton was on the line. Philip cleared the office of everyone but himself and the president. He called the White House operator and told her to put the call through.

The conversation was short and gracious. Amanda thanked the justice for her more than twenty years of service. The timing was right. The Court was out for the summer, and the Democratic majority in the Senate could push through a successor. There had been questions lately about Ross-Braxton's stamina and about some uncharacteristic comments she had made in informal social settings. Of course, none of that came up during the phone call. There was nothing but effusive praise and sincere thanks from President Hamilton.

When she concluded the call, she looked at Philip Kilpatrick, and they both smiled.

"It's about time," Kilpatrick said.

★ ★ ★

Later that day, the president and Kilpatrick carved out thirty minutes to discuss the short list for the vacant slot. The list had been ready for twenty months. As a lawyer, the president desperately wanted to leave her own imprint on the Court. "It may be the only lasting impact I have," she'd said once to Kilpatrick after Congress stopped yet another initiative.

They sat at a conference table with résumés from the top five candidates spread out before them. They talked about credentials and potential land mines in the candidates' backgrounds. They talked about issues before the Court. And not surprisingly, the president kept coming back to the same person: Attorney General Seth Wachsmann. "He's already been vetted, and we know there's nothing to hide," Hamilton noted. "The man cannot be corrupted; he's incredibly smart, and he's a liberal who believes in law and order."

"I'd hate to lose him from the cabinet," Kilpatrick said.

"This position is way more important in the long run." The president shuffled a few résumés, frowning at the others. "Plus, he's got heart. We need justices who will look at cases with their heart as well as their head."

Kilpatrick appreciated the fact that the president was so loyal. She looked at things with the heart too. But Kilpatrick always tried to take emotions out of it. He calculated, one move at a time, playing it out on the chessboard—all of the options. He didn't like where it led them with Wachsmann. "There is a downside," he said.

The president raised her eyebrows, a cue to continue.

"As the former head of the Justice Department, he would be conflicted out if the Court takes up the *Anderson* case."

The president shrugged it off. "Not going to happen."

"Dylan Pierce thinks it will," Kilpatrick said. "He thinks they'll grant an emergency stay before my deposition. If they don't and the district court is allowed to continue conducting depositions, it will be an unprecedented intrusion into our decision-making process. It's always been the prerogative of the executive branch to conduct national security operations free from judicial second-guessing. Some scholars are saying this is the biggest judicial power grab since *Marbury v. Madison*. And if the Court doesn't grant the stay and dismiss the case, it will be kicking around at least through the fall campaign."

He could tell he had the president's attention. The thought of this case hanging around for another year was everyone's worst nightmare.

"It's hard to tell how the justices would vote on a case like this," Kilpatrick continued. "You can usually count on the conservatives to protect state secrets, but then you've got to mix in the political implications. Do the Republican appointees really want to shut down a case that they think might be your Achilles' heel?"

"Who's your pick?" the president asked.

Kilpatrick pulled a résumé out of the stack that had not made the president's top five. He slid it across the table. "Taj Deegan has been on the Virginia Supreme Court for four years. African American. Single mother of teenagers. Former prosecutor. GED instead of high school, worked her way through college while her mom helped with the kids. Attended law school at night while working for a private security company."

The president looked intrigued and started glancing through the bio the staffers had prepared.

"She survived a courtroom shooting while prosecuting a Muslim accused of honor killings," Kilpatrick said. He had done his homework. "Actually took a hit but was wearing a Kevlar vest. Cool story. Real Wild West stuff."

"Does she have enough experience?"

"She's young. But then, so are you."

This brought a smirk to the president's face.

"If you want to leave a legacy," Kilpatrick argued, "you've got to take a chance with someone young. And think of the politics."

"Of course, the politics. With you, it's *always* the politics."

Kilpatrick ignored the barb. She was right. To him, everything *was* political. "Deegan is law and order. She would be the first female African American appointee on the Court. And I think we would have a real ally in the war on terror. Can you imagine the Republicans trying to oppose her at the Senate confirmation hearings?"

The president was warming to the idea, Kilpatrick could tell. But she still wasn't completely sold.

"She wouldn't have a conflict on the state secrets issue," Kilpatrick said. "And I think we could count on her, as a former hard-nosed prosecutor—" he held up a hand—"not that I'm stereotyping hard-nosed prosecutors, but I think we could count on her to uphold the state secrets defense."

The president took a few minutes to read the rest of Deegan's bio, and Kilpatrick could almost see the wheels spinning in her head. He had pushed hard enough for now.

"Let's put her in our top six," the president said. "I'd like to see a couple of her best opinions—see what kind of writer she is."

"Done," Kilpatrick said. He was already thinking about the impact on the African American turnout in November.

"But just so you know," the president said, "I still like Seth Wachsmann for now."

55

Three days later, President Hamilton stood next to Taj Deegan and made history by nominating the first African American woman to serve on the nation's highest court. They cut a striking pose, both tall women who had overcome so much, and the president couldn't resist regaling some of the high points of Deegan's unlikely story. Her kids stood off to the side, dressed in their Sunday best, and even the Republicans must have known there was no way they could keep Deegan off the bench.

The president urged the Senate, controlled by Democrats, to confirm the appointment during its July session, before it adjourned for the month of August. The Court would start hearing cases again in the fall, and Deegan needed time to get familiar with her new job.

★ ★ ★

Now approaching eighty, Chief Justice Leonard had been appointed to the Court during Bill Clinton's first term and ended up being a Clinton clone on the issues. He was pro-abortion, pro–affirmative action, okay with big money in politics, and wishy-washy on LGBT issues. As far as Paige could tell, he had no discernible judicial philosophy other than his deep love for the institution of the Court itself.

Leonard was a Southern gentleman from the Palmetto State who wore seersucker suits and white shoes from Memorial Day until Labor Day every year. He was unfailingly polite, gregariously witty, and the only unifying influence on the Court. He looked the part of a Supreme Court justice—neatly combed gray hair, a thin face lined with wrinkles, and thick glasses that gave him an aura of intelligence despite a reported IQ that wasn't going to threaten anyone else on the bench.

His opinions were never quoted as the kind of soaring prose that characterized Justice Augusta Augustini's opinions. But then again, Augustini was a former Harvard law professor and acclaimed fiction author whose opinions sometimes read more like a Steinbeck novel than legal prose. Nor did Leonard's opinions contain the type of biting commentary that came from David Sikes, former White House counsel for George W. Bush, who loved taking shots at the liberals like Augustini. Instead, Leonard's opinions were polite and workmanlike, designed to soften blows and avoid alienation. He was the glue that held the Court together, and it was generally agreed that he was the reason that justices Augustini and Sikes had not yet come to physical blows as opposed to just verbal ones.

The chief justice weighed in on *Anderson* the afternoon before the deposition of Philip Kilpatrick. Paige read the order with a mixture of relief and disappointment. She knew that Kilpatrick's deposition would have been every bit as combative as Marcano's. But she was fully prepared and, in some ways, actually looking forward to it.

Now her questions might never see the light of day.

The three-paragraph order from Leonard was narrowly drafted. It recognized the importance of the case and the need for a speedy resolution. *This case raises constitutional issues of the highest order,* Leonard wrote, *including the role that the courts should play in reviewing foreign-policy decisions made by the executive branch. The president's top-level advisers claim that even the limited discovery authorized by the trial court imposes an undue burden and represents an unconstitutional infringement into state secrets and executive authority.*

Accordingly, Leonard halted the deposition of Philip Kilpatrick and any other government witnesses, as well as requests for any documents that might contain state secrets, while the Court conducted a truncated review of the case. Other discovery could proceed, as long as state secrets were not implicated.

Leonard established an expedited briefing schedule and a hearing that would take place on the first Monday in October. Though the order didn't say so, it was clear that the Court wanted to resolve the issues well in advance of the November elections.

It took Paige a few minutes to absorb the implications. She wasn't even admitted to the Supreme Court bar yet and didn't think Wellington was either. But within forty-five days, her team would be filing a brief, and a month or so later Wyatt would be arguing in front of the highest court in the land.

She quickly researched the requirements for admission and determined that she had been practicing law long enough to be admitted by motion. If Wyatt wasn't already a part of the Supreme Court bar, he could gain admission the same way, assuming that he didn't have any currently pending bar disciplinary issues.

That thought nearly paralyzed her. If Wyatt had disciplinary issues that would keep him from being admitted to the Court, they would need to associate an experienced practitioner to argue the case. No way was Paige ready to be lead lawyer on a complicated case like this.

She got on the phone with Wellington, and they talked about the order and everything that had to be done in the next two-and-a-half months. She could hear the excitement in Wellington's giddy voice. Every lawyer dreamed about appearing before the Supreme Court, and now the two of them would be sitting at counsel table next to Wyatt for one of the most anticipated cases of the term.

But it didn't take long for the euphoria to give way to concern and a building anxiety. It wasn't a good sign that the Court had granted the stay and decided to review the case. Only a minuscule fraction of petitions for review were actually granted by the Court. And it was even more rare for the Court to expedite a briefing schedule and fully resolve a motion for stay on such a short turnaround. What did that say about their chances?

Wellington was prone to worry, but Paige tried to look at the optimistic side. Maybe the Court was ready to rethink its decision in *United States v. Reynolds*, a decision that was over sixty years old. Sooner or later, the *Anderson* case was bound to end up at the Supreme Court anyway. Might as well find out now what the justices were thinking.

Later that day, Paige talked to Wyatt, who didn't seem at all concerned about the legal aspects of the case. "This is gonna be a blast," he said.

56

With the lull created when the depositions of both Philip Kilpatrick and Daniel Reese were put on hold, it was time for the plaintiff's team to pay a visit to Gazala Holloman. The Amtrak train left Norfolk for Washington at 6:10 Monday morning, and both Paige and Wellington were thirty minutes early. Wyatt, of course, showed up at the last possible moment. He slept for the first two hours and spent the last two on the phone, spreading out his stuff in the seat next to him so that nobody else would sit in his row. Once they stepped outside Union Station in D.C., Wyatt lit up a cigar that he puffed on during their walk to the Mediterranean restaurant a few blocks away.

Paige wasn't quite sure what she was expecting from Gazala Holloman, but it wasn't the woman who showed up about ten minutes late and joined the team at their table. She knew Gazala was a Muslim and half expected her to show up in a full-length black *abaya*.

Instead, the woman wore jeans, sandals, and a tight-fitting blouse, with plenty of makeup to accentuate her striking Lebanese features.

Her personality surprised Paige as well. She'd expected quiet and submissive, but Gazala was engaging, bold, and loud. She prodded Wyatt to order something more "interesting" than the steak roti and pita bread he had his eyes on. It took her less than five minutes to begin trading barbs with the old lawyer, matching him wit for wit, sarcasm for sarcasm.

Gazala, like her husband, was a journalist. She wrote for Islamic periodicals and online publications. She was a crusader for women's rights, especially in Saudi Arabia, where women couldn't go out in public without an escort and were not allowed to drive.

"As it should be," interjected Wyatt.

"How do you put up with this?" Gazala asked Paige.

"In small doses," Paige said. She was the only one who wasn't kidding.

When the meal arrived, Gazala turned serious. She talked about U.S. policies in the Mideast and how she and Cameron had wanted to pull back the veil on the shadow war that was alienating so many Muslims. "Yemen is the perfect example," Gazala said. "Saudi Arabia has killed thousands of civilians. The U.S. and its drone campaign have taken out entire wedding parties. The average American citizen has no idea. We should be supporting the Houthis, not trying to restore a discredited dictator."

The members of SEAL Team Nine all resisted the bait, no small feat for Wyatt. This wasn't about defending America's Mideast policies; it was about getting her on board as a witness. Nevertheless, Paige had never expected Gazala to be sympathetic to the Houthis. They had executed her husband and left his body to rot.

"The Houthis said your husband was working for the CIA," Wyatt noted.

Gazala scoffed at the idea. "Cam *hated* the CIA. He compared it to the Nazi SS—the president's own private army that can kill without any congressional oversight. His dream was to expose the CIA. Trust me, he was *not* working for them."

She was convincing, but her protestations didn't dispel all of Paige's lingering doubts. The CIA chose its agents carefully. A journalist like Cameron Holloman, who let everyone know how much he detested the CIA, would provide excellent cover.

Wyatt quizzed Gazala at some length about communications she'd had with her husband during his last weeks in the Mideast. Gazala said she had anticipated the questions and had put together a copy of Cameron's e-mails and Facebook DMs that she would forward to Wyatt. "I wanted to make sure I could trust you first," she added.

Cam had called a few times, she said, but he was basically speaking in code because he had snuck across the border into Yemen. He was with a Muslim imam who was arranging meetings with the Houthi leaders.

"Do you know the imam's name?" Wyatt asked.

Wellington was taking notes. He had hardly touched any of his food.

"Saleet Zafar. I met him at a conference a few years before Cam's trip. He and Cam began exchanging e-mails. They shared a mutual loathing of Saudi Arabia and the CIA."

"Do you know how we can contact him?" Wyatt asked.

"Ask the CIA," Gazala said. "But if they find him first, he won't be of much help."

"He's in hiding?"

"For his life."

"Do *you* know any way to contact him?" Wyatt pressed.

Gazala thought about this for a moment and took a bite of her lunch. "Perhaps. But I don't think you understand what I'm saying. You can't just pick up the phone and call a guy like this or send him an e-mail. The CIA is trying to kill him."

For Paige, the comment was chilling. If Gazala was right, Paige was neck-deep in a case where a critical witness was on the CIA's designated kill list. They didn't go over this kind of stuff in law school.

"I would like to talk with him," Wyatt said. "I'll fly anywhere and meet him anyplace he chooses. His testimony is critical."

Gazala studied the three of them at length. "Your client's husband was part of the military establishment, and at first I had no desire to help you," Gazala said. Her voice had lost some its vibrancy, and her eyes darkened with sadness. "That's why I didn't return your calls or e-mails. But when Patrick Quillen's grandfather stopped by just to pay his condolences, I realized that the SEALs' families were hurting just as much as me. The men were only doing their job—trying to bring Cam home alive."

Gazala turned to Wyatt, and Paige was surprised at how the two of them, so very different, had seemed to form a connection. "From the start, I thought this case was just tilting at windmills," Gazala said. "But to be honest, Wyatt—and don't let this go to your head—you've made some pretty big waves. I don't think you can win, but you're dredging up issues that Cam cared about, and now the American people are talking about them."

"We can win, but we need your help," Wyatt said.

"I don't think you know what you're dealing with," Gazala cautioned. The banter was gone, her tone now subdued. "There are real lives at stake. We can't afford to be reckless."

Wyatt chose not to respond. The charge of him being reckless was self-authenticating.

"We know how to be careful," Paige interjected. "And we are well aware of the stakes."

A long silence followed while Gazala considered her options. "I'll see what I can do to connect with some of the people Cam spent his final weeks around," Gazala said. "And I'll send you copies of his e-mails and DMs."

★ ★ ★

On the way back to Norfolk, the three lawyers discussed their takeaways from the meeting. If Cameron Holloman was working for the CIA, his wife surely didn't know it. Wellington speculated that the CIA had been monitoring the e-mail and text communications between Cameron and his wife. That's how they'd learned about his meeting with the Houthi leaders.

Not surprisingly, Wyatt took a darker view. "They knew he was going to pull the curtain back on the CIA's secret war in Yemen. They probably followed him around and then bombed the Houthi leaders he had met with. Then they leaked information to the Houthis to make it look like Cameron was working for the CIA. Then, after he was in prison, they probably leaked information about the upcoming raid so that the Houthis would move him before the SEALs went in. That way, the Houthis would execute Holloman so he wouldn't be talking, and our government would look like they had tried to rescue him."

There were a lot of holes in Wyatt's analysis, but Paige didn't bother pointing them out. When it came to conspiracy theorists, Wyatt Jackson could spin shadowy plots with the best of them. After all, he had plenty of practice as a criminal defense attorney. The cops planted evidence. The prosecutors rushed to judgment. The snitches just wanted a better deal. Other paranoid defense lawyers might have graduated from Conspiracy University, but Wyatt Jackson was the dean.

57

The confirmation hearings for Taj Deegan got off to a rocky start. Republicans complained about the Democrats convening the judiciary panel just four days before the August recess. This was no emergency, they said. They needed time to vet the candidate. Taj Deegan could be confirmed on a normal timeline, just like every other justice.

They accused the president of trying to rush the proceedings to help win the *Anderson* case. Though they didn't have the votes to stop the proceedings, they decided to make a spectacle of it and boycott. Thus, when Taj Deegan sat down to be questioned by the senators, she stared at a number of empty seats on the dais, all behind the name tags of Republicans.

Undeterred, the chairman of the committee made a nice little speech. He claimed that the Republicans knew Taj Deegan was eminently qualified and so, instead of asking questions, "just took their ball and went home." He excoriated them for playing politics with such an important matter. He asked Taj Deegan if she had an opening statement.

She did, and by the time she was done, there wasn't a dry eye in the place. She talked about her struggles as a single mom. She assured them of her commitment to law and order. She couldn't believe that an African American woman like her who had grown up poor would one day be wearing the robe of a justice of the United States Supreme Court.

She told the story of the honor killing case she had prosecuted and how a terrorist had opened fire in the courtroom. Taj was hit but, "by the grace of God," she had been wearing a bulletproof vest. She always carried a gun in her briefcase. Later, when the coroner performed the autopsy on the shooter, he found one of her bullets in the terrorist's chest.

"I was hoping your Republican colleagues might be here to hear that part of my story," she quipped, and the room erupted in laughter.

Having a brush with death changes a person, Taj said. It had her more committed than ever to her family and more thankful to God for the gift of each new day. She cared about the people who brought their cases in front of her, and she would do her best to help the high court live up to its motto: "Equal justice under law."

When Taj was finished, the chairman sat back, satisfied that there would be a lot of video clips of Justice Deegan's eloquent remarks on the news that night. And just to be sure there were no lingering doubts, he took the privilege of the chair to ask the first set of questions. Justice Deegan was direct and convincing in her answers.

No, the president had never discussed specific issues with her. In fact, she had not even met the president before being nominated for this position. Justice Deegan insisted that she had as yet formed no opinions on the *Anderson* case and the issue of state secrets.

The proceedings could have been over by lunch, but the Democrats dragged them out so that nobody could claim they had failed to perform due diligence. By 5 p.m., Taj Deegan was unanimously recommended by the Senate Judiciary Committee for the open seat on the U.S. Supreme Court. The full Senate took up the nomination four days later, on the last day of the July term. The vote split along party lines with only three Republicans joining the Democrats, who put Deegan over the top.

Paige thought it was bad news for the *Anderson* case. "It's why the president nominated her in the first place," Paige said to Wellington.

"You're just being paranoid," Wellington told her.

★ ★ ★

The program was one of John Marcano's favorite initiatives. The CIA had hired a number of Yemeni doctors to travel around the country and immunize school-age and preschool children. There was no shortage of diseases that required immunizations, and the parents anxiously brought their kids to the doctors in every village. Unknown to the villagers, the doctors were paid handsomely by a "humanitarian organization" that was in turn funded by the CIA. And as part of the immunization process, the doctors collected DNA samples from several million Yemeni children.

Those samples were entered into an enormous CIA database at Langley and cross-referenced against the DNA of known CIA targets. The program, code-named Operation Harvest, had produced more than its share of drone targets in the last two years.

During the same week that Taj Deegan was promising judicial restraint and equal justice to the Senate Judiciary Committee, Operation Harvest yielded another hit. And this time, it was a big one.

In one of the remote villages in the northeast corner of Yemen, doctors had immunized two boys whose DNA suggested they were the sons of Saleet Zafar. Excitedly, Marcano directed as many assets as possible into the area. They would immediately begin creating a matrix of satellite images and drone surveillance footage, using facial recognition technology to find the imam when he went to visit his sons.

He had slipped through their net before. This time, they would bring him into the boat.

58

For Paige, there was nothing quite like running the Cape Henry Trail at First Landing State Park early in the morning. One of the perks of being self-employed was that she could come back to her apartment sweaty and take her time starting her work.

In many ways, her morning run was the most important part of her workday. It gave her a chance to think, the endorphins triggering an ability to focus and be creative in ways that she found impossible when sitting behind her desk.

Paige was running hard, lost in her thoughts, her playlist pushing her forward, when she noticed a man in her peripheral vision. He startled her. Instead of running by, he fell into stride.

"Good morning," he said.

Paige left her earbuds in and nodded. She hadn't seen another runner in several minutes, and she was alone in the middle of a large swampy park with a strange man whom she could clearly not outrun. Her heart started beating faster, and she picked up the pace.

"Mind if I run with you for a bit?"

She glanced over and immediately recognized him. Handsome face, short dark hair, a strong jawline, and dark-brown eyes. He was wearing a T-shirt that was too tight only around the arms, showing off biceps and a V-shaped torso.

Daniel Reese.

"This is a pretty mean pace," he said. "About seven and a half?"

Paige took her earbuds out. What was he doing here?

"Something like that," she said. "Why are you following me?"

"I thought this might be a good place to talk. Someplace where we wouldn't be seen."

"Seems like a phone could have done the trick," Paige said. Her breath was coming in short, labored bursts.

"Can we walk awhile?" Reese asked. "I think if you let me explain, you'll understand why I chose to do it this way."

Paige shook her head and looked down at her watch as if she were gunning for a personal record. These military guys sure loved the cloak-and-dagger stuff. But she still didn't know what to make of Reese. The sooner they got to the end of the trail, the better she would feel. "I'll tell you what, Mr. Reese. If it's all the same to you, you can talk while we're running."

"Okay," Reese said. "But please call me Daniel."

Paige decided she would push the pace as much as she could and at least get *Daniel* breathing hard. If he wanted to talk, he would have to do it while running these 7:30 miles.

Over the next few minutes, she found that he was entirely up to the task. He stayed step for step with her for the next mile while telling her more about his lifelong dream of being a Navy SEAL and how he had served four tours in Iraq. Then he had met Admiral Towers and was assigned administrative responsibilities, eventually becoming chief of staff. He missed the combat missions but felt a real sense of purpose serving his country.

He admired Patrick Quillen and the other members of SEAL Team Six, an elite team that he had never qualified for himself. "Everybody loved and respected Q," Reese said. "He was cut from a different cloth."

By the time they reached the large pavilion at the end of the trail, Paige felt more comfortable with her new running partner. Nevertheless, as she turned to head back, running another three miles to her car, she decided to push the pace even more.

Reese kept up and continued to talk. He told Paige that at first her lawsuit had made him angry. He thought it was a publicity stunt and a money grab by Wyatt Jackson. But the more he watched Paige and Wyatt, the more he became convinced that they might actually have a chance. At the very least, he knew they weren't going down without a fight, and he wanted to help.

Paige immediately thought about the Patriot and wondered if she was perhaps running next to him at that very moment. The Patriot had expressed the same kind of thoughts. But Reese had turned against them with his affidavit. "You've got a strange way of helping," she said.

"I know. But everything I said in that affidavit is true, and they could have proven it a thousand other ways. I had to earn their trust."

Paige didn't know if she believed him. Maybe he had been sent by the CIA to gain inside information about her case. There was so much misdirection going on. She decided she wouldn't give anything away. Besides, she didn't have the breath to talk much right now.

"I'm about to tell you some things that could get me in a lot of trouble," Reese said. "I'm doing this for Q and the rest of his team. But I need you to understand that we never had this conversation unless the case goes to trial. If you get that far, I'll come in and testify to everything I'm about to tell you even though it will put my career at risk."

He paused for a moment to let that sink in and to catch his breath. "I won't share classified information, but I can point you in the right direction to get everything you need."

Paige took off her sunglasses, wiped the sweat from her eyes with her shirt, and kept running. She put her shades back on. "I can keep a secret. And I could really use the help."

Reese began by confirming the news accounts about the night of the raid. He had been on video conference with the Situation Room. Towers and President Hamilton had always had a rocky relationship, but that night it exploded.

"I'm not telling you anything that hasn't already been reported," Reese emphasized. "Towers wanted to send in the Quick Response Force to extract the bodies of the SEALs after the mission went south, but the president wouldn't let him. There was a tense standoff, and she removed him from command the next day. Now he's in an administrative position at the Pentagon."

Paige could hear the frustration in Reese's voice. Every SEAL and former SEAL knew the mantra: *Nobody left behind.*

"Admiral Towers is a good man, one of the most honorable people I've ever known. He deserves better," Reese said.

They passed a runner coming from the opposite direction, and they both ran in silence for a few minutes. The only sounds were their running shoes hitting hard-packed dirt and their heavy breathing. To her satisfaction, Paige noticed that Reese was starting to have a harder time catching his breath as he talked.

"Is there any chance you could slow this down to a mere sprint?" he asked.

Paige suppressed a smile and backed off just a tad. "Thought you were a SEAL," she said.

"A SEAL. Not a track star."

They talked for nearly sixty minutes—thirty while running, five while gasping for breath afterward, and another twenty-five on a long walk. Reese had a disarming manner that relaxed Paige, and she found herself letting down her guard.

"You're lucky I didn't have a can of pepper spray," she said after he apologized again for running up beside her earlier that morning.

"You didn't seem like a pepper-spray kind of girl," he said.

He helped Paige understand the relationship between the military and the CIA and how things generally worked on a mission like Operation Exodus. He reiterated that he would be willing to testify for Paige at trial "within lawful parameters." Primarily, he said, he wanted to meet with Paige and see if there was anything informal he could do to help—any questions he might be able to answer.

Paige asked a bunch of questions, but the main one she had—about the president's and Director Marcano's knowledge of whether the operation had been compromised—he couldn't help her on. Still, she was starting to trust this guy. He was giving her too much information for it to be a setup.

"I've received a couple of phone calls from a drone pilot," Paige told him just before they parted ways. "Claimed the CIA asked him to lie about how long they had conducted drone surveillance before a certain drone strike."

This definitely piqued Reese's interest. "Lie to whom?"

"Anybody who asked about it," Paige said. She gave Reese the details of the phone calls. "If I gave you copies of the recorded calls, could you find out who it is?"

Reese said that he would try. They arranged a place where Paige would drop off a thumb drive later that morning.

She thanked him and they shook hands.

That's when she asked him, watching carefully for the slightest flicker of recognition.

"Have you ever heard of a person nicknamed the Patriot?"

Reese didn't blink, though he took a second to respond. "No. Who is that?"

"Good question," Paige said. She turned and headed for her car. "See you in a couple of hours."

★　★　★

Paige gave Reese the thumb drive later that morning and only then called Wellington to let him know what she had done. She knew

Wellington would report to Wyatt, and she didn't want the two men trying to talk her out of it.

The gamble paid off two days later when Paige received a call at nine o'clock at night.

"My name is Brandon Lawrence," the man said. "I'm a drone pilot in the U.S. Air Force." He hesitated and took a deep breath. "I'm the one who's been calling you."

59

Fortune favors the bold, Philip Kilpatrick thought. And sometimes the cunning. And often those who have spent a lifetime nurturing relationships, never knowing when you might need someone to cover your back.

That was the case now, and for nearly a month Kilpatrick had thought it through like a grand master of chess, anticipating moves and countermoves and a decision tree of endless possibilities. It wasn't hard with Wyatt Jackson and Paige Chambers—they were amateurs, street players against Bobby Fischer. But John Marcano was another matter. He was unpredictable and canny, an expert at using deception, and one of the most powerful men in Washington, D.C.

But he wouldn't be ready for this. How could he be? Kilpatrick had played the scenario out many times, anticipating every reaction, and always came to the same conclusion. Checkmate. This was a way Kilpatrick could avoid testifying, put the *Anderson* case behind him, and get back to saving the country.

Four days before Labor Day weekend, Kilpatrick called Harry Coburn, a reporter for the *New York Tribune*, a man he trusted more than anyone else in the Fourth Estate. He couldn't even count how many confidential tips he had given this guy over the past few years. In the process, Kilpatrick had been building up the favor chips one by one, and now it was time for a big withdrawal.

He got Coburn on the phone and told him the stipulations. *You must be willing to go to jail before burning your source. If necessary to reduce the heat, you can make it look like the information came from the plaintiff's lawyers. You must release the story on my timetable.*

Coburn made every guarantee with the eagerness of a young child promising to keep his room clean in exchange for a trip to Disney World. Kilpatrick could almost hear it over the phone—the dreams of a Pulitzer Prize now within reach.

Kilpatrick said he wouldn't send the document electronically. He didn't want to leave a digital trail that would point back to him. If Coburn wanted the story, he would have to come and get a hard copy.

Coburn said he would arrive via Amtrak the same day. "How long is it?" he asked.

Kilpatrick had a hard copy of the document sitting on his desk. He checked the last page. "Four hundred eighty-two pages."

"Wow! Are you sure no one else has access to it?"

Kilpatrick was sure. The court orders were very specific, the recipients were all classified, and the number of people who had access to this document could be counted on two hands. "I think you should shoot for the weekend edition," he said.

He hung up the phone and smiled, then tucked the bound document into his briefcase and headed out the door to a local OfficeMax. He would handle the copying of this one himself, using gloves, so there would be no fingerprints on what he handed to Coburn.

The deposition of John Marcano, protected by court order under pain of fine and imprisonment, was about to hit the press.

60

As August drew to a close, Paige and Wellington spent every spare moment working on their Supreme Court brief and analyzing the justices. They researched prior decisions and backgrounds, looking for hints at how the justices might rule on the state secrets issue.

Some of them were easy. The three justices in the Court's conservative bloc had never met an alleged criminal that didn't belong behind bars. In the balancing act between security and liberty, they came down hard on the side of law and order. In this case, they would be reluctant to pull back the curtain on the CIA, even if doing so meant they could embarrass a Democrat in the White House.

Justice David Sikes, one of the younger justices on the Court and former White House counsel for George W. Bush, had defended the CIA's interrogation program under Bush and would certainly defend the agency now. Justice Barton Cooper, a seventy-two-year-old conservative appointed by Bush Sr., was a former Texas judge who had affirmed the death penalty dozens of times. The only justice with facial hair, he had been dubbed "the Beard" by the creatively challenged lawyers who practiced before the Court. The Beard wasn't going to be in Paige's and Wellington's camp. Nor was the woman who sat to his immediate left, closest to the chief justice because of her seniority. Justice Kathryn Byrd, gray-haired, thoughtful, and quiet, could be counted on to vote with the conservative bloc every time.

There were four liberals who would probably help Paige and Wellington despite the fact that a win for SEAL Team Nine would be a loss for the Democrats in the administration. Justice Augusta Augustini, a brilliant jurist who had taught at Harvard Law and managed to pump out a novel every other year, would be an outspoken ally. So would the two veteran African American justices—Reginald Murphy, a former Innocence Project lawyer, and William Martin Jacobs III, a large man weighing in at almost three hundred pounds who had made a career arguing civil rights cases. Jacobs had been appointed by President Clinton, and the word around the Court was that he never wrote a word of his own opinions but had a knack for hiring Ivy League clerks who shared his crusading ideology and did all the work for him.

The fourth liberal was less certain. Justice Evangelina Torres was the Court's only Hispanic justice. A former senator from California, she had been nominated by President Obama during his last year in office and confirmed by a Democrat-controlled Congress in the months following Hamilton's election. Philosophically, Paige and Wellington thought she would side with them. But she had served on the Foreign Relations Committee during her days in the Senate and might be particularly sensitive to exposing classified CIA information.

That left two potential swing votes—Chief Justice Cyrus Leonard and forty-five-year-old Taj Deegan. Wellington was about 90 percent sure that the chief, given his faithful adherence to Supreme Court precedent, would not be willing to overturn the 1953 *Reynolds* case. And if Wellington was right, they could only win if they carried the vote of every liberal justice, including former senator Evangelina Torres, and also won over Taj Deegan.

It was a monumental challenge, and it didn't help that Wyatt seemed disinterested and unprepared during their prep sessions. He didn't grasp the nuances of prior case law and, in Paige's opinion, kept making statements that sounded more like jury arguments than points of law that would sway seasoned judges.

The sessions became tense, and Paige exacerbated the problem by intentionally asking questions she knew Wyatt couldn't answer. After one particularly poor performance inside his RV, Wyatt lit up a cigar, declared himself tired of the process, and said they should take a few weeks off so he could come back to the case with a fresh perspective.

"I think we need to practice every day," Paige insisted. "There's a lot to cover, and we only get one chance at this."

Wyatt scoffed at the notion. "I work better under pressure. I won't even remember anything I read a month ahead of time. Besides, I've got other cases."

His attitude had long since worn Paige's patience thin. It grated her that she and Wellington were working around the clock when the man who would actually argue the case had such a cavalier attitude.

"Have you even read these?" she asked, pointing to the black notebooks full of prior cases. She brushed away a stream of smoke from Wyatt's cigar. She glared at Wellington for a second—*I thought you said he never lit up inside.* "Our entire case hinges on your argument, and you haven't even cracked these notebooks."

Wyatt shrugged and took another puff. "You don't get it," he said. "You actually think we can win this case?"

Wellington spoke up. "If we can convince both Justice Torres and Justice Deegan, we can win. Why don't Paige and I just finish the brief and then you can read that and start there?"

"Because you don't get it either," Wyatt said. "I hate to break it to you two, but we stand no chance of winning this case." He watched Paige swat away some more smoke, frowned, and snuffed out his cigar in a nearby ashtray. "We're going to the Supreme Court, where we hope that we can somehow get five justices to say that we can take a few depositions. We'll probably lose that argument, but even if we win, then what? Kilpatrick will deny and obfuscate and hide behind state secrets just like Marcano did. We've been at this for months, and we still don't even have a clue whether the CIA told the president that the mission was compromised."

"We've got the park-bench conversation," Paige countered. "We've got a drone pilot who was told to lie."

"How is the drone pilot even relevant? And the park bench? We have no idea what Marcano said, only what Kilpatrick asked him. They'll both come to trial and testify that Marcano confirmed the sources were solid. Marcano will say they had this meeting before the National Security Council meeting so he could share details with the president's chief of staff that he didn't feel comfortable telling the whole team. Then where are we? If we ask what details, they claim state secrets."

Like the smoke from his smoldering cigar, Wyatt's brutal assessment hung in the air. It was the last thing Paige had expected. This was the same guy who always thought he could pull rabbits out of a hat and part the Red Sea. If he didn't think they could win, what chance did they have?

"This case has never been about winning," Wyatt continued. "This case is the Alamo. Those men knew they were going to lose but fought anyway because they were trying to rally people to something bigger."

He had a beer on the table in front of him—another thing that bothered Paige about their prep sessions—and paused to take a sip. His eyes went from Wellington to Paige.

"Let's face it; we're going down. So I'm not interested in some legal nuance that might nudge one justice closer to a narrow opinion that allows us to take one more deposition before the case gets dismissed. I'm interested in using the Supreme Court argument as a platform to rile up this country and get the laws changed by Congress.

"Don't you see what's happening? Every dictator in history always had their own private army. The Roman emperors and the Praetorian Guard. Napoleon and the Imperial Guard. Hitler and the SS. And now our president has the CIA. Those guys are accountable to no one, and every time we try to hold them accountable, they claim state secrets and hide behind national security. They can kill anybody they want anywhere in the world without a court granting them permission beforehand or exonerating them of guilt afterward. They don't even have to go to Congress to declare war."

His voice had risen with emotion as he talked, and when he stopped, neither Paige nor Wellington uttered a word. Comparing the CIA to the SS was way over the top, but that wasn't his point, and Paige knew it. She had been down in the weeds, but Wyatt was talking about something way bigger than a single Supreme Court case.

"So you're right," he said, his voice softer. "I haven't read those cases. I'll read them before I argue, but it's not going to change what I say. My audience isn't those nine people in the black robes; my audience is the American people. Because they don't know what's happening, and they'd better wake up real soon. I've spent my entire life fighting the government. I've seen innocent men railroaded by the system and good men and women lose their reputations even if they're found innocent. We get scared because there are some legitimately bad actors out there, and we hand over our freedoms one at a time."

Paige chewed on it for a moment, her frustration dampened by how much he cared. "Why can't we do both?" she asked. "Why can't we speak to the people *through* the Court? How else are we going to change the law if we don't take advantage of our best opportunity?"

"I didn't say I'm not going to try," Wyatt said.

He took another swig of his beer and switched into storytelling mode. "Colonel James Bowie was sick in bed when the Alamo was attacked. They say that he was killed on his cot, firing pistols at the Mexicans who barged into his room, and when he ran out of bullets, he pulled out his knife. You know what Bowie's mother said when she was informed of her son's death?"

Paige shook her head. Of course she didn't know.

When he answered his own question, Wyatt's eyes were distant with admiration. "She said, 'I'll wager you didn't find any wounds in his back.'"

Wyatt raised his beer in a solitary toast. "Here's to going down fighting."

61

The lead article in the *New York Tribune* hit the streets on the Saturday of Labor Day weekend. Paige found out about it from a text message and immediately checked online. The story was at the top of the *Tribune* web page, and it came complete with several photos, including one of her and Wellington entering the courthouse. The article already had accumulated more than two hundred comments. And following the story, embedded online for the entire world to see, was the full PDF transcript of John Marcano's deposition.

The article, written by Harry Coburn, described the contents of the deposition, which Coburn said he had obtained from a confidential source with inside information. A few paragraphs later, the article quoted Paige, who had made a few innocuous comments about the upcoming Supreme Court hearing to some local Virginia reporters. Coburn made it seem as if he had interviewed Paige himself.

The article described how duplicitous Marcano had looked when claiming a state secrets privilege for this mission when movies had been made and books had been written about similar missions in the past. It also highlighted the CIA's practice of eyewashing its own agents and even cabinet members so that confidential information would not spill out.

After showing how powerful the CIA had become and noting that there was virtually no congressional oversight for the agency's military activities, Coburn ended his article with a quote that dated back almost two thousand years: "Who guards the guards?"

Paige knew the article and the leaked deposition would stir public sentiment in their favor. But it seemed like the reporter was hinting at Paige as the confidential source. Thinking about how Judge Solberg might react made her stomach turn.

She worried about the article incessantly that morning but couldn't focus on it all day. She had a date at the beach with Kristen and her two boys. The outing had been in the works for two weeks, and Paige couldn't call it off now. Besides, there was nothing like the squeal of kids in the ocean to make you forget about your legal troubles.

★　★　★

The broad white sands of Virginia Beach were crawling with people and, for Labor Day weekend, blazing hot. Kristen and Paige set up two beach chairs in the wet sand close to the water and settled in to talk while Justin and Caleb played.

That plan didn't last long. The boys begged them to go swimming, and soon Paige and Kristen were bodysurfing while the boys rode their boogie boards. Then the boys wanted to build a castle. Then they needed another layer of SPF 30, and Paige made sure to lather it on herself again as well. She had a faint runner's tan, and the parts of her skin that were covered when she was running but exposed in her swimsuit were as white as they had been in March. It had been that kind of summer.

And then, as soon as the boys got new sunscreen on, they wanted to go into the surf again. They couldn't go alone, of course.

All in all, it was an exhausting day, and it made both Paige and

Kristen miss the men who had been in their lives. It wasn't until nearly four o'clock, with the boys finally playing in the small waves and hunting for crabs, that Paige and Kristen had a chance to talk.

It had been a rough summer for Paige. Her law practice wasn't generating the income she'd thought it would. Kristen's case seemed to sprout a new set of problems every day. And Paige didn't feel like she was mending from Patrick's death the way she should. There were still days when the sadness was just overwhelming, Paige confided. Days like today when her heart felt like it had been ripped out of her chest all over again.

"I know what you mean," Kristen said with a huge sigh. She had on sunglasses but Paige suspected she was tearing up. "I look at these two little guys and my heart just breaks for them without a father. And then I get mad at myself because I lose my patience with them and think I'm a horrible mother."

"You're the best mother I know," Paige said.

"You need to get out more," Kristen responded.

They talked about how summers would never be the same again. Kristen and Troy used to go to the beach even before the boys were born. "He loved the water," Kristen said. "We would walk on the beach for miles. This is where we found our peace."

Paige didn't have the same kind of memories, but for her it was an opportunity missed. She had imagined herself raising a family with Patrick, the kids attacking the ocean the same way Kristen's boys had done today. For her, it was the pain of dreams that would never be realized. For the first time, she told Kristen about Patrick's proposal the night before he left for deployment and about her own regret at saying she needed more time.

"He knew you loved him," Kristen said. "He knew you were going to say yes eventually."

By five o'clock, Paige was pretty sure her skin was scorched despite her best efforts to stay covered in sunscreen. They left the beach tired, sunburned, and surprisingly refreshed. The time with Kristen helped Paige remember why she had left her old job and taken this case in the first place. Kristen was a good woman, and she had lost something that could never be replaced.

When they parted ways, Paige hugged the sandy bodies of Kristen's little boys. She had wanted to buy them some ice cream, but Kristen said it would ruin their supper. So she settled for a quick squeeze and watched the boys follow their mother to the parking garage.

Paige thought about the words of Wyatt Jackson—his firm belief that they could never really win this case. She didn't share that same sense of fatalism. It might take a miracle, but unlike Wyatt, she actually believed in miracles. She turned left on Atlantic, walking toward her car, which was parked two blocks away in an uncovered lot. She prayed as she walked—a plea for justice for Kristen and the boys and strength for herself. How could God turn down a humble request like that?

★ ★ ★

The day after Labor Day, a $10,000 check from Kristen arrived in the mail. It was accompanied by a handwritten note.

> I haven't seen a bill yet. Knowing you, you probably aren't going to send one. But I never expected you to do this for free. Wyatt and Wellington certainly aren't.
>
> I've enclosed a $10,000 retainer. Please let me know if you need more.
>
> I could never do this without you, Paige. Thanks for being a great lawyer and an even better friend.

Paige hated cashing the check, but ramen noodles were getting old. This would keep her new firm afloat for the next several weeks. By then maybe she would have a few more paying clients.

That same day, she received an electronic notification from federal court with an attached order from Judge Solberg. The judge had apparently read the article in the *New York Tribune*, and she was not happy about it.

She ordered all parties and all lawyers who had worked on the case to appear in her courtroom at nine o'clock Friday morning to answer a rule to show cause. The purpose of the rule, according to Judge Solberg, was to find out who had violated her protective order by leaking the deposition of Director Marcano.

Paige knew that everyone, including Judge Solberg, probably thought it was either her or Wyatt Jackson. But she had followed the protective order to the hilt, not even giving Wyatt a copy of the deposition. She would be prepared to defend herself, though she expected the judge to be skeptical.

It was the last thing she needed in a case that was growing more difficult to win every day.

62

Paige showed up in federal court on Friday hopeful that she could clear her good name. She had never danced close to the ethical lines the way Wyatt did, and she was far more stressed about the hearing than he was. For Wyatt, it had been an enjoyable week of increased media scrutiny on the actions of Director Marcano and more pressure on the administration to tell the American public exactly what happened on the night of the failed rescue mission. There were even rumblings from various congressmen and congresswomen about holding hearings once they returned to D.C.

The media was out in force again for the rule to show cause hearing. The case continued to capture the attention of the American public, and the politicians were using it as fodder for their campaigns. But there was also the intrigue of how the deposition got leaked to the press, and the fingers of blame were pointing everywhere.

Paige couldn't figure it out. Wyatt swore that he had never laid eyes on the deposition. Paige had Wellington check her own computer to make sure she had not been hacked. Harry Coburn, the *Tribune* reporter who had authored the story, was giving no hints about his sources. There was a possibility that Solberg might subpoena him and threaten him with contempt if he didn't disclose his source, but most legal scholars thought she would avoid that scenario. She was a big fan of free press and didn't want to be the judge who threw a prizewinning reporter in jail for protecting confidential sources.

The hearing started with the usual fanfare as Judge Solberg took the bench. This time she brought no coffee, and Paige could see the smoldering anger in the judge's eyes as she surveyed her courtroom.

She began the proceedings by reading from her notes.

"We are here today on the court's rule to show cause for violation of this court's protective order regarding the deposition of Director John Marcano taken on July 13. That deposition was attended only by myself, the court reporter, counsel for the parties, Mr. Kilpatrick, and Mr. Marcano. This court's order prohibited dissemination of that deposition or its contents beyond a select group of people listed in the court's protective order, all of whom had national security clearance. Contrary to that order, the deposition was leaked to a reporter for the *New York Tribune*, who published the entire deposition last week. The court subsequently issued its rule to show cause in order to determine the source of that leak."

Paige thought that Solberg glanced briefly at her when she finished reading, or maybe she was just being paranoid. She knew for a fact that most of the eyes in the courtroom were on the plaintiff's lawyers. What good would it do for Marcano's lawyers or Kilpatrick's lawyers to leak the deposition?

Nevertheless, Judge Solberg began by questioning lawyers for the defense. She interrogated all seven lawyers from Dylan Pierce's firm who had been working on the matter and had access to the deposition. She did the same with the four lawyers from Kyle Gates's office. She then called Wyatt to the podium for his grilling.

"Mr. Jackson, you do not have security clearance, is that right?"

"That is correct, Your Honor."

"Have you seen or reviewed the deposition of Director Marcano?"

"I have not."

"Have you learned from your cocounsel or otherwise about the contents of that deposition?"

"I have not."

"Do you have a copy of that deposition on your computer, your iPad, your smartphone, or any other device, or do you have a hard copy of any kind?"

"I do not."

"Do you have any idea how the deposition got leaked to the *New York Tribune*?"

"Your Honor, I have no idea."

The judge stared at Wyatt for a moment, and it was apparent to Paige that she did not believe him. Many people assumed this was Wyatt's doing, and why wouldn't they? The man used publicity like just another legal tactic. Even Paige assumed that Wyatt had somehow accessed the deposition and leaked it.

She was called to the podium next. Like the others, she was grilled by Judge Solberg about whether she had shared the deposition with anybody or stored it electronically in any area where it could be accessed. She answered each of the judge's questions directly and decisively, denying that she had anything to do with the deposition leak.

Wellington then took his turn. But instead of giving short, direct denials, he went to great lengths to explain the encryption system he had set up for his own computer and the fact that he had searched Wyatt's computer—with Wyatt's permission, of course—and found no trace of the deposition. He was nervous and stumbled over his words, and the whole thing made it seem like he was protesting too much and covering for Wyatt.

When the interrogations were complete, Judge Solberg let the courtroom know that she had already examined each of her court clerks and the court reporter and was satisfied that the leak had not come from any of them.

"So where does this leave us?" Judge Solberg asked. "This court is handling a case that involves, at least peripherally, the most sensitive classified information imaginable. And this court decided early on that the case would proceed anyway because we would conduct confidential depositions that would protect those state secrets while at the same time getting at the truth of the allegations in the complaint. But now Director Marcano's deposition has been released to the public, calling into question the integrity of the entire process."

There was no mistaking it this time—Judge Solberg looked at Paige, Wyatt, and Wellington before she returned to her notes.

"At this point, the court cannot determine who breached its confidentiality order—" she paused for emphasis—"though it stands to reason that the plaintiff benefited the most from the deposition's release.

"I have had my clerks perform extensive research regarding this court's ability to mandate disclosure of the confidential source by the reporter. After reviewing that research, the court is of the mind-set that it should not subpoena Mr. Coburn and attempt to compel the name of his confidential source. He has First Amendment rights that would protect the anonymity of the source under these circumstances.

"But this court is not satisfied to simply lecture the parties involved and proceed forward without getting to the bottom of this blatant disregard of the court's order. Therefore, I am asking the U.S. attorney's office to conduct an investigation and report back to the court with the results."

Judge Solberg flipped a page and allowed that news to sink in. Paige felt a chill cascade down her spine, its tendrils branching out and squeezing her heart. She knew that the U.S. attorney would draw in the FBI. She would tell them the truth, but how many times had she seen zealous investigators put together a case where none really existed? Wyatt was her cocounsel. The feds would love to see him disbarred.

"The report will include whether or not the U.S. attorney's office intends to file charges, and this court will decide what sanctions are appropriate for the breach of its confidentiality order. I anticipated that counsel today would deny any knowledge of the leak, and I have therefore already asked the U.S. attorney's office to be ready to start this investigation immediately. Counsel can expect to be hearing shortly from that office or its investigators."

63

Paige hadn't been home five minutes Friday when her cell phone vibrated. Wyatt Jackson.

"Are you alone?" he asked.

"Yes."

"I got a call from the Patriot. He thinks the FBI is after more than just who leaked Marcano's deposition." Wyatt paused to let this sink in. "Says we need to get rid of any traces of classified information. I think he's right."

"Like what?" Paige asked. She didn't like the direction this was heading.

"Like recordings of phone calls from the Patriot. Any notes mentioning him. Any classified information he gave us. Check out 18 U.S. Code Section 798, Paige. Both disseminating and using classified information are felonies."

Paige started mentally cataloging the evidence she had received from the Patriot. The original tip about the president calling off the Quick Response Force. The confidential deliberations in the Situation Room. The thumb drive with the video of the meeting between Kilpatrick and Marcano. The picture of Admiral Towers sacrificing a lamb. The fact that the imam in Yemen had been killed by American forces. The inside tips about the state secrets defense. The unredacted copy of the Senate Intelligence Committee's report on the CIA. It was a long list, and a lot of it was probably classified.

"Right now, there's no search warrant or subpoena for any of our computers or anything else," Wyatt continued. "And no reasonable person would think there was already an investigation about our confidential sources of information for this case. So now's the time to make sure we're clean.

"I've told Wellington to get three new computers and cell phones, one for each of us. Told him to bleach the old hard drives and destroy them. Same for the SIM cards and phones. The feds aren't entitled to know how we get our information. If they ask you about it, just tell them you want to talk to an attorney. We can huddle up and take it from there."

Alarm bells were going off for Paige. She didn't want any part of this. "I won't answer questions about our sources. But I'll take care of my own computer and phone," she said. "I don't think bleaching and destroying the hard drives and phones is a good idea."

"Do you remember Clinton's e-mail scandal?" Wyatt asked.

"Of course."

"Neither Clinton nor her lawyers ever got in trouble for destroying e-mails. The issue that wouldn't go away was the way she handled classified information."

Wyatt let Paige's silence help make his point. "Paige, I've been through this drill before. We've got to act quickly, but we've got a window of time where there's nothing illegal about deleting information. For obstruction charges to stick, they have to prove we knew that there was an ongoing criminal investigation about classified information.

Right now, we only know about a possible contempt investigation into the leak of Marcano's deposition. But if we don't act now, I can assure you that we'll regret it later. And you'll be the one explaining to Kristen Anderson why her case got dismissed."

By the time the phone call had ended, Paige's anxiety had been stoked into a full-blown fire. She would never obstruct justice—that was for sure. But under the obstruction laws, you could destroy anything you wanted *unless* you had a reasonable belief that a criminal investigation had been launched. She could probably make a legal argument that she had no way of knowing that a federal investigation would include anything other than the issue of who leaked the Marcano deposition. But she didn't play the game that way. She had ethical standards that went beyond the mere letter of law, and she wasn't going to lie under oath.

She played out the consequences of the FBI discovering her conversations with the Patriot. He had exposed state secrets; there was little doubt about that. And from her training on classified documents that she had received for her security clearance, she understood that knowingly receiving those secrets was also a crime. Especially here, where she had used them to advance a legal case.

And it was worse than the Patriot even knew. Paige and Wellington had audio recordings of the Patriot's voice on her computer, including the phone call where he had told Paige that the defense attorneys would be using the state secrets defense. She thought about how embarrassing it would be for this to be released. She was getting illicit information from a source inside the defendant's legal team.

This couldn't come out. In hindsight, she should have confidentially told the judge about the Patriot early in the case. But it was too late now.

And there was another problem. If Wyatt and Wellington destroyed their computers and Paige did not, the FBI would find the information about the Patriot and then charge Wyatt and Wellington with obstruction of justice. She would have to decide whether to testify against them, including the conversation she had just had with Wyatt, or take the Fifth. It would create an irreparable rift in the legal team. And what about Bill Harris and Kristen, who had also received classified information from the Patriot?

Sick to her stomach, Paige considered the implications from every angle. As the minutes ticked by, she dreaded the visit from the FBI agents, knowing she wasn't ready to deal with them. She called and talked to Wellington, who was more worried than she was.

She had never been on this side of an investigation before—the hunted, the accused. She thought about her years as a prosecutor. It had all seemed so clear then. But now everything was murky. Was her duty to Kristen and the case? Was Wyatt right that she could skirt around the law by destroying everything now?

It didn't feel right. And she wanted to do the right thing, not just the legal thing. But the consequences of delay felt even worse. She couldn't betray her team.

64

The FBI didn't show up Friday afternoon, and Paige began to wonder if she was overthinking this. Wyatt's paranoia had her worried, but in her calmer moments, she reminded herself that the only thing Solberg really cared about was who had released the Marcano deposition. All the other stuff on her computer had nothing to do with that.

Still, she couldn't sleep Friday night. Instead she patched together a plan that would preserve her options, though it felt a little too much like something Wyatt would cook up. She couldn't bring herself to destroy the videos, her hard drive, or documents that might somehow be relevant to the case or to an FBI investigation down the road. But she knew that the FBI could get a warrant for her condo, her car, Wyatt's RV, or anyplace else that Paige might think to store her computer and phone in the short term. Plus, it would look more than a little deceptive if they found the computer stashed away someplace.

She wanted to hide the items somewhere that the FBI wouldn't consider. She wouldn't lie about their whereabouts, but she could refuse to answer their questions. That way, if she needed the evidence later, she would have it.

And so, at 5 a.m. on Saturday, she dressed in her running gear, loaded up her backpack, and drove to First Landing. It was still dark when she walked down the Cape Henry Trail, a path she had run dozens of times, perhaps hundreds, and stopped at a place marked by a large cypress tree on the right. According to her GPS, it was 1.4 miles from the start of the trail. She used the flashlight on her cell phone to navigate past the cypress tree, into the woods, through the briers and brush and fallen limbs. She counted an even one hundred steps. It was a good distance from the trail, but she knew she could find it later, using a metal detector if necessary.

She put her phone in the same garbage bag that contained her computer and the documents. She had wrapped them in three layers of plastic and tied the top in a secure knot. She dug deep with the small shovel that she had brought along for the trip. It took her nearly thirty minutes to bury the items, fill in the hole, and rearrange the leaves and pine needles so that it didn't look like anyone had been there. She stumbled back to the path in the dark.

When she returned to her car, she stayed there until the sun started peeking over the eastern horizon. She needed a long run this morning to clear her mind and conscience. She told herself that she could always go back and get these things whenever she wanted.

After her run, and before she left the park, she threw the shovel in a large trash bin. She understood forensics well enough to know that they could study the dirt and narrow down the location. She wasn't worried about her sneakers—they would expect to see the swampy soil of the Cape Henry Trail on them. Later today she would buy a new cell phone and computer. She had saved almost everything she needed on a single thumb drive.

Everything, that is, except for evidence that might link her to the Patriot. She prayed she was doing the right thing.

★ ★ ★

When Paige returned to her condo, they were waiting for her. Her running clothes were still sweaty, and she hadn't yet settled on answers to all the questions she might be asked. But now she was out of time.

Unfortunately, she didn't see them until she had parked. A man and a woman in a black sedan a few rows over, sipping coffee, watching her.

She tried to act normal as she walked to the elevator, knowing the agents were staring at her back. She pushed the button and the man called her name.

"Paige Chambers?"

She turned. They were walking toward her and pulling out their badges.

"Yes."

"FBI Agents Vaughn and Diaz. Mind if we ask you a few questions about the Marcano deposition?"

They made it seem as if it were natural to show up at a lawyer's condo at 8 a.m. on a Saturday. The timing concerned Paige.

Agent Vaughn looked like he was several years past retirement. He was thin, his leathery face wrinkled and worn, and he limped as he approached her, keeping his left leg relatively straight as he swung it around.

Diaz was young, petite, and pretty. Her hair was pulled back in a ponytail, and she exuded energy and confidence.

Paige shook their hands and noted the smell of smoke from Agent Vaughn. "No problem," she said, hoping they wouldn't notice how cold her hands were.

They rode with her in the elevator, making small talk, asking her about her run.

"Where do you run?" Diaz asked.

"The oceanfront."

"On the boardwalk?"

"Sometimes. Other times I just run Atlantic Avenue."

"What about today?" Vaughn asked.

"Mostly the boardwalk," she said, stepping off the elevator. It was her first lie, though she didn't consider it an official part of the interview.

She wondered if they were looking at her shoes.

They followed her into the condo, and she knew that she had now consented to their entry, meaning they could ultimately use anything in plain sight against her. Man, she hated being on this side of an investigation!

"Is it okay if I change?" Paige asked.

"Of course," Agent Diaz said quickly.

She must be the good cop.

"Make yourselves at home," Paige said.

She hustled into her bedroom and pictured the agents walking around her condo—checking out her study, the living room, the kitchen. She changed quickly into another pair of shorts and a T-shirt. She wanted to seem as casual as possible.

The agents began by explaining the reason for their visit. They had been asked by the U.S. attorney to determine who had leaked the deposition of Director Marcano. As one of the few people present at the deposition, Paige was a person of interest. But she shouldn't be worried. They knew her background and didn't think she had anything to do with it. Still, they had to ask their questions—a matter of formality, you understand.

"Technically, this is a criminal investigation," Agent Vaughn said. "So I'll have to read you your Miranda rights."

Paige said she understood, but she found it odd that they had called it a *criminal* investigation. Nevertheless, she affirmed that she was willing to speak to them without a lawyer. Diaz pulled a form out of a thin manila folder.

"We need to get it in writing," she said, flashing a quick, apologetic smile. "Paperwork."

Paige pulled a book from a nearby stand to write on as she signed the Miranda waiver. She braced the heel of her hand against the book so they wouldn't notice it was shaking. She handed the document back to Diaz.

"You don't mind if we record this, do you?" Vaughn asked. He placed a digital recorder on the small table next to Paige and flicked it on.

"No problem," Paige said.

Vaughn did an introduction for purposes of the recording, describing the time, who was present, and the purpose of the interview. Then he and Diaz took turns asking Paige questions.

The first ten minutes were friendly enough as the agents probed how Paige had handled Marcano's transcript—whom she had shared it with, how she stored it on her computer, and similar issues. They seemed particularly interested in whether she had shared it with Wyatt Jackson.

"Where is your Microsoft Outlook hosted?" Diaz asked.

Paige named the company that hosted her Outlook e-mails in the cloud.

"What security protocols do they use?" Diaz asked.

"I'm not sure. I could check."

"Did you send a copy of the transcript to anybody via e-mail?"

"I don't think so. If I did, it would only have been Wellington."

Diaz had a little black book, and she made some notations. "What kind of security firewall do you have to keep people from hacking into your computer?"

Paige shrugged. She had no idea. "My password?"

Diaz furrowed her brow. "No. I mean . . . you're handling classified information, right?"

"Not really. I didn't consider the deposition transcript to be classified. It was subject to the confidentiality order, but—"

"You don't have any classified information?" Diaz cut in.

Paige scowled. And this was the good cop? "I'm not handling classified information," Paige said.

"Well, good. Because it doesn't sound like you have any kind of security to prevent others from hacking into your computer," Diaz said.

Paige didn't appreciate the snarky attitude, but it wasn't an area where she felt comfortable fighting back. "I mean, I've got the usual antivirus and spam protections." She knew she sounded defensive, but this was a stupid line of questioning. She was sure her computer had not been hacked. "Wellington is my go-to guy for IT issues, and he thought we were pretty secure."

"Yeah, we intend to visit him later today," Vaughn said.

"But a copy of the deposition is on your computer, right?" Diaz asked.

"Yes, the court reporter sent it to me via e-mail."

"Oh, so it's on your e-mail system. And you don't know what the security protocols are for that server, either?"

"I said I'd find out for you."

A certain iciness had developed over the last several questions, and Paige was getting a little fed up with the haughty attitude of these guys. She sat up a little straighter in her chair and frowned at Diaz. The FBI agent was too busy taking notes to notice.

"You mind if we take a look at your computer to see what kind of security protocols are in place?" Diaz asked after scribbling a few notes.

Paige needed to be careful here. "I told you I would let you know."

"Does that mean no?"

"Yes. That means no."

Diaz and Vaughn exchanged a glance.

"What about your cell phone," Vaughn asked. "You mind if we look at that?"

"Yes, I mind."

"Do you have it with you?"

"No."

"Is it in your car?"

"No."

"Do you always go out running in the morning without your cell phone?"

"Not always."

Vaughn shook his head, frowning his disapproval.

"Would you mind giving me your administrative password so that I can check out the protocols for your home Wi-Fi network?" Diaz asked.

"I'll let you know that as well," Paige said.

"I take it that's another no," Vaughn said.

"That's right."

Agent Vaughn shifted in his seat. "You understand that we're not working with the CIA or anyone in the executive branch who are on the other side of this lawsuit. Anything you tell us or show us cannot be shared with anyone outside the context of this investigation."

"I understand that."

"Then why don't you want to let us see your phone or computer?"

Paige had been trying to avoid directly taking the Fifth, but now she felt boxed in. "I just don't."

"Are you asserting your Fifth Amendment rights?" Diaz asked.

"If that's what it takes, yes."

Vaughn slid forward on his seat. "The U.S. attorney is also concerned about your team's access to classified information," he said, his voice foreboding, as if invoking the specter of the U.S. attorney should provoke great fear. "So I need to ask you a few questions about that as well."

"What's that got to do with Marcano's deposition?"

"The judge asked us to look at the Marcano deposition issue. But the U.S. attorney is also curious about a few other things, and so are we. So let me get right to it: Has anybody from the government provided you with classified information?"

Technically, Paige didn't know whether the Patriot was a government employee. But she knew better than to play word games with these guys. "That exceeds the scope of the investigation authorized by Judge Solberg. I'm not going to answer questions about that."

"Are you asserting the Fifth?" Vaughn pressed.

"Yes."

"So you think answering questions about whether someone has provided you with classified information might incriminate you?" Vaughn asked.

There was no longer a pretense of this being a friendly interview. Paige was determined to shut it down.

"I'm asserting my Fifth Amendment rights."

"But I thought you said there was no classified information on your computer," Diaz said.

Paige could feel her face turning red. This was why attorneys always told their clients not to talk to investigators *at all*. "I said I'm not answering any questions about this."

Diaz flipped back a few pages in her notes. "Here it is, right here. I asked whether you had any classified information on your computer and you said, 'No.'" She looked down at the digital recorder. "Do you need me to play it back for you?"

"I think this interview is over," Paige said, standing. "I've answered your questions about the Marcano deposition. I'm not talking about anything else."

Vaughn let out a big sigh. "Paige, please. . . . Sit down. We didn't come here to give you a hard time. There's nothing in your background to suggest that you would intentionally violate the law. But you're running with some guys that have a—how shall I say this?—a more checkered history. Wyatt Jackson is not going to have your back if somebody has to take a fall."

Paige stared at him for a moment. Everything in her—all of her law enforcement background—was screaming that she should cooperate.

"Work with us, Paige. You're in over your head here, and we can help. We're talking about some serious felonies and, at the very least, a violation of Judge Solberg's protective order."

Paige took a deep breath and ignored her instincts. "I *have* worked with you," she said, her voice more resigned now, though she was still standing. "I've answered every question about Marcano's deposition as fully and honestly as I know how. These other questions are invading attorney-client and work-product privileges, and I'm just not going to answer them."

"If you received classified information from a third party, that's not covered by attorney-client privilege or the work-product doctrine," Diaz insisted.

"I'm done answering questions."

Vaughn pulled himself up by the arms of his chair and limped over to the recorder. He dictated the time that the interview was ending based on the decision of the witness to invoke her Fifth Amendment rights. He shut the recorder down and placed it in his pocket.

Diaz pulled another document out of her manila folder and handed it to Paige. "This is a search warrant for your condo and vehicle," Diaz said. "You can see the things we're after."

Paige pretended to study the document, though she couldn't focus on the words. She wanted to call Wyatt or another defense attorney but knew there was nothing anyone could do to stop the search.

"Have at it," she said.

65

The agents left after ransacking Paige's condo and car. She sat on her couch for several minutes, thinking. She had lied to the FBI. In the pressure of the moment, and with circumstances pinning her down, her self-preservation instincts had taken over. She had spent her entire professional life prosecuting people who committed crimes and lied to cover them up. Now she *was* that person.

Beating herself up wasn't going to solve the problem. She prayed for forgiveness, a heartfelt prayer borne of desperation and guilt, then hopped in her car and drove straight to Wellington's apartment. Nobody answered the door. She got back in the car and headed to the KOA campground, where she parked out of sight because she saw the agents' black sedan sandwiched between Wellington's Fiat and Wyatt's truck in front of the RV.

Forty-five minutes crawled by as she watched the RV, waiting for Vaughn and Diaz to leave. Eventually they emerged, carrying a computer and cardboard box to the car. She watched them pull away, waited another five minutes, and then went inside.

Clients was happy to see her, jumping on her legs, trying to lick her, and wagging his tail like crazy. After Wyatt settled the dog down, the three lawyers traded notes.

Wellington had told the agents that he wasn't willing to talk to them without his attorney, Wyatt Jackson, present. The agents had taken his cell phone and computer pursuant to their search warrant and followed Wellington to Wyatt's RV. They had interrogated both lawyers there, but Wyatt had shut down any questions that didn't pertain to Marcano's deposition.

"Did you tell them why you weren't answering those questions?" Paige asked.

Wyatt gave her a smug look. "I told them it was none of their business. We were taking the Fifth on anything that didn't have to do with Marcano's transcript."

"What did they say?"

"They just frowned and stared a lot. It got to the point where they would ask a question and I would say, 'Fifth,' and then they would move on to the next question. They're not the sharpest tools in the shed, but after a while they got the gist of it."

And you looked 100 percent guilty, Paige wanted to say. But there was no sense arguing about it. They were all on the same team, and this was serious.

"I saw them with a computer and a box full of stuff," Paige said. "I thought you were destroying your computers."

"They didn't get mine," Wyatt said. "I pounded it to shreds last night with a rock and then melted it in a fire."

"Did you tell them that?"

He scoffed. "Of course not. I didn't tell them anything."

Paige turned to Wellington. "But they got yours?"

"Yeah, but I deleted anything having to do with the Patriot and erased any trace of him from my hard drive."

Paige didn't like the sound of that. Wellington was good, but this was the FBI, and they had unlimited resources. Her stomach was already in knots, and this conversation wasn't making it any better.

"They got our cell phones, too," Wyatt said. "But there's nothing on there about the Patriot."

"You don't think they can trace the number that he called from?" Paige asked.

"I certainly couldn't," Wellington said.

"Even if they do, they'll only get the name of the man giving us the inside information," Wyatt said. "They won't know what he told us."

They speculated for the hundredth time about who the Patriot might be. Wyatt favored someone from the military establishment, like Defense Secretary Simpson, who didn't like the extent of the CIA's growing power to wage war. Wellington thought it was someone involved with the legal team or in the attorney general's office. Paige didn't know what to think—she bounced between a dozen different possibilities.

The three attorneys discussed their predicament for a long time. There was a general consensus that the failure by Paige and Wyatt to produce their computers would lead to all kinds of suspicions and probably result in the FBI concluding that they had released the Marcano transcript. The U.S. attorney would issue a stinging report to Judge Solberg, who might well find them in contempt. But Wyatt was of the firm opinion that a finding of contempt was far better than the criminal charges they might face if the FBI found out about the Patriot.

And Paige knew he was right. One of the last things she had done before burying her computer was to look at the code section dealing with the disclosure of classified information. There wasn't a lot of wiggle room.

Whoever knowingly and willfully . . . makes available to an unauthorized person, or publishes, or uses . . . any classified information . . . concerning the communication intelligence activities of the United States . . . shall be fined . . . or imprisoned not more than ten years, or both.

She had received classified information, no doubt about that. And the three of them had all used it and published it as part of their lawsuit. But the Patriot was the one most at risk. He was the one who had provided the information in the first place.

And that wasn't the only statute that was causing Paige to spin dark scenarios of humiliation and imprisonment. There was also 18 U.S. Code Section 1519, which prohibited anyone from knowingly destroying, concealing, covering up, or falsifying any record, document, or tangible object with the intent to obstruct or influence a criminal investigation. And that statute had a maximum term of twenty years.

Paige drove away from the RV with her thoughts about Kristen's case entirely eclipsed by worries about her own personal freedom and reputation. Her mind played out the drama of being arrested, the headlines that would follow, and the agony of a public trial. She envisioned herself sitting in the witness box with prosecutors asking questions that had no good answers: *Why did you lie to the FBI? Why did you bury your computer? Didn't it dawn on you while you were studying to obtain security clearance that you could not use classified information in order to obtain an edge in litigation?*

Paige longed for the days when she had been working as an assistant attorney general. She'd been one of the good guys. Now she was teamed up with Wyatt Jackson, a renegade attorney who liked to fly so close to the sun that he was sure to get burned.

Only this time, he wouldn't be the only one feeling the flames. Paige and Wellington would be consumed right along with him.

★ ★ ★

Five days later, Agents Vaughn and Diaz returned with a grand jury subpoena that required Paige to produce her old cell phone and computer within one week or show cause why she could not.

She thanked them for the subpoena and generally kept her composure until they left. Her hand trembled as she read through the document and realized the legal import of what she was holding in her hand.

This investigation was now well beyond Judge Solberg's rule to show cause. A federal grand jury had been impaneled; a full-blown criminal investigation was under way. From the gist of the agents' questions and these subpoenas, the grand jury would be investigating both the unauthorized use of classified information and obstruction of justice charges.

She called Wyatt, who had received the same kind of subpoena. He'd told the FBI agents that he had destroyed his computer because it contained attorney-client confidences that he was not about to turn over to them. "I can't produce what I don't have," he said.

When she got off the phone, Paige knew she was in way over her head. She needed a criminal lawyer to give her some objective advice. She had been resisting hiring someone because she didn't have the funds, and she was too embarrassed about the circumstances to ask for a favor.

But none of that mattered now. She would promise payment as soon as things turned around. She could no longer navigate this alone. She and Wellington could hardly concentrate on their Supreme Court brief while they incessantly worried about what the FBI might do next.

During her time in the attorney general's office, Paige had seen a lot of local defense attorneys in action. There was no question whom she wanted on her side.

She called Landon Reed that afternoon. As a college quarterback, Landon had been caught in a point-shaving scandal and had served two years in prison. Following his release, he went to law school, passed the bar, and after an arduous review process was deemed of sufficient trustworthiness to practice law. Paige had seen his work firsthand and knew he was always prepared. More importantly, at least from Paige's perspective, Landon really seemed to care about his clients. Other lawyers might look down on their clients, but Landon never forgot that he had once been in their shoes.

Landon was in court, and Paige only talked to his assistant, setting up an appointment for first thing Monday morning. But when she hung up the phone, she felt like she could take a deep breath for the first time since the FBI agents had shown up at her door more than a week earlier.

66

Paige woke early Monday after another fitful night of sleep, put on a black dress with red trim that she normally reserved for court, and arrived a few minutes early at the address for Landon Reed and Associates, less than a mile and a half from the beach. It was a tasteful, three-story office building with impressive pillars framing the front door. She pulled into the parking lot with her mind churning through the challenges of the *Anderson* case. What had started as a crusade now felt like a cancer.

She met with Landon in the firm's large conference room, which featured a huge marble table, paintings of beach scenes on the walls, and handcrafted bookshelves populated with old volumes collecting dust. Landon looked the part of a former quarterback—handsome and tall, white shirt neatly pressed, and a red tie snug around his neck. He had probably put on a few pounds since his playing days, but he still moved with athletic grace and confidence.

He offered Paige something to drink, and they sat down at one end of the conference table, each nursing a small bottle of water. At first Paige was nervous and somewhat embarrassed, but Landon had a calming demeanor that soon put her at ease. She told him everything, and when she had finished, she felt a flood of relief from just having shared her story with someone as empathetic as Landon. There were no easy ways out, but talking through it out loud somehow made her feel better.

"Talk about no good deed goes unpunished," Landon said, shaking his head. "I know you probably can't sleep at night, but you need to know that people like me look at this and think you're heroic, not some kind of criminal."

At some level, Paige knew Landon was just trying to reassure her, but at another, his words were like balm. Landon had faced his own high-profile trial and at a young age had developed quite a reputation with the local bar. To have someone like him on her side, not just because he was getting paid but because he believed in her, made Paige sit up a little straighter.

"Unfortunately, these classified information laws are not very forgiving," Landon continued. "And hindsight is always twenty-twenty. I'm sure that if you had it to do all over again, you would have reported this confidential source early in the process."

Paige wasn't so sure about that, but she didn't want to pick a fight with her new lawyer. "I guess so," she said. "But at the time, this person just felt like a good inside source. I really didn't think of it as a classified information problem."

"Most of it probably wasn't," Landon said. He pulled a thick document out of a file folder. "After you called, I read Marcano's deposition. Ninety percent of what your source told you was ruled not to be a state secret by Judge Solberg. There are a few exceptions, like the unredacted CIA report or the imam being killed by a drone strike. But to be honest, I'm a lot more concerned about potential obstruction of justice charges than I am about mishandling classified information."

They segued into a discussion of the obstruction charge, and Landon studied the subpoena for Paige's computer. Knowing that the ethical rules were fuzzy about lawyers helping their clients conceal evidence, Paige had only told Landon that she could access the computer if she needed it. She didn't tell him the location.

"Is your law practice a professional corporation?" Landon asked.

"Yes, I incorporated just a few months ago."

Landon made a face. "I wish they had addressed the subpoena to you individually," he said. "Individuals have a Fifth Amendment right not to produce documents or electronic devices that might incriminate them. But corporations don't have Fifth Amendment rights. The FBI knows this, so they've addressed this subpoena to you as the officer and director of the Chambers Law Firm, meaning that if you have access to the computer and don't produce it, you can be held in contempt."

Paige felt her spirits sinking again. She couldn't give them the computer.

Landon stood and walked over to a window, his hands in his pockets as he gazed out at the trees behind his office building.

"You're making me nervous," Paige said.

"Sorry about that. But I wanted to think this through because you might not like what I'm about to say."

He sat back down, looked Paige straight in the eye, and told her that they needed to come clean with the U.S. attorney's office. Mitchell Taylor, the U.S. attorney for the Eastern District of Virginia, was a straight shooter and a good lawyer.

"Let me talk to him," Landon said. "You'll need to be ready to produce your computer."

He apparently saw Paige flinch because he held up his hand. "I know you don't want to burn your source, but my job is to protect *you*. You didn't dig this person up and convince him or her to divulge this information. Your source came to *you*. And you shouldn't feel duty-bound to go to jail to protect him."

"It's not just the Patriot," Paige said. "If we go to the U.S. attorney and agree to cooperate, they'll ask me about Wyatt and Wellington, right? And I'll have to tell them that Wyatt destroyed his computer and advised me to destroy mine knowing that the FBI would want to see if we've received classified information."

"Not necessarily," Landon said. "If we give them your computer, I might be able to convince Mitchell that your conversations with cocounsel are protected by the counsel work-product doctrine. It's worth a try."

Paige asked for a few days to think it over. She couldn't agree to any scenario that would incriminate Wyatt and Wellington.

"Sure," Landon said. "But the return date for the subpoena is Friday."

Paige left the office feeling the same tight vise squeezing her that she'd had when she first arrived. Landon was the right lawyer to help her; she had no doubt about that. But even he couldn't make the subpoena disappear. The only way out was straight ahead, and the road was littered with land mines.

67

Paige rolled out of bed at 6 a.m. on Tuesday. She had already been staring at the ceiling for nearly an hour. She pulled her hair back in a ponytail, brushed her teeth, and put on her running clothes—black shorts, a tank top, and an old black sweatshirt with a hood. A brisk September wind would keep the temperature down until sunrise.

She fixed a cup of coffee for the road and then did her best Jason Bourne imitation, driving around the back roads of Virginia Beach for thirty minutes, checking her rearview mirror, making sure she wasn't being followed.

Eventually she wound her way to First Landing State Park, grabbed her backpack and a new small shovel she had stashed in her trunk, and started jogging down the Cape Henry Trail. She tracked the mileage with her GPS until she came to the large cypress tree near the spot where she had buried her computer and phone. She took twenty steps into the woods, then stopped and listened. She took another twenty and stopped, waiting and listening again. The sun was just starting to peek over the eastern horizon, filtering its way through the mossy branches of the cypress trees. Paige took another twenty steps and listened a third time. Nothing but the sound of crickets and the wind rustling through the trees. Forty steps this time and a final pause to listen. Finally she convinced herself that nobody was around. One hundred paces into the woods, she began to dig.

The area looked the same as it had nine days earlier, but she had done such a good job that it was impossible to tell exactly where she had buried the stuff. She made her best guess and started with a hole about four feet by four feet, hitting nothing but roots. She moved to her right a few steps and started digging again. Then back to her left, where another hole came up empty. She methodically dug up a grid, forward a few paces, back a few paces, to the right, to the left. The sun warmed things up, and Paige took off the sweatshirt and kept digging, panic notching up with every shovelful of dirt. Occasionally she would hear somebody on the trail, and though they were out of sight, she stopped digging until they were past.

After an hour of this, Paige left the shovel and her sweatshirt and walked back to the trail. She paced again from the same cypress tree, retracing her steps, making sure she was digging in the right place. She ended up at the exact same spot where she had started and for the first time began accepting reality. Somebody had found her computer and cell phone!

She spent another hour digging until her grid was large enough that there was no way she could have missed it.

Her first thought was that it had to be Daniel Reese. He knew this was her running trail. Maybe he had followed her out to the path that Saturday morning.

But there was another possibility. The FBI had shown up the same morning that Paige had buried her stuff. What if they had followed her earlier that morning and then headed back to the condo and waited? What if Diaz and Vaughn had known all along that she had buried her computer? Everything else would have just been springing the trap.

Or maybe her phone was tapped. Maybe they had heard Wyatt tell her to destroy her computer and ditch her cell phone and then followed her on Saturday morning. Maybe her computer was sitting in the FBI offices even now.

Perhaps she had just watched too many movies, but Paige felt like she was living in a house of mirrors and trapdoors and optical illusions. It was ridiculous to think that she and Wyatt Jackson could litigate against the CIA and take down some of the most powerful people on the planet. Now they were paying the price.

Later that morning she stopped by Landon's office and told him the computer was gone. His advice was still the same. Let him call the U.S. attorney and explain. Like Paige, he thought it was entirely possible that the FBI already had the computer. The whole thing would be a much tougher sell now, but it was still possible they could work out some kind of deal.

It was the first time that Landon had used that word, and it frightened Paige. "What sort of deal are you talking about?"

"Nothing involving a guilty plea. Just an agreement to cooperate fully, and they would take that into account in deciding whether or not to press charges."

"You mean I would testify against Wyatt and Wellington?"

"You would have to tell the truth on everything. Without the computer, it's all we've got."

Paige didn't have to think about that one. Landon wasn't saying it explicitly, but he was suggesting that she trade her freedom for theirs. She shook her head. "I'm not turning against them," she said emphatically. "There's got to be a different way."

★ ★ ★

AL MAHRAH GOVERNORATE, YEMEN

The small brick hut in the mountainous eastern region of Yemen had no air-conditioning, and the place was stifling. Saleet Zafar was meeting with tribal leaders, dispensing advice late at night, when he heard the buzzing sound that froze his blood. The others heard it as well. The talking stopped, and the men scampered from the house, climbing into trucks and running in every direction.

If the tribal leaders had learned one thing during the constant drone wars in Yemen, they had learned that drones couldn't hit moving targets. The lag time from the relay of satellite images back to the pilot eroded the accuracy of the missiles. But there was no time to spare.

In the chaos, Saleet made sure his two boys got in a different vehicle, one headed the opposite direction from the truck he boarded. A minute later, he leaned out the window and watched as the drone circled overhead and fired, creating a crater in the road less than a hundred meters in front of the speeding truck. He could feel the heat on his face.

The missile had destroyed the road, and the driver jammed on the brakes and began turning around. Saleet opened his door, rolled out on the hard ground, gathered himself, and started sprinting toward the mountains. He glanced over his shoulder, just in time to see the truck in which he had been riding get obliterated, consumed in a tower of flames. Another missile destroyed the brick hut. Saleet turned and kept running.

A few seconds later, the drone whirled away, locked on another truck, and disappeared in the distance.

Later that night, Saleet circled back and found that his two sons had survived. With tears of gratitude, he kissed them both on the forehead and told them how proud he was of the young men they had become.

The three of them spent the night at the home of a different tribal leader. Saleet and the men stayed up all night—deliberating, watching, talking of revenge. After breakfast, with a vehicle waiting, Saleet asked for a few moments alone with his sons. He told them to take care of their mother. He had business to do and would not be able to see them, perhaps for a long time. He would pray to Allah for their safety, strength, and courage.

"You must not be afraid," he said as he watched their lips quiver.

They held their heads high, trying to make their father proud. "Allah will give you strength."

He left them and rode away without looking back. He blinked away tears, feeling like someone had separated his heart from his body. Allah demanded great sacrifices. Saleet prayed that he would be equal to the task.

68

The report filed by U.S. Attorney Mitchell Taylor was factual, decisive, and crisp. Based on the FBI interviews, he concluded that the deposition had most likely been leaked by one of the plaintiff's lawyers. They certainly had motive. Moreover, while each of the lawyers denied ever speaking to Harry Coburn, Wyatt Jackson had destroyed his computer, Wellington Farnsworth had bleached certain files, and Paige Chambers had refused to produce her computer, though it was subject to subpoena. All other persons interviewed by the FBI had voluntarily allowed access to their computers and personal devices.

The report and any appropriate sanctions would be considered by Judge Solberg at a hearing she had scheduled for a few days later. And all of this was separate from the grand jury that was now investigating other charges against Paige and her colleagues.

Paige had steeled herself for the report, and Taylor's conclusions did not surprise her. If anything, she was relieved that he didn't go into greater detail about the obstruction of justice charges he was now investigating or the grand jury he had convened. Judge Solberg had asked for a report solely about the leaking of the deposition of John Marcano, and that's what Taylor had given her.

But it didn't take long for the press to jump on the story and blast Paige and her colleagues. The same reporters who had been pounding John Marcano since the release of the deposition now turned their guns against Wyatt, Paige, and Wellington. As one might expect, Wyatt took the brunt of the criticism because he was lead counsel and had a history of shady tactics. In almost every article, his old transgressions were summarized so that this new piece of red meat could be properly digested. The ineffective assistance of counsel petitions were trotted out again, including the one that described Wyatt napping during trial. There was even a quote from an old prosecutor who suspected that Wyatt had leaked information to the press in a different case.

Paige couldn't stop herself from reading the articles one by one and watching videos from the TV reporters. They were devastating hits, and Paige dreaded the upcoming hearing in front of Solberg, but she knew her team would survive. She thought about how the old Paige would have reacted just a few months ago. She probably would have curled up in the fetal position and refused to get out of bed. But hanging out with Wyatt and going through the battles in this case had already thickened her skin. Sure, she was still going to obsess over every article that hammered away at her reputation, and she hated every minute of it, but in her better moments she knew this attack would pass and that somehow they would manage to strike back.

Wyatt was right about one thing—there was a certain nobility in the mind-set of the Alamo. If you're going to lose, you might as well at least go down fighting. It's what Patrick and Troy and their teammates had done. And it's what Paige owed them on the most important case she had ever handled.

★ ★ ★

Chick's Oyster Bar was one of the most popular hangouts on the Chesapeake Bay side of Virginia Beach. It was located at the intersection of the Lynnhaven River and the bay, overlooking the water so that people could pull up to the dock and have the waiters serve them on their boats. It had a rustic feel, with picnic tables on the back deck, an old bar with local beers, and a small T-shirt shop to take advantage of tourists who thought they had stumbled onto a local watering hole. It was also the place where Navy SEALs hung out to meet local girls, so it featured more than its share of great-looking women.

"I can't tell you how many times Troy and I ate here," Kristen said as she and Paige settled at one of the picnic tables on the screened-in back deck. Paige had called her earlier that day, after Taylor's report came out. The two women decided to meet for dinner, and Kristen got a sitter. They had both been ignoring calls from the press.

It was a cool autumn night, and Paige wore a sweatshirt, though the women at the bar were still in spaghetti-strap tops and short skirts. Lit up on the other side of the river was a mansion that belonged to Pharrell Williams, the famous R & B artist. Paige ignored the televisions hanging in every corner of the bar and restaurant.

As so often happened when they got together, Paige found her own spirits lifted by Kristen's sarcastic yet optimistic view of the world. Kristen had now decided that if she and her lawyers were SEAL Team Nine and the defendants were the Houthis, then the media must certainly be ISIS.

The two covered a broad range of subjects that night. The boys were starting to do better. The other SEAL families were still very supportive. And they couldn't forget that the case was still alive—almost miraculously so.

Kristen asked about preparations for the Supreme Court argument, and Paige felt the need to be honest. Wyatt wasn't very focused, and this FBI investigation hadn't helped. But Paige promised Kristen that Wyatt would be ready by the time the hearing rolled around. It was the way he operated—always waiting until the last minute to prepare for anything.

It wasn't until nearly thirty minutes later, after Kristen had had a few drinks and the waitress had brought the bill, that Kristen circled back around to the issue.

"Paige, I've been giving this Supreme Court argument a lot of thought today. And what you said earlier confirmed some things for me."

"What I said about what?"

"Wyatt not being focused."

"No, I said he would be fine—"

"Just hear me out for a second," Kristen said. "All of this press coverage, and these allegations against Wyatt . . ." She hesitated, pulled her napkin from her lap, and placed it on the table. She pushed her plate aside. "I don't think I want him arguing at the Supreme Court. He wouldn't just be representing our family; he's representing all the SEALs, in a way. I know he's good at what he does—and he's a fighter, something that Troy appreciated."

Paige could tell where this was headed, and she didn't like it. For all his weaknesses, she had grown to admire Wyatt. She never had to worry about whether he would wilt under pressure or shrink back. Nobody else could take on the justices of the Supreme Court like him.

"I just think you'd be better arguing the legal aspects of this case," Kristen said. "Especially after today. Is that even possible?"

Paige nearly choked on her drink. She had sensed that Kristen wanted to replace Wyatt. But she thought it would be with someone who specialized in Supreme Court arguments. "Replace him with *me*?" she asked. "Wyatt has a lot more experience than I do, and his credibility at the Court will be far greater. I mean, I just got admitted a few weeks ago. I've never even *been* to the Supreme Court, much less argued there."

"I've seen you in court," Kristen said. "I read what you did at Marcano's deposition. And from what you've told me, the arguments at the Court don't really matter all that much. It's the written briefs that count, and you and Wellington are doing a great job on those. I just think I'd rather have the spotlight on you than him."

They discussed it for another ten minutes, nursing glasses of water as Paige did her best to talk Kristen out of this. It wasn't just a fear of making her first argument on such short notice, or a reluctance to disappoint Wyatt, but Paige legitimately believed Wyatt was the better choice. Sure, he was way too casual about his preparation—but she and Wellington would get that fixed.

Unfortunately, the client had other ideas, and she was stubborn. They didn't resolve the matter at Chick's, but Kristen did ask a critical question just before they got up to leave.

"As the client, do I get to make this decision? Or is this something the lawyers work out?"

"It's your call, Kristen. But I think Wyatt is the right guy."

Kristen agreed to think about it, and Paige thought she had bought some time. But after Paige drove her home that night, sitting in the car in Kristen's driveway, Kristen brought it up again. "Paige, I know you don't agree with me, but I think it's the right thing to do," she blurted out. "I want you to argue this case. We don't have much time, and I'm not going to change my mind."

Paige stared out the front windshield and frowned. This was the last thing she needed on top of everything else.

Kristen reached over and touched her shoulder. "You're the best shot we have. I need you to do this for me and the kids and for Troy and Patrick."

"I'll talk to Wyatt about it," Paige said.

The women hugged, Kristen thanked her, and Paige stayed in the driveway until Kristen had disappeared inside her house. Paige drove away thinking about the conversation she would need to have with Wyatt. She felt like somehow she was betraying him. Maybe she had been too critical when Kristen first brought the subject up.

Paige had dreamed of arguing before the U.S. Supreme Court, but not like this. This entire case felt snakebit. She bit her lower lip, fighting back tears.

It was nearly ten o'clock, and she knew she wouldn't be able to sleep if she headed home. And so, instead of stopping at her condo on Laskin Road, she drove by and headed to the ocean. There were some things she had to get straight, and they couldn't wait any longer.

69

Paige parked a few blocks from the beach, crossed the concrete boardwalk, and took off her sandals so she could feel the cool sand on her feet. There was a strong breeze blowing in from the water, creating small whitecaps on the waves. She pushed her hair out of her face and filled her lungs with the smell and taste of salty beach air, a purifying blend that seemed to clear her mind and reduce the pressure squeezing her from every side.

She rolled up her jeans and walked down to the wet sand next to the rolling waves, sandals in one hand. She walked along the beach, letting her mind wander. The reflected light from the nearly full moon danced on the water and, together with the distant light from the high-rise hotels on the boardwalk, lit her way. There were a few tourists hanging out, some kids with glow-in-the-dark bracelets and light sabers, a couple holding hands, even some teenagers swimming unsupervised. Paige felt like she could pick out the locals—like the guy with a dog off-leash, in and out of the waves, chasing a tennis ball. But for the most part, the beach was deserted, Paige's private ocean sanctuary. So she walked, thinking about the challenges ahead and feeling Patrick's loss on a deeper level than she had in a very long time.

Somebody had told her that grief was a companion on a journey, not just a moment in time, and tonight it walked heavy beside her, reminding her of everything she had lost. She longed to have him here with his arm around her shoulder, pulling her tight, telling her that everything would be okay. She would find strength from his confidence and security in his love. She would know that whatever was about to happen—whatever people said about her or believed about her—*he* would know the truth and *he* would love the person she really was. He would remind her of that, and she would know that nothing could tear them apart.

But tonight, all of that was replaced by the sudden grief that had made a roaring comeback, cutting through all the pressures and dangers in her life and reminding her that no matter what happened, it could never be worse than what she had already endured. The suffocating loneliness. The shattering of dreams.

It was in this moment, walking close enough to the water that an occasional wave would wash up and lap over her feet, that she thought about Patrick's faith. It was stronger than hers, and she knew he would have taught her by example. This God who had grown distant to Paige had permeated nearly every aspect of Patrick's life, every strand of his thinking. He had talked about praying on the battlefield and how God had sustained him in SEAL training when he felt like quitting. Patrick's strength had been drawn from a well of prayer and Bible verses and a healthy dose of God's Spirit.

Paige stopped and turned to face the sea in front of her, staring out at its vastness, letting the rhythmic churning of its waves remind her of God's cathartic power. Patrick had told her that he came here often, maybe not to this exact spot, but to this same shore, and had developed his own unique prayer ritual to remind him that God's power was greater than anything he faced. It was time, Paige knew, for her to do the same.

She turned and took a few steps away from the water, kneeling in the wet sand. At first, she looked around to see if anyone might be watching and then decided that she didn't really care. With her finger, she wrote the words in the sand. She wrote them large, starting with the things that had driven her out there that night. *Contempt. Obstruction. Telling Wyatt. The Supreme Court.*

The words were out of reach of the waves, the same way Patrick had described writing them when he first told her about this ritual. She took a few steps and, a bit farther from the waves, wrote again. *Fear. Reputation.* These were the things eating at her soul. A desire to have men and women speak well of her. Endlessly climbing to achieve and to prove herself worthy.

The last thing she wrote, and the word she placed farthest from the water, was Patrick's name. She wrote it deep in the sand, with large block letters, because the scars from his death were deep, and in part of her soul she knew that she blamed God.

When she had finished, she took a few steps away from the water and sat in the dry sand, wrapping her arms around her knees, watching the waves wash in. Patrick had done this too. The waves reminded him of God's power and sovereignty washing over everything he faced. He would inscribe in the sand those things that struck fear into his own heart or represented his darker nature. Then he would sit on the beach and pray as the waves did their inevitable work, smoothing over the crevices that formed every word, replacing the challenges and heartaches with ten thousand new grains of sand.

And now Paige watched it happen herself—while she prayed, the words began to fade and disappear. The tide was coming in, and she began to spot the larger waves as they made their way to shore, crashing through the ones rolling out, increasing the reach of the tide, swooping up the small incline of wet sand, covering the things Paige feared.

It didn't take long for the water to erase the first set of words, and

Paige found that what they represented began to feel less dreadful. Her apprehension about telling Wyatt that Kristen wanted her to replace him, the upcoming hearing in front of Judge Solberg, her fear of being charged with obstruction, her angst about arguing at the Supreme Court. None of that seemed quite as daunting as before.

After several more minutes of praying—more confession than anything else—the words *fear* and *reputation* began to erode as well. It took a while for a wave that was large enough to reach that level of the sand, but Paige was patient, and she found the prayer time surprisingly intense and empowering. The same Spirit that Patrick had talked about invading his life became a part of hers as well.

It was, she knew, the Spirit of Christ, the same Spirit that had sustained him before his own hour of challenges and sacrifice. She had prayed to Christ when she was younger, but never quite like this. This was new and different and more personal, reflecting an intimacy and reverence she had learned from a few short months with the man whose name was still etched in the sand just a few feet away from where she sat.

Eventually all the words were gone except for Patrick's name. She had carved it at the very edge of the wet sand, and even the strongest waves had not come near it. She had done so intentionally because she knew that this would be the hardest wound of all. Even if everything else could somehow be washed away, this one gaping hole would remain.

She lost track of time that night, praying and mourning but somehow in the process also gaining strength. After two hours she stood and walked a few steps to Patrick's name. She knelt, kissed her fingers, and touched the sand. Then she stood, took a long, final look out over the ocean, and headed back to her car.

She knew nothing had changed in the physical world that night, but her steps felt lighter and more certain than they had before. The pain still stabbed at her heart, yet the fear wasn't there anymore, squeezing her and scrambling her thoughts. Things would not be any easier in the days ahead and there were still a lot of mountains to climb. But as she trudged back through the dry sand, the cool grains sifting through her toes and the wind blowing her hair across her face, she somehow knew that she would be equal to the task.

Or at least that's how she felt right now. She would sleep tonight. Tomorrow could take care of itself.

★   ★   ★

Two hours after she left, in the quiet night air of a deserted beach, a wave crashed ashore at the height of high tide and washed farther up the bank than any wave before it. It crested far above the place where Paige had written Patrick's name, making its way almost to the impression left in the dry sand where she had been sitting. And when it washed back out, the sand where Patrick's name had once been recorded was as smooth and flat as every other area around it.

70

Early the next morning, Paige headed to the KOA campground on General Booth Boulevard. She wasn't looking forward to her talk with Wyatt, but there was no sense putting it off. No matter how much she practiced the lines, she couldn't really think of a diplomatic way to phrase it. The client had decided that Paige should argue the case before the Supreme Court. They would both have to honor that request. It was as simple as that.

The rain pelted her car on the way, forcing her to keep her wipers on full speed. When she arrived at the campground, the place was a muddy mess. She parked as close as possible to Wyatt's RV, pulled up the hood on her raincoat, and walked quickly to the door. Wyatt let her in, and Clients came bounding over to get some love. She rubbed Clients and took off her shoes. The place smelled like cigar smoke and wet dog.

"Want some coffee?" Wyatt asked.

"No, I'm fine."

"Nice of you to drop by," Wyatt said. He was wearing jeans and a long-sleeved untucked button-down shirt rolled up at the sleeves. It didn't look like he'd bothered combing his hair.

Paige took off her raincoat and hung it over a chair. As much as she had grown to appreciate Wyatt, it was still awkward trying to engage him in small talk. She decided to just get to the point before she lost her nerve. "I wanted to talk to you about the Supreme Court argument."

Wyatt leaned back and crossed his arms. "What about it?"

Paige explained it as best she could. Kristen had requested that Paige argue the case. She had tried to talk Kristen out of it but to no avail. Kristen was worried that Wyatt's credibility had been hurt by all of the recent publicity. Paige had not asked to be lead counsel or even planted the seed. Kristen was adamant about it, but to be honest, Paige was scared to death.

She was nervous, and she knew Wyatt could hear it in her voice. He stared impassively at her as she spoke, making it impossible to read his thoughts. When she was done, he simply shrugged his shoulders, got up from his seat, and went over to a box of notebooks sitting near the small table in the RV. He pulled them out and placed them on the table one at a time.

"These are all the cases you'll need to review," he said, his back toward her. "This first notebook deals with state secrets. The second covers the Feres Doctrine, which will probably not come up, but just in case. This one here has a copy of the transcript from our hearing in front of Judge Solberg, the Fourth Circuit's opinion, and a copy of our briefs."

Paige got up and looked at them, opening them to see that Wyatt had been reading the cases and highlighting key passages. He had scribbled notes in the margins. The man had been working a lot harder than Paige thought.

"Are you okay with this?" she asked.

"You mean getting fired by the client?"

"She's not firing anyone, Wyatt. She's just switching which one of us argues the case."

"It's her call," Wyatt said. "And it will make my life a lot easier."

Paige didn't know what kind of reaction she'd been hoping for, but this wasn't it. Their alliance had started off on rocky terms, but she had developed a grudging respect for the man. Now he probably thought Paige had undercut him with the client. "Looks like you've done a lot of work already," she said.

Wyatt placed the notebooks back in the box and put the lid on it. "Gazala Holloman called," he said, changing the subject. "Said that she had been in touch with Saleet Zafar through an intermediary. He's agreed to meet with me if I fly into Dubai and follow his instructions."

This was all news to Paige. "Dubai?"

"It's in the UAE. I can fly there with just a passport. There will be someone to smuggle me across the border. Not only that, but Zafar is going to take me to meet the owner of the home where that lamb was sacrificed by Admiral Towers. I've been trying to figure out how I could do this trip and argue at the Supreme Court at the same time. I guess Kristen just simplified things for me."

It seemed to Paige that he said it with a hint of resentment, but what did she expect? "Are you going alone?"

"That's one of the terms," Wyatt said.

Then he changed the subject again. He had received a subpoena to appear before a grand jury on September 25, less than a week before the scheduled Supreme Court argument. Paige hadn't received one yet, but Wyatt assured her that one was coming. The feds were looking at obstruction charges against all of the plaintiff's lawyers. Wyatt, of course, saw it as a grand conspiracy. They would all get indicted, and their Supreme Court hearing would be toast.

Paige wasn't surprised by the news of the grand jury, but Wyatt's prediction of an indictment put a lump in her throat. "I've got an attorney," Paige said. "Landon Reed."

"I know. He's good."

"How did you know about him?"

"Can't say," Wyatt replied. "In fact, we shouldn't discuss the grand jury at all. Anything we say is not protected, and I don't want someone accusing me of coaching witnesses."

Paige sat back down and Clients came over for some more attention. He put a paw on her leg and she took the hint, rubbing his head and scratching his back. "You really think we'll get indicted?" Paige asked Wyatt.

"Hard to tell," he said casually, as if he were discussing whether the rain would soon blow over. "But you can't rule it out."

It was his opinion, he told Paige, that they needed a plan B for the Supreme Court argument, just in case. And he just happened to have one. Starting in two days, on Saturday, Paige should begin practicing her argument every morning in front of a panel consisting of Wyatt, Wellington, and Landon Reed. "I'll hire Landon as a consultant on the case. That way, if they indict us, he can argue the case at the Supreme Court."

Paige didn't respond. She was having a hard time getting past the thought of a federal indictment.

"Every afternoon I'll review the tapes of the practice arguments with you," Wyatt continued, as if the sword of an indictment hanging over their heads was just a small annoyance. "We'll go over the questions and critique your answers. In the evenings, you can study some more and get ready for the next day."

Paige had her own style of preparing for oral arguments, and this wasn't it. But she had just delivered some hard news to her cocounsel and didn't want to reject his proposal out of hand. She agreed to give it a try, at least for a few days. She was thankful he was still engaged, and she could learn a lot from the guy.

Before she left, he hit her with one last question. "You're not producing your computer pursuant to that grand jury subpoena, are you?" he asked.

"I thought we weren't supposed to talk about it."

"There are exceptions. I need to know that you're not producing your computer. And I need to know for sure that you're not the one who leaked the Marcano deposition."

Paige bristled at the suggestion. "Of course I didn't leak it."

"What about your computer?"

She didn't know how much to tell him, especially without checking first with Landon. "They're not going to be getting it."

He looked at her suspiciously, narrowing his eyes. "Whatever you do, don't give it to them before the rule to show cause hearing tomorrow," he said. "And don't cut any deals with them either. I think I've got some ideas."

Just what I needed, Paige thought. *Wyatt putting on a big show at the hearing tomorrow.* But what did it matter? She couldn't produce her computer even if she wanted to. "Don't worry about me," Paige said. "They're not getting my computer."

"Good."

The spark in Wyatt's eye worried Paige. Tomorrow was going to be a long day.

71

Paige just wanted to stay curled up in her bed all day. She hit the snooze button three times. She stayed in that half-conscious state between sleep and wakefulness, her thoughts a tangled web of defiance, resignation, and dread. Images flashed through her groggy mind. A pack of reporters asking questions. An angry Judge Solberg. Marshals escorting her off to prison. She prayed and summoned her resolve for the day ahead.

By the time she got ready for the day, she was running behind and had to skip breakfast and fight aggressively through the interstate traffic, tailgating every slow driver who blocked her way as if by force of will she could make them speed up. She hit the parking lot at 8:45, and court started at nine. She knew there would be a crazy-long line at the metal detectors and that she would need to elbow her way to the front, explaining that she was one of the lawyers involved in the *Anderson* case, as if that gave her a free pass. She would ignore the harsh, condemning stares of the people behind her.

Walking quickly, her heels clicking against the pavement, she turned the corner on Granby Street and found that the chaos outside the court building was even greater than she'd anticipated. The media had turned out in full force again, and soon they would come rushing her way, a herd of cameras and microphones and glammed-up reporters shouting questions. She had known this day was coming for two weeks, but she still wasn't ready for it. This morning she had thrown her hair up in a messy bun, put on a light foundation with a little eye shadow, and nothing else. She had chosen an old black pin-striped suit. She was humble Paige today, a hardworking lawyer who needed a little sympathy from the court.

She kept her eyes glued to the sidewalk in front of her as she pushed her way through the media horde like a seasoned pro, lips pursed, ignoring every attempt to bait her into commenting. She managed to elbow to the front of the metal detector line, letting the snarky comments fall on deaf ears. After getting cleared, she hurried up the steps and took her place at counsel table just a few minutes before nine. Even Wyatt Jackson had arrived before her.

Landon Reed was in the front row, and she had a brief conversation with him before the hearing started. He had coached Paige to be respectful but firm when questioned by Judge Solberg. No, she had not leaked the deposition of Director Marcano. But with all due respect, she was not going to produce her computer. It contained client confidences and attorney work-product. An attorney's first responsibility was to represent her client zealously, and Paige, though she would love to prove her innocence by turning over her computer, could not do so in this matter. If necessary, they had agreed to have Landon stand and introduce himself to the court and make arguments on her behalf. The less Paige said the better.

There was a chance, Paige knew, that she could actually get carted off to prison after this hearing. If she did, Landon would be ready to file an emergency appeal. But more likely, she and the rest of the team would be scolded and fined. She would hunker down, take it like a soldier, and hope that the media found something else to divert their attention in a few days.

On Paige's advice, Kristen had not attended the hearing. There were no SEALs or their families in the first few rows. This was not going to be a good day for the plaintiff, and the fewer people who had to endure Judge Solberg's tongue-lashing, the better.

On the other hand, the defense team had shown up in force, most likely to gloat. The lawyers were all there, including what seemed like fifteen attorneys from Dylan Pierce's firm. Even the ultra-busy Philip Kilpatrick and John Marcano had somehow managed to put aside their important governmental duties to attend the dressing-down. They could hardly conceal their glee.

Just before Judge Solberg took the bench, Wyatt slid a piece of paper in front of Paige. "Sign this," he said.

"What is it?" Paige asked.

"Read it. But make sure you sign it before I get up to talk."

Paige was only halfway through the document when Judge Solberg blew into the courtroom. She was angry, and she made no effort to conceal it. Her face was drawn and tight, eyes darting around the court-room. The marshal called the court to order, and Judge Solberg wel-comed everyone with a terse "Be seated."

The judge leaned forward on her elbows and, without greeting the lawyers, explained the reason that court had been convened. Her protective order had been violated. She had received a very thorough report from U.S. Attorney Mitchell Taylor, who was sitting in the sec-ond row on the defense side of the courtroom. She thanked him for his thoroughness and thanked the FBI agents who were also in attendance for their diligent work.

She spent a few minutes dictating portions of the report into the record while Paige sat grim-faced, staring at a spot in the well of the courtroom. Paige heard some whispering in the back and Judge Solberg must have heard it as well. Her head snapped up and she fixed a death stare on two people who were quietly talking to each other. Like the rest of the courtroom, Paige turned to look at them as they realized a second too late that the entire courtroom had gone quiet. They stopped talking and Judge Solberg let them have it.

"Quiet! If you have business to transact, do it out in the hallway." She glared at the two men, whose faces were both turning red. "Do you two gentlemen understand that, or do I need to ask the marshals to escort you out?"

They both apologized and told Judge Solberg that they understood.

"Very well, then." Judge Solberg went back to reading the report, and the courtroom was deathly quiet.

Wyatt leaned over to whisper in Paige's ear, and she wanted to elbow him in the gut. "Her Honor seems a little testy today," Wyatt said.

Paige gave him an almost-imperceptible nod. No way she was going to say a word. She was already in enough trouble as it was.

She finished reading the document in front of her, signed it, and slid it over to Wyatt.

72

After Judge Solberg had outlined the case against the plaintiff's team as contained in the report filed by Mitchell Taylor, she stopped reading and fixed her gaze on Wyatt, Paige, and Wellington.

"The court is sorely disappointed in the conduct of counsel," she said. "This court bent over backward to accommodate counsel's request to take the depositions of the defendants despite the fact that those depositions might potentially reveal state secrets. Relying on the integrity of counsel, this court allowed plaintiff's counsel who had obtained security clearance to take those depositions under seal. This court trusted counsel to keep those depositions confidential."

Paige could hear the anger riding on Judge Solberg's every word. She was working hard not to raise her voice, but her words were clipped, her facial muscles strained. Yet Paige was now staring back. She didn't like being lectured like a middle schooler, especially for something she had not done. She knew the strategy was to be contrite and say very little. But she was getting angry, and it was going to be hard not to fight.

"Based on this report and the lack of cooperation by plaintiff's counsel during the investigation, I am inclined to hold all three of you in contempt. However, before I do so, I want to give you an opportunity to explain yourselves and provide the court with any evidence I should consider to the contrary."

The words were no sooner out of her mouth than Wyatt Jackson was on his feet. "Thank you, Your Honor," he said, with a great deal of confidence and aplomb. It was as if the court's scolding had never occurred. "I call FBI Agent Bryant Vaughn to the stand."

The judge blinked back her surprise. Paige turned to look at Vaughn, who had his brow furrowed in confusion.

"Who said anything about calling witnesses?" Judge Solberg asked. "And for what purpose?"

"For the purpose of defending myself," Wyatt said matter-of-factly.

Solberg frowned, unimpressed. "Agent Vaughn, please take the stand," she said.

Vaughn stood, buttoned his suit coat, and limped up to the well of the courtroom. His eyes were wary, and he paused for a moment to look at Wyatt as if promising the lawyer that he would be sorry. Wyatt was shuffling papers and ignored him.

Vaughn took the oath and settled into the witness box, a cagey veteran ready to play cat and mouse.

"Good morning, Agent Vaughn," Wyatt said.

"Good morning."

"This *New York Tribune* article was written by a man named Harry Coburn; is that right?"

"Yes."

"And Mr. Coburn would know for sure who leaked the information to him, wouldn't he?"

Vaughn shifted in his seat. "Of course. But as Judge Solberg previously mentioned—" he turned slightly to look at the judge—"there are serious First Amendment concerns with making a reporter reveal confidential sources. Our job was to determine who leaked the deposition without implicating those concerns. So we didn't interview him, if that's what you're getting at."

Wyatt smiled. He had handled a few crafty witnesses before, ones that wanted to give speeches instead of answering questions. He took a step closer to the witness box. "How about if I just signal to you what I'm getting at by asking my questions? You can just answer them and save the speeches for later."

"Objection!" Dylan Pierce said.

"Sustained," Solberg ruled. But Wyatt had made his point.

"So instead of questioning Mr. Coburn and making him choose between protecting his confidential source and possibly going to jail, you decided to question me and the other lawyers on my legal team—" Wyatt made a sweeping gesture toward Paige and Wellington—"and make *us* decide between protecting the confidential information of our clients or going to jail. Is that right?"

Vaughn frowned as if he were explaining something obvious to a four-year-old. "That's completely wrong. We would have protected any confidential information on your computers, if you had produced them instead of destroying them."

"And we have *what* to prove that? Your word?"

"My word and the word of the U.S. attorney."

"Exactly. The word of the government." Wyatt said it with disgust, as if everybody knew the government could never be trusted. Paige was getting more nervous by the second. He was only making things worse.

"Director Marcano and Mr. Kilpatrick over there—they work for the same government; is that right?"

"It's not unusual for the FBI to set up a firewall to protect information it obtains from other branches of government."

"And we have what to ensure that this firewall is set up—your word again?"

"Trust me—this is the way it works."

"That's the problem I'm having. I don't trust you."

Vaughn's face turned a shade of red and Solberg could no longer restrain herself. "Stick to asking questions, Mr. Jackson, or I'll end this examination right now."

"Thank you, Your Honor," Jackson said sarcastically.

He took a few steps in silence, letting the tension build. *Always the showman,* Paige thought.

"Would you agree that if Mr. Coburn had the permission of his confidential source to reveal his or her name, he wouldn't be facing this journalistic dilemma any longer?"

"I don't understand what you mean."

"Well, the source is only confidential because the person who gave Mr. Coburn the information made Mr. Coburn promise that he would not release the person's name. Isn't that true?"

"I suppose so."

"So if that same source now said it was okay for his or her name to be released . . ." Wyatt threw open his arms, as if he had just discovered something incredibly profound. "Problem solved!"

"I suppose. But the source is never going to do that. That's why they asked to remain confidential in the first place."

"Aha," Wyatt said. "Precisely! So anyone who is not the source would have no problem signing an agreement waiving any rights they might have to confidentiality and giving that agreement to Mr. Coburn. Isn't that right?"

This caused Vaughn to think for a moment. He seemed to be chewing the inside of his cheek. "I'm not sure that type of agreement would be enforceable."

"Because you're not a lawyer, right?"

"I'm not a lawyer; that's correct."

"But your partner is a lawyer, right?"

"Agent Diaz, who worked with me on this investigation, is a lawyer. That's correct."

"So did you or Agent Diaz ever suggest that all of the people you are investigating simply sign an agreement waiving their right to confidentiality? Hang on." Wyatt walked over to his counsel table and picked up a few sheets of paper. "An agreement like this one authorizing Mr. Coburn to disclose the name of the source? Did you ever even think about that?"

"No. We didn't consider that."

"Exactly," Wyatt said, sounding excited. "So I thought of it for you. And better yet, I signed one voluntarily. And I've got one here from every member of our defense team."

Wyatt pivoted and looked at the court. "And I will represent to the court that we are putting copies of these agreements in the mail to Mr. Coburn this very day, return receipt requested, telling him that he can disclose our names or the name of our client if one of us was the source of the leak."

Judge Solberg studied Wyatt as if looking at some interesting insect. "Let me see that," she eventually said.

Wyatt walked up to the bench and handed her the document. "Why don't we mark that as Exhibit 1," he said. "A signed copy of my agreement to waive any confidentiality promise Mr. Coburn might have made to me. And I'll hand up signed agreements from my cocounsel and my client that we can mark as Exhibits 2 through 4."

"All right, I'll mark them as exhibits," Judge Solberg said. It seemed to Paige that her tone had softened a little.

"I'm done with this witness, Your Honor," he said. "Now I'd like to call each of the defendants and defense counsel to the stand one by one and present them with a copy of the same agreement to sign."

This brought both Dylan Pierce and Kyle Gates to their feet. But their reactions were tellingly different. Gates spoke first, anxious to beat Pierce to the punch. "We have no problem signing those agreements. But we think this is just showmanship because Harry Coburn will never burn his source, agreement or not. But we certainly didn't release that deposition and we have no problem signing."

"Mr. Pierce?" Judge Solberg asked.

He hesitated just for a second, and Paige knew from that moment that Pierce or his client had released the deposition. Yet he didn't want to be the only one in the courtroom arguing that the agreement shouldn't be signed.

"This is just another distraction," he said. "They're the ones who won't produce their computers or cell phones. We've produced every computer and shown the FBI every e-mail sent since the deposition of Director Marcano. We're certainly happy to sign whatever other documents the court might desire, but I agree with Mr. Gates—it's not going to make any difference. Mr. Coburn is not going to reveal his source no matter what."

"May I respond?" Wyatt asked.

"Of course."

"I would like the court's permission to take the deposition of Mr. Coburn," Wyatt said. "I will press him on just this point. Instead of assuming that Mr. Coburn won't do the right thing, let me depose him. If he still refuses to divulge the source, Your Honor could hold him in contempt without implicating any First Amendment concerns, because his source would have signed a document waiving confidentiality."

Paige sat back in her chair. She was actually enjoying the show now. Somehow, Wyatt had put the other side on the defensive.

"And further," Wyatt continued, "I want to call every one of the defense lawyers to the stand and both of the defendants so that I can ask them under oath whether they leaked this deposition. My team and I are willing to testify under oath. If somebody is lying, they ought to face not just contempt charges but also perjury charges when their lies are discovered."

Paige studied the faces at the defense counsel table. Wyatt had expertly laid the trap. None of them knew whether Coburn would burn his source once he was provided with waivers of the confidentiality agreement. And now Wyatt had raised the stakes. Perjury was punishable by up to a year in prison.

"More showmanship," Pierce complained. "Your Honor can already hold the person in contempt. Sworn testimony is not necessary."

Judge Solberg, however, seemed intrigued by the idea. After several minutes of legal bantering, she required every lawyer and every party to take the stand, be sworn in as a witness, and individually answer two questions: "Did you leak the deposition of Director Marcano?" and "Do you know who did?"

Every lawyer and the two defendants answered without blinking. And when it was Wyatt's turn, he couldn't resist editorializing just a little.

"No, but I sure hope you find out who did."

At the end of the hearing, Judge Solberg took the matter under advisement for another thirty days. She asked Wyatt to submit a statement signed by Kristen Anderson, taken under oath, that she had not leaked the deposition. She granted Wyatt permission to depose Harry Coburn after everybody had signed an agreement authorizing him to reveal his source. She said she would reconvene the proceedings once that deposition was completed.

Wyatt, Paige, and Wellington all left the courtroom with their heads held high.

Uncharacteristically, Wyatt did not stop on the courthouse steps and hold an impromptu press conference. He did, however, throw a few nuggets to the reporters as he and the rest of the team walked away.

"We're looking forward to the Supreme Court hearing in two weeks. Whoever leaked that deposition ought to be locked up for a year." And then there was Paige's favorite quote of all. Somebody had asked whether he thought they were going to win. Did he have any predictions?

"Take the Redskins and the three points," he said.

Even Paige smiled at that one.

73

For Paige, the next seven days were a sleepless blur of preparation for the Supreme Court argument and for her grand jury appearance. She read cases until her eyes blurred and endured grillings from a moot court panel of Wyatt, Wellington, and Landon. They held four-hour sessions in Landon's conference room, with the three lawyers sitting on one side of the large marble-topped table while Paige stood behind a podium on the other side and fielded questions. Wyatt had insisted that she be prepared to call each justice by name and not act like a rookie who just referred to everyone as "Your Honor."

"But I am a rookie," Paige had protested.

"You don't have to sound like one," Wyatt countered.

To help her memorize the justices' names, Wellington came up with a system. They put a computer monitor in the middle of the table facing Paige. Each time one of the three lawyers asked a question, they first clicked a name on their computer, which popped up a picture of the Supreme Court justice who was supposedly asking the question. Paige would then refer to the justice by name when she answered.

She got used to the hardest questions coming from Justice David Sikes. He was young and brash, a true law-and-order type, and whenever Wyatt had a tough question, he would click on Sikes's picture. The other justice Paige got tired of seeing, and had no problem remembering, was the Beard, the seventy-two-year-old former Texas judge named Barton Cooper. He was another sure vote against Paige and someone who would certainly try to trip her up.

The two justices whom Paige always mixed up were Justice Torres, the former senator from California, and Justice Augustini, the Harvard law professor who was also a novelist. They were both in their fifties, and Paige kept forgetting which one was which.

"Augustini has the curly hair and the mole," Wellington said as if that solved everything. It also scared Paige to realize she would be close enough to use a mole as a distinguishing feature.

"Right," said Wyatt. "Augustini is Italian, and Italians like spaghetti, so you'll be able to remember the curly hair." Typical Wyatt Jackson—profiling an entire nationality. But for some reason, it worked.

Every four-hour session was followed by a ten-minute break and another hour of tips from Paige's three tormentors. Nothing was off-limits. Stand up straighter; project more; more eye contact; don't shuffle your papers—and then there was the substance of her answers, which never seemed to satisfy anybody. She took notes on all of it and then ignored most of the comments on the theory that the best advocate was one who tried to be herself.

After the critique sessions were over, she would spend the next few hours alone with Wellington, listening to the audio of each question and answer, discussing ways to improve what she had said. It was exhausting work, but she liked it better than the sessions she spent with Landon Reed discussing her grand jury testimony.

Landon wanted Paige to take the Fifth Amendment in response to almost every question, but Paige thought that if she answered the questions fully and honestly she could pull off a miracle and talk the grand jury out of indicting her. After they debated this, Landon suggested that they see how well she might hold up on cross-examination. He took the next two hours questioning her about why she hadn't produced her computer and what information she had obtained from the Patriot. He raised an eyebrow when she testified truthfully but the answer seemed hard to believe. And Landon knew how to lay on the sarcasm. There were lots of those "When did you stop beating your wife?" types of questions for which there were no good answers.

When they had finished, Landon showed Paige how much additional jail time she could be facing if the U.S. attorney tacked on a charge of lying to the grand jury. She was completely deflated. The best course, she acknowledged, would be to take the Fifth.

It seemed surreal that they were even having this conversation.

Because the law did not allow someone to assert a blanket Fifth Amendment privilege at the grand jury hearing, Paige and Landon spent the next session going over the types of questions she would answer and the ones where she would plead the Fifth. Defense lawyers weren't allowed in the courtroom, but Landon would be just outside in the hallway, and if she had any doubt, she should ask for a break to consult with him.

"Won't that look bad?" Paige asked.

"Paige, you're going to be taking the Fifth Amendment to almost every question. It already looks bad."

Her testimony was scheduled for Tuesday, and she began to obsess over the fact that she might be indicted just a few days before she was scheduled to argue at the Supreme Court on the first Monday in October. How could she stand up in front of the justices as an accused felon?

Wyatt didn't seem concerned about it, but then again, he would be either out of the country or in prison. "You're innocent until proven guilty," he reminded Paige. "If it comes up, show a little righteous indignation. Heck, if it were me, I'd bring it up in court myself to show how desperate the government is to keep the truth buried in this case. Wear it like a badge of honor."

Only Wyatt would view a pending indictment for obstruction of justice as a badge of honor, Paige thought. The justices certainly wouldn't look at it that way.

★ ★ ★

WASHINGTON, D.C.

Philip Kilpatrick had created a monster. He'd been afraid that might be the case, but he knew it for sure when he received the phone call from Harry Coburn.

"I got your waiver of the confidentiality agreement today," Harry said. "Very accommodating of you."

"Nice of you to call, because I'm revoking that waiver right now," Kilpatrick said.

This brought a sarcastic laugh from Coburn. "Obviously you didn't read the document. Wyatt Jackson is pretty clever. Says it can only be revoked in writing."

"We both know you've still got an obligation to protect your sources."

Kilpatrick didn't like the way Coburn let the silence linger before responding to the comment.

"I'll still protect you," he eventually said. "But not because I have an obligation. It's just that I always protect sources when I can count on them for future stories."

"I've always sent my best scoops to you, Harry," Kilpatrick said calmly. But even as he said it, he knew the dynamics had changed. Before, he would send the stories and Coburn would be gracious, almost fawning. Now Coburn had all the leverage.

"I heard something about a grand jury investigating the plaintiff's lawyers for obstruction. What do you know about that?" Coburn asked.

Kilpatrick knew plenty. But he didn't want to leak that story to Coburn. The man already had enough to hold over his head with the confidentiality waiver.

"I'll look into it," Kilpatrick said.

"If it's true, I'd like to break the story before the Supreme Court argument."

"As I said, I'll look into it."

"I appreciate your help. And I'm pretty sure they have a term for this new relationship we've developed," Coburn said.

"What's that?" Kilpatrick asked, somewhat caustically.

"We're codependent, Philip. Have a great day."

74

Tuesday was one of the longest days of Paige's life. She sat on a hard wooden bench in the marble hallway of the federal court building, just outside courtroom 1, clutching her subpoena to appear before the grand jury. Landon, Wyatt, and Wellington were there as well, and Wyatt did his share of pacing, complaining to Mitchell Taylor every time Mitchell came out the courtroom doors. It was a sign of disrespect to keep them waiting, Wyatt said. Mitchell should have planned things better. When was Mitchell going to call Wyatt and his team? They had lots of things to do, including preparing for a Supreme Court argument.

Mitchell said little and gave nothing away. Paige watched as other witnesses came and went, including some she did not know. Landon approached the witnesses after they testified to see if they would brief him on what they had said. None of them seemed willing to cooperate.

Paige was the first of the three plaintiff's lawyers called to testify. It was nearly noon when the U.S. marshal came into the hallway and called her name. She wiped her sweaty hands on the sides of her dress, nodded at Wyatt and Landon, and marched toward the door of the courtroom. She entered with her head held high and walked down the middle aisle, staring straight ahead. The marshal administered the oath, and Paige swore to tell the truth.

Twenty-four grand jurors stared at her, gauging her every move. Twelve were seated in the jury box and twelve in the first few rows of the courtroom. There was no judge, and there were no lawyers at the table for defense counsel. The courtroom was empty except for the jurors, the marshals, a court reporter, Mitchell Taylor, and FBI Agents Vaughn and Diaz.

Paige settled into the witness chair.

"Good morning, Ms. Chambers," Mitchell Taylor said. He looked like a Marine—ramrod straight, hair clipped short, his suit tight and pressed.

"Good morning." Paige's voice was high and nervous.

"Please state your name for the record, spelling your last name."

"Paige Chambers, *C-H-A-M-B-E-R-S*."

Many of the jurors were taking notes, and the body language was not good. Some had their arms crossed. Others scowled.

"I'd like to ask you a few questions about whether or not you received and used classified information."

"Okay."

Mitchell began by establishing some background facts. He questioned Paige about her familiarity with the prohibition against receiving and disseminating classified information. Paige and Landon had anticipated this line of questioning, and she answered his questions, carefully focusing on each one, taking her time before responding. She knew that the pauses made her appear guilty, but Landon had convinced her that there was no way to persuade the grand jury anyway, and the only thing that mattered was the resulting transcript of her testimony. She couldn't afford to make any mistakes.

Mitchell next asked a series of questions to help the jurors understand Paige's role in the *Anderson* case and the alleged leaking of the Marcano deposition. Paige answered each of those questions as well—carefully, methodically, like someone trying to hide something.

Then Mitchell shifted to the FBI interview with Paige. He handed her a copy of the transcript from that interview.

"Ms. Chambers, the jurors have already heard the recorded interview between you and FBI Agents Vaughn and Diaz. This is a written transcript if you need it to refresh your memory."

"Thank you."

"At the time Agents Vaughn and Diaz interviewed you on Saturday, September 8, you were aware that this office was conducting an investigation into a violation of Judge Solberg's confidentiality order; is that right?"

Paige wanted to answer the question. She wanted to explain that she had known about the investigation into the deposition leak but hadn't known they would be questioning her about classified information. But she was under strict orders from Landon not to answer such questions. *"Don't be a hero,"* he'd said. *"You'll only get yourself in more trouble."*

Paige paused, swallowed hard, and repeated the line that Landon had made her memorize: "I'm asserting my rights under the Fifth Amendment to the United States Constitution not to answer the question."

Landon had told her to keep it short and simple and to act confident as she asserted the Fifth. Still, she felt sleazy doing it.

Mitchell Taylor feigned surprise. "You're refusing to answer?"

"I'm asserting my privilege under the Fifth Amendment of the Constitution."

"So you're claiming that something about the question might incriminate you?"

"I'm asserting my right under the Fifth Amendment," Paige said, with more authority this time. But as soon as the words were out, she knew that her tone had been a mistake.

Mitchell frowned for his little audience of jurors. "Okay then, let me ask you this: Did you deny to Agents Vaughn and Diaz that you had received any classified information from any source?"

"I decline to answer the question on the basis of my rights under the Fifth Amendment of the Constitution."

"But the jury has already heard you say it on the recording," Mitchell insisted. "It's right there in black and white in front of you. Are you denying that you said it?"

Everybody in the courtroom seemed to be frowning at her. Mitchell Taylor. The FBI agents. The jurors. "I'm asserting my right under the Fifth Amendment of the United States Constitution not to answer the question."

Mitchell had been pacing around the courtroom, holding a legal pad full of notes. He now walked over to his counsel table and set the notepad down. He returned to the well of the courtroom empty-handed and crossed his arms, a look of disdain on his face.

"Isn't it true that you knew an official federal investigation was under way when you talked to the FBI, and you knew that the investigation went beyond the question of who had leaked Director Marcano's deposition?"

"I'm asserting my rights under the Fifth Amendment of the Constitution not to answer the question."

"And isn't it true that you received classified information prior to that interview and then obstructed justice by lying to the FBI about it?"

"I decline to answer the question."

"You used classified information to advance your case, didn't you?"

"I'm asserting my rights under the Fifth Amendment of the U.S. Constitution."

"And you're on a contingency fee, meaning that if your client wins a stash of money, you get one-third?"

"What's that got to do with anything?"

"Ah—a question that you can answer?"

Paige shook her head, mad at herself for taking the bait. "I'm asserting the Fifth."

Mitchell smirked. "Here's what it has to do with anything," he said. "You are illegally using classified information to advance a case in which you will personally profit. Isn't that true?"

"I'm asserting my rights under the Fifth Amendment of the U.S. Constitution."

And so it went for what seemed like an eternity. Mitchell Taylor making accusations, Paige refusing to answer the questions, the jurors scolding her with their body language. Even before he was done, Paige knew for certain that she would be indicted for obstruction of justice and the unauthorized dissemination of classified information.

"One more set of questions," Mitchell said. "From whom did you obtain the classified information?"

"I refuse to answer and I assert my rights under the Fifth Amendment of the U.S. Constitution."

"Was it Daniel Reese?"

It felt to Paige like she had been hit with cannon fire. Her jaw dropped a little at the mention of Reese's name, and she scrambled to regain her composure as the blood rushed to her face.

"I refuse to answer and assert my rights under the Fifth Amendment of the U.S. Constitution."

Did they know that she had met with Reese on the Cape Henry Trail? That he had given her background information about the case? What else did they know?

"You're sure you don't want to answer that question?" Mitchell asked.

"I'm sure."

Mitchell made a great display of walking back to his counsel table, leafing through his notes, and shaking his head. "In light of the witness's invocation of the Fifth Amendment, that's all the questions I have for now," Mitchell said.

Paige stood but Mitchell held out his hand. "Wait; one more thing. Did you bring the computer and cell phone that we subpoenaed?"

Paige stared at him. He knew she didn't have it. "Obviously not."

"Why not?"

"I'm taking the Fifth Amendment on that, too, Mr. Taylor."

"I thought maybe you would."

★　★　★

It seemed to Paige that Wyatt's and Wellington's time with the grand jury was shorter than hers. They all huddled up and compared notes afterward. Landon tried to reassure Paige, but his words rang hollow. She was steeling herself to be indicted later that day or at the very least prior to her Supreme Court argument. "Landon, you'd better be ready to go on Monday," she said.

They were huddled at one end of the hallway when Paige heard footsteps coming around the corner. She looked past Landon's shoulder and saw him—dressed in his military whites, his shoes shining, his hat tucked under his arm. Daniel Reese was surrounded by a small army of military lawyers, each carrying a briefcase. They formed their own huddle, and Reese avoided looking in Paige's direction.

Landon turned, took in the scene, and asked Paige if it was Daniel Reese. When Paige nodded, Landon walked over to the group of men. He talked to them quietly, and Paige couldn't hear a word that was said. When he came back, he told Paige that they weren't willing to tell Landon anything about why Reese had been subpoenaed or what he might say.

A few minutes later, a marshal came into the hallway and called Daniel Reese's name. He walked alone into the grand jury room.

When he reemerged nearly an hour and a half later, Landon approached his team again. This time, Reese had a message for Paige.

"Tell her I was just responding to the government's subpoena to testify," Reese had told Landon. "I was just doing my patriotic duty."

75

Daniel Reese was the Patriot. What else could he possibly have meant?

Paige and her team kicked that question around for nearly two hours back in Landon's conference room. There were still things that didn't add up. Why had he denied being the Patriot on the day that he snuck up on Paige on the Cape Henry Trail? Why had he risked his job to provide them with classified information? And what had he told the grand jury?

Had Mitchell Taylor and the FBI somehow figured it out? Were they about to indict Daniel Reese along with Paige, Wyatt, and Wellington? Reese had been in that grand jury room for a long time. Maybe he had cut a deal and was going to testify against the others. Was that his "patriotic duty"?

After Wyatt and Wellington left, Landon told Paige his theory. "The government has your computer," he said. "They probably used some kind of complex voice recognition software to figure out that Daniel Reese was the Patriot. And if they have your computer, they know what he told you."

The next day Landon called Mitchell Taylor, who did not return his call, and Daniel Reese's lawyers, who stonewalled him. Landon told Paige he had no idea if the grand jury had returned any indictments or whether they would continue meeting the next week.

★ ★ ★

After a fitful night of sleep, Paige got up early Friday, put on her sweats, and went for a run at First Landing. When she returned to her condo, she drove by the parking lot twice to make sure there were no strange-looking sedans with FBI agents waiting to arrest her. She finally pulled in and parked, showered and changed, and headed to Landon Reed's office for another day of prepping for her Supreme Court case. She didn't want to stay at her apartment during the day, get arrested by the feds, and do a perp walk in broad daylight.

She returned to her apartment after dark and checked around the parking lot again before going inside. Landon had finally gotten through to Mitchell Taylor late Thursday, but Mitchell wouldn't tell him anything.

Friday night, Paige lay awake in bed, weighed down with worry about the FBI and the Supreme Court. She finally dozed off at 2 a.m., and her cell phone's alarm startled her to life a mere three hours later.

Under cover of darkness, SEAL Team Nine left for Washington, D.C., early Saturday morning, crammed into Paige's small Honda. Wyatt had a plane to catch out of Dulles International Airport, and the rest of the team, absent Landon Reed, had decided to settle into a Washington hotel with an extra day before the Supreme Court argument. Paige just wanted to get out of town a step ahead of the FBI, and Kristen seemed excited about having a break from the boys.

The crew was pretty quiet as they left Hampton Roads. Paige was driving and deep in thought. Next to her, Wyatt was sprawled out in the front passenger seat, his mouth open as he snored. Riding in the backseat next to Kristen, Wellington waited until the sun came up and then started rereading cases. Paige had her cell phone connected to the car stereo system, cycling through her most inspirational running songs, trying to get ready for her big day in court.

Paige stopped at a pancake house on I-95 just north of Richmond, and the team came to life. Once they were seated, Wyatt started in with one of his stories, and Kristen laughed along, providing all the audience Wyatt needed. Even Paige loosened up a little, though the sinking feeling came back whenever her thoughts turned unprompted to the possibility of an indictment. If the government wanted to play it out for maximum impact, they would arrest the entire team today, or maybe even tomorrow or Monday, on the streets of Washington, D.C. Landon would be forced to argue the case while Paige and the others waited for their bond hearing.

"If the government has indictments against us, I might just stay in Dubai," Wyatt said between bites. "I hear it's nice there."

"Just keep an eye on the sky," Paige said. "Now that they have drones, they don't have to worry about extradition."

Wyatt laughed. "We're going to make a defense lawyer out of you yet."

Later that morning at the airport they were met by Gazala Holloman, who handed Wyatt a handwritten letter for Saleet Zafar. "Make sure he reads this as soon as you see him," Gazala said. "He'll like you better after he does."

Wyatt thanked her and promised everyone he would be in touch. He had packed everything he needed for the trip in his backpack—a computer, a couple of changes of clothes, toiletries, some legal pads, a baseball cap, and a pack of Phillies cigars. He stopped and gave Paige a quick pep talk about her Supreme Court argument before heading through security.

"You're one of the smartest lawyers I know," he told her, his arms on her shoulders. "And we're on the right side of this. Don't get intimidated.

Stare those old geezers down and show them you belong up there. And whatever you do, don't back down on anything."

"I won't," Paige promised.

"Did I ever tell you the story about James Bowie and the Alamo?" Wyatt asked.

"About a hundred times."

"Long live the Alamo," Wyatt said.

Paige blinked back the tears. This was sounding too much like a last good-bye. "Be careful over there," she said.

"Don't worry about me. The Houthis are nothing compared to that snake pit you'll be in."

"Thanks. I feel a lot better now."

Wyatt gave Paige a hug, wrapping her in the smell of cheap cigars. She was already missing the man, and he hadn't even left. He had an infectious boldness, and just having him around made her feel more confident.

After he pulled away, he retrieved a letter from his backpack and handed it to her. It had a single name on the outside. "If anything happens to me, would you give this to my son?" Wyatt asked.

"Of course," Paige said.

"Thanks."

He turned, walked toward security, and didn't look back. Silently, Paige prayed that she would see him again.

76

Wyatt had paid extra for a direct flight on Emirates Airlines, but he was still in the air for thirteen straight hours. His flight left Dulles at 10:55 Saturday morning, and he arrived in Dubai on Sunday morning at a few minutes after eight. He was haggard and exhausted and kept wondering what he had been thinking when he agreed to take this trip. They had served no alcohol on the flight, and he was squeezed into a window seat next to a big man who should have been required to buy two seats himself. Wyatt's neck was stiff and he felt scuzzy as he exited the airplane into the Dubai International terminal.

It was not at all what he expected. The terminal was glistening and spotless and teeming with people from every part of the globe. All of the signs were in both Arabic and English, and he heard lots of travelers speaking his native tongue. The airport featured lush little gardens of palm trees and shrubs set off by glass railings. It was a sharp contrast to the arid and brown landscape he had seen as the plane came in for a landing.

Wyatt was wearing a pair of jeans, boat shoes, and an old gray T-shirt, yet he didn't feel at all out of place. Walking toward customs, he saw only a few women in traditional Arab garb with their heads or faces covered. He passed a Starbucks and stopped for breakfast at the cleanest Burger King he had ever seen. He used the bathroom because he knew it might be a long time before he had accommodations like this again.

He traded in his dollars for local dirhams and passed through customs without a glitch. Wyatt had steeled himself during the flight for life-threatening dangers once he hit the ground, but he was starting to think this might not be that bad.

On the other side of customs stood a wall of people waiting for travelers, holding signs in a variety of languages. Wyatt stopped and looked around. The plan, according to Gazala Holloman, was for somebody to meet Wyatt right here, carrying a sign with his name on it. That person and a few others would sneak Wyatt across the border and take him deep into Yemen, where he would meet with Saleet Zafar and the people who knew about the drone strike at the adobe house where the sheep offering had taken place.

But Wyatt saw no signs with his name. He looked around for a few minutes and was finally approached by a short man with a full black beard and bright brown eyes.

"Mr. Jackson?" The man had a thick Middle Eastern accent.

"Yes," Wyatt said, extending his hand.

The man shook it. "Come with me," he said, nodding toward the doorway. "May I take?" He grabbed for Wyatt's backpack but Wyatt pulled it back.

"No. I've got it."

Wyatt followed the man, who continually turned and peppered Wyatt with questions. *Good flight? You sleep? How is your family? You are hungry?*

Wyatt learned that his bubbly and energetic host was named

Mahmoud. And according to Mahmoud, Wyatt was looking at a nearly thirty-hour road trip along the northern coast of the United Arab Emirates, through Saudi Arabia, and into Yemen. It wasn't the most direct route, but it was apparently the fastest.

"Are you going with me?" Wyatt asked.

Mahmoud smiled and gave his head a vigorous little shake. "Oh no. I stay here in Dubai."

"Will anybody speak English on the trip?"

"Yes. Sure. Saleet Zafar speak English."

"No, I mean, will anybody in the car with me during the thirty-hour car ride speak English?"

Mahmoud smiled, shaking his head again. "It's okay," he said. "They show you what to do."

For some reason that he couldn't put his finger on, Wyatt instinctively trusted Mahmoud. The man was cheery and making every effort to be helpful. It was like Wyatt was some kind of celebrity and it was Mahmoud's job to keep him happy. Wyatt didn't like the fact that Mahmoud was not going with him into Yemen.

"What are the roads like?" Wyatt asked.

"They okay. Pretty good."

"Rocky?"

Mahmoud looked puzzled.

"Rough. Lots of stones and rocks," Wyatt explained, using his hands to show the shape of a rock.

Mahmoud nodded. "Yes. Yes. Very many stones."

Wyatt let it drop. He decided it was better to just be surprised.

★   ★   ★

His first unpleasant surprise came at a small house on the outskirts of Dubai when he met the three men who would be escorting him into Yemen. As Mahmoud introduced them, he was the only one smiling and nodding. The others looked harsh and weathered, staring at Wyatt as if they would rather beat him to a pulp than give him a ride anywhere.

Mahmoud had blitzed through the introductions so fast that Wyatt couldn't remember any of their names. But it became immediately clear that none of them spoke English.

Each wore a long white robe and a red-and-white head scarf tied with a black cord. They were broad-shouldered, and two were nearly as tall as Wyatt. They had long knives tucked into their waistbands, and there was a table in the house full of AK-47s and loaded magazines.

One of the men said something to Mahmoud, who in turn translated for Wyatt. "They want your backpack," Mahmoud said. As he was talking, one of the men reached for Wyatt's backpack, but Wyatt stepped back and stared him down.

"No," Wyatt said sternly to Mahmoud. "Nobody touches it."

The men immediately frowned and started arguing with Mahmoud in Arabic.

Mahmoud turned to Wyatt. "They say they must have it."

"Tell them to pound sand," Wyatt said.

Mahmoud tilted his head and furrowed his brow.

"I am not giving it to them," Wyatt said.

Mahmoud relayed the message, which precipitated another animated discussion between Mahmoud and his hosts. Finally Mahmoud turned back to Wyatt. "They say if you do not give backpack, they not take you to Yemen. It is not for negotiation."

Wyatt glanced from one face to the next. He was a master negotiator, but he was dealing with a culture that he didn't understand. "They can look inside, but they cannot have it."

Mahmoud sighed and translated again. After another argument with the three men, this time more animated than before, he turned back to Wyatt. His hand gestures indicated that he was at the end of his rope. "They say it must stay here. They cannot trust Americans."

There it was—out in the open. These three men didn't trust Wyatt, and Wyatt didn't trust them. He had spent thirteen hours flying here, and Saleet's testimony had the potential of winning the *Anderson* case hands down and exposing Director Marcano. But at what price?

Wyatt decided to do what he always did—try one more bluff. He shook his head no. "Take me back to the airport," he demanded.

This time Mahmoud didn't bother to interpret. He just looked at the three men and shrugged and their body language said it all. They weren't going to give an inch.

"As you say," Mahmoud said, his formerly energetic voice flat and resigned. "Let us go."

Wyatt walked out the door with Mahmoud but stopped before they got in the car. "I don't have any weapons," Wyatt said. "I don't understand why I have to leave everything here."

Mahmoud turned and looked at him. This time the little man was frowning. "Drones fall from skies," Mahmoud said. "Those men in the house have seen friends—" Mahmoud stopped and signaled an explosion with his hands, mimicking the sound of a Hellfire missile. "They have good reason not to trust Americans."

Wyatt thought about it for a moment. Even if the Supreme Court ruled against them, Wyatt and his team might be able to prove their case through these witnesses in Yemen. He had come this far. He had waited all his life for a case like this where he could expose the corruption of the government, the same government that had always refused to cut his clients any slack. He was getting old. When would he ever have another chance like this?

"Okay, you win." He opened his backpack and stuffed a few cigars in his pocket. Then he handed it over to Mahmoud. "Let's go back inside and get this trip started."

77

The unpleasant surprises didn't stop there. Before he left, Wyatt had to follow Mahmoud into a small and dingy bathroom where Mahmoud handed Wyatt a razor and soap.

"I am sorry to say but you must shave eyebrows," Mahmoud said. He was shaking his head from side to side as if apologizing for the request. "You will cross border into Yemen as a Muslim woman. We have passport for you. You will wear a *niqab* and *abaya*." Mahmoud shrugged as if it were natural for a man to shave his eyebrows.

"Are you kidding me?" Wyatt asked. "I'm not doing this." The only asset he would have in Yemen would be his tough-guy American persona. If he shaved his eyebrows, he would look like a clown.

"You must do. These men have worked very hard for planning this trip."

Wyatt looked in the mirror and then at his host. He grabbed the razor from Mahmoud's hand, then wet his eyebrows and soaped them up. Within a few minutes the bushy gray eyebrows, as much a part of Wyatt as his caustic personality, had been rinsed down the sink.

"You look very beautiful," Mahmoud said, chuckling.

"Shut up."

Mahmoud giggled some more. Then he pulled out a black eyebrow pencil and handed it to Wyatt. "You may need later."

When Wyatt returned to the main room, one of the other men broke into a broad grin. He said something in Arabic to the other two and they all had a good laugh. Wyatt pulled a pair of shades out of his backpack and put them on along with his baseball cap.

"Now can we go?" he asked Mahmoud.

"Of course," said his host, as if they had all just been waiting for Wyatt to ask.

Wyatt watched the men put the AK-47s and ammo in the deep trunk of a black sedan along with a couple of gym bags. He sat in the back on the passenger side while the youngest of the three men joined him in the backseat. As they rode, his hosts engaged in little conversation, none of which Wyatt understood. He spent his time looking out the window, studying the scenery in the United Arab Emirates and thinking about the next few days of his life.

The roads were paved and smooth, and people drove on the right-hand side of the road, though it seemed like his vehicle was going exceptionally fast. The scenery was arid but breathtaking, with red rock formations that resembled the Arizona desert. They passed loose camels on the side of the road; one time a camel crossed not too far in front of the sedan. The driver braked, swerved, and continued on as if it happened all the time.

To keep his sanity, Wyatt nicknamed his three captors. The driver was Moe because he seemed to be the boss and was older than the others. His sidekick in the front seat was Larry—a wiry man, taller than Moe and all business. Curly, in the backseat, was probably in his twenties—the apprentice who carried the bags. He laughed hard at Moe's jokes and seemed like he was trying to impress. He was restless and full of energy, shifting in his seat, trying to get comfortable. His beard was straggly and spotty, his skin pockmarked. His eyes seemed wary but not as hard as the others', more open to mirth and sympathy. If there was a weak link, it would be Curly, and Wyatt made a mental note.

After about an hour, Wyatt pulled out a cigar and held it up to see if it was okay. Curly said something to Moe, and after Moe approved, Curly nodded his head. Using hand motions, Wyatt explained that he needed a lighter, and soon one was handed back from the front seat. Wyatt lit up and instantly started to relax. He offered a cigar to Curly, who smelled it, nodded, and lit up as well. Soon, all four of them were enjoying a nice American Philly.

For Wyatt, it started to feel like home.

The weather was hot and dry and apparently the vehicle had no air-conditioning, because the men rode with the windows down. Wyatt finished his smoke and leaned back in his seat. He was hungry and exhausted from the long trip and from the adrenaline that had coursed through his body. He let the hot, dry desert air blow in his face, and before long he had dozed off to sleep.

He woke when the car came to an abrupt stop. He looked around, gathered his bearings, and discovered that they had pulled over on the shoulder of some deserted road. He wanted to ask a few questions but what was the use? Curly got out of the car and grabbed one of the bags from the trunk. He threw a large black robe and head covering to Wyatt. He motioned with his arms for Wyatt to put it on.

Wyatt stepped out of the car and pulled the black robe over his head. He put the head covering on as well so that only his eyes were exposed and he threw his sunglasses and hat in the backseat. Curly motioned for Wyatt to take his shoes off, and Curly threw them in the trunk. Curly then retrieved Wyatt's eyebrow liner from the backseat and had Wyatt lean over so he could get a new thin set of eyebrows. Larry inspected the work and nodded. Then they all climbed into the sedan and started back to the main road.

About fifteen minutes later, they approached an area that looked like a customs checkpoint, and Wyatt assumed they were heading into Saudi Arabia. The men handed Wyatt a passport as they waited in a long line of cars. When they finally pulled up to the booth, two customs officers approached the car, one on each side. Everybody spoke rapidly and brusquely, and it seemed to Wyatt like they were all talking at once. His eyes shot back and forth from the customs officers to his escorts. The driver handed one of the men some papers that he glanced through. Another customs officer came to the back door and stared at Wyatt for a moment. He said something in Arabic and held out his hand. Wyatt handed him the fake passport and the man looked it over, his eyes shifting from Wyatt to the passport and back again. He stamped it, grunted something, and tossed it back in the car.

Wyatt let out a breath, and within minutes they were on the road again, driving through Saudi Arabia. Wyatt started to take his head covering off and Curly reached over and jerked it back down.

"What are you doing?" Wyatt asked.

Curly grunted something that Wyatt didn't understand.

It was time to test the young man's resolve. Wyatt started taking the head covering off for a second time, and Larry turned around and pointed a pistol at his head. He barked an order that Wyatt didn't need translated. *Leave it on while we're in Saudi Arabia.*

When Larry turned back around, Wyatt glanced over at Curly. The young man had an I-told-you-so look on his face. This was going to be a long ride.

At noon the men stopped on the side of the road, pulled prayer mats out of the trunk, and conducted their midday prayers while Wyatt watched from the backseat. An hour later they stopped at some kind of restaurant but made Wyatt stay in the car. This time Curly stayed with him, a pistol on his lap to keep Wyatt in line.

While Wyatt waited, his concerns mounted about the way he was being treated. He was alone in a foreign country, and nobody in America knew his precise location. These three men were supposed to be on Wyatt's side, taking him to Saleet Zafar, but they were treating him more like a prisoner. Somewhere near the border with Saudi Arabia, things had gone from cordial to hostile.

Wyatt thought about his meeting with Mahmoud at the airport. Why no sign as they had originally planned? Had some other group found out about Wyatt's arrival and kidnapped him? Were they taking him to an al Qaeda or ISIS leader? Why wouldn't they let Mahmoud, the one man who also spoke English, go along on this trip?

When Moe and Larry returned to the car with two plates of food, Wyatt decided it was time to act. He got out of the car and started arguing with them—English and Arabic flying like missiles. Wyatt ripped off his head covering, drawing the attention of a rapidly growing crowd, staring at a tall American with white hair wearing an abaya. Moe and Larry threw their plates down and shoved Wyatt into the vehicle. In the chaos, Larry pistol-whipped Wyatt, stunning him, then climbed into the backseat along with him and held the gun to his temple.

The others jumped in and they sped away, leaving a gawking crowd behind. Larry and Moe were both yelling at Wyatt, who touched the wound on his forehead gingerly as blood trickled down his face. From the front seat, Curly handed Wyatt some type of rag, and Wyatt put pressure on the wound, stanching the flow of blood, eyeing Larry suspiciously as he did so.

They eventually pulled over to the side of the road and forced Wyatt to get out of the vehicle. They handcuffed his bloodstained hands in front of him, using plastic ties that they had apparently brought for just such an occasion. They pulled the *niqab* back over his head, but this time put it on backward, covering his entire face. They tied the bottom of it around his neck. Then they shoved him back into the vehicle and drove off in silence.

It was hot, dark, suffocating, and painfully uncomfortable. And it was how Wyatt would ride for the next several hours as the foursome made their way across the barren landscape of Saudi Arabia to its border with the sovereign nation of Yemen.

78

Paige woke early on the biggest day of her professional life. She had slept for maybe a grand total of two hours the night before, tossing and turning, staring at the ceiling, cases churning through her mind. When she finally dozed off, she found herself answering questions in her dreams after arriving late for court and confusing the names of all the justices.

She made coffee using the in-room coffeepot at the Marriott hotel. Before Wyatt left, he had given them his firm credit card to pay for three separate rooms. On her budget alone, Paige would have shared with Kristen. She reviewed some cases and avoided looking at her phone. The morning's headlines would only make her more nervous.

She got ready quickly, going light on the makeup, pulling her hair back, and putting on some low heels and a gray suit that doubled as courtroom armor. She checked herself out in the mirror and pronounced it good, or at least good enough, given the red eyes. Paige wasn't hungry but she had agreed to meet Kristen and Wellington for breakfast. Maybe some time spent with the others would calm her nerves.

Before she headed out the door, she reached into the zipper compartment of her luggage and pulled out a small box. She carefully removed the diamond ring and strung it on the small gold necklace she was wearing. It hung just below her collarbone, and she tucked it inside her blouse.

Today, she felt worthy of wearing it. And like Patrick, she prayed for courage.

When she arrived downstairs, Wellington and Kristen were already there. Wellington's face was more pale than normal, as if he'd been visited by the ghosts of the justices the prior night.

"Have you seen this?" he asked, handing his phone to Paige. The headline from the *New York Tribune* was like a gut punch: "Anderson Family Lawyers Are Targets of Grand Jury."

The story was written, of course, by Harry Coburn. It talked about how Kristen's lawyers had destroyed or bleached their computers in the middle of an FBI investigation into whether they had illegally obtained classified information. According to confidential sources, the lawyers had used top-secret information, unlawfully obtained, to advance the *Anderson* case, and the lawyers stood to make one-third of any recovery. The person who provided the classified information was unknown. But Wyatt, Paige, and Wellington had been called before a Norfolk grand jury on Tuesday, and it was presumed that indictments would soon be handed down. Even so, U.S. Attorney Mitchell Taylor had refused to comment. The article ended by saying that the sentencing guidelines for the misuse of classified information would range from five to six years with the possibility of an additional year for each obstruction count.

Paige instantly lost what little appetite she had. "Great" was all she could muster as she handed the phone back to Wellington.

A perky waitress showed up and asked Paige if she wanted coffee.

She hadn't intended to drink another cup because she didn't want to be too jittery. But now she turned her cup right-side up. "Please."

As they discussed this latest blow, it was Kristen who asked the pertinent question: "What would Wyatt do if he were here?" They all agreed that he would storm into court that morning as bombastic as ever. The government was so desperate to hide its illegal conduct that it was now trying to shut down the case with a grand jury indictment. Not only that, but it proved that the *Anderson* legal team had not leaked the Marcano deposition to reporter Harry Coburn—he was obviously no friend of theirs. It was logical to assume that whoever was feeding Coburn information had both given him Marcano's deposition and told him about the grand jury.

It all sounded good in theory, but Paige knew the reporters could twist the story any way they wanted. And the plain truth of the matter was that Wyatt wasn't here; she would be the one getting swarmed on the courthouse steps that morning. She would be the one facing the Supreme Court justices with this damning information floating around in the atmosphere, serving as the subtext to every question. Paige knew that by the time "May it please the Court" had crossed her lips, every person in that courtroom, including every single justice, would know that the lawyer about to argue for Kristen Anderson was being investigated for obstruction of justice.

But what could she do? It was too late to switch lawyers now. And Kristen had no desire to do so.

"This is the reason I wanted you to argue today," Kristen said to Paige. "No offense, Wellington, but those justices might have believed that Wyatt was playing games and obstructing justice. They will never think that about Paige."

Paige appreciated the vote of confidence. But she wasn't so sure.

They were only a few blocks from the Supreme Court, so the three of them decided to walk. Paige and Wellington each carried fat briefcases full of black notebooks, and Paige's briefcase also held the one thin manila folder that contained the outline of her argument and several pages of references to the record. She knew that she would never get a chance to deliver a scripted argument; there would be too many questions coming at her too fast. But being from the obsessive side of the tracks, she had decided to type one out anyway.

Their case was scheduled to be heard first and would be followed by an antitrust case and two criminal procedure cases. On the way to court they speculated about the size of the lines outside the building and how much interest their case might engender. "It's not an abortion case," Paige said. "I don't think it's going to generate that kind of chaos."

"It was the top story for every newspaper in the lobby," Wellington said, unhelpfully. Paige didn't need any more pressure right now. "Except for the *New York Tribune*, of course," he added, as if Paige could somehow forget.

"This case will determine the balance of power between the courts and the president in foreign affairs," Wellington continued. "Is there any check on the president's power? I mean, if we win this case, Hamilton could be impeached."

"Can we change the subject?" Paige asked.

A few minutes later, they turned the corner and crossed the street with the light. Wellington was right. Maybe it wasn't an abortion case, but you couldn't tell that by the crowd.

Paige now had an unobstructed view of just how much interest the case had stirred up. On the sidewalk in front of the Supreme Court building with its grandiose steps, massive plaza, and giant marble pillars emphasizing the grandeur of the law, there were two long lines spreading out in opposite directions. The line on the left at the bottom of the steps was for lawyers admitted to the bar; it snaked along the sidewalk for more than a hundred yards. But it was dwarfed by the line on the opposite side, which was for the few hundred ordinary folks who might be lucky enough to grab a seat for the entire argument and for the several hundred more who would rotate through for three minutes each. That line stretched around the entire block, and it looked to Paige like the people at the front had been camping out all night.

In addition, there were cameras and satellite trucks, protesters with signs, and hordes of reporters that all made Paige's throat feel a little tighter and her heart beat a little faster.

She and Wellington had scoped the place out the day before, and they knew the door they were supposed to enter was at the top of the plaza on the right-hand side of the building. There was no way to get there without plowing through the mob.

The three of them stayed on the opposite side of the street until they were even with the entrance. They waited for a break in traffic and got ready to jaywalk into the madness that would consume them in just a few minutes.

"Let's go," Paige said.

"Hooyah," Kristen responded.

Paige kept her chin up as she crossed the street and the media converged on her. Cameras whirred and questions flew. Most of them dealt with the grand jury investigation. She saw a few signs from protesters bouncing around behind the reporters—*Why did you make the soldiers die?*

Paige, Wellington, and Kristen kept moving up the steps, ignoring the reporters. Paige veered across the plaza to the right, staring straight ahead, her jaw set. Wellington was half a step behind, but Kristen was right there by her side and at one point started yelling at the reporters to get out of the way.

It was an adrenaline-laced moment, one that most lawyers dreamed about, but Paige would have preferred to be almost anywhere else. She fought her way to the top of the second set of steps and then stopped, realizing that she wasn't sure exactly where the door she was supposed to enter was located. It had all seemed different the day before.

Kristen grabbed her elbow. "It's right over there," she said.

Paige couldn't help but smile. They started moving again, and the reporters grudgingly gave way. "You don't think I look like a rookie, do you?" she murmured to Kristen.

"Maybe a little," Kristen admitted. "But at least you're a pretty one."

79

It seemed to Wyatt like he had been riding for an eternity in the backseat, hands cuffed, the hood covering his eyes, seeing nothing. He could tell that it had been dark for several hours. The others rode in silence. The roads had become rough, and the vehicle bounced around at a slower speed.

They had stopped only for prayers and twice to go to the bathroom—both times on the side of a deserted road.

He dozed in and out of sleep as the night wore on. He heard only a few cars passing in the night. The desert air became cool, and his guards rolled up the windows. The car smelled like stale sweat.

Wyatt was half-asleep and half-awake when the vehicle slowed, pulled off the road, and stopped. Larry untied the *niqab* and yanked it off Wyatt's head.

Curly got out of the front seat and opened the back door. Larry motioned with his gun for Wyatt to step outside. Slowly, Wyatt obliged.

The old lawyer had been waiting for a break like this. In the last several hours, he'd had plenty of time to think, and he had come to a few conclusions. If these men were al Qaeda or ISIS, they probably planned to behead Wyatt and post a video of it on the Internet. It would be better if he died trying to escape. But if these men were operating under orders from Saleet Zafar to keep Wyatt safe, they wouldn't rough him up too much if Wyatt made a run for it. Either way, he had everything to gain by trying to get away and not much to lose. At least he would know if they were going to kill him.

He glanced over his shoulder as Larry opened his door and started to get out the other side. He seemed to be the only one of the three with a gun. Wyatt's only chance would be to take him out first and grab the gun, but that would be nearly impossible to do with his hands cuffed.

They pushed Wyatt toward the back of the car and opened the trunk. Larry shoved a few of the AK-47s off to the side, pulled out all of the ammunition and a few of the canvas bags, and motioned for Wyatt to climb in.

Wyatt scowled at him and told him where to go. Curly had pulled out Wyatt's passport and motioned to the road ahead of them, apparently saying that they were approaching another border check. Regardless, Wyatt wasn't about to voluntarily climb in that trunk.

He furrowed his brow as if he didn't understand, and Curly started explaining again. Wyatt took a step toward him and looked at the passport in the dim light coming from the trunk. Then, without warning, he whirled and lunged at Larry, landing a vicious head butt just above Larry's eye. He swung back around with a kick to take out Curly, the way it was done in the movies, but Curly grabbed his foot and pushed him off-balance. He fell halfway into the trunk and saw Larry coming at him, blood streaking down his face. The injured man grabbed Wyatt by the front of his robe and pulled him straight up.

Wyatt was helpless, his hands cuffed in front of him. Larry cursed and spit and then punched Wyatt in the gut, doubling him over as the wind went out of him. It felt like every rib had been shattered. The two men then shoved Wyatt into the trunk as he gasped for air, sharp pain shooting through his side with every breath.

Larry reached down and pulled a needle and syringe out of one of the backpacks he had put on the ground. He came at Wyatt, and Wyatt started kicking and bucking, his eyes wide with horror. But Moe had joined the others, and there were arms and elbows pinning Wyatt down while one of the men pulled up Wyatt's robe and jammed a needle into his thigh.

They slammed the trunk shut and Wyatt moaned in pain as the darkness engulfed him. He wiggled around and pushed the AK-47s aside, trying to get more room. The vehicle took off and the road jostled Wyatt, pain piercing his side with every bump, while the trunk seemed to shrink in on him. For a few minutes, he thought he would pass out from the pain. But soon enough, the drug did its work, and he drifted off into a deep, hard sleep.

★ ★ ★

WASHINGTON, D.C.

Once inside the Supreme Court building, Paige, Wellington, and Kristen wandered the halls, looking at the marble statues, reading plaques about the Court's rich history, and killing time until they had to report to the lawyers' lounge. Maybe it should have intimidated her to be walking the same halls that Thurgood Marshall had walked before his argument in *Brown v. Board of Education*, or Leon Jaworski had walked in his battle to subpoena Richard Nixon's tapes. This was the stage where history was made, and in a few minutes Paige would be staring down nine justices who would decide a case that would probably appear in every constitutional law book studied by students for an entire generation.

But for some reason, she felt equal to the task. Yes, she was worried sick about what the justices might say or think about the grand jury proceedings. Yet she was still confident in her argument. She had used her time to prepare well, and she believed in the rightness of her cause.

And a few times, as she studied the pictures and read the plaques memorializing the great decisions that had been made here, she closed her eyes and saw the waves washing up on the beach, smoothing over the words she had written in the sand. There were larger forces at play here. Her job was to do her part and do it well.

At nine thirty, her team of three entered the lawyers' lounge, where they joined the other lawyers whose cases were being heard. SEAL Team Nine was outnumbered by at least a dozen lawyers milling around for the defense, including Dylan Pierce and Kyle Gates. Philip Kilpatrick and John Marcano were there as well, huddled with their lawyers, talking softly, smiling, and occasionally stealing a glance at Paige, Kristen, and Wellington.

Paige found a seat on the ornate furniture and pulled out the folder she would be taking to the podium in just under an hour. She glanced through her argument and the case cites as well as the excerpts from the record. Out of the corner of her eye, she watched a relaxed Dylan Pierce chatting with his team. Everything about his demeanor was designed to send the message that this wasn't his first rodeo.

After ten painful minutes, the clerk of the Court came in and gave all the lawyers a final briefing.

"The Court does not allow computers, cell phones, cameras, or other electronic devices in the courtroom. You may leave them here. The chief justice likes to keep things moving quickly. Do not wait to be prompted to take your place at the lectern. When your case is finished, please clear your table quickly so the next set of lawyers can get started. The chief will recognize you by name, and once he has done so, begin by saying, 'Mr. Chief Justice, and may it please the Court.' Do not introduce yourself or your cocounsel. Refer to the justices as Justice Sikes or Justice Augustini or Your Honor. Do not use the title *judge*. If you are in doubt about the name of a justice, it is better to use Your Honor than to make a mistake in the justice's name.

"With five minutes left in your argument, a white light will come on at the lectern. Five minutes later, when the red light comes on, you are finished. If you are in the middle of an answer, ask the chief for leave to finish your answer and then sit down.

"There are quill pens at each counsel table, and they are gifts for the lawyer making the argument—a souvenir from your time before the Court. Take them with you. They are handcrafted and usable as writing quills."

The man spoke like a tour guide rattling through a lecture he had given hundreds of times before. When he finished, he asked if there were any questions.

It seemed to Paige that everyone in the room looked at her.

"Then in five minutes I'll walk you into the courtroom. Please take your seats right behind counsel table. As soon as your case is called, move up to counsel table and prepare to make your argument."

The butterflies were out in full force now, and it was hard for Paige to get them in formation. She knew that once the argument started, she would be fine. Once she was up there, she wouldn't focus on the occasion, only the case. But that didn't help her now.

As they lined up to walk into the courtroom, the lawyers placed everything they were leaving behind on the side tables. And on top of a pile of documents left by Dylan Pierce, placed prominently on a table that Paige would walk by, was a copy of the *New York Tribune* with the front-page story about the grand jury prominently displayed. Kristen was standing next to Paige and saw it too.

"You're ready," Kristen whispered to Paige.

Paige reached up and touched the ring on her necklace. "I know."

80

YEMEN

Wyatt regained consciousness and blinked. The fuzzy world came into focus around him, taking its time, one pixel after another. He was lying on a striped couch, low to the floor, in a long, rectangular room with a Persian carpet in the middle. Similar sectional couches with the same striped design lined the other walls. There were three large stained-glass windows and a beautiful chandelier with bright lights that made Wyatt squint. His head throbbed, and he touched his forehead where he had been struck with the butt of a pistol. They had bandaged the wound and wrapped a linen cloth around his head.

It dawned on him that his hands were no longer cuffed. Slowly he sat up and focused on the other man in the room, sitting on the couch on the opposite wall no more than fifteen feet away with a pile of books next to him. He wore a white robe and a white headdress. He had a broad forehead, a thin and wiry beard, serious eyes, and small oval glasses. He smiled, and there was a slight gap between his front teeth. Wyatt recognized him immediately.

"Welcome to Yemen," said Saleet Zafar.

Wyatt glanced around. The three stooges were nowhere to be seen. He rubbed his eyebrows to check that everything had not just been a nightmare, but he could feel no hair and wondered if the pencil-thin eyebrows of a woman were still visible.

"I trust you slept well," Zafar said, cracking another smile.

Wyatt's ribs still ached, though he could breathe better now. "Like a baby."

It was light outside, and Wyatt could see a city of mud and clay built into the side of a mountain. He tried to cement the image in his mind, little details that might provide a clue to where he had been brought. "Your men were a little rough," he said, rubbing his eyes.

"They are not my men. But I knew they would get you here."

Zafar spoke good English, with the kind of pure diction that marked somebody who had developed English as a second language in the classroom rather than living in the country.

"I understand that you were a friend of Cameron Holloman," Wyatt said. "I'm a friend of his wife and have come to see if you would help us in our case against the director of the CIA."

"We will talk in time," Zafar said. "But first, you must be very hungry."

Wyatt hadn't come this far for a social visit, and he had no real desire to get to know the radical imam across from him. But he also knew the *Anderson* case hinged on two things: what was happening in the Supreme Court and what would happen in the next few hours with Saleet Zafar. Wyatt had come too far and suffered too much to lose an opportunity because he was trying to rush things.

Zafar shouted some instructions in Arabic, and before long, two women with everything covered except their eyes and hands were scurrying around and bringing in lunch. They spread a mat on the floor in the middle of the room and then, while Zafar and Wyatt talked, brought in the meal. They started with unleavened flatbread in a black iron skillet, the smell of which made Wyatt remember how hungry he actually was. They brought a glass of something that looked like the weakest coffee Wyatt had ever seen.

"It is *shahi haleeb*," Zafar said. When Wyatt gave him a quizzical expression, the imam simply said, "Milk tea."

Wyatt took a sip—it was flavored with mint—and surprisingly, he liked it. Meanwhile, the food kept coming. The women brought potatoes, eggs, and lentils. The main dish was what Zafar called *mandi*, lamb meat topping a plate of rice. The whole thing looked like a feast fit for a Persian king.

Zafar and Wyatt sat on the floor and ate together, taking their time, while Wyatt asked questions about the culture in Yemen and the country's civil war. Taking a deep breath still hurt, and the dull headache wasn't going away, but he made himself focus on the conversation.

After the men had finished eating, the women cleared the meal and brought in a small bowl of a leafy substance. Wyatt had read about this before his trip. The entire male population of Yemen would apparently eat a big lunch and then start chewing qat, a mild stimulant that created a feeling of euphoria, at about two o'clock. The men would continue chewing until about six or so at night, when they would finally spit it out. It was, Wyatt thought, an unusual phenomenon—the whole country with a mild buzz for most of the working day. Right now he could use something like that.

He took a few leaves and stems, placed them in his mouth, and chewed the leaves slowly, squeezing out the juice. He was careful about how much he took because he would need to be on his game the next few hours. After about ten minutes of talking while chewing the qat, he spit it back onto a plate. Zafar chuckled and shoved a few more leaves into his own mouth.

"Americans never appreciate the finer things in life," he said.

"Tell your goons to go get my cigars out of the car and we'll experience one of the finer things."

"Phillies cigars?" Saleet asked skeptically. "Not exactly Cuba's finest."

How did this guy know about American brands?

"Have you ever had one?"

"I don't smoke."

But you chew on an amphetamine all day, Wyatt wanted to say.

"I had a letter from Gazala Holloman," Wyatt said instead. "But your men wouldn't let me bring it with me."

Saleet reached over to his pile of books and, to Wyatt's surprise, pulled out the letter. "I read it. They brought it along. And remember— they are not my men."

"I need your help," Wyatt said. "Gazala wants you to help. Together we can expose what really led to the deaths of Cameron Holloman and several American servicemen."

"I may need your help as well," Saleet replied.

The comment surprised Wyatt, though he didn't show it. And he realized immediately that he should have known something like this was coming. Everybody always had an angle. "In what way?"

"You may know that your government is trying to kill me. It seems that any imam who preaches the whole truth of the Quran ends up on an enemies list and can be executed without a trial at the mere word of your president. I want to hire you, Mr. Jackson, as my attorney. I will give you everything you need to prosecute the case against Director Marcano and Mr. Kilpatrick. But in exchange, I want you to advocate my cause in the American media. I need you to help your country see what is happening."

Zafar reached over his pile of books and pulled out pictures of two young boys. He placed them on the floor, facing Wyatt.

"These are my sons. They have also been targeted by American drone strikes. I have studied your history as an attorney, Mr. Jackson. I know that you are always loyal to your clients." Saleet paused, searching for the right words as he continued. "I am not an enemy combatant of your country. I command no troops. I plot no strategy. I plant no bombs. I preach that there is no god but Allah and that Mohammed is his Prophet. I preach about the glory of the martyrs. I preach that we are in a spiritual war. These are ideas that are not so different from the ideas spread by your American pastors. When did your country start executing religious leaders for preaching their conscience?"

Wyatt could think of a thousand rejoinders. American pastors didn't instigate suicide bombings and terrorist attacks. Maybe American pastors spoke of spiritual warfare, but they didn't advocate the subjugation of all Muslims by force. But now was not the time for debate. Wyatt was a lawyer, and he needed to cut a deal.

"Tell me what you know about the death of Cameron Holloman," Wyatt said. "In our system of justice, we call it a proffer. You would need to be willing to testify about it from an undisclosed location on video. But if you tell me the substance of what your testimony might be, I'll tell you whether I can take your case. And believe me, Mr. Zafar, if I take your case, I'll advocate for you to the best of my ability."

"You say I must tell you first. But then you will have the information already," Saleet said. He studied Wyatt for a moment, his jaw working the qat, and then his lips formed into a small, sly smile. "This issue of trust is a difficult thing to establish, no?"

"Indeed it is," Wyatt said. "But there is a question in my country: Is the enemy of my enemy my friend? We both want to expose the events that caused the death of Cameron Holloman. Our common enemies are the director of the CIA and the president of the United States. Does that not make us friends?"

Saleet smiled broadly at the suggestion, exposing a mouthful of qat. "Here in the Middle East, Mr. Jackson, we have been asking that question for thousands of years."

81

Paige entered the packed courtroom at 9:45, trailing behind the clerk and Dylan Pierce's team. The folding chairs that were jammed in the well of the courtroom behind counsel tables were filled with members of the Supreme Court bar who had waited in line for hours to hear this case. It seemed that they were all staring at her.

Immediately behind them, on rows of hard wooden benches, sat the spectators who were lucky enough to get a seat. The ones in the front row were likely those who had camped out all night.

But to Paige's surprise, when she entered the courtroom, the entire first two rows of the spectator section rose as one and stood at attention. She recognized many of the faces as members of the Virginia Beach–based SEAL teams. They had shown up today, she knew, to show their support and loyalty. The SEAL family coming through again.

Before she sat down in the front row, Paige glanced over her shoulder and nodded at them. They all sat down at once, as if she had saluted them, and it made her heart swell with pride.

"That was pretty cool," Wellington whispered.

Minutes later, the clerk called the Court to order and the justices came out from behind a huge scarlet curtain, taking their respective seats on the bench. Paige was struck by how intimate the setting felt. In most appellate courtrooms, the podium was a good distance from the justices, conveying a feeling of respectful separation. But here, in the nation's highest court, the lawyers and justices were just a few feet away from each other. Other lawyers had said that they could hear the Court's oldest member, Justice Kathryn Byrd, wheezing from the bench. You didn't have to raise your voice to be heard—this argument would be a conversation, not a courtroom lecture.

Paige studied the looks on the justices' faces, but they gave nothing away. Before she knew it, Pierce was at the podium and the questions had started flying. He handled them with great aplomb, the perfect mix of formal respect and confident advocacy. He emphasized the separation of powers in the Constitution and how the Court had always honored the role of the executive branch in matters of foreign policy. Our country was at war, he said, and we could not jeopardize the lives of those serving abroad by spilling state secrets every time a plaintiff wanted money in a lawsuit. That was why, from the days of the *Totten* case in 1875, this Court had dismissed such claims instead of forcing the executive branch to divulge its state secrets.

As expected, Pierce's argument did not sit well with the more liberal members of the bench. Justice Augustini, who was one of the newer members of the Court and therefore sat in the second-to-last seat on the right, led the charge. As a novelist, she had a knack for imagining hypotheticals that showed the danger of Pierce's logic. Sitting on the opposite end of the bench was David Sikes. Every time Augustini made a point, he would lob a softball question to make a counterpoint.

Justice William Martin Jacobs III, a bulky man sitting close to the chief, actually scoffed at one of Pierce's answers. "Seems to me that you're saying the courts just have to take the words of politicians at face value and can't even test whether state secrets are actually at issue," he said, peering over reading glasses. "Just like the old days in the South when the politicians claimed that segregated schools weren't the result of racist motives and we should stay out of the busing business. We should just take their word for it."

"That's not what I'm saying," Pierce replied calmly. "This Court has a constitutional duty to ensure that the citizens of our country are treated equally, and segregation did not pass that test. But it also has a duty to ensure that the executive branch has the latitude it needs to protect our citizens from terrorists without being harassed by plaintiff's lawyers and tort lawsuits."

It was obvious to Paige that the Court's three conservatives—Sikes, Barton Cooper, and Kathryn Byrd—were all firmly on the side of Kilpatrick and Marcano. The chief was hard to read, but he seemed concerned about the prospect that Judge Solberg's procedure might result in the inadvertent disclosure of state secrets. "Once that genie is out of the bottle, you can't put her back in," he said. Paige knew she couldn't count on him.

That left the four liberal justices for Paige's side—Murphy, Torres, Augustini, and Jacobs. But she would also have to win the vote of the Court's newest justice, Taj Deegan, sitting all the way to the right, who had not yet asked a single question.

What is she thinking? Paige wondered.

Deegan gave a clue just before Pierce's white light came on. "Isn't your appeal premature?" she asked. "Judge Solberg was only trying to figure out whether there are state secrets that would require dismissal of the lawsuit. She hadn't definitively ruled that it can go forward. Isn't it a little extreme to say that a judge can't even hold closed-door depositions to test the government's claims about state secrets?"

Pierce jumped on the question as if he had been waiting for it all morning. "What you've seen happen in this case is exactly the problem with such a procedure," he claimed. "A deposition that was supposed to be sealed from the public has been leaked to the press, and the state secrets that Director Marcano testified about under a promise of confidentiality have been spread across the front page of the *New York Tribune*. We can't risk the country's safety the way Judge Solberg did."

With perfect timing the white light came on. "I would like to save my remaining time for rebuttal," Pierce said. The chief nodded, and the lawyer took his seat.

Paige stood quickly, gathered her folder, and took her spot. She paused for just a second, taking it all in. Paige Chambers, representing the warriors of SEAL Team Six, at the Supreme Court of the United States.

"Good morning, Ms. Chambers," Chief Justice Leonard said.

"Mr. Chief Justice, and may it please the Court . . ."

82

YEMEN

When Saleet Zafar got rolling, Wyatt could see why he was such a powerful imam. The man could tell a story. He was all hand gestures and facial expressions and voice inflections. Smiling one moment, scowling the next. Leaning in to make sure Wyatt followed everything he was saying. He could have been a good lawyer, Wyatt thought.

Saleet was cerebral, and he peppered his story with words and descriptions that displayed a keen intellect. It was his intellectual curiosity, he said, that had first drawn him to Cameron Holloman. Cameron was not a Muslim, but he was sympathetic to the cause and distraught at the devastation Saudi Arabia and the United States were leveling against civilians in Yemen. Indiscriminate aerial strikes, Saleet called them. He began corresponding with Cameron and talked with him via Skype.

"My goal was to convert him to Islam," Saleet said. "It was a goal I shared with Gazala."

He and Cameron met during the reporter's trip to Yemen. Cameron wanted to meet with some Houthi leaders to better understand their side of things.

"So I arranged that meeting," Saleet continued. "Cameron asked questions for hours and took notes. I think he uploaded that information to the cloud, where he stored his research. He may also have sent text messages and e-mails, which I now believe were being monitored by your government. Eight days after we left the compound where he met with the Houthi leaders, a drone strike killed all three of them, as well as two women and one six-year-old child."

He paused for a moment and weighed his words. "After that strike, Cameron was arrested by the Houthis on suspicion that he worked with the CIA. A few weeks later I was contacted by an intermediary working on behalf of the United States to see if I could negotiate Cameron's release."

This was news to Wyatt, though he was now to the point where virtually nothing surprised him. "Who approached you?" he asked.

"Another imam who had connections with the U.S. ambassador in Saudi Arabia," Saleet said. He chewed his qat. "Do you know the story of Raymond Davis?"

Wyatt racked his memory. "Never heard of him."

Saleet shook his head. "I would think that you, of all Americans, should be aware of the Raymond Davis story."

Once again Saleet launched into his mesmerizing storytelling mode. Raymond Davis had been a CIA operative in Lahore, Pakistan, during the administration of President Obama. One day, after he withdrew cash from an ATM, a motorbike pulled up beside him at a stoplight. One of the men on the bike pointed a gun at Davis. They were just common street thieves, but they had chosen the wrong victim. Davis pulled out a Glock and killed them both.

The Pakistani police arrested Davis and accused him of being a CIA operative, though Mr. Obama would never admit it, saying only that he worked for the American State Department. Eventually a solution was reached. Davis was transported from his prison cell to a Sharia court in a remote area of Pakistan, where he faced the families of the victims. Under the Sharia custom of *diyat*, or "blood money," the families forgave Davis after the CIA paid 200 million rupees, or approximately $2.3 million. In this secret court proceeding, family members approached Davis, some of them sobbing, and announced that they forgave him. Davis was released and returned to the United States.

"I tried to negotiate a similar resolution for Cameron Holloman," Saleet said. "I was authorized to offer *diyat* of up to $10 million. But the relatives of the victims were not willing to have their forgiveness purchased. And so your country sent in a strike force to free my friend. Even after the deaths of the American soldiers, I pleaded with the Houthi leaders to release Cameron. But they would not listen and threatened me as well. I never saw Cameron alive again."

It was this part, Wyatt could tell, that bothered Saleet most of all. Not just the fact that Cameron had died but that he had died as an infidel and would thus, according to Muslim theology, spend eternity suffering in hell. From the look on his face, Saleet held himself personally responsible.

"How did the Houthis know the American Special Forces were coming?" Wyatt asked. "Did you know?"

Saleet gave Wyatt a sad smile. "If you're asking whether I told the Houthi leaders that the Americans were on the way, the answer is no. I myself did not know. And I wanted to see Cameron released more than anyone."

"Then how did they find out?"

Saleet let the question hang in the air for a moment. He was undoubtedly smart enough to understand that this was the real issue in the case. Wyatt could never win unless he could show that the administration *knew* the raid was doomed from the start.

Studying the imam's expression, Wyatt could sense that he was close to the truth. His heart started beating faster, and he had to will himself to stay calm. This man knew! Wyatt could make his case right here, with witnesses from Yemen, and the state secrets defense could not stop him. "You know, don't you?" he persisted.

"Yes. I know. And I will take you to the person who can provide the evidence you need."

Saleet chewed his qat a little before he continued. "You asked in your letter to talk to the relatives of victims who were killed in the drone strike that led to the sheep sacrifice by Admiral Towers. Do you remember that?"

"Of course."

"You will get your wish. But first, there is a condition."

There were always conditions. And now, so tantalizingly close to the truth, Wyatt was ready to agree to anything. "Which is?"

"I have now given you a preview of my story. A—what do you call it?"

"A proffer."

"Indeed, I have given you enough so that you can decide. I need to know that in exchange for meeting this man who will make your case, you will act as my attorney upon your return. I need to know that you will do everything within your power to remove my name from the president's list."

Wyatt looked Saleet in the eye, reached out his hand, and shook on the matter.

"What is your retainer?" Saleet asked.

"How about a new set of bodyguards to escort me back to the Dubai airport when we're finished?"

"I'll tell the men to be more gentle," Saleet promised. "They are only doing this because I told them that together we might be able to destroy President Hamilton. To be honest, Mr. Jackson, they have no love for Americans."

"I've noticed," said Wyatt.

83

"This case presents a simple question: Can the president conspire for political purposes with her chief of staff and the CIA director to send our forces on a rescue mission knowing full well that they will die?"

Paige asked the question forcefully and paused for a breath. She had been warned that this would be an active bench and she should try to summarize her argument in the first minute or so before they started peppering her with questions. She never got that chance.

"If that's the issue, how can you possibly prove your case without knowing what the president knew?" The question came from Justice Sikes, who was leaning forward and had drowned out a question by his older colleague, Justice Cooper from Texas. "And that would implicate all kinds of state secrets, would it not?"

"No, Justice Sikes, it wouldn't. State secrets are limited to military or espionage secrets that, if divulged, would endanger the security of our country. The mission in question is now history. Divulging what the president knew going into the mission—as long as names of CIA operatives and specific engagement strategies are kept secret—would not endanger our country or help our enemies."

The words were barely out of her mouth before the Beard asked his question again. This time he wasn't going to let anyone speak over him. "It's naive to think that you don't have to get into the details to prove your case, Counsel. You'll put on witnesses to say the president knew the plan was doomed. The defendants will say that's not true. And the only way for the jury to figure who's right is for them to know the precise intelligence information the president had and to know who provided that information so they can weigh the credibility of the sources. All of that information qualifies as state secrets."

To Paige, that sounded more like an argument than a question. But she kept her composure, responding as if she and the Beard were best friends.

"That may be the case, Justice Cooper, or it may not be. The point is that we'll never know unless this case is allowed to proceed. Judge Solberg was doing a good job of letting us take depositions without divulging state secrets or classified information. Once those depositions are completed, we may find there is no dispute about what the president knew and we don't need to test the sources. Or we may be able to prove our case without government witnesses, thus negating the state secrets defense. We should at least be allowed to take enough discovery to find out."

"And as soon as those depositions are taken, they get leaked to the press," Justice Sikes interjected.

"Which we didn't do," Paige shot back. It was a cheap shot from the justice, and Sikes was starting to get under her skin.

"I guess that remains to be seen," Sikes said, intent on having the last word.

Two justices chimed in at once and Justice Deegan, as the junior member of the Court, deferred. Justice Torres, the former senator from

California who had served on the Senate Foreign Relations Committee, was a critical vote if Paige had any hope of winning the case.

"Doesn't the result you want go directly contrary to our *Reynolds* decision?" she asked.

Reynolds was a 1953 case in which widows of civilians aboard an Air Force plane tried to get information about what made it crash. The Air Force claimed military secrets, and the case was not allowed to proceed.

"We think the procedure employed by Judge Solberg is consistent with *Reynolds*," Paige explained. She and Wellington had carefully crafted this answer. They knew the Supreme Court didn't like to overturn its own cases, especially ones more than fifty years old.

"In *Reynolds*, this Court said that it should treat state secrets like it treats a defendant's assertion of the Fifth Amendment privilege in a civil proceeding. You don't have to accept the privilege at face value; you can inquire into the circumstances and decide whether answering the question might tend to incriminate that person. That's what Judge Solberg was doing here—inquiring into the circumstances."

"But the trial court in *Reynolds* did not allow depositions like Judge Solberg did," Torres responded.

Before Paige could answer, Chief Justice Leonard chimed in. It felt like questions were coming from every direction. "In *Reynolds*, the Court assumed from the circumstances that there was a reasonable danger the evidence would expose military matters of national security. Can't we assume the same thing here?" he asked.

"I don't think the Court should assume any such thing, because we already have the deposition of Director Marcano," Paige said quickly, anxious to answer before another question popped up. "And Judge Solberg did a good job conducting that deposition so that we were able to get the information we needed without exposing state secrets. I think it's obvious she can do the same with other depositions because Director Marcano's was the trickiest one."

"If I believe the reports from the *New York Tribune*," Justice Sikes said caustically, making Paige pivot to the left to face him, "you've already received classified information that you've used in this case. And there is supposedly a grand jury looking into the matter. Are those reports true?"

The question stunned Paige. She knew that the specter of the grand jury proceedings would hang over her argument, but she didn't expect to field a pointed question about it. She had taken the Fifth in the grand jury, but she certainly couldn't do that now.

"It would be inappropriate for me to comment on that article, which, by the way, was written by the same reporter who leaked the Marcano deposition," Paige said. She could feel her face turning red. "But I can assure you that we did nothing wrong."

"Aren't grand jury proceedings secret, anyway?" Justice Deegan asked from the far right end of the bench. Her question seemed to be directed at Sikes. "As a former prosecutor and trial court judge, I certainly agree that it would be inappropriate for counsel to comment on grand jury proceedings, no matter how badly you would like to do so." Deegan shot a quick glance at Sikes, and he scowled back.

The exchange emboldened Paige, not just because she had an ally on the bench but also because Deegan was likely the swing vote.

"Precisely," Paige said. "The *Tribune* article seemed insidiously timed to cast doubt over today's argument. If anything, Justice Sikes, that article makes it clear that the source of information for the reporter who leaked the Marcano deposition was not anyone on the plaintiff's team."

It was a high point of her argument, one she would take pride in later. A chance to put the loquacious Sikes in his place was rare for even experienced Supreme Court practitioners, much less someone as inexperienced as Paige.

Her low point came about five minutes later, when Justice Augustini asked a question and for some reason Paige slipped and addressed her as Justice Torres. This brought an awkward smile from the justices and an immediate apology from Paige. But Augustini deflected it graciously: "I've been called a lot worse." Her comment broke the tension in the courtroom and brought a laugh from the gallery far out of proportion to the humor of the statement.

Paige's time flew by, and ultimately her preparation paid off. She probably hadn't changed any minds during her time at the podium, but she had held her own. With the exception of the slipup in names, she had acted like someone who had been there before. The SEAL team members in the front two rows of the gallery would be proud.

When the white light came on, Paige fielded two more questions and then launched into her final arguments. "Justice Torres mentioned the *Reynolds* case earlier. But when *Reynolds* was decided, the CIA did not have drones and Special Forces teams killing thousands of enemy combatants. Our military is accountable not just to the president but also to Congress, who alone has the power to declare war. But the CIA and all of its firepower are under the direct control of the president and no one else."

They were letting her go, and Paige took full advantage of it. "The office of president has more power today than it has ever had in the history of the republic. But one thing has not changed since *Reynolds*; indeed, one thing has not changed since the founding of our nation. There are checks and balances in the Constitution. And the job of this Court is to ensure that everyone in our country complies with the law— from the president to the poorest beggar on the streets of the capital. Equal justice under law—isn't that what it says on this very building?"

Paige paused and caught her breath. She knew the red light would soon stop her midsentence, and she wanted to finish strong. She and Wellington had spent hours wordsmithing her final plea. To her surprise, the justices seemed content to hold their questions and let her deliver it. The conservatives leaned back and gave her skeptical looks. The others were clearly engaged.

"As Abraham Lincoln once noted, this nation will never be destroyed by outside forces. He said, 'All the armies of Europe, Asia, and Africa combined could not by force take a drink from the Ohio or make a track on the Blue Ridge.' But Lincoln also warned, 'If danger ever reach us, it must spring up amongst us. If destruction be our lot, we must ourselves be its author and finisher. As a nation of freemen, we must live through all time or die by suicide.'"

Paige took one last glance at the Court, surveying the members from left to right. The red light came on, but she ignored it. "To place the president and her cabinet above the law is suicidal. We urge this Court to reject that approach and affirm Judge Solberg."

84

Wyatt rode blindfolded in the backseat between the two guards he had dubbed Larry and Curly. Moe was driving, and Saleet Zafar rode shotgun. Wyatt's captors had switched vehicles; they were now in an old Land Rover with much more room. Wyatt was not handcuffed, and as far as he knew, nobody was pointing a gun at him. They had started late in the afternoon, and Saleet said they would be arriving at their destination right around dusk.

The ride was bumpy and the seat uncomfortable. The springs and shocks in the SUV had long ago deteriorated, and every jolt reminded Wyatt that his ribs had not yet recovered.

But he wasn't complaining. He had asked to go to the site where the drone missile had killed innocent civilians who were not even aligned with the Houthis, the site where a photo had been taken of Admiral Towers sacrificing a lamb. As they rode, Saleet and Wyatt talked in English, raising their voices to be heard over the wind blowing in the windows.

"In our culture, sacrificing sheep is asking for forgiveness," Saleet explained. He told Wyatt that the parents of the young men and women who were killed by the drone strike had met with Admiral Towers. The admiral told them the strike had been a terrible mistake and that his heart grieved for them. He offered reparations to the families, though he acknowledged that no amount of money could make things right. The fathers said that they would not keep anything in their hearts against the American soldiers, even though they had hated them since the moment of the drone strike. One of the fathers, through a translator, told Admiral Towers that he had planned to be a suicide bomber until the sacrifice was made.

"But unknown to Admiral Towers, there was another father who was not there on that day. His only daughter, annihilated by the drone strike, had been twenty-two years old and pregnant at the time. Her father swore to take his revenge on America, and you will be meeting him in just a few hours."

This was more than even Wyatt had expected. "Is it safe to do that?"

"Safety is a relative thing, my friend," Saleet said. "Allah's will must be done. But this man has the same interest in keeping you alive that the rest of us do. You are the one who will tell our story. You are the one who will expose the American president and her advisers who caused such great heartache. If we harm you, we would destroy any chance of punishing the ones responsible for such atrocities."

Wyatt had instinctively understood this to be the case, but it was still a little troubling to hear it stated so bluntly. "Is this man now working with the Houthis?" Wyatt asked.

"I should let him answer that," Saleet said.

They hit a major pothole, bouncing Wyatt around, and he cursed loudly.

The guards started arguing in Arabic, and for a moment, Saleet joined them. He then switched to English for Wyatt's sake.

"These men guarding us are with the al Islah party, composed primarily of Yemen's Muslim Brotherhood," Saleet explained. "They are sworn enemies of the Houthis and at times work with al Qaeda in the Arabian Peninsula. They are doing this only as a personal favor to me because they know that you are the only hope to keep me alive."

"Are you working with al Qaeda?" Wyatt asked. The tribal alliances in Yemen were confusing, but there was nothing ambiguous about al Qaeda.

"I do not work with anyone, Mr. Jackson. I preach what Allah tells me to preach. Al Qaeda would like me to continue preaching. In that respect only, our interests are aligned. But I have never recruited for al Qaeda or tried to justify their terrorism or suicide bombings."

Over the years, Wyatt had learned not to judge his clients. If they paid the retainer, he was their man. But this one would not be easy. Even he understood that anyone aligned with al Qaeda was an enemy of the United States. He suddenly felt the urge for a smoke. "Ask these guys what they did with my cigars," he said.

Saleet spoke to the men in Arabic. Then, to Wyatt: "They said they kept them as payment. But they are happy to share some of their qat."

"I'll pass."

They rode in silence for a few minutes before Saleet picked up where he left off. "The man you will meet in a few hours swore revenge on the Americans. He found a way to connect with the CIA and began providing valuable information. He played the role of informant for nearly eighteen months, waiting and praying for the right opportunity. When Cameron Holloman and Prince Abdulaziz were captured, he provided the Americans with information on where they were being held and the layout of Sana'a Central Prison. But he also informed the Houthis that the Americans were planning a rescue operation."

It took Wyatt a second to digest this last piece of information. If Saleet was telling the truth, Wyatt was about to meet the double agent who had betrayed the CIA and caused the death of the American SEALs.

"What's his name?" Wyatt asked.

"Mokhtar al-Bakri. The Americans called him Pinocchio."

"Why haven't the Americans killed him?"

At this, Saleet laughed. "For the same reason they have not killed me. They have not yet found him."

"Why is he willing to meet with me?"

"Because he wants the world to know that he has exacted revenge for his daughter."

Wyatt thought about this. "And he knows that I will tell the world as part of my case."

"Precisely," Saleet said.

The whole thing was starting to make sense now. Perhaps the CIA had tapped Holloman's phone or had been illegally monitoring his e-mail. However they did it, they had learned that Holloman had met with the Houthi leaders. When the CIA killed them several days later, other Houthis believed Holloman had been working with the CIA, so they arrested him and sentenced him to death. Then this man nicknamed Pinocchio, who had been building credibility with the Americans, told the CIA where Holloman was being held and then double-crossed the Americans by telling the Houthis that the Special Forces were on their way.

But it still left one huge question. "Did the CIA or Director Marcano know that Pinocchio was going to betray the mission? Because if they didn't, our entire case falls apart."

"I realize that, Mr. Jackson," Saleet said. "And I would like for you to hear that straight from the lips of al-Bakri himself. I will translate for you, and if he has no objection, I will videotape what he says on my phone."

For once, Wyatt was out of questions that his host could answer. He sat back and tried to relax, getting jostled about by the guards on both sides. If al-Bakri provided the testimony that Saleet believed he would, Wyatt would have to find a way to preserve it and get it in front of Judge Solberg.

But even though he had personally filed the lawsuit and traveled halfway around the world to locate witnesses, Wyatt still found the whole thing hard to believe. Did Marcano and the president really know that al-Bakri was going to betray the American mission? And were they so coldhearted that they would order the men to go forward anyway, knowing that they were sending them to their death?

In a few hours, Wyatt would have his answer.

★　★　★

After the morning session, Paige left the Supreme Court building and held an impromptu press conference on the plaza out front. With Wellington and Kristen at her side, she expressed confidence that the Court would allow the case to go forward. The families of the men who died for their country deserved their day in court.

After she completed her brief remarks, the first question dealt with the grand jury proceedings. "As Justice Deegan noted, it would be inappropriate for me to comment on that," Paige said. She deflected a few more questions, and then Kristen stepped up to the bank of microphones and told everyone what a great job her lawyer had done. She too expressed confidence in the outcome and said that Troy would be proud. She took a few questions of her own, mostly softballs respectfully lobbed at a gold-star wife, and then the three members of SEAL Team Nine made their way through the mob of reporters, down the steps, across the street, and back to the hotel.

They agreed to change into comfortable clothes and grab some lunch. Paige was suddenly starving because she had eaten so little in the last few days. When she walked into her hotel room, she fell backward on the bed, closed her eyes, and said a prayer of thanks. She felt the tension seep out of her body for the first time in weeks. Sure, she still had to worry about the grand jury and a possible indictment and a thousand other things. But she had acquitted herself well at court today, and she had done everything possible to salvage the case. She thought about Wyatt and wondered how things were going in Yemen.

She couldn't wait to give him a blow-by-blow of the argument, embellishing her answers a little—the same way he would have if he were telling the story.

She still didn't know what had happened on Good Friday and why everything had gone so wrong. But right now, in this moment of post-argument euphoria, she actually felt like they might have a chance to win this case. Justice Torres had asked some troubling questions, but if she stuck with her friends on the liberal side of the Court, and if Taj Deegan joined them, Paige would have a historic five-four decision in her first case at the high court. And if Wyatt could get testimony from Saleet Zafar, they might blow this case wide open.

It was nice to dream, if only for a moment. She allowed herself to bask in the glow of imagined victory and then willed herself to rise from the bed. She removed the diamond ring from her necklace and placed it carefully back into the box. She changed into her jeans and a sweatshirt, then headed out the door to join the others for lunch.

85

The roads started smoothing out, and soon Wyatt could hear the sound of a city. Vehicles passing by, horns blaring aggressively, hawkers in the street. The Land Rover stopped and moved again, zigging and zagging around the traffic.

Finally the vehicle came to rest, and one of the men in the backseat removed Wyatt's blindfold. It took a minute for his eyes to adjust. They were parked outside a light-brown oblong brick building with steel grates protecting the windows. There was a sign shaped like a dove on the roof and lettering on the side of the building in both English and Arabic. *National Bank of Yemen.*

"What city are we in?" Wyatt asked.

"Aden," Saleet said. "I'll be right back."

Saleet hurried into the bank, leaving Wyatt in the vehicle with the three guards. Wyatt knew Aden was a port city, located at the eastern approach to the Red Sea. Mountains towered behind the city, located on a peninsula formed by a dormant volcano, like a miniature replica of the boot of Italy. Wyatt also knew that President Hadi had fled here from the Houthis after they attempted to take over the government. The city was battle-scarred and partly in ruins. The Saudis, backed by American dollars and technology, had concentrated many of their air strikes here, targeting Houthi fighters.

Still, the downtown area was active, with people motoring around in small European cars, riding bicycles, and selling their wares from makeshift kiosks. The architecture Wyatt could see was an odd mix of splendid Arabian palaces built into the hills above the city, a few towering mosques, and thousands of concrete pre-fab apartments that dominated the area nearest the bank. Yemen was the poorest country in the Mideast, and Aden reflected that.

Saleet was gone for about ten minutes and came out carrying a computer. He settled into the front passenger seat and pulled a battery out of the glove compartment. He put the battery in the computer and handed it to Wyatt along with a flash drive.

"This is Cameron Holloman's computer," Saleet said. "I've stored it here in a safe-deposit box. Do not turn on Internet access or wireless capabilities. Just download everything onto this flash drive."

Wyatt turned on the computer and inserted the flash drive.

"What's the password?"

"Mohammed," Saleet said.

Wyatt shot him a surprised look. "That was Cameron's password?"

"I changed it. Something easy to remember."

"How did you end up with this?"

"He told me where it was after his arrest. I was able to see him once during the negotiations."

Wyatt downloaded everything he could—Word documents, Cameron's e-mail folders, photos, videos, Internet search results. Saleet told him to hurry up. They needed to get to the site of the drone strike before dusk or they would be interrupted by evening prayers.

Wyatt finished quickly and handed the computer back to Saleet.

"Give me ten more minutes," Saleet said.

★ ★ ★

Director John Marcano was in the middle of a 10:30 a.m. briefing when he was interrupted by his chief of staff. "A word with you, sir?"

Marcano looked up at the young man, perturbed. "Can it wait?"

"I don't think so, sir."

The man wasn't normally given to panic, so Marcano excused himself and stepped into the hallway.

"There's a secure call from the head of the bureau in Saudi Arabia, sir."

A few minutes later Marcano was in his office and on the phone with one of his top men on the Arabian Peninsula. The computer that had belonged to Cameron Holloman had been removed from the vault at the National Bank of Yemen.

Marcano knew that a CIA operative had placed a GPS chip on Holloman's computer when he first went through customs. They had followed him into Yemen and located the compound for the Houthi leaders that way. After Holloman's arrest, they knew that the computer had been placed in the vault. It had never been accessed—until now.

"Do we know who took it?" Marcano asked.

"We're working on that. Checking through satellite imagery. Drones are on their way."

"Where's the computer now?"

"Back in the vault. It was only out for about ten minutes. The signal stayed right next to the bank. We think they might have copied the hard drive."

"We've got to find the people who accessed it," Marcano said. "There's classified information on that computer, and we've got to quarantine it."

"We're working on it."

Marcano had worked with this associate for a long time. The man would know that the order to "quarantine" meant to find anyone who had seen Holloman's computer and take them out.

Fifteen minutes later, Marcano got the best piece of news he had received in a very long time. An analyst came to his office and put the grainy satellite photos on his desk.

"We ran these through facial recognition software." The man pointed to a bearded figure leaving the bank. "That's Saleet Zafar."

Marcano maintained a poker face. Even with news like this, he would never let anyone see a reaction. "Were we able to follow him?"

"No. But we know he got into this vehicle, and we're searching for it through satellite images. Drones will be there soon to provide additional imagery."

"Thank you; that will be all," Marcano said. When the analyst left, Marcano called his man in Saudi Arabia. He told him about Saleet Zafar and reminded him that there was a standing order to take the imam out.

"We'll have drones in place within an hour," the man said. "He won't escape this time."

86

Saleet had the guards stop the vehicle on the outskirts of Aden in a bombed-out warehouse complex on the mountainside overlooking the harbor. They pulled behind some abandoned buildings, where they could have some privacy, and the men all got out of the car.

Moe opened the trunk and pulled out a shoulder-fired missile launcher. Larry grabbed an AK-47.

"You think we need that?" Wyatt asked, staring at Moe's huge gun.

Saleet shrugged. "I hope not. But it is hard to say."

Next Saleet retrieved a long, rectangular piece of red-and-white cloth. "Covering your head is a sign of respect," he said to Wyatt. He folded the cloth diagonally. "We need to show respect to Mokhtar al-Bakri."

"I had a hat in my backpack," Wyatt said.

"You are no longer in America, my friend."

Wyatt stepped forward and bent down so that Saleet could wrap the cloth around his head, letting part of it hang loosely on the back of Wyatt's neck. Saleet tied it with a black cord and stepped back to admire his work.

"It also hides your wound and those hideous eyebrows." Saleet adjusted the kaffiyeh and pronounced it perfect.

He then handed Wyatt a long brown suit coat made of lightweight linen. It was similar to what the other men were wearing over their robes. The arms were a little short, but otherwise it fit well.

"Still the American with your jeans and T-shirt," said Saleet. "But maybe you don't stick out quite so much now."

The imam spoke to Moe and Larry for a few moments, and then they took off on foot. "The house is down that way," Saleet said to Wyatt. He pointed down the mountain, toward a crowded neighborhood of larger homes built into the mountain with concrete or mud walls, trimmed with white brick columns and adorned with domed windows, many of them featuring stained glass. There were five- or six-foot-tall brick fences around most of the properties and intricate carvings colored with deep red and purple hues.

"We will give them a head start, and then the three of us will head to the house. We do not want to look like we brought an army."

A few minutes later, Saleet climbed back into the Land Rover, and Curly got behind the wheel. This time Wyatt had the entire backseat to himself.

Following directions from Saleet, Curly made his way to a house that had been destroyed by Hellfire missiles and never rebuilt. There was still rubble and debris everywhere, and it looked like someone had chopped the house nearly in half, exposing the elaborate archways of the interior and the colorful tile walls, now falling apart panel by panel. There were steel beams exposed in the upstairs circular bedroom as well as in several rooms downstairs.

The three of them got out of the vehicle and walked toward the ruins. A man Wyatt assumed was al-Bakri stood in front of the house, staring sullenly as they approached.

Behind him were several bearded men hanging out in the ruins, eyeing Saleet and Wyatt, AK-47s at their sides. In the shadows of the first-floor rooms, Wyatt saw three or four more men with rounds of ammo strung across their chests, holding their guns casually. He counted another two upstairs. Curly followed a step behind Saleet and Wyatt, carrying his own AK-47, a lone gunman against al-Bakri's small militia.

"Are you sure you trust this man?" Wyatt asked Saleet under his breath as they walked toward al-Bakri.

"I am certain that I do not," Saleet said. "But Allah is in control."

That thought didn't do much to comfort Wyatt. He knew Larry and Moe had taken up positions somewhere nearby, but if they had to use that missile launcher, Wyatt didn't like his chances of getting out alive.

Al-Bakri looked to be about forty-five or fifty with a thin nose and close-shaven beard that had turned half-gray. His eyes were set deep, and he regarded Wyatt with a mixture of disdain and suspicion. He wore a blazer over a long white robe, and he had tucked a short dagger into the front of his belt.

Saleet and Wyatt stopped a few feet away, and Saleet exchanged greetings with the man. They shook and then al-Bakri extended his hand toward Wyatt. Wyatt looked him in the eyes and shook hands, surprised by the strength of al-Bakri's grip.

"Do you speak English?" Wyatt asked.

Al-Bakri waited a beat before he answered. "A little. I prefer translation." He looked at Saleet.

Saleet said a few words to al-Bakri in Arabic, and al-Bakri nodded. The two of them sat down, and Wyatt followed. Curly took a few steps back but remained standing. Wyatt noticed that the men in the bombed-out residence were now leaning against the walls, not missing a thing.

"Please thank him for coming," Wyatt said. "Please let him know that I am sorry about the death of his daughter."

Saleet spoke to al-Bakri, who kept his eyes glued on Wyatt. Al-Bakri said a few words in return, his face expressionless.

"He thanks you for your condolences," Saleet said. "He would like to know more about your fight with the U.S. president. Do you mind if I explain it to him?"

"Be my guest."

Saleet began talking, contemplative at first and then faster, and eventually al-Bakri turned his attention from Wyatt to Saleet. It was a lively interchange, as the two men cut each other off several times, their conversation gaining intensity as they spoke. Al-Bakri shook his head a few times and it was driving Wyatt crazy not to know what they were saying. After a few minutes, he put a hand on Saleet's arm. "Why is he so upset?"

Saleet turned to Wyatt with a slight smile. "He is not upset. I am only trying to explain that he can trust you."

A few more words were exchanged between the men and Saleet translated for Wyatt. "He wants to know what will happen if you win your case against the president. What will be her punishment?"

Wyatt paused to think it through. He didn't really have a case against the president. But that surely wasn't the answer al-Bakri wanted. "Tell him that the man who caused this destruction, the leader of the CIA, will lose his job. And if I get what I'm after, we will take every dollar he has. The president might lose her job too." Wyatt knew it probably sounded like little solace to someone who had lost his only daughter.

Saleet began explaining, silhouetted by the sun setting low in the sky behind him. Wyatt wondered how long they had until the call for prayer at dusk. And what would happen then? Would everything stop while the men bowed toward Mecca and recited their evening prayers?

"Okay," Saleet said after another series of exchanges with al-Bakri. "He says he is ready for your questions."

"See if we can record it," Wyatt said. Saleet nodded and pulled out his phone. He asked al-Bakri a question in Arabic.

But before al-Bakri could respond, his head jerked skyward. He had apparently heard it before anyone else, and it took Wyatt a second to realize what the buzzing meant. He looked up as al-Bakri rose, pulling his dagger from its sheath.

A drone, barely audible, flying high above them. Wyatt scrambled to his feet as al-Bakri lunged at him. It was an unexpected move and Wyatt barely dodged it. He heard the pop of gunfire from behind him and saw al-Bakri take the hits, getting blown backward, blood spurting from his chest and neck.

Wyatt and Saleet turned and sprinted toward their car as al-Bakri's men returned fire, the bullets spraying the ground around Wyatt.

"Keep your head down!" Saleet shouted.

Curly fired back, but his resistance was short-lived. One second he was returning fire; the next he was blown back, his AK-47 flying out of his hands. Almost instantaneously, Wyatt heard a terrible explosion behind him and turned to see smoke pouring out of the house—Moe's rocket launcher finding pay dirt.

In the chaos, he grabbed the AK-47 next to Curly's body and raced with Saleet to the Land Rover. He jumped into the passenger seat and ducked down. He heard the window break and metal ping as bullets riddled the car. Saleet hit the gas and spun the vehicle around, spitting dirt from the tires. Wyatt poked up his head and fired out the window in the general direction of the house where al-Bakri's men had been keeping watch. It felt like a scene out of the movies, but Wyatt was pretty sure his bullets were landing nowhere near their target.

As they sped away, with Wyatt firing as fast as he could at the bombed-out structure, he saw a second explosion, far more powerful than the first. A missile pulverized the building where al-Bakri's men had been stationed, reducing the shell of the house to heat and smoke and ashes.

"Hang on!" Saleet yelled.

They quickly left the house behind them, flying down the road, jerking around steep curves, trying to put as much distance as they could between their vehicle and the drone that had wiped out al-Bakri's men.

But when Wyatt cleared out the rest of the glass from his window with the butt of the gun and leaned out, cutting his arm as he did so, he saw the drone now chasing them at a distance, making up ground, like a hawk sweeping in for its prey.

"I thought you could outrun these things!" Wyatt yelled.

At that moment, Saleet misjudged a turn and the right wheels hit the ditch. The car jerked to the right and bounced around, spitting up dirt and dust until Saleet got it back on the road.

His face was white, eyes wide. "You want to drive?" he shouted.

"It's a little late to be asking now!" Wyatt shouted back.

Saleet pulled into the left lane and passed a slower vehicle. He had a death grip on the wheel. The road was steep going back down to the city, the turns sharp, and the drone was closing the gap.

The first drone strike had taken out al-Bakri and his men. It probably could have killed Saleet and Wyatt as well before they fled in the Land Rover. But he was an American citizen. Surely they wouldn't launch a second Hellfire missile at him right in the middle of the city of Aden.

Saleet slowed down behind a string of three or four cars in the right lane.

"Pass them!" Wyatt shouted.

Saleet shook his head, murmured something in Arabic, and pulled out to go around. He was on his horn when a car coming from the opposite direction nearly crashed into them head-on but veered off at the last second, bouncing into the ditch.

An explosion rocked the road behind them and Wyatt felt the heat. The drone was locked on now. The soulless hawk flew behind them, moving ever closer. They were nearly at the foot of the mountain, but the traffic would be heavier ahead of them, slowing them down, and the chase would soon be over.

"How can they do this?" Wyatt yelled. "I'm an American!"

87

John Marcano watched dispassionately as the whole scene played out on a computer screen in a dark-paneled conference room at Langley. He had two of his top assistants with him; they were under instructions to keep the circle of those who knew about this very tight. There were decisions being made in split seconds that would have to be explained later, and Marcano only wanted those he trusted to be in the know.

He had watched the satellite imagery and drone footage of the rendezvous between Saleet Zafar and a man the face-scanning technology had identified as Mokhtar al-Bakri. There had been brief moments of panic as his team tried to identify the man sitting next to Zafar—a man with a traditional Muslim head covering who appeared to have a mustache and a long, lean build. They could not get a good visual on his face.

Marcano's associates had been smart enough not to say what everyone was thinking. They knew Wyatt Jackson had flown into Dubai. They had lost him somewhere in the UAE. But he would have had time to make it to Yemen, and Saleet Zafar had been friends with Cameron Holloman. Marcano couldn't be sure—it might be Jackson, but then again, his face was not part of the CIA database, and the drone videos were too indistinct to make a definitive ID. For all they knew, it could have been any one of a thousand associates of Zafar.

But if it was Jackson, he had made a fatal mistake. He had entered Yemen illegally. He was working with a sworn enemy of his country, an imam who preached jihad. He was meeting with a traitor who had cost twenty men their lives.

If Marcano had believed in such things, he might have called it a miracle. Three of his country's greatest enemies all gathered in a single spot, all within the destruction zone of a single Hellfire missile. He had immediately authorized the strike against al-Bakri. But a firefight had erupted, and al-Bakri was dead before the missile launched. Marcano authorized the drone to fire anyway, taking out al-Bakri's men.

The director had watched as the drone took up the chase with the vehicle driven by Saleet Zafar. Marcano had authorized a second strike, knowing that the man with Zafar would be collateral damage.

Though Marcano did not believe in divine intervention, he did believe in fate. Wyatt Jackson had pried where he didn't belong. In Wyatt's smug self-righteousness, he had embarrassed Marcano and trashed the CIA director's reputation.

Now, if Marcano's hunch was right, Jackson would pay with his life.

The director dispatched another drone that would arrive at the scene and take up the chase shortly. This drone, a newer prototype, used guided munitions technology that combined the GPS and satellite-driven navigation of the Hellfire missiles with laser-enhanced precision. Once the drone fixed its laser on an identifiable person on the ground, the laser would stick—driven by readings of light wavelength—and the Hellfire would adjust midflight to hit the target regardless of how fast or in what direction it was moving. The problem the CIA had experienced for nearly ten years with targets outrunning the drones would be a thing of the past.

With the Hellfire 3, you could run, but there was nowhere to hide.

* * *

ADEN, YEMEN

I won't die from a drone strike, Wyatt thought. *Saleet's driving will kill me first.*

The imam had reached the bottom of the cliffs and turned onto one of the main four-lane roads running through Aden. Weaving in and out of traffic, Saleet stayed on the horn, running red lights, swerving into oncoming lanes, and even jumping up on the sidewalk to get around cars. He was frantically checking the mirrors and praying in Arabic, or least Wyatt assumed he was praying. People scattered to get out of the way, vehicles screeching to a halt. They flew through one intersection, causing a car to swerve and miss them and crash into another vehicle.

Wyatt assumed the drone was still behind them, but for some reason the remote-controlled aircraft held its fire, its pilot perhaps worried about civilian casualties.

"Where are you going?" Wyatt yelled.

"To the mosque," Saleet replied, breathless.

"A mosque?"

Saleet jerked the car to the left, and Wyatt banged his right shoulder against the door. He tried to look out the window but couldn't see the drone.

"They won't blow up a mosque," Saleet said.

"What makes you so sure?" Wyatt shot back.

"Allah won't let them."

A few seconds later, Saleet turned hard to the right and Wyatt was able to see the sky behind them. He had lost sight of the drone. He heard the mournful call to prayer beginning on loudspeakers all over the city—melodic, distorted, insistent. Cars began pulling over to the side of the road, thinning the traffic.

"There!" Saleet said, pointing to the sky in front of them.

Wyatt saw it too—another drone, or maybe the same one coming at them from a different angle. Out of the corner of his eye, Wyatt noticed a red dot coming through the front windshield, flickering on Saleet's chest.

A laser! They were marking him with a laser!

The call to prayer grew louder, and cars stopped in front of them. Wyatt felt trapped. They were surrounded by multistory buildings, backed up by traffic. Ahead on the left was an apartment complex that looked like it had been bombed out by the Saudis. On the right were half-finished construction sites and deserted sidewalks as the call to prayer continued.

"We're stuck!" Saleet yelled.

The drone dove toward them. Would it fire here in the middle of the city?

"Hang on!" Saleet shouted. But before Wyatt could brace himself, Saleet drove up on the sidewalk and bounced along for a hundred feet before turning right into a small parking garage. He crashed through the gate arm and swerved to the right, barely missing the cars parked at an angle, squeezed in next to each other.

They were safe here for a moment, shielded from the drone by the concrete of the garage. But Wyatt knew one missile could probably level the entire structure.

"They'll expect me to exit over there," Saleet said, pointing toward the other side of the garage. "But we will surprise them."

He began a clumsy three-point turn, hitting at least two other cars in the process, and circled back to exit the same way he had come in.

"You've been watching too many movies!" Wyatt yelled.

"Allahu Akbar," Saleet said, with a sudden calm that frightened Wyatt. The prayers filling the air seemed to give the imam a source of strength. He looked straight ahead as if in a trance.

"I am ready to die for Allah," he said.

★　★　★

John Marcano popped a mint in his mouth as he watched the video feed from the drone, now hovering over the parking structure, waiting for the Land Rover to exit. It was just a matter of time. The vehicle would emerge and the drone would lock on again. This time, once the laser hit the imam's chest, the pilot had instructions to fire. Yes, there would be collateral damage. But there was always collateral damage.

Surprising no one, the Land Rover came bounding out the same way it had entered. It raced across the sidewalk and clipped the front fender of an oncoming car before swerving into the other lane. A white flash filled the screen—a silent explosion that seemed sterile and surreal. The Land Rover was reduced to ashes as the blast formed a massive, smoking crater in the road, destroying other vehicles and damaging nearby buildings. Smoke rose from the street and people got out of their cars, screaming and running in every direction.

The pilot confirmed that he had locked on with the laser and destroyed the target. Collateral damage had been kept to a minimum. The passenger in the Land Rover was a given. Perhaps two or three other drivers. Otherwise, the strike had been clean.

Marcano knew that he would have a lot of explaining to do, but it would all be worth it. He would have to convince the Saudis to take credit for the strikes. The Yemenis would complain about civilian casualties and claim that the missiles had killed dozens of women and children. They would make lots of noise on the international stage. But ultimately they would be ignored. There was a civil war in Yemen, and this was the price to be paid.

The real explaining would take place a few miles away. Marcano thanked the men who had assisted in the operation and then prepared some notes for his briefing. He dialed a secure line to the White House and requested a meeting with the president.

"It's urgent," he said. "She'll want to be interrupted."

88

The ghost of Wyatt Jackson haunted Marcano as he rode in the backseat of the sedan to the White House. As he had done before, he would have to eyewash the president on these latest developments.

He would have to let her know that there was at least a chance Jackson had been killed in a drone strike. That way she would understand how critical it was to convince the Saudis to take responsibility for the bombings. But Marcano would need to be careful about the way he explained this. He would paint a scenario where the CIA had no reason to believe that Jackson was in the Land Rover at the time of the strike. Only in hindsight, only after reviewing additional satellite and drone photographs, had they developed their suspicions. It would be a difficult line to walk, but the critical point was this—nobody could ever prove that Jackson had been killed. There would certainly be no DNA in the ashes.

White House security processed Marcano, and he joined the

president's other grim-faced advisers in the Situation Room. Philip Kilpatrick was there. He looked like he had aged fifteen years in the last week alone. The gray beard seemed more haggard than before, and his eyes bugged out behind the black-rimmed glasses. He had his shirtsleeves rolled up and his tie loosened, as if he were a blue-collar workingman trapped in a white-collar uniform.

Perhaps it wasn't so much that he had changed but that the air around him had changed. From confident to wary, the man who was always two steps ahead suddenly finding himself struggling to keep up.

Marcano's nemesis, the young and cocky vice president, was in the room as well, looking like he had dressed for church. Marcano knew that Leroy Frazier would jump at any chance to discredit the CIA and spout his moralistic tripe about the need for America to lead in the fight for global justice. He was too young and idealistic to understand the complexities of global engagement, the shades of gray that colored international espionage.

Defense Secretary Simpson was also present. But the man who concerned Marcano the most was Attorney General Wachsmann. He was no fool and undoubtedly assumed that such a hastily called meeting would involve some CIA shenanigans he would be asked to support. He had argued against putting Saleet Zafar on the kill list in the first place, and now Marcano would be reporting on the imam's death.

The president entered the room, and a second round of handshaking commenced. She took her seat at the head of the table and didn't waste a second. "John, you called this meeting. Let's get started."

Marcano handed confidential folders to everyone. He knew that once they had the memos and satellite photos, he would lose their attention. But this was all about creating a paper trail anyway, so he didn't really care.

He explained that earlier that day, they had confirmed a sighting of Mokhtar al-Bakri, aka Pinocchio, in Aden, Yemen. Amazingly, he was meeting with Saleet Zafar and a few other men. Marcano had authorized drone flights to obtain surveillance video and await further orders.

"The first photo in our package is from our satellite feed. It's hard to tell who's there. The second photo is from our drone. It's taken from behind Saleet and his men but you can see al-Bakri facing them. The third photo is a close-up of al-Bakri's face."

The others in the room leafed through the photos. It was possible to discern the vague contours of al-Bakri's face and the back of Saleet Zafar. A man stood behind Zafar with a weapon, and another man stood next to him wearing a traditional head covering and a long brown coat.

Not included in the folders—because Marcano had left them out— were any shots taken from in front of Zafar, any shots that would show the gray mustache on his sidekick.

"A firefight erupted during the meeting, and al-Bakri was shot," Marcano continued. "The next photograph was taken a few seconds later. Everybody scattered, so I authorized a drone strike on Zafar, who, as you all know, was on our list of enemies."

Marcano waited a minute as they riffled through the next few pages showing the crater and the aftereffect of the missiles.

"Saleet Zafar escaped into the city, but we had one of our drones run him down. We missed once when we fired at his vehicle, thinking it was clear of others. It was prayer time and we were afraid that he was headed toward a mosque and would disappear into a crowd. You'll remember that we had already lost this man once."

By now, virtually everyone around the table had already leafed through the other photos, well ahead of Marcano's narrative. They had seen the devastation of the street in Aden and they knew that Saleet Zafar had not survived.

Marcano finished his narration anyway, photo by photo, explaining that the Hellfire 3 missile had struck with precision, keeping casualties to a minimum. He admitted that it wasn't ideal, but their only alternative would have been to let Zafar escape.

"The Saudis have in the past admitted to firing their missiles at mosques and commercial districts. If they agree to take responsibility here, it will be just one more example of their insensitivity to collateral damage. There will be international condemnation for the killing of a Muslim cleric, but the noise will die down quickly as long as the strike is blamed on the Saudis rather than the United States."

There was some halfhearted debate, but eventually they adopted Marcano's proposal. The president would direct the secretary of state to cut a deal with the Saudis. The U.S. would continue its support of the Saudi bombing campaign in Yemen, and in turn the Saudis would take credit for these two hits. They would need to do it quickly. Photos of the devastation were already circulating.

"Who was with Zafar?" Seth Wachsmann asked.

"The man behind him was probably al Qaeda in the Arabian Peninsula. We tried to run a facial recognition on the man beside him but came up empty."

Wachsmann took off his glasses and leaned closer to the photo. He looked up at Marcano and narrowed his eyes. "Was that man part of the collateral damage?"

"He was. He fled with Zafar and was in the vehicle when the missile hit."

Wachsmann looked at the president, but she didn't return his gaze. The conversation soon shifted to a plan B—what if the Saudis weren't willing to take credit? And finally, for the first time since the meeting started, the ever-composed John Marcano took a deep and relaxing breath.

★   ★   ★

After the meeting, he pulled the president aside and spoke with her privately in the West Wing. "I need you to know about a possible worst-case scenario," Marcano said.

They were both standing. Marcano had told her this would be very short.

"Wyatt Jackson flew to Dubai last week. We have no record of him crossing into Yemen, but it's possible." Marcano watched the president's face tighten, her eyes wary. She could apparently sense what was coming.

"We don't know why he went, but it's possible he might have been meeting with Saleet Zafar. We know Zafar was a friend of Cameron Holloman's."

"What are you saying? Get to the point."

"That the man with Zafar might have been Wyatt Jackson."

"And you knew this at the time you authorized the strike?" The president's voice was sharp and accusatory.

Marcano stayed calm, his own voice low and even. "Of course not. There was no record of Jackson flying anywhere near Aden. At the time we were focused on Zafar. The men with him were an afterthought. In hindsight, looking back through the photos, I'm just saying there is a possibility it might have been Jackson."

The president sighed, exasperated. She began to speak but stopped herself. When she did, her voice was soft and ominous. "John, Wyatt Jackson better make it back to the United States alive. There is no rationale that could justify taking him out if we had even the slightest hint that he was the person with Zafar."

"I assure you, Madam President, we did not. But with respect, if it *was* Wyatt Jackson, then he had entered the country of Yemen illegally and was conspiring with our terrorist enemies. Under our rules of engagement, we *would* have been justified."

"He's an American citizen, John. He's entitled to due process."

"This is a war, Madam President. If he was conspiring with our enemy, he is entitled to no such thing."

89

When she returned from her run on Wednesday morning, Paige had a text message waiting from Wellington. **Saleet Zafar was killed in Yemen!** Wellington had embedded a link, and Paige immediately clicked on it.

The link was to an Arabian news source complete with pictures that showed the smoking crater on a city street in Aden, Yemen. The Saudis had taken responsibility for the strike, but the locals were saying they saw an American drone.

Still sweaty, Paige sat down at her computer and searched for every article she could find. Wyatt was supposed to have met with Zafar. But he was also supposed to be returning to Dulles International Airport tonight, flying out of Dubai.

The articles were confusing and contradictory. Some said that American drones had bombed a car during the evening prayer time on the busy streets of Aden. Innocent civilians, including many small children, had been killed. But the news agency for Saudi Arabia said the missiles had been fired from Saudi planes resulting in precise hits on Saleet Zafar and one of his lieutenants. Both of the men were allegedly plotting a terrorist attack in the port city of Aden.

Paige surveyed the photographs, but they were not helpful. Whoever had fired the missile had created a gaping crater, but there was no way of telling how many people had died. Nor was there any mention of an American among the casualties.

She called Gazala Holloman, but Gazala had not heard a word from Wyatt either. The news of Zafar's death was a shock to Gazala. "He was a good friend to Cameron," she said, and Paige could hear the sorrow in her voice. "He was a faithful servant of Allah."

Paige, Wellington, and Kristen burned up the phone calls and text messages all day Wednesday, trying to piece together what had happened. The real panic set in early Wednesday evening, when they learned that Wyatt had not boarded his scheduled flight to Dulles. They talked about calling the State Department, but they didn't want to jump the gun. They would have to reveal that Wyatt had planned on meeting with Saleet somewhere in Yemen. What if Wyatt was just delayed in his return? They kept texting and e-mailing him, hoping against hope that he would eventually respond.

After a sleepless night, everyone agreed that Paige should call Congressman Mason. He had been helpful in the initial investigation; maybe he could pull some strings now.

It took him most of Thursday to return Paige's call. She explained that Wyatt had flown to Dubai and was planning on meeting with Saleet Zafar in Yemen. She told him what little she knew about Zafar's death and the fact that Wyatt had not returned on his Wednesday-evening flight. Mason said he would look into it right away and get back to her.

Meanwhile, Paige and Wellington checked every flight from Dubai to D.C. and other East Coast cities, telling the airline representatives that they were supposed to pick up Wyatt at the airport. But nobody at the airlines had heard from him.

Congressman Mason had given Paige his cell phone number, and she called him back Thursday evening. The State Department seemed to be stonewalling him. There was a record of Wyatt clearing customs in the UAE when he entered the country but nothing more. Mason promised to call Paige as soon as he heard something.

That same night, Wellington called Wyatt's son, but he didn't even know that Wyatt had flown to the Middle East. He asked Wellington to let him know as soon as he heard any news.

By late Thursday night, a sense of foreboding had descended on Paige. She pulled up the photos of the devastating air strike again, just to make sure she hadn't missed something. On the one hand, it would be just like Wyatt to come bounding back into the country two days late and wonder why everyone had been so worried. But that faint hope faded as Paige dissected the circumstances, trying to stay as objective as possible. This attack had all the markings of an American drone strike. It was a precise hit on a Muslim cleric, something her country had done before. And if they knew that Wyatt Jackson was in the vehicle with Saleet Zafar, the CIA could have annihilated every piece of evidence against them with one strategic missile.

Lawyers learn early in their careers that coincidence is the first cousin to cover-up. Coincidence should never be trusted—closer inquiry almost always revealed the fingerprints of manipulation and deception.

It was too coincidental that a drone strike against Zafar had occurred so soon after he had been scheduled to meet with Wyatt. Too coincidental that Wyatt had not been heard from since. A more plausible explanation was that CIA agents had followed Wyatt and that Zafar had walked into their trap. The only question in Paige's mind still to be answered was whether Wyatt had been killed along with him.

★ ★ ★

Paige woke on Friday morning too emotionally drained for a run. She had been up most of the night glued to her computer, searching for any new information on the Aden attack. She had managed only a few hours' sleep, and even that time had been racked with nightmares.

She drank her coffee and got dressed before the sun came up. She stepped outside and surveyed the parking lot, looking for nondescript sedans that might belong to the FBI. Every day since the grand jury hearing had been a day that Paige spent looking over her shoulder. Today would be no exception.

She stepped back into her condo and tried to force down a bowl of cereal. She had eaten very little in the last two days, worried sick about Wyatt and the FBI and the impending Supreme Court decision.

The pundits had predicted that the Court would act quickly, within just a few days. It was election season, and the chief justice would not want this decision hanging out there during the last few weeks before people went to the polls. Moreover, it was an emergency appeal, and the only question was whether Judge Solberg had adopted the right process or whether she should have dismissed the case on the basis of state secrets. Most experts believed the Court would issue a quick and concise ruling. Even those experts who predicted more lengthy written opinions speculated that two opinions had already been drafted—one supporting Solberg and the other throwing the case out. The only question was which side Justices Torres and Deegan would join. Which opinion would become the majority? Which would be the dissent?

Paige checked the SCOTUS blog that morning as she had done every day that week, but there was no announcement that the decision would be coming down that day. At 8 a.m. she got into her car and drove to Pungo Kennels, where Wyatt had boarded Clients for the week that he was gone. Paige explained to the lady at the desk that Wyatt had been delayed and that she was there to pick up Clients. The woman had Paige sign several documents and, after going to the back, reappeared a few minutes later with Wyatt's big golden retriever pulling at the leash. Clients jumped up on Paige and started licking her as if Paige had been his lifelong friend.

"Clients is the best dog," the woman gushed. "He loves everyone."

Paige thanked the lady and left with Clients. She put him in the backseat, but before she could climb in the driver's seat, Clients had bounded up front and was riding shotgun, his head swiveling this way and that, excited to have his freedom.

"If you're going to stay with me for a few days, we've got to have an understanding," Paige said. "No licking. No shedding. And no riding in the front seat."

Clients leaned toward her as if he understood every word. He put a big yellow paw on Paige's arm and leaned over to lick her.

"No! What did I say?"

Clients tilted his head as if he didn't quite understand—a pathetic, endearing look that Paige couldn't resist.

"Okay," she said. "You can ride up front. But this licking stuff has to stop."

Clients wagged his tail and sat straight up, his tongue hanging out. It actually made Paige feel a little better just to have Wyatt's dog with her.

"We'll have to stop at the puppy store and get some food," Paige said as she backed out of the parking spot. "If you're good, maybe we can get a bone and a toy as well."

She glanced over at the happy dog riding next to her. She wasn't exactly a dog person, but she couldn't leave Clients in the kennel indefinitely.

"Wyatt Jackson, you owe me," Paige said.

Fifteen minutes later, in the pet store, getting pulled from one aisle to the next by Clients, Paige received a text from Wellington.

SCOTUS blog says one opinion to be issued today.

She stopped and sent a reply. **What time?**

10 a.m.

Paige looked at her watch. There were no other emergency cases on the Court's docket to be decided. In less than ninety minutes she would know if her case against Philip Kilpatrick and John Marcano was going to survive or whether it would die at the hands of the nation's highest court.

90

Clients made himself right at home. He spent an hour eating, doing his business outside, and sniffing around the small condo. He dragged a few dirty clothes out of the closet and presented them to Paige in her study.

"No!" she scolded. "Bad dog!"

He wagged his tail.

At 9:45 Paige logged on to the SCOTUS blog. Her hands were sweaty, her mouth dry, her heart beating as fast as it had on the day that she argued the case. A few years ago, lawyers in big D.C. firms would find out the results of cases by sending a low-ranking associate to the steps of the Court. The clerk would rush out of court with the results, and the associates would call back to their offices. Reporters would snag copies of the opinion and leaf through it, trying to quickly get the gist of what the Court was saying so they could be first on the air.

But now everybody sat hunched over a computer and watched the live SCOTUS blog titled #waitingforlester. Lester was the clerk of the Court, and the bloggers were sitting in the Court's press room waiting for him to bring in the latest opinion as the results were simultaneously announced from the bench. And today there was only one opinion it could possibly be.

Commenters on the blog were all speculating about whether such a quick decision was good news for the plaintiff or good news for the defendants. Most believed that it meant a victory for the Anderson family. It would be easy for the Court to issue a short opinion saying that Judge Solberg was handling the dicey issue of state secrets properly and that the Court would issue a full opinion once the case was completed and came back up to the Court a second time. Other commenters were sure that a quick turnaround meant the Court was going to dismiss the entire case. It was obvious, they wrote, that state secrets were involved and that the Court could simply cite its prior precedent under the *Reynolds* case and dispense with this hot-button issue expeditiously.

Paige wanted to log on under a fake name and argue with the commenters, but what good would that do? Instead, she shot a text to Wellington. **Are you nervous?**

Terrified!

Wellington had been great, but on days like this he didn't do much to boost her confidence.

Right at ten o'clock, almost on cue, Clients started pawing at the front door.

"Are you kidding me?" Paige asked.

Clients looked forlornly over his shoulder. He paced back to Paige and then returned to the door again, pawing at it some more.

Paige checked the screen. "You're going to have to wait," she said to Clients. This time he moaned as if he were talking to her, telling her that he couldn't possibly wait. "All right," she snapped. It wasn't like sitting in front of the screen was going to change the outcome.

She put Clients on a leash and took him outside, where he wandered around in the grass and the bushes lining the parking lot, sniffing here and there as if he had to find the perfect spot to pee.

"Oh, for goodness' sakes! Just go!"

Finally he stopped and lifted his left leg. Then he decided that it wasn't quite the right spot and started walking around some more. It seemed like forever before he finally settled on a spot and peed for all of about two seconds.

"You'd better pray Wyatt makes it home," Paige said to the stupid dog. She quickly took him back inside and sat down at her computer, scrolling through the comments she had missed. To her relief the opinion had not yet been released. The Court was apparently swearing in some attorneys who had just been admitted to the Supreme Court bar. Clients sat obediently at Paige's feet, staring at her. He raised a paw and put it on her leg. She remembered how Wyatt had always given Clients treats when he came back in from outside.

"I don't have anything," Paige insisted. She immediately felt bad when Clients's face drooped in sadness. He was already growing on her, and it had been less than two hours.

Back to the screen.

Here's Lester with today's opinion. *Estate of Anderson v. Kilpatrick et al.*

Paige sucked in a breath. This was it!

Fourth Circuit is reversed.
The vote is 5–4.
Justice Augustini dissents joined by three others. Deegan writes separately.

Paige stopped reading, stunned, as if someone had knocked the wind out of her. The screen began to blur and she had to blink away the tears. Five months of work, everything she had risked, and they had lost! The case would be dismissed. It seemed like the world was crashing around her. There was a finality to the Supreme Court that could crush a person's spirit. There was nowhere to go from here.

The commenters were lighting up the blog, but Paige ignored them and clicked on a link to the opinion. Justice Sikes wrote for the majority. Paige felt sick as she thought about Kristen. She began to read the opinion but then decided there was no use. Who cared if the reasoning was logical or flawed? To whom would she complain? What did it matter?

She looked at the justices who had joined the majority. Chief Justice Leonard and the Beard were no surprise. Paige had never expected them to vote her way. Justice Kathryn Byrd, the quiet eighty-one-year-old conservative, had aligned herself as usual with the other right-wingers on the Court. But it was Evangelina Torres, the former Democratic senator from California, who had swung the opinion. Appointed by Obama, she had justified the drone program and secret CIA wars that he had relied upon so heavily during his two terms.

Paige scrolled down until she came to Augustini's dissent and started reading there. The former Harvard professor wrote with palpable frustration that mirrored the emotions Paige was feeling at that very moment. At one point, she called the majority opinion "cowardly" for its failure to even question the executive branch about claims of executive privilege.

According to Augustini, the entire CIA drone program was troubling, an end run around the constitutional requirement that Congress declare war. It was a slippery slope from a constitutional republic to a dictatorship, and we were halfway down when the executive branch could command its own army with no oversight from Congress or the courts. At times like these, the novelist said, she felt like she was living in the land of *Animal Farm*, written by George Orwell in 1945 to mock the events leading from the Russian Revolution to the Stalinist era in the Soviet Union.

Paige felt somewhat vindicated reading Augustini's arguments, though it did nothing to lessen the impact of the Court's decision. Her phone was blowing up with calls from reporters and Kristen and

Wellington. She ignored all of them and began reading the short separate dissent from Taj Deegan.

Deegan was new to the Court, and Paige knew it took guts for her to write her own dissent. Deegan lamented what this case said about the rule of law. She wrote eloquently about the Court's motto of "equal justice under law" and how much that meant to the American system of justice.

The lowliest child from the most disadvantaged neighborhood would get the same treatment in this building as the president of the United States. Until now. Today's decision obligates the president and her advisers to follow the rule of law only when they are operating domestically. But in international affairs, they have a get-out-of-jail-free card called "state secrets," which allows them to do anything they want without judicial review.

The state secrets doctrine was never intended to be so broad that the courts cannot even inquire into the truth of a case. The safeguards Judge Solberg put in place appropriately ensured that state secrets weren't revealed while at the same time holding high-ranking officials accountable in the same way as ordinary citizens.

When a plaintiff comes into this Court and claims that the chief executive of our country, aided by her top advisers, knowingly sacrificed the lives of American troops to advance her political agenda, this Court cannot and should not wash its hands of that matter under the pretext of state secrets. In times of war, the executive branch will feed on fear, and the people will willingly sacrifice their constitutional rights in hopes of achieving greater safety. It is this Court's sworn duty to prevent the executive branch from devouring those rights that so many men and women have died to protect. It brings me shame to see our once-strong Court cower behind the doctrine of state secrets and believe, as Pontius Pilate once did, that history will not judge us harshly.

> I may be on the wrong side of today's opinion, but I am more concerned with being on the right side of history. When today's opinion ultimately takes its place among the *Dred Scotts* and *Plessy v. Fergusons* of our jurisprudence, which it surely will, I will be proud to say that when the votes were taken, I told Chief Justice Leonard that I respectfully dissented.

Paige finished reading and paused to collect her thoughts. She could remember few cases where the justices had shown more emotion than this. She swallowed hard as she thought about Wyatt Jackson and his analogy of the Alamo. Winning hadn't been the goal here. The debate was now raging just the way Wyatt would have wanted.

She wished he could have read what she'd just read. She wished he could see what was happening on the Internet even now. If he were around, he would probably be on the steps of the Court denouncing the five justices in the majority and calling for Americans to sit up and take notice. He would vow to expose the CIA's shadow war and the kill list and the lack of transparency by the Hamilton administration.

But he wasn't here, and for the first time Paige allowed herself to admit what she knew in her heart to be true. Wyatt Jackson wasn't coming back. He had flown too close to the flame, and the CIA had taken him out.

It made her angry and frustrated and filled with regret all at the same time. Wyatt had literally died fighting for his client. And now, the case had died along with him.

She leaned over and started rubbing Clients's ears and scratching his back. The dog wagged his tail like he didn't have a care in the world.

"Your master was a brave, brave man," Paige said, her eyes filling with tears. "I'll bet they didn't find any wounds in his back."

91

Paige woke while it was still dark Saturday morning and took a few seconds to gain her equilibrium. She reached over and grabbed her phone. It was not quite six. Clients was sprawled out next to her in the bed, crowding Paige into a corner. Last evening he had lain at the front door, his head on his paws, waiting for his master. Paige had finally coaxed him back to the bedroom and then had to chase him off the bed twice. But sometime in the night, after she had fallen asleep, he had apparently snuck back up.

"Clients, get down," Paige said, pushing the dog.

He ignored her and continued to sleep. She finally shook him awake, and he looked at her with sleepy eyes as if put out that she had the audacity to wake him up. She snapped her fingers on the side of the bed. "Get down," she said, pushing the big lug.

Clients finally sauntered off the bed and immediately started begging for breakfast. Paige fed him, fixed coffee, and began scrolling through stories on her laptop. The Supreme Court's opinion had touched a nerve with both liberal and conservative journalists who believed that the executive branch was accumulating too much power. They were joined in their criticism of the Court by Republican politicians who were livid that the president would never have to account for the deaths of the SEALs.

Several of the articles mentioned Paige. She had issued a brief written statement yesterday, saying that she respected the Court but was disappointed that she would never be able to expose the truth about what happened. Kristen had been less circumspect. Reporters had shown up at her house, and she'd gone on camera expressing her profound disgust at the ruling, saving her harshest criticism for Justice Sikes.

Paige spent some time thinking about her own future. She still had to deal with the contempt citation hanging out there from Judge Solberg, and she prayed that the grand jury would not indict her for obstruction. But even if she could get past all of that, she knew her own law practice would never prosper. She wondered if her old boss at the attorney general's office would even want her back given all the allegations floating around against her.

She threw on her running clothes—black tights, a dry-wick shirt, and a long-sleeved cotton pullover since it had dipped into the low fifties overnight. She put on a headband and snapped on Clients's leash. "Come on; we're going for a run."

She and Clients parked at a garage near 31st Street, and she stretched under the King Neptune statue on the boardwalk. She started with a slow jog, and Clients did fine until he wanted to stop and sniff. For the next several minutes, he was the most erratic running partner Paige had ever had. He would slow down to sniff the shrubs along the boardwalk and then Paige would yank him away, causing him to jump up on her and let her know how much fun he was having. Paige shortened the leash and tried to keep him right next to her. After a while she won the battle of wills, and he settled in beside her at a somewhat-even pace, looking up occasionally for approval.

"Good boy," Paige would say, reaching down to rub his head.

She picked up the pace a little, and Clients followed along, though he still tried to sniff people as they ran past.

They ran for a few miles with the sun coming up over the ocean, and Paige felt some of the pressure dissipate. She was exhausted from all the tension that had been building up in the last few weeks, and Clients was going to make sure that she didn't go at a record pace. But it still felt good to get out and fill her lungs with the saltwater air. There was something comforting about seeing the waves roll onto the beach a hundred yards away across a wide expanse of white sand. There were lots of people out walking and running, enjoying the morning, and it made Paige remember why she loved Virginia Beach.

Because this was Clients's first run, Paige had left her iTunes at home. But she was still deep in thought and didn't hear the man coming until he was running beside her, on the other side of Clients, almost step for step.

"What's his name?" the man asked.

Paige turned sideways.

Daniel Reese?

She was stunned, momentarily speechless, but kept running. "What are you doing out here?" she asked.

"The Navy likes us to stay in shape."

A number of conflicting emotions hit Paige all at once. She thought about the obstruction charge and her unauthorized use of state secrets. "I don't think we should be talking to each other," Paige said.

"If I were you, I would be thinking the same thing," Reese responded, but he didn't slow down or peel off.

"I can't talk to you, Daniel. We're both under investigation."

Paige stopped abruptly and pulled a U-turn on the boardwalk, taking Clients with her and walking in the opposite direction.

Reese turned as well.

"I'm serious. Leave me alone."

She was hoping that Clients might sense her frustration and growl at Reese, but instead he just pulled on the leash so he could get closer and lick his new buddy.

"My lawyer cut a deal with the prosecutors," Reese said, falling into step. He looked straight ahead as they walked, his eyes hidden behind sunglasses. "I agreed to spill everything to the grand jury and plead guilty to the unauthorized disclosure of classified information. I'll get the same sentence General Petraeus did—a hundred-thousand-dollar fine and two years' probation. I might be dishonorably discharged."

They walked a few more steps and he looked sideways at Paige. "In exchange, they agreed not to seek indictments of you or Wyatt or Wellington."

Paige stopped in her tracks and turned toward Reese. "They what?"

"Mitchell Taylor cut a deal when I told him how it all happened— me calling you guys out of the blue as the Patriot and everything. He never really wanted to go after you in the first place. I don't think he believed he could get a conviction."

Paige was stunned by all this. It seemed too good to be true. The threat of indictment could be over—just like that?

"Can we sit down?" she asked, nodding to a nearby bench.

"Sure."

"Why did you do that?" she asked.

"Because I wasn't going to let you and Wyatt take the fall. Your team had already made so many sacrifices to expose the White House and CIA." He paused, looking out over the ocean. "And because it was the right thing to do. SEALs don't leave their teammates flailing in the wind."

They took a seat, and Paige took a minute to process this. She wanted to say something to Daniel about Wyatt, but she wasn't sure that was a good idea. "Why didn't you tell me sooner?" she asked.

"Before the deal was finalized, I got a late-night visit from someone that added another layer of complexity. For reasons that will become clear a little later, I couldn't say anything until today."

Paige furrowed her brow. "Do you have my computer?"

"Yes."

That meant he must have been following her the morning she buried it. "Why did you take it?"

Reese was scratching Clients's head and the dog's tail was wagging like crazy. "For your own protection," he said, leaning back on the bench. "If you turned it in, they would have the evidence they needed to prosecute you. I needed to be the guy controlling the evidence so they had to deal with me if they wanted an indictment of any type."

"Do they have it now?"

"No. I'll give it back to you when all this is over."

Reese stood and Clients got excited, dancing around. "Is this Wyatt's dog?" Reese asked.

"Yes."

"Is he a good runner?"

"Horrible."

Reese reached for the leash. "Can I have him for a minute?"

"You can have him period," Paige said, though she knew she didn't mean it.

Reese took the leash and stood in front of Clients. "Sit," he commanded, raising his palm in the air. Clients obeyed as if he had just spent the last three years of his life in obedience school.

Reese shoved his shades on top of his head and bent over so he was looking the dog in the eye. "Now, we're going to run back the way you came, and this time there will be no fooling around. You stay right at my side. Miss Paige is going to need a good running partner."

Reese stood straight up and winked at Paige. "Heel," he said and he pulled Clients around to his right side. "Sit." Clients obeyed like a champ.

Paige stood as well, secretly hoping that Clients would give Daniel Reese a hard time.

"You okay to run some more?" Reese asked Paige.

"Why not?"

Reese looked at Clients. "Let's go!" he commanded. He started running, pulling on the leash a little as he did so. To Paige's chagrin, Clients fell in step immediately. Paige joined them and Reese picked up the pace. Clients loped along with a fluid run that Paige didn't know he had in him.

"Where did you learn to train dogs?" Paige asked.

"I didn't," Reese said. "But the SEALs taught me how to show tough love."

On the way back to 31st Street, Reese asked about Kristen and how she was doing. He told Paige that he already knew about Wyatt and that it had the full attention of the State Department and even the president. He also told Paige that she had done a masterful job at the Supreme Court. He had listened to the audio recording of the hearing online and had thought she was going to win.

They stopped running at the small park located on the boardwalk near the statue of King Neptune, the same place where Admiral Towers had delivered a speech on Memorial Day. It was bordered by a Hilton hotel with an outdoor restaurant.

Paige bent down, hands on her knees, trying to catch her breath. Reese petted Clients and told him what a good job he had done. He looked at Paige. "I didn't realize you'd be bringing a dog," he said, handing her the leash. "Can you wait here for a second? I'll be right back."

"I guess so."

He disappeared into the side door of the Hilton, and Paige looked around to see if they had been followed. This whole thing felt so bizarre. Everything about Daniel Reese had been strange from the very beginning. She still wasn't 100 percent sure she could trust him. Were her legal worries really over?

In a few minutes, another man came out the same door and walked up to Paige. He was in his thirties with a military buzz cut, a tight shirt, and the ripped muscles of a SEAL. He spoke with crisp authority, as if Paige had no choice but to do what he said. "Commander Reese said I'm supposed to take care of your dog," he said. "He asked you to meet him on the second floor, conference room D."

Paige handed the man the leash. She pulled a small plastic bag out of the pocket of her running tights and gave that to him as well. "You never know."

She found the conference room, and the two men standing guard outside nodded to her. When she walked in, Reese was sitting at the conference table in his shorts and long-sleeved running shirt. He was sweating and had a towel draped over his shoulder, a computer in front of him.

"Have a seat," he said, motioning toward a chair opposite him. "Sorry for all the secretive protocol, but we've got a secure link in this conference room, and there's something I need to show you."

Paige tilted her head, the posture of a skeptic, but nevertheless sat down opposite Reese. She wiped her brow with the sleeve of her shirt and readjusted her headband.

He slid the computer across the table. "There's a document on here I'd like you to read."

"What is it?" she asked before touching the computer. She suddenly had a sense of foreboding. Reese was going to great lengths to explain something in a very controlled setting. This couldn't be good news. Was this the way they would tell her about Wyatt?

"It's a lawsuit that Gazala Holloman is going to file," Reese explained. "The whole thing can be proven without access to any state secrets."

Still skeptical, Paige opened the computer. "What's the password?"

"ThePatriot. All one word."

"Of course."

Paige typed in the password and opened the document. It was titled, *Gazala Holloman, as the Executrix and Next Friend of Cameron Holloman, Deceased v. Philip Kilpatrick, Chief of Staff to the President of the United States and John Marcano, Director of the Central Intelligence Agency.*

"Is this real?" Paige asked.

"Just read it."

With Reese watching, Paige quickly scanned the first page and scrolled through to the second and third. The complaint laid out detailed facts about what had happened not just to Cameron Holloman, but also to Patrick and the other SEALs. It was stunning in its precision and in the allegations being made against the defendants. Paige leaned in and began slowing down as she read—this was the case they had been trying to prove! And somehow Gazala Holloman and her lawyer had pieced it all together.

There were exhibits attached via links in the text of the document. She clicked on them, reviewed them, and then returned to the text of the complaint.

When she clicked the link for exhibit D, the computer took longer than normal to pull it up. And when the screen finally changed, she jerked back in her chair, her hand over her mouth, blinking, reeling, a cross between shock and pure, unmitigated . . .

92

FIVE DAYS EARLIER
ADEN, YEMEN

Saleet crashed through the gate of the parking garage and swerved to the right, barely missing the bumpers of the cars parked at an angle. He stopped for a moment as the call to prayer echoed in the garage, so loud Wyatt could barely think. Wyatt knew they couldn't stay here. One drone strike would take out the entire three-story structure, and they would be buried in the rubble and ashes.

"They'll expect me to exit over there," Saleet said, pointing to the other side of the garage. "But we will surprise them."

He hit two cars as he turned around in the cramped space.

"You've been watching too many movies!" Wyatt said.

But Saleet was staring straight ahead, his face calm, as if the call to prayer were putting him in a trance. "*Allahu Akbar.* I am ready to die for Allah."

"Not if I have any say in it," Wyatt said. "How far are we from that mosque?"

Saleet did not respond. His hands were frozen on the wheel, arms straight, as if steeling himself to exit the garage.

"Let me drive," Wyatt suggested, trying to break through to the man. "You can give directions."

Still the imam didn't move.

"Saleet, they're going to kill us here!" Wyatt reached over and shook the imam's shoulder.

Saleet turned to him. "You should drive," he said.

Wyatt jumped out of the vehicle to change places with Saleet. But as soon as he did, Saleet reached over and pulled the passenger door closed. Too late, Wyatt realized what was happening.

"The world will listen to you," Saleet said through the passenger-side window that had been shot out earlier. And before Wyatt could climb back in, Saleet took off.

"Stop!" But the imam wasn't listening.

He hit the gas and burst through the same entrance they had entered a minute earlier, and the world slowed down for Wyatt. As if choreographed to the final Arabic strains of the evening call to prayer, Saleet bounced across the sidewalk and turned left in front of oncoming traffic.

"Hayya alal Falah . . . Hayya alal Falah . . ."

Wyatt felt the heat and the ground shake at the same time that he saw the blinding blast. He ducked away, covering his eyes. Ashes and smoke filled the air.

"Allahu Akbar . . . Allahu Akbar . . ."

Wyatt breathed in and started coughing. On the street where Saleet's vehicle had been was a crater and smoke and chaos. People were screaming and running and the concussion from the blast had crumbled part of the facade of the parking garage.

"La ilaha illallah."

The call to prayer ended, but the air was filled with the bleating of horns and the shouts of desperate people running scared. Wyatt's ears were ringing, but he gathered himself and walked out the back of the garage, keeping his head down, avoiding eye contact with anyone. He had nowhere to go, but he knew the locals would be taking pictures of the devastation and the American drones would capture the scene in high definition. The farther away he could get from the devastation, the safer he would be.

For the next two days, he lived in the shadows of Aden—hungry, tired, and thankful he was still alive. Though he was bone-weary and famished, he began to develop a sense of invincibility. For some reason, his life had been spared. He had no doubt that he would get out of Yemen alive.

Forty-eight hours after the explosion, Wyatt took matters into his own hands. He made his way back up to the nice houses on the cliffs overlooking the city. He stayed in the shadows and watched for an entire day to better understand the rhythm of life here. He waited until the evening prayer time and then broke into two of the houses whose owners had gone to the mosque, helping himself to a meal and taking whatever money he could find. He didn't even understand their currency, but he figured he had enough now. Before he left the second house, he also invaded the man's closet and took a long white robe, a belt, sandals, and another red-and-white cloth to cover his head, replacing his grimy and charred head covering.

That evening he took a chance. He tried four different stores before he found somebody who spoke English. He negotiated for a phone that could make international calls and pulled the currency from his pocket, spreading it on the counter. The man looked him over and eventually started separating the pieces that he needed to pay for the phone. To avoid doing paperwork, Wyatt bribed him and told him he could keep the rest.

He believed that Paige's and Wellington's phones were tapped and so he called Gazala Holloman and swore her to secrecy. Following instructions from Wyatt, she drove to the home of Daniel Reese and told him what had happened. Within hours, Reese called Wyatt back. He said he would go to Admiral Towers, who would run it up the chain. Reese was fairly certain they could have a Special Forces extraction team in Aden within twenty-four hours.

The following night, the SEALs landed just up the coast and met Wyatt at a designated rendezvous spot. Six hours later he was at the U.S. military base in Stuttgart, Germany, decompressing. He was questioned by Navy intelligence and a special investigator for the Justice Department. Notably, he did not talk to anyone from the CIA.

When he learned the outcome of Paige's argument at the Supreme Court, he hatched an idea. Wyatt knew that either Cameron Holloman's computer had been illegally tagged by the CIA with some kind of GPS device or else the journalist's e-mails and phone calls had been illegally monitored. Either way, Wyatt had downloaded the information from Cameron's computer, and he knew where the computer itself was located. Gazala was entitled to possession of it as a matter of law. Once he obtained it, forensics would be able to tell him whether it had been hacked or tagged. He might have lost the *Anderson* case, but now he had an even better one.

He quickly put together a rough draft of the lawsuit for the wrongful death of Cameron Holloman and talked Daniel Reese into allowing him to use it to add a little drama to his Skype reunion with Paige. Wyatt embedded a link on exhibit D, which would take Paige to a Skype call. Wyatt would be waiting on the other end.

★ ★ ★

VIRGINIA BEACH, VIRGINIA

. . . joy. Pure, unmitigated *joy*. Her hand cupped over her mouth, Paige stared at the screen, speechless.

"I heard you lost our case while I was gone," Wyatt said.

"Oh. My. Gosh. Is that really *you*?"

"I mean, a man goes out of the country for a week and it all hits the fan. His case gets blown away and his star witness has to plead guilty for divulging classified information."

Paige looked up at Daniel Reese, who was smiling broadly.

Paige took her hand down but couldn't take her eyes off the screen. "Wyatt Jackson, you had me worried sick."

He didn't look well. He had dark circles under his eyes, and his face looked more drawn than it ever had before. He had a bandage on his forehead. And there was one other thing.

"What happened to your eyebrows?" Paige asked.

"It's a long story," Wyatt said, cracking a smile. "And unlike a lot of my stories, this one is mostly true."

93

The last thing that Amanda Hamilton did before taking a seat at her desk in the Oval Office was to kiss Jason, her husband of twenty years. Last night, over a glass of wine, he had calmed her nerves. Americans are a forgiving people, he had said. When they saw her heart, they would like it as much as he always had.

Her press secretary had suggested that she stride down the red-carpeted Cross Hall, then stop at a podium in the stately East Room entryway and speak there, the way she had on other important occasions. She was good on her feet, and it would be a powerful visual. But that was exactly the point, she told him. This wasn't about powerful visuals. This was about being humble and authentic with the American people.

And so, dressed in a blue suit with a credenza behind her featuring family pictures, flanked by the American flag and the presidential flag, President Amanda Hamilton took her seat and faced the cameras.

The cameraman in front of her started the countdown, and she folded her hands on the desk. She remembered her husband's words from last night: tell the truth and trust the people. She swallowed hard and looked straight ahead.

The red light came on, and she envisioned Jason and her kids and her many friends listening with encouraging faces. This was not a proclamation; this would be a heart-to-heart with the American people. The entire speech was on her teleprompter, but she had to do far more than just read the words—she had to somehow *connect*.

"Good evening, my fellow Americans. I am here tonight to talk to you about some recent events in the Middle East and, in particular, my role in those events. I am here because I believe in transparency, and I trust your judgment. I am here because I believe that our American ideals should apply not just at home but in the way we conduct our business abroad."

She paused for a second and tried hard to calm her nerves. Amanda Hamilton was a gifted public orator, but this was different. She felt vulnerable and exposed. Her heart was racing, though she would never show the nerves or even the fear.

"Five days ago, on Monday, October 1, I learned that a radical Muslim imam named Saleet Zafar had been killed by an American drone strike. His sermons and anti-American rhetoric had inspired many to violence and terrorism, including a man who tried to assassinate me. In addition, Zafar had verifiable ties to al Qaeda. His addition to America's list of targeted enemies was certainly justified. However, I was also told that attorney Wyatt Jackson may have been with Zafar at the time of the strike and therefore may have been inadvertently killed as well.

"Thankfully, I would later learn that Mr. Jackson survived, but in the meantime I instructed Attorney General Seth Wachsmann to immediately begin a complete investigation into the circumstances that precipitated the strike. I have now had an opportunity to review his findings, as well as notes from an interview with Wyatt Jackson. In addition, I have personal knowledge about events surrounding the failed rescue operation known as Operation Exodus. Tonight, I want to share the results of Attorney General Wachsmann's investigation and my own conclusions with you."

Amanda knew that Wachsmann was one of the most respected politicians in the country. When she requested that he launch a full investigation within an hour of learning about the possible death of Wyatt Jackson as "collateral damage," she knew there would be no turning back. She knew the investigation would lead to a moment like this— baring her soul to the American people.

"In order to understand why Operation Exodus and the recent death of Saleet Zafar are connected, you must first know the backstory about why we launched Operation Exodus in the first place. Several months ago, American journalist Cameron Holloman traveled to Yemen in order to catalog the suffering of the Yemeni people as a result of the civil war raging in that country. Though travel restrictions prevented him from legally entering Yemen, he found a way to cross Yemen's border with Saudi Arabia and set up meetings with various persons, including a few leaders of the Houthi rebels. Without my knowledge, but with the full authorization of the director of the CIA, a small GPS unit and listening device were attached to Mr. Holloman's computer. This was done without a warrant and without any prior court knowledge or approval.

"With the assistance of these devices, the CIA learned the location of several high-ranking Houthi leaders. Eight days after Mr. Holloman met with them, a drone strike was authorized by the director of the CIA that killed those leaders and several of their family members.

"As a result, the Houthis assumed that Mr. Holloman worked for the CIA. They captured him and scheduled him for execution along with a member of the Saudi royal family. It was only then, after the fact, that I was informed by my chief of staff about the illegal monitoring of Mr. Holloman's computer."

Amanda paused before continuing. This was the hardest part—getting it out in the open, her own role in the cover-up. She had made mistakes, costly ones. But tonight, she would own them and let the American people decide what the consequences should be.

"As commander in chief, I should have immediately asked Director Marcano to step down. My failure to act was a mistake in judgment—one I deeply regret. At the time, I was focused on extracting Mr. Holloman from captivity, and I believed that if the truth came out, his captors would view it as a cover story and it would confirm their suspicions that Mr. Holloman had indeed worked for the CIA. So instead, we attempted to negotiate Mr. Holloman's release by using a Muslim imam as an intermediary. That imam was Saleet Zafar.

"Those negotiations were unsuccessful, and as you know, we ultimately sent a Special Forces team into Yemen in an attempt to free Mr. Holloman. In recent months, there have been a number of accusations associated with those events. I can assure you of this: I did not know that the mission was doomed to failure. I would never have sent those brave men on that mission if I knew our intelligence had been compromised."

Amanda paused, emphasizing what she had just said. She felt the load lifting from her shoulders, the weight of secrets kept and the crushing burden of wondering what would happen if they were exposed. She knew that it would be hard for the American people to believe her, given the mistakes she was admitting in this speech. But she was telling the truth, and she hoped the world could see that.

"I have now learned that the director of the CIA knew, prior to the commencement of Operation Exodus, that the informant we were relying on had lost a family member to a drone strike two years earlier. This cast doubt on the veracity of that source because there was the possibility that he might be trying to double-cross us. That information was conveyed by Director Marcano to my chief of staff, Philip Kilpatrick. But Director Marcano and Mr. Kilpatrick kept that information from me. If I had known at the time, I would never have authorized the rescue mission that put our men at risk."

Amanda could tell that even the camera operators were now hanging on her every word. This speech would be dissected and debated for months and would undoubtedly serve to define her presidency. She had to get it right, not just for her own sake but for the sake of America and its standing in the world.

"Earlier today, I asked for the resignations of both Mr. Kilpatrick and Director Marcano. Among other things, they withheld information from me and from the National Security Council that may have cost men their lives. By doing so, they have proven themselves unfit for the offices they hold.

"Now, there have been a lot of things said about my preparation of a speech that I gave to you, the American people, on the night that our servicemen died. Yes, I did spend more time personally editing the speech that would be given if the mission failed. But that was not because I was part of some grand conspiracy and anticipated the mission's failure. It is relatively easy to announce a successful mission. But it is painstakingly difficult to find the words to describe the sorrow that accompanies a failed one.

"My second mistake was this: As a former attorney general committed to justice, I sat back and watched as my own chief of staff and the director of the CIA hid behind the state secrets defense in the lawsuit filed by the family of Troy Anderson. That defense allowed them to hide the fact that Holloman's computer had been illegally monitored. This I also regret, and it is why I'm giving this speech now, as soon as possible after receiving Attorney General Wachsmann's report. The plaintiffs still have an opportunity to petition the Supreme Court for a rehearing, and I did not want that window to close before this information was made public."

With the hard part over, it was time for Amanda to outline her proposed action plan. She sat a little straighter in her chair and tried to appear as presidential as possible.

"In light of these events, I will be taking the following actions. First, I will reconstitute the panel that considers what targets should be added to the kill list of enemy combatants. I believe we did the right thing in adding Saleet Zafar to the list. And as it stands now, I make the final call. But America has recognized from its founding that human nature requires a balance of power. No one person should serve as judge, jury, and executioner. I will therefore be reconstituting the panel and asking that the Supreme Court appoint one of its justices to sit on the panel and that the House and Senate do the same. Nobody will be added to the target list unless there is unanimous agreement among the three branches of government.

"Second, I will work with a new CIA director to ensure that our elite Special Forces and our drones operate primarily under the command of the military, not the CIA. Our founders did not want the president to have the ability to wage undeclared shadow wars. We will continue to aggressively pursue terrorists at every turn. But I will ask for broad congressional approval to do so through the military chain of command in places like Pakistan and Yemen rather than rely on the fiction that we are not waging war just because the CIA is in charge.

"Third, I will ask Congress to consider the authorization of a special court to adjudicate with complete confidentiality any cases that might implicate state secrets. The judges for this court will have clearance for classified information at the highest level. There will be no juries and no public hearings. In this way high-level executives in our government will not be above the law simply because state secrets could be exposed."

She was almost done now. She had listed the facts, told the truth. Now it was time to trust the people.

"As I have said, I have made my share of mistakes in this chapter of American history. I have already called Gazala Holloman and expressed my deepest apologies for what happened to her husband. At the conclusion of tonight's address, I will call the families of each of our fallen servicemen and express my regrets to them. I believe I will be a better leader because of the things I've learned. But frankly, that is for you to decide.

"This is a critical juncture for our country. It is no time for protracted proceedings assessing blame for what has happened. I am therefore requesting that both the House and the Senate hold a vote of confidence within the next ten days on my ability to continue as this country's leader. If a vote of no confidence is the result, I will step aside with no questions asked. Vice President Frazier is fully capable of leading this country at such a time as this. But if the House and Senate bring back a vote of confidence, despite my mistakes, I promise that I will give everything I have to uphold our American ideals both at home and abroad. This is the greatest country on the face of the earth. And it would be my privilege to continue leading it."

She waited, swallowed, and realized that this might be the last thing she said to the public as president of the United States.

"God bless you, and God bless the United States of America."

94

Paige spent the evening at Kristen's house, watching as the boys put on a wrestling display, with Justin announcing the combatants just like his dad had done. This time, though, Justin wore Incredible Hulk cutoff shorts and introduced himself as "Beef Anderson." Caleb came out in an oversize Captain America outfit, and Justin introduced his brother as "a dairy farmer from New York, soft and cuddly, also known as Uncle Q!" Caleb jumped around and grunted a little, as if it was the greatest introduction anyone could ever have.

The match didn't last as long, shortened by a hard fall by Caleb, who ran crying to his mom. She scolded big brother and suggested they find another way to amuse themselves.

The boys were in bed when the president began speaking. By the time the speech ended, both women were crying. They sat there for a while, staring at the television as the commentators provided analysis. For the longest time, neither of them spoke.

"I guess she'll be calling here in a little while," Kristen said.

"It seems so surreal." Paige's head was still spinning from what Wyatt had told her earlier that day. And now she had seen the president apologize on national TV.

"Do you believe her?" Kristen asked.

Paige tried to shift into lawyer mode, but her thoughts were jumbled. "She says she called for a full investigation as soon as she heard about the drone strike that might have killed Wyatt. That means she did it before Wyatt was found alive. Presumably, Attorney General Wachsmann could attest to all that. And if she's telling the truth about that, she had every intention of coming clean even when she could have just buried all this."

Kristen pondered it for a few moments. "I'll leave the analysis to you, Paige, but I never wanted to believe she sent Patrick and Troy on that mission knowing they would die."

The two women talked about what might happen next. Paige explained that they would petition the Supreme Court to reopen their case. The Court would probably grant the petition, and both Kilpatrick and Marcano were in so deep they would likely settle.

"They're going to need most of their money for legal fees for criminal lawyers. There probably won't be a lot left to pay either you or Gazala Holloman," Paige said.

Kristen shrugged. "It was never about the money, Paige. You know that."

Though the president's speech virtually guaranteed them a legal victory, or at least a favorable settlement, for some reason Paige didn't feel like celebrating. And she could hear the sadness in Kristen's voice, too. Maybe Paige felt this way because the case had somehow kept Paige connected to Patrick. Maybe it was because she knew she had thrown all of her energy into this cause, and now she would have to stop and take time to really mourn his loss.

A few minutes later, she thanked Kristen for being such a great friend and said she needed to spend some time alone. Today was a lot to process, and she was emotionally drained. In truth, she didn't want to be around when the president called. Everything was still too raw for that.

The two women hugged, and Kristen struggled to find the words to let Paige know how much this case meant to her.

"I don't know what I would have done without you," Kristen said, tears welling in her eyes.

"Let's get together tomorrow and maybe we'll feel more like celebrating," Paige said.

She left Kristen's house at ten thirty that night. It was cold and blustery, but the sky was clear and the stars were bright. There was a half-moon hanging low on the eastern horizon, and Paige knew instinctively where she needed to go.

★　★　★

She took off her sandals and rolled up her jeans for the walk from the boardwalk to the water. The sand was cool and moist, squeezing between her toes. She reached the edge of the wet sand and looked out over the foaming waves. In the distance she could see dots of light—huge ships making their way along the shoreline.

The stars were luminescent, and the moon reflected off the water. The steady beat of the waves, tumbling over the undertow, muffled the human noise from the boardwalk. This was *her* ocean, almost a sanctuary, and Paige sat down in the dry sand to take it all in.

She huddled inside her windbreaker. The breeze was stronger here as the prevailing winds skimmed across the vast, open sea. She stayed there for a while, grateful for the day's events, thanking God and sorting things out, her spirit calmed by the steady rhythm of the waves. And she stared for a long time at the smooth wet sand spread out before her, polished by the waves, where once there had been footprints and sand castles and words scribbled in the surf.

EPILOGUE

Paige wore a blue-and-white flowered sundress on Memorial Day, her dark hair pulled back with clips. She sat next to Bill Harris at the Arlington Memorial Amphitheater, listening to the president's speech. She thought about how much things had changed.

The president had survived a vote of confidence, but the Republicans had managed to push it past the election that occurred less than a month after the president's address. The controversy had helped Republicans gain a greater majority in the House and control of the Senate.

As the president had requested, there was a new council, including members from all three branches of government, that determined when somebody could be added to the kill list. And the CIA's firepower had been severely clipped. But the secret court proposed by the president had been voted down by Congress.

Kilpatrick and Marcano did not fare well. They were removed from office and roundly criticized from the left and right. U.S. Attorney Mitchell Taylor lodged perjury charges against Marcano for lying in his deposition. And after Harry Coburn from the *New York Tribune* spilled the beans on Kilpatrick, the former chief of staff was convicted of the unauthorized disclosure of classified information. Wyatt Jackson, of course, parlayed that conviction into a full day of circuit riding on the cable TV shows.

Both Marcano and Kilpatrick served sixty days behind bars and were given two-year suspended sentences. They settled the *Anderson* case and the case filed by Gazala Holloman, but they continued to deny all liability. It was hard for people to take them seriously when they each paid over $500,000.

Justice Deegan was quickly making a name for herself on the Supreme Court. And Kristen's boys, who were sitting just a few rows down from Paige at the memorial service, had become stars on their respective soccer teams.

The weather was hot and muggy that day, the thin, wispy clouds giving little relief in the ninety-degree heat. It didn't keep Bill Harris from wearing a proper sport coat and tie, the perspiration trickling down his brow. And during the prayer at the end of the ceremony, he reached over and placed a hand on Paige's forearm. She had spent a few days over Christmas vacation visiting the man, and she loved him with all her heart.

Paige cried only twice that day. The first time was at the close of the ceremony in the amphitheater. The speeches had been given, the prayers had been said, and there was a flyover with a missing pilot. That was followed by an honor guard firing three volleys in the air and the playing of taps by a lone bugler. It was during that song, while the families sat in reverential silence, that young Justin Anderson, all of five years old, sprang to his feet and saluted. Paige looked down the row and saw the brave young man standing at attention, his bottom lip quivering, and the tears began to flow.

When the ceremony was over and the people began filing out, Bill and Paige headed for Patrick's grave. Only about half of the SEAL families had made the ceremony this year. For some, the emotions might have been too strong. Others might have decided to remember their loved ones in more private ceremonies in hometowns scattered around the country. Bill and Paige, on the other hand, had vowed that they would make the journey together every Memorial Day. It was the least they could do.

Paige thought about the magnificent procession during the memorial service for the SEALs—the twenty flag-draped caskets and the gleaming caissons pulled by sleek white horses. She remembered the thousands of people lining the streets of the cemetery, the servicemen and -women with their uniforms sparkling in the sun. She remembered the children on the shoulders of their dads and the men with their hats over their hearts.

Today there was none of that. She and Bill walked quietly together down the roads of Arlington, past the thousands of white grave markers, all neatly and perfectly spaced, past the other families stopping and bowing at the graves of loved ones. She smelled the freshly cut grass, and it reminded her of the year before and the brutal sorrow that had ripped at her heart. On their right, they passed a grave where a young woman had opened an umbrella and propped it on its side so it provided shade for the tombstone and the area just in front of the grave. She had placed a blanket there and was lying on her side on top of the blanket, flowers in her hand, tears streaming down her face.

When they reached Patrick's tombstone, his grandfather knelt, and Paige knelt beside him. Bill said a short prayer, thanking God for giving him a grandson of such great courage and honor, a grandson who was willing to sacrifice his life for the freedom of others. He thanked God for the full assurance that he would be with Patrick again soon, and he ended his prayer in the name of the Father, the Son, and the Holy Ghost.

He and Paige had chatted like best friends earlier that day, but now they were both at a loss for words. They knelt there for a long time, alone with their thoughts, until Patrick's grandfather placed a hand on the headstone to help him rise to his feet.

"Guess I'd better be going," he said. "Come up and see me again."

Paige assured him that she would, and she gave him a long hug. Her heart ached as the old man slowly walked away, his shoulders stooped from the sorrow life had thrown at him.

She watched him for a very long time and was not at all surprised when he stopped at the grave where the young woman was lying on the blanket. He said a few words and sat down to talk with her.

Paige, alone at Patrick's grave, wanted to do a little talking of her own.

She sat in front of the tombstone, ran her fingers over the inscription, and thought again about the tragedy of a good man like Patrick dying so young. There were so many things he would never do, but she kept herself from going there. She reminded herself that men could live to be ninety and never accomplish half as much.

She knew she probably looked pathetic sitting there, but she didn't really care. "I know you're not here," she said. "But I also know that you can hear me, so this is as good a place as any to get a few things off my heart.

"First of all, I might not have said yes the night before you left, but you knew it was going to happen. I loved you more than any man who has ever been in my life, and I can't imagine ever loving anyone like that again."

She was sitting with her arms wrapped around her knees, sunglasses on, feeling the warm sun beating against her bare shoulders. She looked into the distance, a sea of headstones with people milling about. She sniffed back some tears for the second time that day and continued.

"Thanks for helping me find the courage to be who I am and to embrace my faith again. It took somebody like you to teach my heart to trust.

"You might have heard, but we didn't do half bad in our case. And I know this might surprise you, but I've got a little announcement to make. After everything I went through last year, it's hard to get excited about private practice. So I've decided to join the Navy and be part of the JAG corps."

She had been thinking about this for a long time. She had been inspired by the loyalty of the SEAL team families and the sense that they were fighting for a higher cause. There was nobility in sacrifice; Patrick had shown her that. She would never be a SEAL, but she had other skills. She was a born prosecutor, and she would put those skills to work in the JAG corps, trying cases, protecting the integrity of the Navy and its commitment to honor and discipline.

"So that's it. I've already signed the papers. You're not the only one who can look good in a uniform."

She stood, kissed her fingers, and placed them on his name.

"We would have made a good team, Patrick," she said. "We would have made a good team."

ABOUT THE AUTHOR

Randy Singer is a critically acclaimed, award-winning author and veteran trial attorney. He has penned more than ten legal thrillers and was a finalist with John Grisham and Michael Connelly for the inaugural Harper Lee Prize for Legal Fiction sponsored by the University of Alabama School of Law and the *ABA Journal*. Randy runs his own law practice and has been named to *Virginia Business* magazine's select list of Legal Elite litigation attorneys. In addition to his law practice and writing, Randy serves as teaching pastor for Trinity Church in Virginia Beach, Virginia, and teaches classes in advocacy and civil litigation at Regent Law School. He and his wife, Rhonda, live in Virginia Beach. They have two grown children. Visit his website at www.randysinger.net.

ACKNOWLEDGMENTS

Writing novels is the easy part. This is the hard part—finding the right words to thank the people who make it possible. Nevertheless, I will try.

Inspiration. People ask me where I get the ideas for my books. There is nothing like real life to inspire fiction, and this book is no exception. I live and I watch.

Lately, as a lawyer, I've had the privilege of representing families in lawsuits against state sponsors of terrorism (like Iran and Syria). Many of these families have lost loved ones who served our country valiantly. They have shown me how God can bring good things out of the ashes of tragedy. So much of this story is their story.

Living in Virginia Beach, I also have the privilege of being a pastor in a church with a large military contingent, including members of the Special Forces. It may sound clichéd, but they epitomize duty and valor, never hesitating to risk their lives for our freedom. They know the meaning of sacrifice. The least I can do is write about it.

Gratitude. It takes more than inspiration to write a novel. In my case, it requires an entire team to keep me straight. I'm especially grateful to be part of the Tyndale team and to have editors like Karen Watson and Jeremy Taylor. Their skill is equaled only by their unending patience, and believe me, I've tried it. They don't just doctor the words; they capture the vision and help make it reality. Without Karen's unflagging enthusiasm for this story, it would never have come to fruition.

I'm also grateful for those who help in the earliest stages. For this book, Mary Hartman, Denise Wood, and Andrew Cleveland provided great critique and feedback before I even sent it to the folks at Tyndale to perform their magic. Also, my friends in a Bible study group called Tactical Side Bar (named for the military members and lawyers in it) will probably take credit for this book (as they do my sermons), so I might as well beat them to the punch. Thank you, gentlemen.

Grace. My church, my law firm, and my family bear a disproportionate burden when I launch out on one of my fictional escapades. Every hour spent in the fictional world means one less hour in the real one, and somebody has to pick up the slack. Thank you, Trinity Church, for realizing that writing is a ministry, and for supporting me in it. Thank you to the lawyers and staff at Singer Davis for keeping the real cases on track while I spend energy battling fictional ones. And most of all, thank you, Rhonda, Rosalyn, Joshua, Alisa, and Andrew for putting up with the idiosyncrasies of a fiction author in the family. I have fun writing. But my real joy is knowing that the people who know me best still love me most. That requires no small amount of grace.

ALSO BY RANDY SINGER

Fiction

Directed Verdict

Irreparable Harm

Dying Declaration

Self Incrimination

The Judge Who Stole Christmas

The Judge
previously published as The Cross
Examination of Oliver Finney

False Witness

By Reason of Insanity

The Justice Game

Fatal Convictions

The Last Plea Bargain

Dead Lawyers Tell No Tales

The Advocate

Nonfiction

Live Your Passion, Tell Your Story, Change Your World

Made to Count

www.randysinger.net

CP0232

TYNDALE HOUSE PUBLISHERS IS CRAZY4FICTION!

Fiction that entertains and inspires

Get to know us! Become a member of the Crazy4Fiction community. Whether you read our blog, like us on Facebook, follow us on Twitter, or receive our e-newsletter, you're sure to get the latest news on the best in Christian fiction. You might even win something along the way!

JOIN IN THE FUN TODAY.

 www.crazy4fiction.com

 Crazy4Fiction

 @Crazy4Fiction